She frowned and walked through to the sitting-room, picking up a discarded sneaker as she went, the automatic genuflection of all mothers everywhere. Michael was still sitting in his father's chair; but his can of root beer was spilled across the beige-coloured rug and his half-eaten sandwich was lying on his chest. His eyes were wide open and his lips were blue, and even before she could speak his name, she knew that he was dead.

CONDOR

Thomas Luke

A STAR BOOK
published by
the Paperback Division of
W. H. ALLEN & Co. PLC

A Star Book
Published in 1985
by the Paperback Division of
W. H. Allen & Co. PLC
44 Hill Street, London W1X 8LB

First published in Great Britain by
W. H. Allen & Co. PLC. 1984

Copyright © Thomas Luke, 1984

Printed and bound in Great Britain by
Anchor Brendon Ltd, Tiptree, Essex

ISBN 0 352 31490 7

'Du musst herrschen und gewinnen
Oder dienen und verlieren,
Leiden oder triumphieren,
Amoss oder Hammer sein.'

'You must either conquer and rule
Or serve and lose,
Suffer or triumph,
Be the anvil or the hammer.'

                                    – *Goethe*

ONE

His best friend Bernie had to go to piano lesson that afternoon, and so he spent nearly an hour throwing a ball up against the back of the garage until his mother put her head out of the kitchen window and told him for God's sake to find something *useful* to do, like rake the lawn or clean his bicycle, and so he decided to take his BB gun and explore the woods on the far side of Conant's Acre, like Indiana Jones in *Raiders of the Lost Ark*.

He left his bicycle propped up against the split-rail fence which divided Webster Crescent and its neat new three-bedroomed homes from the downsloping wildness of Conant's Acre; then he walked in his rubbers across the ploughed-up clay, a nine-year-old boy with irrepressible mousy-blond hair, a snub nose just like his mother, and exactly his father's way of squinching up his eyes when he looked into the distance.

He could have been alone on the whole wide planet. There was nothing to the south but fields and trees; nothing to the north-west but the windblown grazing land of the Kelly estate, of which Conant's Acre was the southernmost part. Ahead, to the east, were the woods, tangled and dark, which Bernie had solemnly sworn to him were haunted.

'There's ghosts in those woods, witches and devils and loogaroos,' Bernie had told him. 'If you ever go in

7

there, they'll skin you alive, and throw you out on the Acre for the vultures and the hyenas to eat you.'

He had protested to Bernie that there were no vultures and no hyenas in New Hampshire, but Bernie had not been deterred. Bernie had read every horror novel that ever was, and when it came to witches and devils and loogaroos, Bernie knew it all. Bernie was ten.

It took him almost ten minutes to cross the field. In the spring, it was usually planted for barley, but now it was furrowed and crusty and difficult to walk over. Above him, a flock of crows suddenly wheeled and shrieked, alarming him. They swung around again and then flew away to the west, under a sky that was already pale with the approach of winter. He watched them for a while, and then carried on walking, sniffing from time to time because it was so cold.

The woods were very still, and even more overgrown with briars than he had imagined. He stood in the field, staring into them intently, his BB rifle pumped-up ready to fire. There was a rustling in the weeds at the border of the woods, but it was probably nothing more than a mouse or a shrew. He looked back across the field, and saw the safe and tidy roof-tops of the new crescent, and for a moment he considered turning back. But then he thought: what am I going to tell Bernie? I walked across the field and looked at the woods and didn't go in? I could always pretend that I *had* gone in. I could always say that I did something else this afternoon, like cycled down to the Winant Mall. But he knew that he always told Bernie the truth, even when it was embarrassing or hurtful. Bernie was his best friend and they couldn't keep anything secret from each other, even when they wanted to.

He took an unbalanced step over the weedy under-growth, pushed aside a dense array of brambles with the stock of his rifle, and then hop-skip-jumped into the shadow of the woods themselves. He stood silent, listening, but there was only the wind and the birds and the ticking of dry leaves, and he thought to himself: there's nothing to be afraid of. Witches and devils and loogaroos are only in books. They're only stories. At least, I *hope* they're only stories.

Taking out his penknife, he blazed a mark on a nearby tree. A triangle, with a circle in the middle. He and Bernie always blazed marks wherever they went, even in the corridors at school. He had read in the Children's Section in the *Concord Journal* that a good tracker always blazes marks. He sniffed, and then took another few steps forward.

It was so quiet in the woods. Outside, it had been windy and wild. In here, it was almost like church. He blazed another mark, and then stepped deeper into the silence. He kept his rifle raised, though, just in case there was something around which was worth shooting at. Like a witch, or a devil, or a loogaroo.

'Okay, men,' he whispered, once he was twenty or thirty paces into the woods. 'We'll stop here for rations.'

He hunkered down, propping his BB rifle against a tree, and took a pack of Hubba-Bubba out of his jacket pocket, wrenching a piece out of the wrapper with his gritted teeth, as if he were biting pemmican. 'It looks like the Japs have gone. Maybe we should turn around and head back to HQ.'

While he chewed the first sugar out of the gum, he carved his initials on the side of a tree, so that he would be able to bring Bernie back here and prove that he had ventured into the unknown completely by himself. Bernie may be ten, but Bernie had never ventured into the unknown completely by himself, let alone cut his initials on a tree to prove it.

He stood up, and as he did so, there was a flickering, fluttering sound right behind him. He knew that it was nothing really terrible, but it scared him all the same, and he swung dramatically around and snapped off a

9

BB shot between the dark trunks of the trees. It was only a bird, or a squirrel, but he frantically pumped up the air in his rifle again, and slid the action backwards and forwards to chamber another pellet. His heart pounded against the inside of his ribs as if it wanted to burst out.

He waited, listening. He was pleased with the quickness with which he had reloaded his rifle. An expert hunter, no doubt about it. He slowly retraced his steps, his rubbers rustling through the dried-up leaves, keeping his rifle raised and his eyes squinched up and his face as mean as possible. One look at that face and any loogaroo would know that he meant business.

He was still walking backwards when his foot slipped, and the leafy ground seemed to collapse right under him. He twisted around, but it was too late. A large piece of clay dropped and broke, and he was tumbled into a hole in the ground that was nearly three feet deep. He was followed by a shower of leaf-mould and twigs, and some of it got into his eyes, but he coughed, and sniffed again, and struggled back on to his feet. His first nervous response was to pick up his rifle and look quickly around, in case this was a mantrap. If he wasn't careful, he'd be porcupine-quilled with native spears before he could loose off even a single shot.

'All clear, men,' he said to himself. He threw his rifle on to the edge of the hole, and prepared to hoist himself out of it. But as his feet scrabbled against the clay, he heard a hollow sound, as if he were kicking a pipe, or a tin box.

Frowning, hesitating, he stared down into the hole. He found a long stick, and poked around the sides of it. Treasure? A boxful of gold? It could be. There had been plenty of wealthy people around here in colonial days; and plenty of highway-robbers, too. Maybe he had accidentally come across a hidden cache of gold sovereigns. God, he'd be rich. Not that he was allowed to say 'God', even though everybody at school said it, every other word, some of them. He could buy his father a gold-coloured Cadillac, without his father knowing, and have it driven right up to the front door and nonchalantly say, 'There you are, daddy, it's yours,' and give him the keys. And his mother could have a white fur coat.

He jumped back down into the hole, and started scraping away at the side which had sounded hollow. It didn't take long before he had uncovered a large bare curve of metal, like the side of a trashcan or something, except that it had a row of rivet-heads on it. It looked as if it had once been painted grey or green, but there was hardly any paint left at all. Maybe it was an old water-heater.

Now he dug more and more of the clay and leaf-mould away; and soon he began to realize that what was under the ground here wasn't a trashcan at all, or a water-heater. It was *enormous*. He dug down with his stick as far as he could through the tree-roots which clung around it; and he dug as far as he could in each direction, panting a little, and even after nearly half an hour of digging he still couldn't find the beginning or the end of it. It was cylindrical, and it was metal, and the rivets were arranged in long rows along the top of it, and down the sides as well.

God, he thought, it's like a rocket-ship. Maybe it's a crashed rocket-ship. Maybe it arrived from Mars one night and crashed right into the ground and nobody ever knew. Or maybe it's a secret tunnel that leads right under the woods. Or maybe it's an airplane.

But how did an airplane get buried in the woods? Who would have wanted to bury it, and why? And most puzzling of all, *how* had they buried it? The roots of the trees were ensnaring it as if they had grown around it. Some of the finer root-hairs had even clung

11

under the rivet-heads, so it must have been here for years and years and years.

He thought he heard a branch snap, and he stood up straight, his nose smudged with mud, his face flushed from all that digging, and listened. But it was nothing: just the crickling and crackling of the woods. He wondered what he ought to do, whether he ought to tell Bernie about what he had found, and nobody else, or whether he ought to tell his father. If somebody had *really* buried an airplane here, the police would want to know about it, wouldn't they?

He dug a little further, and it was then that he discovered a muddy, milked-over window. He tried to rub it with his handkerchief, but it had become so discoloured by years of burial in the clay that he was unable to see anything through it at all. There was another window next to it, and when he dug a little further with the point of his stick, another. They were arranged in a curve, like the pilot's windows of an old-fashioned airliner, a Dakota maybe, or a Lockheed Electra. All of the windows were opaque and impenetrable. They reminded him of Mr Ferris, who used to run the newsstand on the corner by Concord Depot – Mr Ferris and his blind white eyes; Mr Ferris who used to reach out darkly and ruffle his hair and say, 'Fine boy you've got there, fine boy.'

He scraped away as much of the mud as he could; but he was growing tired now, and the temperature was beginning to drop, and twilight was thickening the shadows and clotting between the branches of the trees. Maybe he should come back tomorrow, with Bernie; so that they could break open the windows and see what was inside. But then the secret would be Bernie's secret, too; the great discovery would have to be shared. And for this secret, he wanted to take *all* the glory, *all* the attention, because he alone had braved the witches and the devils and the loogaroos; he alone had discovered

12

where the airplane was buried; and he alone had dug it up.

He craned his neck backwards and looked up at the sky above the tree-tops. It wasn't as dark outside as it appeared to be down here in the woods. Four o'clock, maybe; not later. He still had time to break into the airplane and explore inside it before darkness began to fall in earnest, and the *real* ghosties and gremlins started to scurry through the trees. Daytime was one thing: he could be scathing about loogaroos in the daytime. But everybody knew that the night was dangerous: even grown-ups.

Not far away from the trench he had dug around the airplane's windows, he found a heavy piece of stratified rock. He cautiously lifted it up, and he was right to be cautious, for underneath it the soil was alive with centipedes, a whole nest of them. He kept the rock raised until the centipedes had scurried away under the surrounding leaves, and then he brushed the stone off with the sleeve of his jacket, and lifted it up. It was almost too heavy for him to carry, but for fifteen yards he was the Bionic Man, and somehow he managed to heft the rock right to the very brink of the trench, and rest it there, forty pounds of good New Hampshire sandstone.

He spat out his old piece of bubble-gum, and bit off a fresh piece. He sat chewing for a while, getting his breath back. Then he hopped down into the hole beside the airplane fuselage, and turned around, with his back to the side of the hole, and grasped the rock in both hands. All he would have to do now would be to pitch himself forward, keeping the rock upraised, and it would smash straight through the airplane's window.

However, he hesitated. Supposing there were people inside? Skeletons. If the airplane had crashed here, years and years and years ago, supposing the pilot and the crew had all died inside of it, and were sitting there

13

now, trapped behind these blind and muddy windows, just waiting for a boy like him to break open the cockpit and let them out, their bony fingers as tenacious as the roots which clung around their craft, as groping and clutching as Mr Ferris, 'Fine boy you've got there, fine boy.'

Bernie would know what to do. Bernie would have finished his piano lesson by now. He let go of the rock, and stood there in the hole, biting his lip, and thinking of Bernie. Good old Bernie. Maybe he should run back across the Acre and climb on his bicycle and go fetch Bernie, and then at least they could break into this airplane together, in case of skeletons.

But something impetuous inside of him, something that he had inherited from his mother's side of the family, a sudden madness, led him to seize hold of the rock again and think, God, what the hell, I'm going to do it, and smash the rock straight into the window.

The first time, it didn't break. But he smashed it again, and then again, and then again, and at last it splintered and blistered like those mica windows in the front of furnaces, and he had actually made a hole in it, triangular and ragged. He put down the rock, and bent forward cautiously, peering into the hole as if he expected to see Satan himself in there, peering back at him. But there was nothing: only darkness, and a curious smell like very stale sheepskin jackets. He pushed the point of his stick into the hole, and prized away more of the perspex, until at last the whole window was open.

He peered into the cockpit again, but it was still too dark for him to be able to make anything out. God, if only he had brought his bicycle with him: he could have used the front lamp to illuminate the inside of the airplane, and maybe he could have used the pedals to haul out the treasure if there was any, like a winch.

14

Well – even if there wasn't any treasure, there had to be *something* interesting in there.

He cleared away the second window, and broke that, too. It was still very dark inside the airplane's cockpit, but if he kept his head to the side, he could just make out a row of reflected half-moons; dials, they must be, on the instrument panel. And there was something dark and ragged like an incinerated scarecrow; something in a soft helmet with earflaps, and he knew with a silent scream that jangled his spine right inside of him that this was the pilot, the pilot was still actually there, sitting in his seat.

'*God*,' he said aloud, and sat back on the crumbling clay. He was shaking and breathless, and somehow not so much scared as dreadfully excited. He had only seen one dead body before: his grandfather, lying in his coffin, waxen-faced and pink as a prawn, not so much actually dead as something else altogether, not his grandfather at all, but a puffed-up joke grandfather from some loony-minded carnival store. This scarecrow pilot, though, was *death*. Real, undisguised, *death*. Looking back into the cockpit, he could make out a gloved hand that still rested on the throttle levers, and a wrist that gleamed with knobby triangular bones.

He knew that he wasn't going to be brave enough to squeeze through the cockpit window. Supposing the corpse suddenly turned around and snatched at him, and the only way out was through those tiny broken openings? He was tough, and courageous, but he wasn't an airbrain. He would have to come back with Bernie, so that Bernie could cover him with his BB rifle while he scrambled inside. He didn't mind Bernie knowing about the airplane now; not now that he'd thoroughly discovered it, and broken into it and seen the pilot.

Still, he would have to take some kind of souvenir to prove that he'd been there. It was no good climbing to

the top of Everest if you didn't come back with something to show that you'd actually been up there; you
could have been hiding behind a snowdrift for all
anyone knew. And besides, now that he'd dug it up,
maybe somebody else would stumble across it, and
claim that it was theirs, and unless he had a souvenir
he wouldn't be able to prove that the wreck was his.
God, there could even be money in it. A reward for
finding it. I mean it was obviously an airliner; it was
huge. It must have gone missing years and years ago
and nobody had ever found out what had happened to
it. It was probably still full of people, all sitting in their
seats like the pilot, rows and rows of skeletons in ragged
clothes, with all their luggage and bags and hats and
coats, deep underground on a trip that was never going
anywhere.

He shivered at the thought of it. He had no idea how
an entire airliner could have ended up underground,
under the woods off Conant's Acre; but here it was, he
had discovered it on his own, and he was going to take
something back home with him to prove it.

Taking a deep breath, he reached down inside the
broken window of the cockpit and felt around inside.
There were some switches and levers in there, the fuel-
cock and the filter-pump control, although he didn't
know what they were. Then his fingertips touched the
edge of a steel-and-canvas seat, and a loose seat-belt.
The co-pilot's seat was empty. Either the co-pilot had
managed to bail out before the airplane crashed, or else
he had gone back to reassure the passengers.

He tugged at the seat-belt, trying to loosen the buckle
from the rotting webbing, but he couldn't break the
stitches. There had to be *something* loose in there, something he could take back to show Bernie. He reached in
right up to the shoulder, praying that the pilot wouldn't
suddenly decide to come alive and sink his teeth into

his arm; and he groped cautiously around the co-pilot's seat, first around the front of it, and then behind it.

It was then that he touched a leather handle, like the handle of an old-fashioned camera-case. He touched it again, and then managed to hook the tips of his fingers around it. Grunting with the effort of stretching he gently lifted the case out from behind the co-pilot's seat, and at last brought it out into daylight.

At first he thought that it *was* a camera. It was an oblong case of hard brown hide, with a corroded metal clip-clasp on one side, and a lid that flapped up. There was no label on it, no initials, no brand-name – nothing to indicate what might be inside. He sniffed it, but all it smelled was old, like the leather suitcase that his grandmother kept on top of her wardrobe, with all those photographs in, and grandfather's moustache wax.

The clasp was very stiff; so he took out his penknife and gradually eased it open. He didn't want to break it, the case might be valuable. He opened up the lid and looked inside.

It certainly had nothing to do with cameras. Inside, the case was divided into six green cardboard compartments, and in each of these compartments was a small glass bottle, with a glass stopper. Each stopper had been sealed with something that looked like white candle-grease.

He lifted one of the bottles out. There was no label on it, no instructions, nothing at all. It was made of clear glass, and inside there was about a teaspoonful of clear liquid, slightly oily, like Genever gin, or Russian vodka. He shook it, but it didn't bubble or fizz.

Perhaps it was some kind of chemical that old-time airline pilots had needed; perhaps it was the co-pilot's medicine. But the leather case had such strong associations with camera cases that he felt pretty sure that the fluid was something to do with photography. Developing fluid, hypo, something like that. His older cousin Nat did his own developing, and sometimes let him sit on a stool in the darkroom and watch. He was always fascinated to watch the smiling faces gradually appear on the bottom of the developing tray.

He picked away the candle-grease, first with his fingernail, and then with his penknife-blade. He wasn't so dumb that he would drink any of the fluid. There weren't any ridges on the back of the bottle but it could still be poisonous, or make you sick. All he wanted to do was sniff it, to find out if he was right. He tugged the stopper, with a squeak of ground-glass; and there it was, open.

Carefully, he leaned forward and sniffed at it.

It had a very faint odour, not altogether unpleasant, like sugar-water, or boiled candy. He sniffed it again, trying to think what it reminded him of. He dabbed a tiny spot of it on the tip of his finger, and touched it with the tip of his tongue. It didn't *taste* poisonous. It didn't burn or anything. And after he had sat there for five-minutes waiting for any peculiar side-effects, and none had materialized, he decided that whatever the liquid was, it was nothing particularly dangerous. He stoppered it up again, and put the bottle back in the case, and closed it.

It had grown quite dark now. The wind was beginning to stir through the woods; and not far away he heard the call of a saw-whet owl. He brushed himself down, and kicked the worst of the clay off his rubbers, and started to climb out of the hole.

As he did so, however, he heard a rattling, collapsing noise from inside the airplane's cockpit. He turned around in shock, and involuntarily squirted a little pee into his pants. The dead pilot had dropped sideways out of his seat, and was now staring at him out of the broken window of the airliner, smiling an inane and half-mummified smile. His skin was yellow and leathery, but it was still intact, stretched across the angles of his skull like half-roasted chicken-skin; and although his blond moustache was scraggly and bleached by all his years of burial, it somehow gave him a hideous look of being alive.

Slowly, whimpering, taking as much care as he could not to disturb the sides of the hole, the boy climbed away from the airliner, picked up his BB rifle, and stepped away through the woods with all the frozen caution of a rabbit who can sense wolf but knows the consequences of making too sudden a break for it. At last he was out to the knee-high brambles and the sneezeweed, and into the open acre, and then he ran across the ploughed-up furrows with his head thrown back and his arms pumping and his breath piping *hi!hi!hi!* out of his throat.

He climbed over the split-rail fence, jumped on to his bicycle, and tore off home, the leather case swinging from his handlebars. As soon as he reached the house, he skidded into the open garage, leaped out of the saddle, and stood there with his hands on his hips, gasping for breath. God, made it. All the way home without the skeletons catching me. All the way home, and safe.

He walked up and down the garage for a little while, until he had stopped panting. Then he picked up the leather case and took it down to the far end of the garage where his father's tool shelves were. He cleared aside a heap of greasy rags and a few cans of chrome-polish and two cardboard boxes full of old screws and venetian-blind fittings that his father would never use. Carefully he prized away a loose cement brick, and in the cavity there was his secret treasure-store: a dollar in change, a live .22 bullet that he had once found, and a notepad containing the secret code which he and Bernie were trying to learn so that they could communicate without anybody knowing what they were saying.

He just managed to fit the leather case into the hole; then he replaced the brick, and covered it up again with rags and polish.

His mother wasn't home, although she had left the back door open. There was a note on the kitchen table which said, 'Shopping at Winant Mall. Help yourself to Coke and cookies.' He went to the icebox, poked around for anything interesting, squeezed out a little Instant Cream for the fun of it, and licked it, and eventually discovered a carton of Philly cheese. He made himself a thick and messy cheese sandwich, leaving the bread all over the table and the knife sticking upright in the butter, opened up a root beer, and went into the sitting-room to sling his legs over the arms of his father's chair and watch the rest of Star Trek.

His mother came home from Winant Mall a few minutes after five o'clock. She set her shopping down on the kitchen table and shook her head when she saw all the chaos that he had left. She called, 'Michael? I'm home.'

There was no answer, but that wasn't unusual. She took off her red leather jacket and hung it over the back of one of the chairs. She said, 'Ferdie was down at the Mall. It's his birthday next week. His mom was looking for one of those E.T. wristwatches for him. You know, the digital ones?'

There was still no answer. Only Mr Spock, saying, 'The Zarans are unlikely to attack unless they discover that we have Otrak safely imprisoned.'

She frowned, and walked through to the sitting-room, picking up a discarded sneaker as she went, the automatic genuflection of all mothers everywhere. Michael was still sitting in his father's chair; but his can of root beer was spilled across the beige-coloured rug and his half-eaten sandwich was lying on his chest. His eyes were wide open and his lips were blue, and even before she could speak his name, she knew that he was dead.

TWO

It was the kind of triumphant coincidence that could almost have led Humphrey to admit to himself that there *was* a God, after all: not that he had ever been allowed to question it, at least not openly. Even in those tiresome years after the war, when he had doubted everything, religion, rationing, sex, the meaning of socialism, even his own reality, he had been shepherded along by his sister every Sunday morning to St Botolph's Church, well-supplied with a quarter of mint imperials to suck during the sermon and five shillings in shillings for the collection bag; and been obliged to sing at the top of his inaccurate voice *O God Our Help In Ages Past* and *Lead Kindly Light*.

Every Sunday for 53 years to St Botolph's Church, except for the war years (those blessed war years!) looking for a sign from the Lord.

And here it was: the sign. Not at St Botolph's at all, but here, out on this sidewalk café in Stockholm, on a chilly late-September afternoon, with the sun already falling behind the reddish facade of the Sheraton hotel and gilding his glass of Pripps Fatöl as if it were the Holy Grail. Perhaps it wasn't as spectacular a sign as a burning bush or a shower of locusts, but for Humphrey it was nearly as good. He had come out of the café with his sandwich and his beer, said 'excuse me' several times, and 'is this seat taken?', and then realized once he had made himself comfortable that he was sitting right opposite the most wanted German war-criminal since Joseph Mengele.

It was coincidence, of course. Humphrey had never been to Sweden before, and this was the first holiday he had taken in nearly six years. But Humphrey thought there was something wonderfully *appropriate* about it that smacked of Christian destiny. He continued to drink his beer and eat his prawn-and-dillweed smorgasbord, his legs crossed; and to glance from time to time at the 70-year-old man who was sitting opposite him in his dark-brown reindeer overcoat as if the man were nobody more interesting than any other tourist like himself, just another old buffer who had come to visit Sweden for the saunas and the adding-machine exhibitions and the sex shows, and the temporary reassurance that perhaps he wasn't so geriatric after all. The afternoon was sharp; sharp as a scalpel; and ten minutes ago Humphrey had recognized the man as Klaus Hermann, alias Klaus Schreiber, the so-called 'Vampire of Herbstwald', wanted in seven countries for the murder in the autumn of 1943 of more than 3,000 men, women, and children at Herbstwald concentration camp, near Hoyerswerda.

Humphrey glanced across at Hermann with curiosity rather than distaste. Hermann looked older than Humphrey would have expected him to be. White-haired, stooped, with that kind of liver-sausage complexion that only Germans seem to take on when they grow older. Yet he seemed quite animated. He spoke briskly, and laughed a lot, loud enough for Humphrey to hear, and every now and then he would lean forward and say something to his middle-aged female companion that required a suggestive smile, and a touch on the shoulder, and (once) a quick kiss on the cheek.

It gave Humphrey an extraordinary feeling of achievement to have recognized a Nazi of such notoriety. He could scarcely have felt more pleased with himself if he had discovered Hitler sitting at the next table, or Martin Bormann. There had been few triumphs in Humphrey's life, particularly since his retirement, although his fretwork diorama of Chatsworth House had won second place in the 'hobbies' section at the flower-and-vegetable show this summer; and the prize of a bottle of VP Sherry.

During the war, he had worked in South London for BDG 7, known as 'The Budgies', a small team of legal clerks whose task it had been to prepare for the eventual prosecution of hundreds of minor Nazi war criminals, using information brought back by escaped PoWs and reports from the Resistance. Humphrey had enjoyed the work more than almost anything he had ever done. He had learned to identify by sight two to three hundred Nazis by snatched photographs or by artists' impressions alone; and he had also trained himself to recognize the same faces when they were disguised with beards, false hair-pieces, spectacles, or surgically-modified noses.

He was quite surprised that Hermann had done nothing to alter his appearance. He had grown older, of course, and that had made him fleshier, and more wrinkled; and time had changed his jet-black swept-back hair to iron-grey. But the distinctive cleft-tipped nose was just the same, and so was the horselike jawline, and those near-together eyes that had always made him look excited to the point of mania. Hermann had always had the stereotyped face of a 'Nazi butcher,' and 40 years later he still hadn't changed, nor obviously tried to.

Perhaps Hermann felt that, in Sweden, nobody would recognize him; and that the war was too long ago. Perhaps he was relying on the fact that most concentration-camp victims were too traumatized by what had happened to them to want to recall the faces of their captors: they could pass them in the street as if they didn't even exist. For every Jew who could never

23

forget, there were a thousand more who would do anything at all to prevent themselves from remembering. Hermann's face, in particular, was a face which no former internee at Herbstwald could ever think about with any degree of calmness or sanity. They hadn't dubbed him 'The Vampire' for nothing. In 1947, Humphrey had been required to interview a woman in Sennelager whose three children had all been killed by Hermann. When Humphrey had routinely shown her a photograph of him, she had collapsed on the floor of the interview room and vomited uncontrollably, turnips and corned-beef and coffee. It had been a March afternoon, and he had never forgotten it. A man whose very likeness could make people physically sick.

Humphrey finished his beer, and wiped his mouth with his chequered paper napkin. It looked as if Hermann was getting himself ready to go: he kept opening up a grey leather briefcase which was propped up against the white tubular legs of his chair, and closing it again. The woman leaned forward and kissed him, and for a moment they held hands on top of the table, one brown leather glove on top of one rainbow-coloured knitted glove, the sort of Lappish knitwear you could buy in Åhlens or any of the tourist stores, along with reindeer-skin moccasins and handpainted ski-sticks.

Humphrey went back inside the café and paid his bill at the cash-desk. The café was quite crowded, and several people stared at him openly. The Swedes were unabashed starers, and Humphrey sometimes wondered whether the purpose of his holiday was for him to look at the Swedes, or for the Swedes to look at him. Humphrey didn't much care for staring at people directly; if you genuinely liked a person you didn't have to keep inspecting them to make sure that you did, and if you *didn't* like them there wasn't much point in looking at them anyway. His mother had always

24

snapped, 'Humphrey, don't *stare*!' But as the girl behind the cash-desk counted out his change, he did allow himself the luxury of inspecting himself in the mirror behind the counter, a stockily built man peering through shelves of rollmops, salted sild, prawns, and bright-yellow cheese. Not bad, he thought, for 66: ruddy-faced, clean-collared, well turned-out. Rather like James Mason with a bigger nose. Sensitive, even cultured. And nobody could fault the shine on those brown Oxford shoes.

Through the picture window, Humphrey saw Hermann get up from his chair, take the middle-aged woman's arm, and begin slowly to walk up towards Lilla Nygatan, the narrow shopping-street at the back of the café. The pair of them hesitated on the corner, and then Hermann leaned very close to the woman, and whispered something in her ear, and they both laughed. Then, quite abruptly, they separated.

Humphrey had never 'tailed' anybody before. Well, not quite true, he had once followed the 17-year-old usherette of the Regal cinema all the way from Bakewell town centre to Ashford-in-the-Water, on a moonlit night, until at last she had turned around and snapped at him to beggar off. But that had been 52 years ago. Following Klaus Hermann through rush hour Stockholm was something quite different. Now that the sun had dropped behind the skyline of the city centre, the streets became suddenly very chilly, and the buildings were suffused in a strange brick-coloured half-light. Saabs and Volvos sped this way and that across the bridges which connected Stockholm's fourteen islands, their white safety-lights teeming past like a steady meteor-shower. Humphrey fastened the top two buttons of his coat; and then followed Hermann down the narrow sidewalk of Lilla Nygatan to Korn-hamnstorget, and stood right behind him at the kerb as he waited to cross. A young man beside him sniffed noisily, and hawked. That was another Swedish habit which Humphrey found it hard to enjoy. His sister left him a clean initialled handkerchief on the edge of his bureau every single day, without fail – 'bugle for the blowing of', she used to say.

Across the square, the waters of Lake Mälaren were the same chilled-tomato-juice colour as the sky. A train rattled across the sloping bridge that would take its passengers home to the suburbs of Södermalm and Hammarby, and its lighted windows were reflected in the water. Humphrey stayed close up behind Hermann, feeling cold and over-excited but also extremely professional. Hermann coughed, and cleared his throat, and Humphrey coughed, too, and felt that was rather daring.

Hermann swung his briefcase in short, mechanical swings as he walked up the unevenly-cobbled slope of Fünkens Grand to take a short cut through to Skeppsbrön, where the ships from Finland and the USSR tied up. Incongruously on this cold September evening, soap-bubbles floated all around them from a bubble-machine outside a boutique. Hermann looked neither to left nor to right, but walked like a man who came this way often.

Not far away, a busker with a disturbing resemblance to Björn Borg was playing a scrapy folk violin; and a group of teenagers in blue-and-yellow quilted anoraks were hooting and laughing and kicking a Coke can around the cobbles. It was only five o'clock, but already the restaurants had switched on their lights, and there was a Christmas-shopping feeling that didn't usually reach Derbyshire until the middle of December, sometimes later if the snow stayed away. Humphrey watched Hermann walk around the fountain in the middle of the small square at the top of Fünkens Grand; and then continue up the narrow sidewalk of Osterlanggatan. To their right, the tall old-fashioned houses and tenements were divided by a series of dark little streets which led downhill to Skeppsbrön, and as they passed each one, Humphrey could see the pale cold water of Saltsjön, the inlet from the Baltic, and the fretted silhouettes of freighters and passenger-steamers from Helsinki and Leningrad. High up above, sometimes seven or eight stories, gulls perched on the sharply-pitched rooftops, and screamed like discontented eunuchs.

Hermann suddenly took a right turn down one of the narrowest and smelliest of the sidestreets, and then stopped at a shadowy doorway and scrambled around in the pocket of his coat for his keys. Humphrey waited at the end of the street, pretending to read a poster for cheap travel to Denmark. He saw Hermann go inside, and heard the door bang behind him. Cautiously, he walked down the sloping street and stopped outside the house into which Herman had disappeared. No. 17, Pilogatan. He looked up, and after a minute or two he saw a light switched on in the third-floor window, and a pair of beige linen drapes being abruptly drawn.

Well, thought Humphrey, if Hermann has a key, then quite obviously he lives here. There was the usual row of nameplates beside the front doorbell, but only two of them had cards in them, Lars Wahlöö, Gynokologisten; and somebody called Gösta Mokvist. Humphrey stepped back to the opposite side of the street, and stared up at the building's facade. It was cracked and grimy, and streaked with the marks left by 150 seasons of thawing snow. A rusty rainwater gutter hung out from under the eaves, and clanked in the evening breeze. Not the sort of building he would have expected a Nazi-in-hiding to live in. But he remembered that the blonde-haired guide who had showed him around the Gamla Stan on Monday had told him that many of the older tenements had been expensively converted on the inside, sometimes at a cost of millions of kroner.

Perhaps, behind this dingy Strindbergian exterior, Klaus Hermann lived a life of bright Scandinavian luxury.

Humphrey waited outside in the street until his feet began to feel numb. Then he walked back up to Ostlanggatan, turned left, and made his way along Stora Nygatan to the bridge called Vasabrön, which took him over to the main railroad station, and back to his hotel. It was further than he usually liked to walk, and he was sweating and chilled when he arrived, but it hadn't seemed far enough to make a taxi worthwhile.

The Lantona Hotel was a featureless 1940s building which had somehow escaped demolition when they were erecting the Stockholm-Sheraton on one side and the 'Elegant-80' Swedish furniture store on the other. It stood between the two like an unpleasant old grandmother who insisted on accompanying her smart young children wherever they went. Inside its noisy swing doors there was an oval lobby with a red marble floor and an overhead light which gave the lobby all the qualities of an incipient migraine. The old woman with white-cropped hair who muttered and sniffed behind the front desk handed Humphrey his key. Humphrey went up in the rattling elevator and let himself into his room.

The strange loneliness of foreign cities at going-home time. He wasn't quite sure what he ought to do now. Perhaps he should call the British Embassy, and tell them what he suspected. Perhaps, on the other hand, he had made a mistake, and the man wasn't Klaus Hermann at all, but simply an innocent Swedish businessman who happened to look like him. Supposing the British Embassy wasn't interested – what could he do then? Call the Israelis? They must have contacts with accredited Nazi-hunters, people like Simon Wiesenthal who would know how to arrest a man like Hermann and how to arrange to have him deported. He certainly wouldn't be able to tackle Hermann on his own, despite the fact that he was at least five years younger. It was entirely possible that if Hermann *were* Hermann, he would have a gun, and shoot anybody who looked as if they might have uncovered his new identity. What would one more matter, when he had already slaughtered three thousand?

Humphrey took off his coat and his jacket and hung them in the cramped built-in wardrobe beside the washbasin. He switched on the light and inspected his face in the mirror. If Hermann *were* Hermann, it wasn't beyond the bounds of possibility that Humphrey would now become moderately famous, with his picture in the papers, and perhaps on television, too. The quiet man who brought a vicious Nazi killer to book. Derbyshire law clerk in Nazi arrest drama. He pushed up the end of his nose with his finger to make sure that no extralong hairs were protruding from his nostrils. He had always associated extra-long nostril hairs with senility, and regularly plucked them, even though it made his eyes water.

He loosened his necktie and sat down on the edge of his bed. Below his bedroom window, two buses for Arlanda airport drew up with a blurt of diesel noise, and idled their engines while they waited to pick up more passengers. Humphrey sat where he was, thinking, listening to the sound of the buses as if it were somehow important.

Perhaps he ought to confront Hermann himself. Wait for him outside his apartment, and then simply say, '*Hermann! Ich weiß wer Sie sind!*' But of course if Hermann *were* Hermann, such a confrontation would alert him and he might very well escape. It might even be dangerous. And if he *weren't* Hermann, it would make Humphrey look extremely foolish.

And, when it came down to it, what duty did Humphrey actually have to 'shop' Hermann after all these years? Did he have any duty at all? The war had been over for four decades, and if this grey-haired old man had survived until today, who was Humphrey to report him, and send him to inevitable execution? Why not let evil old memories lie? And in any case, what really was the point of hanging a man who had already escaped the consequences of his crimes for more than a lifetime? Humphrey sympathized with the Jews, or believed he ought to, but he had no racial or religious axe to grind, in fact he rather disliked the Jewish piano-tuner who regularly called to adjust his sister's Leafwood.

Humphrey had been a Budgie, of course, but none of the Budgies had associated all those years of identification and compilation with real men and women. They had jokingly referred to all their war-criminals as 'WCs', and had nicknames for some of them. It seemed rather tasteless now, but in wartime attitudes had been different: if you hadn't been flippant you would have been a mental case.

The truth was, the notion of being the only person who knew where Hermann was rather appealed to Humphrey. Every day that he kept the secret of Hermann's identity to himself, he would be exercising over Hermann an almost God-like power. He could say, in years to come, 'I once saved a Nazi war-criminal's life,' and what a story that would be.

Mind you, his sister would disapprove rather a lot. His sister disapproved of Britain being in the Common Market because it meant we had to associate with, well, you know, one isn't supposed to call them Huns any more.

Humphrey looked at the colour photograph hanging over the head of his bed. It was a view of the Gruvon pulp mills on Lake Vanern, and when he had first set eyes on it he had decided that it was by far the most boring photograph he had ever seen.

Suddenly, he picked up the telephone beside the bed, and jiggled the cradle.

'Jes?' asked the old woman on the desk.

'I wish to make a call to Cricklewood, in England.'

'Jes?'

'Can you give me a line?'

'You want to make a telephone call?'

'Yes, to Cricklewood, in England.'

'Krickelvo?'

'No, no, Cricklewood. Near Dollis Hill.'

There was a crackle, and then a dialling noise, and then a very long silence. Humphrey waited for a while, and then jiggled the cradle again and said, 'Hello? Hello?' but there was no reply. He couldn't get through to the desk again, so he sat with the receiver pressed to his ear hoping that the woman would eventually answer. At last a voice came on the line.

'You eat in the hotel tonight, Mr Browne?'

'Yes. Thank you. About eight o' clock, if that's not inconvenient.'

'Jaha.'

'He put the phone down, and immediately picked it up again.

'Jes?'

'That call to London. Can you give me a line?'

The old woman didn't reply, but connected him through so that he heard a dialling tone. He hadn't called the number in eleven years, but he still remembered it without difficulty, the way he had still remembered Klaus Hermann's face. An orderly, clerk-like memory. The code for Britain was 44, the code for Cricklewood was 208. He had a sudden pang for good old CRICKlewood.

It seemed like whole minutes before the telephone was answered. Then, a suspicious English voice that sounded as if it had just been inconveniently torn away from drawing the living-room fire with yesterday's *Daily*

Telegraph said, 'Milner.' Then, even more snappily, 'Milner.'

Humphrey said, 'Major Milner? I'm sorry if I've called at an inconvenient time. It's Humphrey Browne.'

There was a digestive silence. Then, '*Humphrey*! Well, this is a surprise! It must be, what . . . well, years! My dear fellow!'

'Something rather peculiar has just come up,' said Humphrey.

'You sound frightfully far away,' said Major Milner. 'Where are you calling from? Not all the way from Derbyshire?'

'Erm, I'm in Stockholm, actually.'

'*Stockholm?* My dear fellow! What in the world are you doing in Stockholm? This call must be costing you a fortune!'

'Actually, Major, I think I've run into something rather important. Something to do with the shop.'

'Oh, yes? Good God, Stockholm! Well, you're very *clear*, considering it's Stockholm.'

'Major,' insisted Humphrey, 'I saw a man today who answered the description of Klaus Hermann.'

'Who?' Then another silence, as the information was absorbed. Then, 'Hermann? You're sure?'

'As sure as I can be.'

'I can't really believe that it really *is* Hermann,' said Major Milner. 'After all these years. And what's he doing in Stockholm? The last we ever heard of him, he was on his way to Ecuador. Was it Ecuador? Or Nicaragua?'

'Major, I promise you. I might have made some legal mistakes, but I never mistook a WC's face. Not once. You know that. Everybody in the shop knew that.'

'H'm,' said Major Milner. Humphrey could just imagine him puffing out his upper lip so that his moustache bristled like a small hedgehog.

'What do you think I ought to do?' asked Humphrey.

'If I were you, I'd forget about the whole thing. The fellow's probably somebody quite innocent; somebody who just happens to be unfortunate enough to look like Hermann. All krauts look the same to me; don't know how you ever told the difference. Did you say you spoke to him?'

'No, but I followed him home.'

'Where does he live?'

'Major Milner, if you don't think it is Hermann, then where he lives isn't really important, is it?'

Major Milner cleared his throat. 'You're not baiting me, are you, Humphrey?'

'No, major, but – '

'Always had a bit of side to you, didn't you, Humphrey? Well, never mind. If I were you I'd forget the whole thing. Get on with your holiday, have a good time.'

'I can't forget this, Major. At least I thought you could have – '

'Could have what? I can't do anything these days, Humphrey, I'm retired. Don't have reunions for SI8 men; too hush-hush, even today, so I don't have the contacts any more. They put you out to pasture and they close the gate behind you, that's what they do. All I've got now is my garden, and the telly. Do you ever watch *Coronation Street*? Damned good programme, of its kind.'

'Major – '

'Did you say where he lived? Hermann?' Major Milner interrupted.

'No,' said Humphrey.

'Ah,' said the Major. 'Well, mustn't keep you. This must be costing you a fortune.'

Humphrey hesitated. Major Milner said nothing. The long-distance telephone wires warbled their secret and plaintive songs, like messages from distant galaxies, untranslatable and infinitely sad.

'Pilogatan 17, third floor,' said Humphrey, and then put the phone down.

THREE

He was waiting for her when she drove her scarlet Ferrari up to the front steps. He stiffly raised one hand in greeting, and walked around the front of the car to open the door for her. She kept him waiting while she collected her pocketbook, her sunglasses, and her scarf, and slipped on her shoes. Then she gave him a smile like a squeezed lime and said, 'Hello, Reynard. You've put on weight.'

Reynard stopped to kiss her cheek but she turned her head away. He said, 'I always eat too much when I'm lonesome. You remember that time when I had to stay in Brussels?'

'Everybody eats too much in Brussels,' she countered. 'There's nothing else to do in Brussels, but eat. And I can hardly believe that you've been *lonesome*. Not with Chiffon Trent.'

Reynard followed her across the Futura-stone driveway, and up the semi-circular marble steps. Dick Elmwood was waiting for them at the open doors, and he nodded to Greta as she stalked past him, and then made a quick grimace at Reynard.

Reynard told him, 'You can put madame's automobile away for me, please, Dick. That's if madame has really decided to stay.'

'Madame has simply come to negotiate,' Greta retorted, from inside the hallway. 'You can leave the car where it is.'

Reynard hesitated for a second, and then shrugged, and said, 'Okay, Dick. Leave it where it is.'

Inside the grand domed hallway, with its pale Adam-green walls and its elegant white-marble fireplace, Greta was looking around with her hands perched on the hips of her $650 Geoffrey Keene pants-suit, her nose raised up in the air.

'The place hasn't changed any, has it?' she remarked. 'Still the same old smell of death.'

'Some can smell it and some can't,' replied Reynard, trying to sound as if he were amused; but feeling instead as if he had grit between his teeth. 'Was it Carl who told you about Chiffon Trent?'

'Carl?' Greta asked, obliquely, and walked across to the living-room without answering.

'Don't tell me you had Nathan's Discreet Inquiries on to me again,' said Reynard.

'Nathan's Discreet Inquiries only accept inquiries into affairs which are discreet,' said Greta. She looked back at him with a mixture of sharpness and overplayed pity. 'You and Chiffon Trent have been so damned public you might as well have published a picture in *People*.'

'We're dinner-companions, that's all,' said Reynard. 'Come on, Greta, it was *you* who left *me*. You can hardly complain if I find it socially necessary to have a lady on my arm from time to time.'

'Lady!' Greta said scornfully. Then, 'You've moved the Troy. What on earth is it doing over there?'

The Troy was an oil cartoon for *Esther Fainting in Front of Ahasuerus*, by Jean François de Troy, the final painting of which was hanging in the Maurice Segoura Gallery in New York. Reynard had moved it from its usual place over the fireplace to a shadowy corner by the window-seat. Reynard said, 'I moved it because it reminds me of you. A beautiful woman in a synthetic swoon.'

Greta sat down, and entwined her legs. She opened her pocketbook and took out a gold cigarette-case.

Reynard offered her a light, and she glanced up at him as she inhaled.

'You've changed, you know,' she told him, blowing out smoke. 'There's definitely something more coarse about you. Or perhaps you always were coarse, and I never noticed. Even your *pores* are coarse.'

'My pores?' he said. He put down the heavy Dupont table-lighter, and sat down opposite her. 'Well, that's bad news. Who's going to vote for me if my pores are coarse?'

'Oh, don't worry, people will vote for you in their millions,' Greta smiled. 'American voters have always been irresistibly drawn towards the vulgar and the over-blown. It's a kind of electoral coprophilia. If you're really lucky, they'll not only see that your pores are coarse, they'll remember that you were Lyndon Johnson's favourite spitting partner.'

Reynard drummed his fingers on the gilded arm of his chair. 'What about a glass of wine?' he asked her. 'Are you still drinking Sancerre?'

He was trying so hard to be controlled that the muscles in his face would scarcely move when he spoke. His attorney had raised a finger to him yesterday and warned, 'Be patient, that's all I can say to you. Don't commit yourself. And *don't* get angry.' He very much wished that Maurice were here this afternoon, if only to ward off Greta's needles and barbs and relentless sarcasm, but Greta had insisted on a completely private discussion, no lawyers, no toadies, no men-at-arms. She had always loathed his political entourage, his publicity managers and his male secretaries and his adenoidal accountants. She had collectively called them 'The Snake Pit'. She also believed that when Reynard was alone she could hurt him more, even if she couldn't outwit him. Pain was important to Greta, both her own and Reynard's. Most of their married life had been pain.

They had been apart for nearly ten months now,

Greta and Reynard, although nobody knew that their separation was permanent except their children, their close friends, and their respective attorneys. Greta was living in Newport, in the white summer home that Reynard's grandfather Leonard had built in 1884 when he had first made his fortune in railroads. The children were at school in England. Reynard spent most of his time in Washington, or New York, and the weekends when he was able to come back to the family seat in New Hampshire were increasingly rare. This was his first visit to Concord for three months, and as it was he was going to have to fly back to Washington at first light the following morning.

Both Greta and Reynard were wealthy, well-connected, and good-looking: regardless of Greta's gibes about Reynard's lack of refinement. By all the normal laws of nature and American high society, their marriage should have been idyllic and almost everlasting. Greta was a Verrier, second daughter of the Pasquiset Verriers; small and blonde with a face as perfect as a piece of Dresden and blue eyes that could have chipped diamonds. Reynard, of course, was the oldest of the three Kelly brothers, the social and political princes of New Hampshire. He was physically bigger than his siblings John and Lincoln; and since he had chaired the Committee of Ways and Means his hair had grown wirier and whiter. But he was still young-looking for a 63-year-old; and there was *Saturday Evening Post* openness about his face, something American and fresh-looking, as if he had been mixed out of 100 per cent wholesome ingredients. He could jog two miles without losing his wind, and swim 30 lengths like a professional. He was by far the most charismatic of the northern Democrats, although time and time again his flirtations with the Presidential primaries had ended in confusion and withdrawal. In 1980, his name had been connected by *The Washington Post* with the Winnipesaukee drainage scandal; unfairly, as it later turned out, but too late to salvage his bid for the Presidency. In 1976, he had been linked with Ellen Wangerin, the one-time girlfriend of Sydney 'The Pig' Mandello, and that little item of dirty laundry had obliged him to withdraw from the race on grounds of 'discretion' and to make a public announcement on network TV that he and Greta had been through 'temporary marital difficulties, the same kind of husband-and-wife fighting that 80 per cent of all Americans go through'. He had added, however, that his marriage to Greta was now 'firing on all eight, sweet as a nut.'

The Kelly name had been glittering enough to carry Reynard through both of these scandals, and more, with only a slight tarnishing of his shining armour. But his appetite for pretty girls remained insatiable; and his addiction to roulette meant that he was always in the company of men whose reputations were less than honourable, and who were quite happy to provide him with all the creature-comforts he could ask for, sexual, gastronomic, or sensational. He was not a corrupt man, but he enjoyed the pleasures of power too much to be absolutely honest.

Now, however, he wanted to be President. His aides had weighed up all the political chances and checked every last closet for skeletons. He was ready, as ready as he was ever likely to be. He was at a warm and fatherly age, although not as old as Ronald Reagan. He was a Democrat, with policies that touched on nuclear disarmament, social welfare, and a revolutionary new system of medical aid for the poor and the underprivileged. And he was the kind of man who could be presented as the caring champion of the unemployed, a tough and benevolent hero with a legendary name to match.

There was only one immediate drawback: Greta. If Reynard was going to run for President, he needed

Greta. That was why he had asked her to come up to The Colonnades and talk to him. He wanted to be President, and a President required a First Lady. He was prepared to talk money; he was prepared to talk houses and yachts and racehorses. He was prepared to talk anything which would guarantee that Greta would play the part of his adoring and supportive wife, at least for as long as he was sitting behind that desk in the Oval Office.

He knew that Greta found the idea of the White House alluring, otherwise she wouldn't have come here today. But he was still not sure what she was going to exact from him in return for her performance. She was not a forgiving woman, none of the Verriers ever had been, and she had already taken him for a house, a car, and an annual allowance of nearly half-a-million dollars a year. 'My *pour-boire*,' she called those half-a-million dollars. 'My tip.'

So here they were, in the living-room at The Colonnades, two wealthy and suspicious people, surrounded by satinwood antiques, priceless rugs, and pale-blue velvet drapes with swags and tails and silken cords. Outside on this chilly and restless day, the estates stretched for 326 acres, as far as Oak Hill to the north, and Conant's Acre to the south. Trees, pastures, and rough grazing. Fields of Indian corn, red-speckled and whispering in the wind. And beyond, a view of the Highlands Ski Area and the White Mountains.

Two wealthy and suspicious people, on whose agreement the entire political and social future of the United States could fatefully depend.

Greta said, 'You'll have to give up Chiffon Trent, of course.'

'Is there any need for that? Nobody has to know. And I'd hate to hurt her feelings.'

'Girls who are rash enough to have affairs with you deserve everything that's coming to them,' said Greta, caustically. 'You don't feel sorry for the lady lion-tamer, do you, if the lion happens to bite her head off? It's her own fault for sticking her head in its mouth to begin with.'

'Chiffon's . . . different,' Reynard protested. 'She understands me. Nobody ever understood me the way Chiffon does.'

'Is Chiffon her *real* name?'

'Sure it's her real name. What difference does that make, anyway?'

'I don't know. I just thought that any girl who went out with you would be more likely to be called Percale, or Sacking.'

Reynard pursed his lips. 'You're a bitch, you know that?' he told her. 'Once a bitch, always a bitch.'

'Why should you worry? You've got Chiffon. *Chiffon* understands you.'

'Can we get down to business?' Reynard demanded.

'Well, of course,' said Greta. 'Much as I enjoy talking to you, Reynard, I didn't drive all the way from Newport just to share pleasantries. I gather from what you told me on the telephone that you're thinking of running again.'

'The political conditions are perfect,' Reynard nodded.

'You mean that America has been swept by an overwhelming urge to drag itself out of the Slough of Despond and hurl itself into the Chasm of Infinite Crassness.'

'You know something?' Reynard snapped back. 'There used to be a time when you respected my politics.'

'One has to respect the man to respect his politics,' said Greta.

'But you're still a Democrat? You'd still want to see a Democratic President in the White House?'

'Even if it were *you*, you mean? Well, I suppose so.

But I don't think your chances of winning the nomination are very good, do you? You've got two strikes against you already. You're the man who made Winnipesaukee famous.'

'You know I was innocent of that.'

'I know you were *shown* to be innocent of that.'

Reynard stood up, and walked to the French windows. He looked out across the hewn-stone patio, where a pot of flowerless geraniums were shuddering in the mid-afternoon wind.

'By next November, election day, America is going to be reaching a condition of maximum fear. Fear about its future, fear about its safety, fear about its economy. Winter will be setting in, and that means that every unemployed worker will be wondering how to put a turkey on the table at Christmas, and how to scrape together enough money to buy gifts for his kids. Old people are going to be worried about the cold, the cost of heating and lighting, and the prohibitive cost of medical treatment. The young graduates who left college in the summer and who still haven't found a job are going to be facing their first winter on the executive breadline. Fear, Greta, that's what it's all about. Absolute fear. And that's where I come in.'

Greta crushed out her cigarette, half-smoked. 'You mean that you're going to *frighten* the electorate into voting for you, rather than entice it? I shouldn't have thought that you'd have had much difficulty in doing that. My mother always used to say that you would have scared the pants off Lon Chaney; not to mention Lon Chaney, Jr. Your *eyes*, she said. Never trust a man with eyes that bore holes in you.'

'Your mother was an aristocratic basket-case,' said Reynard.

'My mother was good enough to give you her only daughter.'

'Give? Your mother never gave anything. That scarf

41

your father used to like so much? She sold him that. *Sold* him, for 17 dollars. He told me once, when we were having a drink together. And look what *you* cost. An arm and a leg and a sprained back.'

Greta said nothing. Reynard looked at her for a long while, and then said, 'I'm going for the Presidential nomination, Greta; and this time I'm going to make it. The people in this country are afraid; and I'm going to be offering them freedom from fear. Do you know what that means? Freedom from unemployment; freedom from medical costs; freedom from crime and mugging and urban decay. What I'm offering is what every single voter most desperately wants.'

'You're obviously expecting a landslide, then?' asked Greta. 'Don't you think you ought to win the nomination first? After all, you're going to be up against Walter Mondale and John Glenn, to name but two candidates with a cleaner record than yours.' Then she said irritably, 'Did you call for that glass of wine?'

'Whether I'm nominated or not is up to the party,' said Reynard. 'And whether I'm elected to the Presidency or not, and by how much, is up to the people. I don't expect anything more than plain and honest support for plain and honest measures.'

'Plain, I'll give you,' said Greta. 'Honest, I'm not so sure.'

Reynard came back from the window and sat down. 'Greta, this country has to start living like a family again; and the only way we can do that is if we start taking care of our weak and our sick and our defenceless, the way all families have to. I'm running on a ticket that includes an enormously expanded programme of government spending; vastly improved medical care; new building projects; new highways; new handouts for the destitute and the unemployed.'

'All funded by higher taxes, I suppose?' asked Greta.

Reynard looked at her steadily and said, 'Government

is there to help and to serve the people, but for their part the people have to accept all the responsibility, both moral and financial, that a really caring administration requires. Reagan's administration was founded on selfishness. Bread for the rich, stones for the poor. But good government begins and ends with truly human behaviour; true kindness, if you like. I am going to be nominated and I am going to win the Presidency because I am prepared to come up front and say that I care about every single member of this family that calls itself the United States: rich, poor, middle-class, blue-collar, drunkard, dropout, addict, whore, or pimp.'

'You care about *pimps*?'

'I care about everybody equally.'

'I see,' said Greta. 'It's a pity you didn't demonstrate it to your wife and your children. But I guess when you care equally about 226.5 million people, you have to spread yourself pretty thin.'

'Greta – '

'Oh, forget it,' said Greta. 'I know you care for us in your own idiosyncratic way. Well, I think you do. Where's this wine?'

There was a knock almost immediately at the living-room door, and in walked a pretty black girl with cornrow hair and a maid's black-and-white uniform. Her starched apron was stretched tight across extravagantly large breasts, and as she carried her silver tray across the room, her hips moved in a rhythmic glide that had Greta staring in elaborately-feigned astonishment.

'This is, uh, *Eunice*,' said Reynard, as the black girl Bunny-dipped to put down the silver cooler of Sancerre and two Waterford crystal goblets.

'Pleased to know you, madam,' smiled Eunice, all teeth and twinkly eyes.

'Eunice is Mama Rice's little girl. Well, not so little now,' Reynard stumbled.

43

'Quite,' Greta pronounced. And then, when Eunice had closed the door behind her. 'You didn't tell me you were doing any research into racial attitudes. Not first-hand research, at least.'

Reynard's hand trembled a little as he poured Greta a glass of wine. 'Most connoisseurs describe the flavour of this wine as "catty," ' he said as he handed it to her.

'À votre santé,' said Greta.

Reynard said, 'You must have guessed why I asked you to come here.'

'I have,' nodded Greta. 'But I would love to hear you wriggle and squirm as you try to explain it.'

Reynard sipped his wine, and then set it down on the table beside him. He didn't like dry white wine very much; he was a red burgundy drinker. The only problem was, red burgundy always gave him crashing headaches. So too did Greta. He could feel the nagging pain in his left eyebrow already.

'I won't be able to seek nomination for the Presidency as a separated husband,' he said. 'A President with liberal policies like mine has to be seen as a national father-figure, with a happy and integrated family of his own. The family that lives at the White House is the nation itself in microcosm; and that means I have to bring the children back from England, and also that I have to ask you to come back and live with me as my First Lady.'

'Perhaps you should have thought of that when you took such a fancy to Katherine,' said Greta. It had been Reynard's spasmodic affair with the swan-necked Mrs Katherine T. Welsh which had finally driven Greta to pack her trunks and leave The Colonnades for good. Mrs Welsh (syrupy-voiced, achingly beautiful) had been a college-friend of Greta's, and of all people, Greta had been unable to tolerate Reynard going to bed with her. It had been like having her past violated by Reynard, as well as her future.

'I'm putting this whole thing to you like a business proposition,' said Reynard, rotating his hands as if he were trying to describe how a Rubik's Cube worked. 'It's like I'm offering you a job, a four-year contract. Would-be President requires would-be First Lady, with a view to prestigious live-in position at nation's most fashionable address. Plenty of social duties, extensive charity work, constant smiling.'

'And the salary?' asked Greta.

'Well, it depends on whether you're interested.'

'Give me an idea.'

'Well, a great deal of money, obviously. And at the end of the four years, a selection of prime stocks.'

'You're seriously intending to rent your estranged wife's services so that you can put up a fraudulent political front?'

'Fraudulent is the wrong word,' Reynard retorted. 'The word is, "stable." A stable socio-political image. Just because you and I can't personally get on with each other, that doesn't mean that we can't present ourselves as an ideal couple, in order to give millions of Americans the example and the inspiration that they so sorely need. For God's sake, Robert Wagner and Stephanie Powers aren't married, for all I know they don't even like each other, but nobody accuses *Hart to Hart* of being fraudulent.'

'Reynard, if you can't tell the difference between *Hart to Hart* and the Presidency of the United States, then I don't think that you're *fit* to be President.'

'Of course I can damn well tell the difference!' snapped Reynard. Then, with enormous restraint, he said, 'Of course I can tell the difference. I'm simply using *Hart to Hart* as a metaphor. If Mr Wagner and Ms Powers can be convincing as a happily-married couple in a fictional context, then there isn't any reason at all why we can't be equally convincing in a political context. Both fiction and politics are perceived by the general public through the same media; the same devices can be used. What's the perceptual difference between Nancy Reagan giving Ronald a surprise birthday cake and Jennifer Hart giving Jonathan Hart a surprise birthday cake? Absolutely none.'

Greta took a small mouthful of wine, and held it against her tongue for a moment before swallowing it. Then she said, 'I think you're making one false assumption.'

'What's that?'

'You're assuming that I'm going to say yes. You're also assuming that I'm going to say yes under conditions which you find acceptable.'

Reynard said, 'I'm talking in the area of $3 – $3.5 million, in stage payments, according to the progress of the contract.'

'What do you mean by "the progress of the contract"?'

'For $3.5 million, Greta, I expect a First Lady who *acts* like a First Lady.'

'Oh,' said Greta. 'You mean that if I don't kiss you frequently enough or keep referring to you as The Most Unforgettable Husband I Ever Had, then you won't continue to pay me regularly?'

Reynard looked at his glass of wine and decided not to drink any more. He said, 'All you have to do is agree in principle. Once you've agreed in principle, our lawyers can work out the rest. You can have the whole thing down in writing.'

Greta watched him for seconds on end, and then said, 'You realise what a highly explosive document this contract is going to be. How do you know that I won't use it to blackmail you for the rest of your days?'

'For two reasons,' said Reynard. 'The first is that will be a mandatory condition of the contract that, once fulfilled, all copies of it will be destroyed. What's more, neither of us will actually be permitted to keep a copy of it: but two copies will be lodged with a disinterested third party. A bank, for instance; or a Supreme Court judge.'

'But if I tell?'

Reynard said, 'I've already discussed that possibility with Maurice. He agreed with me that if you do that, then we don't have any other option. This won't be written down anywhere, of course, but you can take it from me that if you attempt to use this arrangement to threaten me in any way, or to extort money, then, well, you will be dealt with.'

'Dealt with? You mean *murdered*?' Greta laughed, high and harshly. 'Poor Reynard, I think you should have been a TV detective, instead of a politician. Can't you just imagine it, *Reynard's Law*, 8 pm Central and Mountain. "If you attempt to use this arrangement to threaten me, Greta, you will be *dealt with*." God, you're pathetic sometimes. Worse than pathetic. You're infantile.'

'But?' said Reynard, inclining his head to one side. She could call him whatever she liked, even though it irritated him so much that he could hardly stand to listen to her any more; but she could never accuse him of lacking in perception.

'But?' queried Greta.

'But, you'll accept the contract,' Reynard coaxed her.

Greta lifted her head. That was the trouble with Reynard. He knew her just a little too well: her ploys and her vulnerabilities. In spite of his apparent naiveté, in spite of his pomposity, he was always so perfectly dressed: light-grey mohair suit, socks without a single wrinkle, laon shirt with white embroidered initials. And this immaculate attire was the outward evidence that he was so wealthy that he could afford to be naïve, he could afford to be mawkish. He could even afford to be wrong. He was so untroubled by financial pressures of any kind; so detached from the violent anxieties which daily assailed the American Family of which he spoke so sympathetically, that he could smile and say he cared about whores. That was his strength. Very few other politicians could afford to be so crass.

He could say he cared about *whores*, damn it, when decent hard-working men in Milwaukee and Seattle and Detroit were standing in interminable lines for the chance of $350-a-week job; and respectable middle-class families were having to shop in thrift stores. Yet those same decent and respectable people would vote for Reynard as enthusiastically as if he were an old friend, in exactly the same way that Greta would eventually say yes to his offer of a rented First Ladyship. She knew it, and she hated herself for it, and him. But he was a Kelly; and the Kellys had always been irresistible.

'You'll have to give me some time to think about it,' said Greta.

'Of course,' said Reynard.

'You're a shit, you know,' she said, and sipped fiercely at her Sancerre.

Reynard shrugged. He wondered how his feelings towards her could be so ambivalent: she aroused him, and he loved her cutting classiness, yet at the same time she could annoy him to screaming-pitch. She was the only thing in the whole world, animal, vegetable or mineral that could ruffle him. Perhaps they should never have married. Perhaps they should never have split up. Perhaps – and this was probably the most accurate thought of all – perhaps they should never have been born on the same planet. Or at least, not in the same century.

'I have several conditions,' said Greta.

'I imagined you would,' Reynard told her. 'Is there anything special, or can we leave it all to the lawyers?'

'There's one thing,' said Greta. 'I want you to promise me that you'll find a senior position on your election staff for a friend of mine. An *effective* position, not a sinecure. And if you're elected, I want you to promise me that you'll appoint him to the government post that he wants.'

'Now, Greta – '

'You *know* him,' interrupted Greta. 'He's not a fool; in fact in many ways he's wiser than you could ever hope to be. He also happens to be a Democrat, so I'm not asking you to appoint a man who's going to give you any political trouble. Walt Seabrook.'

'*Doctor* Walt Seabrook? That gynaecologist you've been fooling around with? He's like George McGovern in a white coat.'

'He happens to be a very sensitive and politically-oriented person. He's also very good at mah-jong. You have to be sensitive to be good at mah-jong.'

'*Mah-jong*?' asked Reynard, disbelievingly.

Greta said, 'You can pour me some more wine.' Then, when Reynard hesitated, she raised her empty glass to him and sharply said, 'Please?'

'Where am I going to find a place on my staff for a technicolour charlatan like Walt Seabrook?' Reynard demanded. 'Quite apart from the fact that he's your current stud.'

'Can't you *ever* resist the temptation to be vulgar?' Greta demanded. 'Walt Seabrook is somebody very special; and the fact that we happen to be able to relate to each other both physically and mentally is completely irrelevant. I mean *politically* irrelevant. He wants to be Assistant Secretary for Health, and you know as well as I do that he'll be absolutely perfect for the job.'

'Greta,' Reynard protested, 'Walt Seabrook is 20 years behind the times. He's a political hippie. When I talk about medical aid, I mean improved tax concessions for the building of private health-centres; and government subsidies for expensive courses of medication. I don't mean free Band-Aids for all comers, with a lid of grass thrown in.'

'Walt Seabrook is just the man you need,' insisted Greta. 'Have you ever seen him on television? He was on that CBS special about fallopian disorders. He was so *warm*. He could talk about inflamed tubes and really make you feel that he *cared*. You could see that he lived that pain, along with the women who were suffering it; and that he lived their childlessness, too.'

Reynard said, 'Are you serious?'

'You're asking me if I'm serious? Walt Seabrook is a human being.'

'The implication being that I'm not?'

'Reynard, this is a condition of my signing that contract. Either you say yes, or it's no go.'

Reynard looked across the room towards the window, as if he wished he were outside walking in the fresh air, instead of discussing the sordid details of a political contract. But after a while he said, 'I suppose you'll want to go on seeing him.'

'Walt? Of course. You're not going to ask me to give up Walt, are you?'

'You asked me to give up Chiffon.'

'Reynard,' Greta complained, 'Chiffon is nothing but one of your two-week flirtations. Walt is *real*. There's a strong possibility that Walt and I might get married.'

'Supposing somebody sees you canoodling with the Assistant Secretary for Health? The First Lady making time with the Assistant Secretary for Health? And supposing that they put two and two together, and check on your background? The whole thing could collapse in ruins; and the country with it.'

'Well, what are you asking?' said Greta. 'You're asking me to stay celibate for four years? That's ridiculous. Apart from being ridiculous, I won't do it.'

'All I'm saying is, you're going to have to be discreet. I mean discreet to the point of invisibility. Because if I hear one rumour that the First Lady has been fornicating with her one-time doctor; just one word in the

50

National Enquirer, then believe you me, you're going to die, and so is Walt.'

'You're jealous,' Greta provoked him.

'Am I? Maybe I am. I'm only a human being.'

'You're *jealous*,' Greta repeated. Her eyes were bright with caustic delight. 'You're deeply, woundedly jealous.'

'So?' asked Reynard.

'So I'm beginning to wonder if you're running for the Presidential nomination for the sake of your political convictions; or simply as a means of getting me back.'

'You think I care about that *putz* Seabrook?'

'You must do, otherwise it wouldn't upset you whenever I mention his name.'

'He doesn't upset me.'

'He does too.'

'Listen, Greta!' Reynard shouted. 'He does not upset me! Believe me, whatever you do these days, it's your own affair. Walt Seabrook – I beg your pardon, *Doctor* Walt Seabrook, is your own affair. You're a free agent.'

'Then you won't have any trouble in saying yes.'

Reynard stared at her. His eyes were bulgy with anger. 'You mean yes, Walt Seabrook can work on my staff?'

'That's right. And yes, he can expect to be appointed as Assistant Secretary for Health.'

Reynard rubbed his face with his hands. At last, he looked up at Greta through his fingertips, and said, 'Every time I meet you, I remember why I cheated on you.'

'No, you don't,' smiled Greta. 'You don't even remember what you ate for lunch yesterday. You cheat because you're an incurable cheat; because it's your nature. This plan of yours for winning yourself the Presidency, don't you think that's cheating? You're a cheat by nature, Reynard Kelly, and that's all there is to it.'

Reynard thought for a while, in silence. Greta finished her second glass of wine, and took out another cigarette. The sunlight which had been crossing the floor began progressively to fade; and outside, the New Hampshire landscape took on a dull and threatening appearance, black metallic sky, bright beige soil, hysterical trees, as if it all had been printed in the wrong colours.

At last, Reynard said, 'All right. Walt Seabrook can have what he wants. *You* can have what you want. As long as you promise to keep yourselves silent. Not only you, Walt Seabrook too.'

'Or you'll kill us,' said Greta, lighting her cigarette, and breathing out twin tusks of smoke.

'Yes,' said Reynard, in the flat voice of someone who has given in a long time ago.

FOUR

He held Michael's body in his arms as tenderly as if the boy were his own son, and as if he were still alive. He looked down at the white, sculptured face, at the breathless nostrils, at the blue-veined eyelids; and then he laid him down on the sofa, the head propped up by a cushion, and slowly drew the plaid blanket up to the neck. He didn't cover the face.

'Was there anything I could have done, anything at all?' Michael's mother asked him. Her expression was blurred with grief. Behind her, Michael's father stood tall and silent and stunned, as if he had been caught at the exact instant that somebody had hit him in the side of the head with a gold-beater's hammer. He had moved here to New Hampshire, changed his engineering job, changed his life, just to give Michael a healthier environment to grow up in.

Edmond unclipped his stethoscope from around his neck. 'I'm sorry, Mrs Osman, nothing.' He looked down at Michael again. 'I don't quite understand how he died; or how it could have been so sudden. The coroner will obviously want to make a thorough check of his own. As far as I can make out, he just stopped breathing.'

'Nobody just stops breathing,' protested Mr Osman. He stared at Edmond with a lack of understanding that verged on a peculiar kind of fury. 'I mean – nobody just stops breathing.' He paused, and then he said, '*Do* they?'

Edmond shrugged, not dismissively, but helplessly. 'Mr Osman, I simply don't have the answers. Not at the moment. Michael was feeling quite well the last time your wife saw him, wasn't he? No sudden temperatures? No complaints about stiffness or weakness in his arms and legs?'

Mrs Osman bit her lips. 'He was never healthier,' she said, her voice congested with tears. 'Running, playing with his friends, laughing. He was never healthier.'

Michael lay on the sofa like an alabaster statue of himself. For some reason, Edmond felt for a moment as if the boy might be playing a practical joke on them all; and that suddenly he might open one eye and grin at them, and run out of the house and off down the street, laughing. But there was to be no more running for Michael, no more laughing. Nothing but a medical examiner's knife and an autumn funeral, and a few colour photographs on top of the television in which he would never grow old.

Mrs Osman shuddered with the pain of it; with the sudden and devastating absence of her only child.

Edmond said, 'The reason I asked about the fever was because what appears to have happened here is a paralysis of the intercostal muscles, the muscles which the body uses to breathe. The same thing can happen in attacks of polio; and recently we've had one or two cases around the neighbourhood schools. Parents forget to have their children vaccinated, you know, or else they don't think it's worth it.

He hesitated, and then he said, 'I know that Michael was vaccinated. But there are some remarkable similarities to polio here that I can't ignore.'

'Polio doesn't hit anybody as quickly as this, surely?' asked Mr Osman. He kept on staring at Edmond so that he wouldn't have to look at his son.

'Well, not usually,' Edmond told him. 'The symptoms are usually gradual, and very noticeable. Fever, aches and pains, stiffness. I don't know. Maybe I'm all wrong. I don't have the facilities here to be able to make an expert judgement. But the pathologist will find out what happened for sure.'

He felt desperately inadequate, standing here in front of the Osmans like this, and having to tell them that he didn't know what had killed their son. But what else could he do? The boy had simply stopped breathing. His intercostal muscles were in a state of paralysis, which Edmond would usually have associated with poliomyelitis, yet how could such a severe paralysis have attacked him so swiftly? In the few cases of polio with which Edmond had dealt in the past two months the symptoms had been relatively mild, and with proper bedrest and appropriate medication, none of his patients had suffered paralysis at all. What had happened to Michael appeared to be something ferociously different. A mad dog virus that killed you as soon as you caught it.

Mrs Osman took hold of Edmond's arm, and clutched it so tight that she pinched his skin through his jacket. 'They won't – cut him up or anything.'

Edmond said softly, 'No. They'll have to take a

sample of spinal fluid, but all they need for that is a needle. And they'll probably take a microscopically thin slice of skin, so that they can examine it under the microscope. They have to see if Michael had an excess of cells in his spinal fluid, or an excess of protein, and those could be indications that he's been suffering from polio.'

'Polio,' whispered Mr Osman. 'Who'd have believed it?'

'Well, we don't know for sure,' said Edmond. He went across to the shiny-topped table and opened his bag, tucking away his stethoscope. On the wall in front of him was a reproduction of William Ranney's famous painting, *The Pioneers*, a woman on a horse, a man walking with a musket over his shoulder. Maybe, in some curious way, that was how the Osmans viewed themselves, lone pioneers in a lonely landscape. Outside, he could hear the whooping of a siren as the ambulance from the New Hampshire Hospital came around the corner of Eddy Drive. No sirens necessary, he thought. For Michael Osman, sirens are all too late.

The ambulance drew up outside, and right behind it the khaki-coloured station-wagon driven by Oscar Ford, the pathologist. Oscar tramped red-faced up the sloping garden path, and was just raising his hand to jab at the doorbell when Edmond opened the door for him.

'How are you keeping, E.C.?' Oscar asked him. He grasped Edmond's hand so tightly that he painfully pressed Edmond's wedding-band against his knuckle. 'Didn't see you over at the Motz place last week.'

'I was held up at the paediatric clinic.'

Oscar slapped Edmond's shoulder. 'You work too hard, you know that? Joe Sullivan says that you're building yourself quite a local reputation for conscientiousness. You must remember that this is the boonies, E.C. The pace of life is slower here, and not many of us know how to *pronounce* conscientiousness, let alone get ourselves a reputation for it. Joe said you're becoming the Albert Schweitzer of Concord.'

'I hope he meant that kindly.'

'Joe never means anything kindly. Hey, by the way, Judy ran into Christy at the market last week.'

Edmond gave Oscar an impatient grimace. 'Yes, Christy said that she'd seen her.'

'Judy said that Christy was buying favours for your surprise birthday party next week,' said Oscar. Then suddenly, melodramatically, he clapped his hand to his mouth, 'Hey – oops, I'm *sorry*. E.C., I'm really sorry. Now I guess it's a *non*-surprise party.'

Edmond stared at him tightly. He had guessed that Christy had been planning a party, but he hadn't known for sure. He said, 'You're all class, Oscar. You know that?'

'I probably saved your life,' Oscar told him, winking. 'Surprise parties are the biggest single cause of cardiac arrest after balling your secretary. You remember that mass homicide over at Laconia? That was a surprise party. The wife shouted 'surprise!' and the husband took out his shotgun and shouted, 'surprise to you, too, slimebag!' and blew away his wife, his Borzoi dog, *and* four of his guests, including his broker, before anybody could stop him. It was stress, you see. The human nervous system is not designed to take surprises like that and like them. Now, where's the remains?'

'The dead boy,' said Edmond emphatically, 'is in the living-room.'

'The parents?'

'They're with him.'

'Get them out.'

'Oscar – '

'I said, *get* them out, not throw them out. I'm not totally lacking in sensitivity, whatever you think. You know I'm going to have to do things to that boy that they won't want to see.'

56

'I'll get them out,' said Edmond. 'But let's get one thing straight. These people are on my personal list and they've just lost their only child. Are you listening?'

'You don't think I know how to be tactful?' Oscar demanded.

'I think you sometimes forget that dead people aren't a selection of cold cuts, and that not very long ago they used to be very dear to the people who knew them, that's all.'

'E.C.,' said Oscar harshly, 'I've cradled more weeping widows on my shoulder than you've had satisfactory craps. Now, let's get this thing on the road, before the boy starts decomposing on us.'

Edmond went back to the living-room. Mr and Mrs Osman were kneeling on the rug beside the sofa, both of them saying a prayer over their son's dead body. The last light of the day faded around them, and in the twilight, Michael's face appeared almost luminous; a death-mask of youthfulness.

When Mr and Mrs Osman had finished, Oscar said, '*Amen*.' Edmond glanced at him but Oscar remained impassive, meaty and short and ruddy-cheeked; more like an Irish boatman than a pathologist.

Edmund spoke quietly to Mr and Mrs Osman, and then ushered them out through the door. Before he left, Mr Osman said, in a voice that was trembling unsteadily, 'You'll treat him with respect, won't you?'

Oscar nodded, almost imperceptibly. 'Sure thing, Mr Osman,' and he almost managed to sound as if he meant it.

When the Osmans had gone, Oscar brought over a table-lamp, lifted off the shade, and switched on the naked bulb so that it shone over the dead boy. He tugged off the blanket which covered the body, and expertly stripped off the boy's clothes. Edmond stood in the background and watched him without saying anything.

'Any conclusions?' asked Oscar, as he tapped at Michael's chest, and then shone a torch into the boy's mouth so that his cheeks were lit up in eerie scarlet.

'Any conclusions about what?'

'Cause of death, what else? You have come to *some* conclusions?'

'I made a cursory examination, in case it was anything infectious I ought to have known about.'

'Covering your tracks, huh?'

'Protecting the neighbourhood.'

'Oh, I'm sorry. I forgot you were a D.S.A.?'

'What the hell's a D.S.A.?'

Oscar wiped his hands, and smiled. 'Doctor in Shining Armour.'

'Is that another one of Joe Sullivan's gibes?'

Oscar said, 'Tell me what conclusions, that's all.'

Edmond was silent for a moment or two. Then he said, as steadily as he could manage, 'I'm not at all sure. But it appears to me that Michael died from asphyxia caused by paralysis or traumatic spasm of the respiratory muscles. Without having taken samples of spinal fluid, I would have guessed that he might have died from an unusually sudden attack of poliomyelitis.'

'Was he sick? Feverish?'

'No symptoms whatever, as far as the parents can recall.'

'Hmm,' said Oscar. He closed Michael's mouth and drew the blanket over his head. 'Did the parents have any idea where he might have picked up anything like poliomyelitis in the past few weeks?'

'We've had one or two cases in our local schools, as you probably know. But nothing serious. And nothing sudden, like this.'

'Where was he today?'

'Out on his bicycle.'

'The parents know where?'

Edmond shook his head. 'They said his best friend was having a music lesson, so he went out on his own.'

'Make sure you check the best friend,' said Oscar. 'Preferably, today.'

Edmond said, 'I've already called his parents. His name's Bernie Mayer, lives two blocks to the north-west of here, Strafford Circle. I've arranged to see him this evening.'

Oscar lifted Michael's buttock and matter-of-factly pushed a rectal thermometer into his anus. Then he turned him this way and that, inspecting the bruise-like marks caused by blood pooling in the lower parts of the body, when there was no longer any heartbeat to circulate it. This inspection would help him to corroborate Mr and Mrs Osman's estimate of the time of death.

'You've talked to the parents about the autopsy?' Oscar asked.

'Sure. They seem to accept that it has to be done. Just, no hacking, that's all.'

Oscar looked up at Edmond with immediate hostility, and then realized that Edmond was getting back at him for spoiling the surprise of Christy's party. 'All right,' he said. 'No hacking.' He inspected the dead boy's fingernails. 'I do the neatest job in the business, *and* you know it. One slice around the middle of the head to get at the brain; one slice down the middle of the abdomen, to get at the guts. Divide the sternum, that's all. And always perfect. *Art*, you know what I mean?' He sniffed, and then said, 'Hacking, for Christ's sake.'

They stood together and looked down at the dead boy in silence. Both of them felt unsettled by the death; not so much because Michael was a child who should have had all of his life in front of him. They had both seen too many juvenile fatalities for that. But because the sickness that had killed him had attacked so fast and so uncharacteristically. To be asphyxiated by polio in a matter of minutes was unheard-of; and nothing in years of medical experience had prepared them for it.

'It *looks* like polio,' said Edmond.

'It has all the characteristics,' Oscar admitted. 'From what I've seen so far, death seems to have been caused by virally-induced paralysis of the intercostal muscles. But, well, you know what they say about first impressions.'

'What do they say about first impressions?' Edmond had the feeling that Oscar was trying to tell him something.

Oscar withdrew the rectal thermometer and peered at it carefully. 'The same thing they say about country doctors who used to be city doctors. Don't trust them.'

'Oh, yes?'

Oscar wiped his hands. 'They usually say, nobody moves out to Concord New Hampshire, unless they have to. Especially when they've been running a wealthy practice in mid-town Manhattan.

'You're trying to impart some delicate information, is that it?' asked Edmond. The trouble was, he already had half an inkling of what Oscar was going to say. It had been bound to come out, sooner or later. He hadn't expected it so soon.

Oscar went over to the living-room window, and beckoned to the ambulance crew outside. Then he turned back to Edmond, and thrust his hands into his pockets, and sniffed, and looked down at Michael's dead body again, and said, 'I like you, for some stupid reason. I think you're good although I wouldn't norm-ally admit it. Probably too good for Pembroke, New Hampshire. But something happened to you in Manhattan that you know about and the Concord Board of Health knows about; but which is now becoming the subject of some pretty bizarre rumours down at the hospital, and down at the ambulance station, too; not to mention the Concord Country Club.'

Edmond said, 'What rumours?'

'You really want to know what rumours?'

'I think I have a *right* to know.'

'Well, I don't know whether it's true or not, but the rumours are that you had to leave New York because you tried to perform an impromptu tracheotomy using only a carving-knife, because a woman was choking. And the rumour was that you weren't too steady and you weren't too sober, and you ended up cutting her throat. And the rumour says that you only got away with it because she was the wife of your senior partner, and if the scandal had gotten out, his whole practice would have been sunk.'

Edmond was silent for a long time. Then he turned to Oscar, and said, 'You believe this stuff?'

Oscar made a face. 'It doesn't matter whether I believe it or not, does it? The point is, the rumour's going around.'

'And?'

'And I'm just trying to warn you to keep a low profile, both politically and medically.'

Edmond said nothing; but just as Mrs Osman let the ambulance crew in through the front door, Oscar said, 'It's election year next year. Somebody on the Board of Health approved your appointment, and said you were fit to work for the Merrimack Clinic, in spite of whatever it was you were rumoured to have done. You get what I'm saying? Next year, that somebody is going to be very vulnerable, because of you. So you can bet that the local sharks are going to start circling, and that whatever you did or didn't do that caused you to leave Manhattan so promptly, that's going to be the bleeding meat that brings them in.'

'You have a way of putting things,' said Edmond.

Oscar raised a hand. He hadn't washed it yet, and it seemed to smell of death. 'I'm not saying anything, E.C. I'm just passing on rumours. But if you hear that a storm's coming, what do you do, you go out and buy yourself a lightning-rod, you understand me? Fore-warned is forearmed.'

'Listen – ' said Edmond.

'A friendly caution, that's all,' said Oscar. 'Me, I don't care what you've done, or where you came from, or why. I judge only by results. But this is election season, and there are people who *do* care.'

The ambulance crew brought the gurney into the hallway outside, and pushed open the door, and said, 'Where is he? In here?'

'That's right,' said Oscar, standing up. 'Treat him gentle, will you? Edmond – I'll catch up with you tomorrow. Maybe we should have a drink.'

'Sure,' said Edmond flatly, and picked up his bag and left.

He drove the long way back to his home at East Concord, just off Shawmot Street, even though it was dark, and it was beginning to rain. The radio was playing soft and sentimental jazz, the kind that always made him feel lonely. But he had to think things over before he went back to Christy. He had to think what he was going to tell her, and most critically of all, he had to think how he was going to cope with his own entangled past, a past that never seemed to let him forget. He had somehow hoped that once they were settled in New Hampshire, he was going to be able to live a new life, he and Christy together, Edmond Chandler, M.D., private physician and paediatric consultant to the Merrimack County Clinic.

But his life was still too crowded with memories, and the memories refused to be shut away, like old and ugly clothes which bulged obstinately out of a suitcase.

The most complicated memory of all, of course, was Arabelle Thorne. Dead now for three-and-a-half years, but still as vivid in his mind as the day when he had first made love to her. He could still imagine her standing by that open window in East Hampton in that pale summer dress, with the breeze billowing the nets, her head half-turned towards him, lips slightly parted, and Beethoven's Emperor Concerto filling the room like bars of sunshine. Arabelle: dead now, and gone. Yet hopelessly unforgettable.

She had said to him once, 'Midnight shakes the memory, as a madman shakes a dead geranium.' And she had pursed her lips, her eyes bright with amusement, waiting for him to say *What?*

'T. S. Eliot,' she had whispered, kissing him unexpectedly on the back of his wrist, in that sensitive spot where his Rolex had been. And then she had switched off the light.

Now, on the road between Sugar Ball and East Concord, in the rain, he drew his Camaro over to the verge, and pushed on the parking-brake, and sat there with the windshield wipers making rubbery noises against the glass, while Gil Evans and his Orchestra played *Hotel-Me* as if it were a personal message from Edmond's past.

'If you hear that a storm's coming, what do you do, you go out and buy yourself a lightning-rod.'

Edmond Chandler was 41 years old; although not many people he met believed it, and he could hardly believe it of himself. Right up until the evening before his 40th birthday he had thought to himself: not me, not forty. It can't be me. I'm fresh out of med-school, I've only just begun my career. Thirty-five, maybe; 36, at a pinch. But not 40. But the day had arrived, and the birthday cards had given malicious proof that his life was already more than half-lived. And ever since then, something inside him had somehow slipped, and somehow he couldn't find it within him self to care so much.

He had stopped exercising, although he still played

a desultory game of squash, and he hadn't yet lost his leanness. He had brown, brushed-back, Clint-Eastwood hair, although his face was more oval than Clint Eastwood's, and his eyebrows were denser. When he read, or wrote out prescriptions, he wore thick-rimmed tortoiseshell glasses: when he drove a car, he wore a permanent wincing frown as if he were trying to make out if he could see Comanches on the horizon, or if it was only a mirage.

He was both fascinated and alarmed by the gradual process of falling-apart that seemed to be attacking his body and his mind. Somehow, he didn't seem capable of saying anything original or fresh any more: somehow, every action he performed seemed to be routine, and uninspired. Maybe it was the effect of living and working in New Hampshire. Maybe it was just him. Either way, he couldn't understand how a man of his age and condition could still be so fiercely in love with the girl he had killed; and still be so deeply dependent on the wife who had seen him through it.

He still couldn't really grasp that Arabelle was dead; nor that Christy had stuck with him. Perhaps he had never been worthy of either of them, the living wife or the dead lover. Perhaps he had given up trying to understand what had happened to him; and, most of all, trying to understand himself. He had analysed himself so many times that he felt as if he wrapped himself up in self-examination, tight as a mummy in swathes of bandages, and that now he could no longer move nor think. All he could do was sit here in the rain, listening to the rubbery complaints of the windshield wipers, tired, defeated, and ceaselessly troubled.

At last, he released the parking-brake, flicked down the indicator, and pulled out on to the highway to drive home. 'Home' appeared all too promptly; no sooner driven towards than arrived at. A large modern split-level house with a shingled roof and a line of miniature trees beside the driveway, and a sloping front lawn that shone unnaturally green in the light from the head-lamps. All the lights were on: Edmond could see into the living-room, where the television was flickering, where potted yuccas flourished, and where his medical certificates were hanging tastefully framed in gold on the tasteful natural-stone wall. It wasn't East 85th Street, but then what was, except East 85th Street? Christy appeared briefly, blonde and cropped, and then turned and walked back towards the hallway. Perhaps she had heard his car coming. She was wearing her scarlet house-dress, the one he liked because it was sexy and because it was scarlet. He turned the Camaro into the angled driveway, alongside the miniature trees, pushed on the brake and killed the engine. He was still sitting in the car when Christy opened the front door, and raised her hand not to wave but to shield her eyes from the bright porch light.

He sat in the car for so long that at last she came out into the rain and tapped with her knuckle on the glass. He put down the window and the rainy breeze blew her Arpège perfume into the car. 'Edmond?' she asked him. 'What's the matter? What are you sitting there for? Come on in, supper's ready.'

He gave her a small pursed-up grin, and nodded. 'Tired, that's all,' he told her, as if that were explanation enough. He put up the window again, took out the key, and climbed out of the car. Halfway back to the house, she turned, and looked at him, and said, 'Come on, Edmond?'

Inside the door, he took off his coat and hung it up on the bentwood hatstand that used to grace their hallway in New York. It looked pretentious here in Pembroke; but then so did almost everything they owned, clothes, cars, furniture, and paintings. Their living-room was furnished with elegant Italian chairs and tables they had bought at Acapellas on Fifth

Avenue; there were three splashy de Koonings on the corridor wall, as well as two Richard Lindners and an Andrew Stevovich. The suburban proportions of the house made them all look absurdly pretentious.

Christy said, 'Something's wrong. You look pale. My God, Edmond you look *white*.'

He sat down, and unlaced his shoes. 'Hard day, that's all.'

'Would you like a drink?'

'Yes, I think I would.'

She made a move towards the lacquered Chinese drinks cabinet, then hesitated. 'Edmond,' she said, 'something's *wrong*.'

He looked up at her. For a split-second, his temper almost burst out of him like an ugly ballerina bursting out of a birthday-cake. Then he took a deep breath to steady himself, and attempted a smile.

'A boy died today. Nine years old, that's all. I guess it upset me.'

'Irma told me you were called out on emergency,' said Christy. 'Somewhere by Conant's Acre?'

'Webster Crescent,' Edmond nodded. 'The boy was dead by the time I got there.'

'Anybody I know?'

'I don't think so, the Osmans. Nice couple; hadn't been living in New Hampshire for very long. Newcomers, like us. They took it pretty hard, as you can imagine. The only reason they moved out here was to give their boy some fresh air and fields.'

'What was it?' asked Christy.

'What killed him? I don't know. Well, polio, I think. But not the usual kind of polio. This morning he was fine; this afternoon he was dead.'

Christy opened the drinks cabinet and poured Edmond a stiff three fingers of bourbon. He rarely drank these days; he didn't trust himself. But every now and then he needed a short hard belt, and this was one of those moments.

Edmond watched Christy as she screwed the lid back on the bottle. She seemed to have grown calmer since they had relocated to New Hampshire. She was very slim, wide-shouldered, and still highly stylish, especially for a community like Pembroke, where most of the women wore jeans. Even the casual house-dress she was wearing looked '40s and fashionable. But she conducted herself with far greater serenity these days, and both of them drank less and had fewer prickly arguments. Maybe she was growing older, gracefully. Maybe the countryside had a settling effect on her: the trees, the forests, and the dark, reflective lakes.

And although this was one thought that he didn't usually allow himself to think – maybe she was calmer because Arabelle was dead, and because she knew that Edmond wouldn't dare to tangle himself up in another affair if he wanted to remain in practice. Harold Bunyan had warned him when he first recommended his appointment that all his outstanding favours had now been repaid; and that if there was ever one whisper of scandal, one suggestion of misconduct, he would be out on his own, and probably out of medicine, too.

Christy said, 'It's not catching, is it?'

'The polio? Well, I don't know. It's usually transmitted by contaminated faeces. I won't be able to tell for sure until Oscar makes all his tests. Even then he probably won't tell me the whole story. Oh – he told me one thing, though.'

'What was that?'

'Judy saw you at the market, shopping.'

'So?'

'He told me what you were shopping for.'

Christy opened and closed her mouth in exasperation. 'He *told* you? He told you about the – ?'

67

Edmond nodded. 'The surprise party, yes. I'm sorry. It's just Oscar's way of trying to be funny.'

'Well, ha, ha. Oh, Edmond, I'm *sick* about that. I've gotten so much ready.'

Edmond swallowed bourbon, and coughed. 'It's okay. I didn't want to be 42 anyway.'

'Thank you for nothing. Why on earth did Oscar have to tell you? And why did Judy have to tell Oscar? Oh, I'm so damned annoyed.'

'Have you invited many people?' asked Edmond.

'Forty.'

'Well, maybe I could pretend to be surprised. I don't want to spoil *their* fun.'

'It's not the same,' Christy protested. 'The whole point about a surprise party is that you're really surprised.'

'Who's coming? Anybody from New York?'

Christy went over to the drinks cabinet and poured herself a gin-and-tonic. Then she knelt down on the carpet beside him, and rested one elbow on his knee. He bent forward and kissed her forehead. Her eyes were the colour of pasqueflowers, almost violet. Her house-dress was slightly open, and Edmond could see the full bulge of her breast. For a moment there was no sound but the faintest sprinkling noise of effervescence in her drink.

'I'll probably cancel it,' she said.

'You didn't invite the Forbes, did you?'

'I did, as a matter of fact.'

'Who else?'

She took his hand, and stroked it with gentle absent-mindedness. 'I invited your brother,' she said.

'*Malcolm*?'

'You only have one brother, don't you?'

'I really don't believe you sometimes,' Edmond told her. 'I haven't spoken to Malcolm for three years and I don't intend to start now. What the hell kind of a party were you planning? The New Hampshire Chain-Saw Massacre?'

Christy sat up straighter and flushed a little. 'I thought it was time that you two made up. He's your brother, Edmond, you can't ostracize him for the rest of your life.'

'For what he did to me, I think I'm entitled to blood.'

Christy could easily have made the sharp remark that drawing blood was something at which he excelled; but she pursed her lips and looked away, and said nothing at all.

'I'm sorry,' said Edmond. 'But none of my family have ever been particularly close, and I really don't feel much like cozying up to them now.'

'Well, then,' said Christy, 'I suppose it was just as well that Oscar told you about the party. It obviously would have been a resounding flop.'

'Christy – '

'For Christ's sake, Edmond,' she said, tiredly. 'You can never take things as they come, can you? You never like anything that anybody does for you, no matter how hard they try to please you. The trouble is, you're not even a perfectionist. You just have to do things your own way.'

Edmond held her shoulder, touched her neck with his fingertips. 'Listen,' he said, 'let's have the party anyway. Just as a normal party.'

'I don't know. It seems like it's spoiled now.'

'Well, think about it. But I'd like to have it. I'll even try to unclench my teeth to speak to Malcolm.'

Christy finished her drink, and then stood up. 'I'm not sure. Let me think it over. Do you want anything to eat?'

'Let me take you out. I have to go back to Webster Crescent in any case to take a look at the dead boy's friend. You know, just to make sure that there's no infection. We could call in at the Penacook Lodge.'

'I'm not dressed,' said Christy.

Edmond put down his glass, and stood up beside her. He unfastened the four small flower-shaped buttons on the front of her house-dress, and then slipped his hand inside, cupping her bare breast. She stared into his eyes for what seemed a very long time. Then she said, '*hm*', and turned away. Edmond stood and watched her as she walked out of the living-room and up the stairs.

At the top of the stairs, with only her ankles and her red-thonged sandals in view, she paused, and turned, and said, 'Aren't you coming?'

As Edmond was following Christy upstairs, young Bernie Mayer was cycling around Webster Crescent on his way to see Michael. He skidded to a stop outside Michael's house, but he was surprised to see that the garage was open and empty, and that all the windows in the house were in darkness.

He laid his bicycle down on the lawn, and went to the front door and pushed the bell. He heard it chiming but there was no reply. He pressed it again, but there was still no reply. That was weird. Double-weird.

He went into the garage to see if Michael's bicycle was there. It was, parked against the wall. Bernie pressed the button which was supposed to activate the bicycle's siren, but the battery must have been dead.

Oh well, maybe Michael had gone out with his parents for a hamburger. He hadn't *said* they were going to go; but maybe they'd just decided to, on the spur of the moment. It wasn't really fair, though: they'd known he was coming back later, and they might have waited. It wasn't *his* fault he had to go to any stupid old music-lesson.

He went to the back of the garage. Maybe he should take out the dollar in change which they always kept in the treasure-store in case of emergencies. This was a sort of emergency, after all. Well, if not an actual emergency, it was the kind of situation which could definitely be improved by a few bars of candy.

He moved aside the rags and bottles of polish, and prized open the loose brick. It was dark down at that end of the garage, but he didn't want to put on the light in case any of the neighbours saw him poking around. Nevertheless, as soon as he put his hand inside the cavity and groped towards the back of it, he found the leather case with the bottles in it, and thought, *treble*-weird. Michael's found a new treasure, something I've never even seen before, and he's hidden it.

He drew out the box and held it up, gently shaking it to hear what kind of noise it made.

Bottles, definitely. But bottles of what? And why was Michael hiding them?

Well, thought Bernie, there's only one way to find out. Open them up and take a look. *That* would teach Michael for going out for a hamburger without even waiting for his best friend. That would show him that he couldn't pull a fast one on Bernie Mayer. I mean, who did Michael think he was?

FIVE

He was stalking like M. Hulot around the cold, court-yard of the Swedish Royal Palace, taking erratic photographs of the grey, uncompromising buildings, and the oddly long-haired sentries in their white-painted helmets, when he became aware quite acutely, that he was being watched. A tall young blond-haired man in a putty-coloured windbreaker was leaning against one of the palace walls, his arms folded, making no attempt to disguise the fact that he was staring at Humphrey with the kind of raptness that Italian Romeos reserve

71

for fat but likely English girls. The young man was tanned, and extremely handsome in a ski-lodge kind of way, and Humphrey's first thought was: oh my God, a homosexual.

Humphrey put away his cloud filters and his Nikon camera, and carefully snap-fastened the cases. Then he walked at a brisk diagonal away from the palace walls, his shoes tapping sharply on the cold early-evening cobblestones. I must resist the temptation to turn around, he thought. That will look like a come-on. I must keep my back to the man, and leave the palace promptly but unhurriedly.

Humphrey was not a homosexual himself, although he sometimes wondered if his celibate life with his sister had led some of his friends and his neighbours to believe that he was. He had loved a girl once, a clippie. Her name had been Marjorie, and she had been perky and pretty with bubbly curls. He had caught her 85 bus every morning, and once he had taken her out for tea. They had kissed by the park gates. But, of course, she had been hopelessly unsuitable. Her sister had said, 'not really our type, dear,' although in some ways she had been quite nice about what she had always referred to afterwards as 'Humphrey's little spot of wild-oats sowing.'

In every memory of those post-war years, it seemed to Humphrey that it had always been August and that he had always been hopelessly hot in a Fair Isle sweater, floundering in wool. These days, he felt the cold, especially in his feet.

He reached Stortorget, the old square. He was surrounded on all sides by flat-faced medieval buildings, and there were tubs of white flowers shuddering in the wind. He turned, and to his alarm the tall young blond-haired man was only a few paces away from him, and worse, he was *smiling*.

72

'Mr Browne?' the young man asked, in an American accent.

Humphrey stood where he was, his hair lifted by the wind. The young man appeared even taller now that he was close up, and by the way he walked he was evidently something of an athlete. A jock, wasn't that what the Americans called them? The word *jock* had terrible connotations with *straps*. Humphrey sniffed, but said nothing. He didn't know what to say that wouldn't sound either vixenish or coy.

'You *are* Mr Browne?' the young man asked, smiling to show Humphrey his threatening white teeth.

'What's it to you?' asked Humphrey, and then immediately wished that he hadn't. What's it to you, dear, 'scuse me for asking.

'My name's Bill Bennett,' the young man told him. He held out his hand 'I've been watching you for most of the afternoon.'

Humphrey ignored the outstretched hand. My God, he thought, what could be more homosexual than 'Bill Bennett'? He let out a peculiar whinnying laugh, more out of nerves than anything else, and then said, 'I'm not interested, you know. Just because I'm English.'

'I don't think you understand,' said Bill Bennett, frowning. 'I was sent here to talk to you because of something you said to Major Milliner.'

'*Milner*,' Humphrey corrected him. Then, more slowly, 'You were sent here? By whom? You were sent here because of what I said to Major Milner?'

Bill Bennett glanced around the square. On a bench in the far corner, four old Stockholm winos were drinking vodka out of brown paper bags, and having what sounded like a hawking contest. 'Listen,' he said, 'maybe I can buy you a drink.'

Humphrey hesistated. 'I was intending to go back to my hotel for a bath.'

'You're right next door to the Sheraton, aren't you?

73

That's where I'm staying. Go take a bath and then meet me in the bar at seven. How's that?'

'Well,' said Humphrey, feeling dreadfully uncertain. 'All right. But I wish you'd give me some idea of what this is all about.'

Bill Bennett smiled. 'Do you play tennis?' he asked.

'Tennis? What has tennis got to do with it?'

'Nothing. But I like to keep my game up, even when I'm working.'

Humphrey took a taxi back to the Lantona, locked his door, undressed, and took a very hot bath. Afterwards, crimson, he sat on the bed in his bathrobe and wondered whether he ought to call Major Milner to find out if 'Bill Bennett' was genuine. Yet for some reason he felt reluctant to do so. How could 'Bill Bennett' be anything *but* genuine, especially since Major Milner was the only person who knew that he had identified Hermann? And Major Milner had always intimidated Humphrey. There was something about his crisp but evasive way of talking; his cheery golf-club manner; that always made Humphrey feel as if he were inferior, as if he hadn't been to quite the right school, and as if there was tomato soup on his tie. His sister would have adored Major Milner, and perhaps that was why Humphrey didn't want to call him now.

Humphrey gnawed at the edge of his thumbnail. He didn't like this spy stuff at all. At least in John le Carré novels everybody played out a dreamlike but infinitely controlled existence. This business with Hermann was all too random, and frightening, too. It was quite possible that a fellow might get killed; and then who would ever know about it? Only his sister, and what would she do? Nothing, except sit in church and suck mint imperials while the Reverend Johnson talked about death being 'a mist of darkness forever'.

Sod that, he thought; and surprised himself with his own vulgarity. He picked up the phone and asked for a line, then dialled Major Milner's number. The phone rang and rang but there was no reply. Major Milner was probably down at the Three Tuns, drinking Bell's-and-water and telling everybody what a jolly nice chap he was. Humphrey was annoyed, but also vaguely relieved.

Bill Bennett was waiting for him on one of the black leather barstools in the Sheraton Hotel. There was soft Muzak playing in the background, and the rustle of travellers arriving and leaving on the polished concourse below them sounded almost like the sea. Through the wide plate-glass window, the lights of interminable Volvos passed along Klara Strand; but beyond the lights there was nothing but the darkness of Riddarfjärden, and the night.

'Lager, please,' said Humphrey, as he awkwardly perched himself on the barstool next to Bill Bennett. In front of Bill Bennett was a large glass of Perrier water with a slice of lemon in it.

'You don't drink?' asked Humphrey, as the girl brought him a Pripps.

Bill Bennett smiled. 'Not on duty.'

'You're not a policeman.'

'No.'

'Then I suppose you're a spy. A secret agent.'

'Hardly. I work for the U.S. Information Service; mostly in Central and South America. I tell starving Indians in Nicaragua that Palm Springs is a lovely place to visit in the fall, and that they really should make an effort to fly to New York at Christmas, so that they can sample hot buttered Medford rum at the Plaza, and take their children for hansom-cab rides in the park.'

Humphrey drank a little of his beer and then patted his mouth with his handkerchief. 'It seems curious that they should have sent someone from South America.'

'Not really,' said Bill Bennett. 'I also happen to be a

minor expert on identifying one-time Nazis. When you're working in South America, it's part of the job. It was me who spotted Barbie, originally; although I didn't get the credit for it.'

'Well, that's interesting,' said Humphrey. 'I used to work for BDG 7 during the war, 'The Budgies' they called us. I spent years training myself to identify Nazi war criminals. I would have picked out Martin Bormann in a crowd, even if he was wearing a Chaplin moustache. I pride myself that I still could. Well, if he was still alive.'

'You saw Hermann,' Bill Bennett smiled at him. 'Leastways, you thought you did.'

'Oh, I saw him all right. No doubt at all that it was him. Very nasty piece of work, Hermann.'

'Major Milner – Milner, is it? – he said that you were always one of the best. Cream of the team, he called you.'

'Well, that's a compliment,' said Humphrey. He was suddenly beginning to warm to this young Bill Bennett, especially now that it was quite clear that he wasn't going to make a pass. 'It takes a special sort of eye, you know. Not everybody's got it. You have to look for the shape of the head, and the ears, and particularly that point between the eyes where the nose and the eyes and the forehead all conjoin. That single square inch is the most distinctive part of a person's features; and even if they dye their hair and undergo rhinoplasty, they can never change the appearance of that central spot. I was thinking of writing a treatise on it once: Browne's Law of Criminal Identification. But, well, you know how it is. Other things press. Time goes by.'

Bill Bennett watched Humphrey carefully as he spoke. 'Why did you call Major Milner?' he asked.

Humphrey shrugged. He didn't quite know why himself. 'Sense of duty, I suppose,' he suggested. 'Showing off, perhaps. Quite a feat, don't you know, recognizing a man after 40 years, especially when you've never seen him in the flesh. Three photographs we had, of Hermann; and a drawing made by an inmate from one of his camps. But there's no doubt at all that it's him. Not in my mind.'

'The apartment at 17 Pilogatan is a rental,' said Bill Bennett. 'It belongs to a Swedish trading company called Södertälje Exports. They deal mainly with the Soviet Union. Electronics, plastics, pharmaceutical goods things like that. Hermann – if it *is* Hermann – is renting it under the name of Rangström.'

'Have you been round there?' asked Humphrey. He was surprised and a little alarmed that the Americans should have taken so sudden and enthusiastic interest in his discovery. He took another swallow of beer and realized that he had finished it long before he meant to.

'Give Mr Browne another one,' Bill Bennett told the barmaid. Humphrey started to demur, but Bill Bennett said, 'Go on. You deserve it.'

'Well, if you put it that way . . . But I must go to the men's room in a moment. This Swedish beer goes right through me.'

Bill Bennett said, 'The reason I've contacted you is because we want to make an absolutely positive identification.'

'You're going to arrest him?'

'It depends.'

'I see. Then you might want me to stand up in court, point him out and suchlike?'

'That's right. The main thing is to be sure that he is who we say he is; and to make sure that we can make the identification stick.'

'I see,' Humphrey repeated. Then, suddenly, 'I was thinking in bed last night, you know – or the night before last, I mean – I was thinking how unusual it is for a Nazi war criminal to have fled to Russia. Most of

77

them went to South America, didn't they, Barbie and Mengele and Eichmann? It was very unusual for Hermann to go to Russia. I'm surprised they didn't tear him to pieces.'

Bill Bennett said, 'Hermann had something the Russians wanted. He was the medical equivalent of Werner von Braun, if you understand what I mean. He and Mengele had been working for years on all kinds of medical experiments, and of course they made tremendous progress because they had all those Jews to work on. Living human subjects, not rats, nor guinea-pigs, nor white mice. For instance Mengele found out as long ago as 1941 that saccharin was carcinogenic, from the work he did on concentration camp inmates; but of course his report was discredited because he was a Nazi war criminal, and also because the big U.S. pharmaceutical companies had a vested interest in keeping his medical records under wraps.'

Humphrey said, 'Is that really true?'

Bill Bennett nodded. 'It's true, Mr Browne, and it's only the tip of the iceberg. Think about it: for at least ten years the Nazi doctors could do anything they wished to anyone they wished. Any serious research scientist worth his sauerkraut couldn't have failed to make enormous steps forward, given those facilities. The Nazi work on genetics stands as one of the great socio-medical achievements of the twentieth century, although nobody is actually allowed to say so. But who else could have cut open living people, to see how their organs worked? Who else could have injected human beings with any poison or virus they felt like; sometimes two or three thousand people at a time? If it hadn't have been for the Nazis, you still would never have heard of the double helix, or test-tube babies, and you still wouldn't have heard of alpha-phthalimido-glutarimide.'

'I'm not sure I've heard of it yet,' said Humphrey.

'Thalidomide,' said Bill Bennett. 'A colleague of Hermann's called Mietzner was working on the synthesis of a similar drug for the specific purpose of shortening the limbs of inferior races, deliberately giving them phocomelia, so that they could be employed in tunnelling and mining work. Sounds bizarre today, doesn't it? But it happened. Of course, the German chemists who synthesized thalidomide in 1953 had no access to Mietzner's records, so they couldn't have known what was going to happen.'

Humphrey was silent for a long time. Bill Bennett kept watching him, and kept on smiling. At last, Humphrey said, somewhat heavily, 'You're an expert on this, aren't you? I mean, you're an expert on Hermann?'

'Nobody can be an expert on somebody who hasn't been seen for 37 years. If anybody's an expert, *you* are.'

Humphrey shook his head. 'All I know is what the man looks like. You know all about him. You know what he *means*.'

'Well, I guess,' said Bill Bennett, cheerfully. 'But then I was trained to. It's my work.'

'He means a lot to America, then? He must do, or they wouldn't have trained you so carefully.'

'Shrewd point, Mr Browne.'

'You may, if you wish, call me Humphrey.'

Bill Bennett held out his hand for the second time. 'You can certainly call me Bill.'

Humphrey said, 'Does Hermann still represent some kind of threat to America? I mean, in the same way that Werner von Braun must have represented quite a threat to the Russians, when he was helping you to build your missiles? I mean, would that be an accurate way of putting it?'

Bill Bennett put down his drink. 'Hermann *does* represent a danger, yes, in a certain sense. We're not sure how much. He helped the Soviets to build up their chemical-warfare arsenal, and as far as we know he's still improving it, if you can use the word improving. He was the first person to develop a method of spreading rabies by missile, and one of his greatest achievements was to breed and develop a psittacosis virus that could be added to a nation's water supply. He's also done work on poliomyelitis and smallpox, although we've never been able to locate his wartime records, so we don't know how far he's got. Yes, he's a dangerous man; even at the age of 71. There's no age-limit on treachery, is there?'

'I suppose not,' said Humphrey; although he hadn't quite understood what Bill Bennett had meant.

Bill Bennett poked at the lemon floating on the surface of his Perrier water. 'The amount of freedom which the Soviet régime allows its citizens is in direct proportion to their loyalty and usefulness to the State. If Hermann is being allowed to travel to Stockholm, and to keep an apartment of his own, then all I can say is that the Soviets must trust him a very great deal; and value him, too.'

'So you're really more interested in what he's doing now than what he did during the war?' asked Humphrey.

'The two are closely interrelated,' said Bill Bennett. 'But, yes, you could say that.'

'So what do you want *me* to do?'

'We don't want you to do anything.'

'But you must, otherwise you wouldn't have told me any of this. You're trying to recruit me, aren't you? I'm not a fool, you know. I had to do it once or twice myself during the war. It's an old technique. The trouble is I'm rather too old to go along with it. At least until I know what it is that you want, and what you might be offering.'

'I didn't say I was offering anything,' said Bill Bennett, trying to be offhand.

'Then you expect me to help you out of the goodness of my heart?'

Bill Bennett was about to say something in reply, but then he caught his breath, and shook his head, and smiled. 'All right,' he said, 'we need your help. That is, we would very much appreciate it if you could see your way clear to assisting us. That's a good evasive English way of asking, isn't it?'

Humphrey said, 'You mustn't take too much for granted, you know.' It sounded prissy, but he couldn't help it.

'I'm not taking anything for granted. I'm asking you to help us, simply because you're the best at what you do. I can recognize Nazis like Vogel and Kress; I even picked out Hörlich once, although the Argentinian police had to let him go on a technicality. But I'm not at all sure about Hermann, and people like that. I need you to finger him for me.'

'Supposing I'm not interested in fingering him?' asked Humphrey. The beer may have been passing through his kidneys quickly, but it was also going to his head just as fast. He felt lightheaded, and a little sick. 'Supposing I refuse to identify him, whether he's Hermann or not?'

'Why would you want to do a thing like that? The man's a war criminal.'

'An *alleged* war criminal.'

'All right, an alleged war criminal. But you know as well as I do that he's guilty of murdering people in thousands. Innocent people, men, women and children. You're prepared to let a man like that stay free?'

'I didn't say I was and I didn't say I wasn't. All I said was, supposing I decline to co-operate with you? After all, there's no reason why I should. Supposing I decided that I was mistaken; or supposing that I decided to go to the newspapers, and make a big splash of it?'

'You're not making any sense,' said Bill Bennett, tensely.

'I wasn't aware that I was obliged to,' Humphrey retorted. 'You – follow me about – on my holiday – and then tell me that you need my help to identify Klaus Hermann – well, what are you going to do then? Arrest him, kill him, or what? And what are you going to do to me? You've probably told me too much already.'

Bill Bennett said, 'Everything I've told you has already been openly reported in the *International Journal of Biology*. There's no secret about it.'

'Still,' protested Humphrey, petulantly. 'I don't see why I should do it.'

'You were pleased you identified him, why are you backing out now?' Bill Bennett wanted to know. 'Come on, have another drink.'

'No, no thank you. Well, just a small one. Half-litre.'

Bill Bennett beckoned to the barmaid. 'Give this gentleman a small beer and I'll have a Perrier.' Then he laid his hand on Humphrey's arm, and leaned forward, and said in a confidential voice, 'You'll still get the credit.'

'What credit?'

'You know what credit. For finding Hermann. That's what you're worried about, isn't it? If I take over, you're worried that the media are going to say that Hermann's capture was all down to me.'

Humphrey looked down at Bill Bennett's hand, and then turned away, his mouth working as if he were chewing cashew-nuts. Bill Bennett was disturbingly right. The whole thrill of recognizing Hermann had been that he, Humphrey, had done it alone; and that it had given him the first opportunity in his whole life to seek a little personal glory; the first chance to exercise power and influence over another human being. He shouldn't have called Major Milner, he knew that now. At the time, of course, he had been prompted by a mixture of pride and fright; but it had obviously been a mistake. Now his achievement had already been taken out of his hands by this tall, tanned, intelligent, and unbearably good-looking American, and he would get nothing for it, not even the satisfaction of seeing his name in print.

Bill Bennett said, 'Let me tell you something, Humphrey, you'll get the credit. I promise you. In fact, I don't even want to be mentioned at all.'

Humphrey glanced at him, then looked away again.

'Just tell me you'll help us, that's all,' Bill Bennett urged him. 'Then you can have the kudos for the whole damn thing.'

'What exactly do you want me to do?' said Humphrey. It was more of a statement than a question.

'You have to identify Hermann, that's all. Point him out. I'll do the rest. But I have to be absolutely 108% sure that it's him.'

Humphrey politely lifted Bill Bennett's hand away from his sleeve, nodding towards his beer to indicate that he wasn't offended by the personal contact (although he was) and that he simply wanted to free his arm to have a drink.

'I'm really not too sure,' he said. 'I mean, I haven't seen your credentials, have I?'

'Humphrey, my credentials are that I know what you said to Major Milner.'

'Well, I'm really not too sure.'

Bill Bennett said, 'I'll tell you what we'll do. We'll drive over to Pilogatan and say hi to Hermann and make sure that it's him. What do you say to that? After that, I'll buy you dinner at the Opera-Kallaren; and then we can go to the Chat-Noir for the sex show. What do you say?'

Humphrey said nothing. This all sounded terribly wrong and terribly complicated, yet he didn't know how to back away from it without losing his dignity. God, his dignity.

'I must just go to the loo first,' he said.

SIX

Bill Bennett waited for Humphrey with the patience of a man who is used to waiting. He ate one or two olives from the dish on the bar, and stared at the traffic outside the window; but his eyes and his mind were both blank.

He disliked Stockholm. He found the Swedes boorish and provincial; and their preoccupation with alcohol reminded him of his father's sweaty, loud-voiced workmates in Mankato, Minnesota, where he had been born and raised. He was 34 now, and he had spent all his adult life striving hard not to be like his father. He had studied relentlessly hard at High School; and at the first opportunity he had joined the Army. The Army had disciplined him, trained him, hardened his body and straightened his mind. By the time he had left the service, at the age of 29, he had grown into a tough and capable young captain.

For a year after his discharge, Bill Bennett had worked for a security corporation in San Diego. He had used that year to teach himself some of the finer ways of the world; to appreciate wine, and music, and good food, and most of all to appreciate other people. He had dated three women, one of them seriously; and if at the end of that time his sophistication had appeared as if it had come straight out of the *Playboy Advisor*, that was only because much of it did. At least he was a more cultured and sensitive man than he had been when he was in the Army.

One of his girlfriends, Yvonne, had called him, 'A

male stereotype of a male stereotype,' although she hadn't meant it unkindly. He knew the difference between a Volnay and a Vouvray; a châteaubriand and a Châteauneuf-du-Pape. He also knew the optimum rate at which a man should tongue-flick a woman's clitoris, 1,840 flicks per minute. But there was more to him than that. Beneath that captain's crispness and that playboy's statistical *savoir-faire*, there was a man of considerable sentiment and emotional strength.

He was a better man, in fact, than he believed himself to be. And that was probably why the Army Intelligence people had got in touch with him only seven months after he had left the service, and suggested that he help them. They were looking for prominent Nazis whose wartime activities might have been, well, embarrassing. You know what we mean by embarrassing? Well, they might have compromised some of today's more respected citizens. It's a good, worthwhile, patriotic task. Besides that, it pays $68,000 a year, which is more than most three-star generals are entitled to.

Bill had just broken up with the intensest love of his life, Karen Windom. Brown eyes, breasts like beach-balls. It had been easier to say yes than no; and within a week he had been sent to Omaha to be trained to identify all those Nazis who were still thought to be in hiding in Central and South America. Scores of them: Adler, August, Berthold, Bergen . . . 196 of them altogether, and only four of them positively identified.

He had sat at his desk in Omaha overlooking Fontenelle Park, and he had tried to picture all of these men in his mind's eye, as they might be today. But he had only been able to conjure up a quorum of wrinkled, white-haired old monstrosities; warped by their past atrocities, and hysterical about their future. He hadn't really been able to believe that they were still alive, or that it made any difference to the United States if they were caught and tried, or allowed to go free. The war had begun and finished before he was born. He had been a toddler during Korea. Sometimes he felt as if he had been sent to look for Bismarck. Who cared about Hermann, or Barbie, and how many they had killed? They were so old they were scarcely worth hunting; and they weren't the men they used to be, for sure.

But, well-paid, with good expenses, he had sat in the bar of the Hotel Concepcíon in Managua, his eyes shaded by the brim of his white straw hat, watching while three former SS officers toasted each other in apricot juleps and talked about Munich before the war; and he had sweated his way on the back of a mule up the side of the Cerro Gaitál in Panama, to a small steaming community they call El Valle, just to talk to a shuddering old man with Parkinson's Disease who had once crushed living children under the wheels of railroad cars.

He had done these things because he had been ordered to; and because he valued the experience; and that was mostly why he was here in Stockholm, making contact with Humphrey Browne.

He found Humphrey tiresome, and too English to be anything but awkward. But he believed that he was professional enough to know how to handle him, and the *Playboy Advisor* had once said that Englishmen are deceptively strong in all of their personal relationships, both male and female. At least 77.2% of Englishmen have sexual intercourse (homo- or heterosexual) three times a week; and 61.1 have it four times a week. Bill was lucky these days if he averaged 0.5; somehow his relationships with women seemed to have become oddly fractured, like boxes of hopelessly mixed-up jigsaws.

After Karen, not very much had made sense; but then, did it ever?

Humphrey came back from the men's room with the

tail of his shirt protruding through his fly. Bill smiled tightly at him, and said, 'Your zipper.'

Humphrey blinked at him. 'Is that Californian for pissed?'

Bill's car was parked in the basement; a rather shabby Grand Prix that belonged to the U.S. Embassy. 'I could have a rented Volvo,' said Bill, as they pulled out of the exit ramp on squealing tyres. 'But, you know, a *Volvo*?'

'I always thought Volvos were rather splendid,' said Humphrey. 'Very safe, I understood.'

Bill glanced at him as they drove across Vasabron back to the old town. Lights, darkness, water. 'Real men don't drive Volvos,' he said. The Grand Prix' suspension clunked as they hit the cobbles of Stora Nygatan. 'Shocks are shot, that's all,' he explained.

They parked outside the Enskilda Banken on Kornhamnstorget, and walked the rest of the way to Pilogatan. The night was very cold, and Humphrey turned up the collar of his coat. For no clear reason he felt quite afraid: more afraid of Bill Bennett than he did of Klaus Hermann.

At last they reached the dark smelly canyon of Pilogatan, and stood outside No. 17. Up on the third floor, the lights were shining through the blinds, and an occasional shadow moved across the waxed linen like an Indonesian puppet-theatre. Bill Bennett fumbled in his pocket and produced a selection of lock-picks, and then quite openly began to ease back the levers of the front-door lock. Humphrey watched him dubiously. 'We won't get arrested for this?' he asked.

'Arrested?' asked Bill, and pushed the front door open so that it softly groaned on its hinges. 'Come on, all you have to do is take a look at him, and tell me you're sure that he's Hermann.'

'I'm not sure I like this,' said Humphrey.

'You're not sure?' Bill retorted.

'Well, I have to think of my sister.'

There was no elevator; the building was too old. They mounted the winding stone steps, passing private and tightly-closed doors from behind which they could just hear the faint strains of hi-fi music or the lilting sound of the Swedish television news. Swedish television runs Zimbabwe television a close second for the worst broadcasting station in the world: if the viewers are really lucky, their Sunday-evening viewing in Stockholm will include a re-run of *Madigan* and an hour-long feature on skating children.

They reached Hermann's door. There was a small brass slot on the front of it, with a neatly-penned card which read. *A. Rangström*. Bill looked back at Humphrey and smiled. 'All you have to do is say, "that's him", and we can get this over with.'

'Very well,' said Humphrey, although he felt just the opposite.

Bill produced another of his lock-picks, and delved into the door, whistling between his teeth as he did so. He had enjoyed his lock-picking course at Omaha more than any other: there was something extraordinarily exhilarating about knowing that he could walk into practically every house or office that he passed, undetected, and that he could steal almost any car that was parked by the kerbside.

The apartment door opened. From inside, there was light and music and dry, fragrant warmth, almost like a sauna. Pale beige walls, and a shaggy cream carpet. Just in view, a black-and-white etching of dancing satyrs.

'Shouldn't we announce ourselves?' Humphrey suggested. 'I mean, ring the doorbell or something?'

Bill put his finger to his lips, and then tucked back his putty-coloured windbreaker to lift out a nickel-plated Smith & Wesson .38. Humphrey said, 'That's it. I'm going. You didn't tell me there were going to be guns.'

Bill snatched out with his left arm and caught Humphrey's shoulder. 'You stay where you are. I need you.'

'What are you doing?' Humphrey protested, flailing at him. He fell back, stumbled on the stone steps, and thumped his back against the curving wall.

'For Christ's sake, stay calm,' Bill hissed at him. Then he beckoned with the gun, and ordered, 'Get back up here.'

Humphrey, miserably, stayed where he was. Bill snapped at him, 'Get back up here, do you hear me?'

At that moment, a voice inside the apartment said, 'Who's there? Birgitta the door's open!'

The music suddenly blared loud, and then softened. Humphrey pressed himself back against the wall and stared at Bill in fright. Another voice a woman's voice, very Swedish, said, 'I locked it. Don't be so ridiculous.'

Again, the man's voice called, 'Who's there?'

'Nobody,' laughed the woman. 'Go and close it, and then come back here.'

Humphrey whispered, 'That's not him. That's not him at all. His accent – quite different – very German.'

'You couldn't have locked it,' the man said, as his voice came closer. Bill eased himself away from the middle of the doorway, and stood just out of sight with his revolver raised in both hands. Humphrey repeated, in a scared whisper, 'It's not – ' but Bill's concentration was total, and he didn't even hear him.

A hairy naked bald-headed man suddenly stuck his head out of the lighted doorway, and stared straight at Humphrey in complete disbelief.

'What the hell is happening?' he demanded, his eyes wide. But at that moment Bill snatched him around the neck and pushed the muzzle of his revolver hard up against his temples. The man sagged, tried to struggle, and then knocked his shoulder against the door-jamb, and said, 'Shit, what are you doing? What the hell are you doing?'

'Is this him?' Bill asked Humphrey, in an off-key, over-excited whisper.

'Of course not,' said Humphrey. 'Hermann's old, 70 years old. This man can't be more than 45.'

'Get that fucking gun away from my head,' the man protested. Bill kept it where it was, so hard against his skin that it was pressing it up into a ridge. Humphrey said, 'It's not Hermann. Hermann's old, really old.'

'Get inside,' Bill ordered the man, and twisted him back into the open door. 'Humphrey, come along; and close the door behind you.'

'Bill, I'm not really sure that I – '

'Get in here and close the door behind you before I blow the idiot's brains out!' Bill barked at him. The 'idiot' didn't take kindly to this at all, and screwed his head around, and pleaded with Humphrey, 'Come, will you, for God's sake.'

Silently, biting his lip, Humphrey followed them into the apartment, and closed the door. Bill shoved and frog-marched the naked man into the open-plan living-room, and the first thing that Humphrey heard was a woman's scream. Then Bill saying, 'Keep quiet, and nobody's going to get hurt. Do you hear me?'

Humphrey came into the room and found that it was as white and modern inside as it was dark and forbidding outside. The walls were off-white, the carpet was pure as snow. There were Swedish-style lamps everywhere, glass-and-wooden furniture, and overlit pieces of Boda and Orrefors crystal. All the furniture was upholstered in white hide.

In the corner of the white-hide sofa sat a very ample dark-haired woman with a mouth as purple as smashed raspberries. She was wearing a black laced-up basque, over which her huge white breasts bulged like duck-down pillows; black garters, black fishnet stockings, and black patent stiletto shoes. Something golden protruded from the black fur between her thighs and it took Humphrey two or three discreet but mesmerized glances to understand that it was a vibrator. He was shocked: he looked away from her and couldn't bring himself to look back.

The naked man said, 'What is this? A robbery? You want money? I don't have any money. You want my American Express card? Take it.'

'Sit down,' said Bill, and then, to the woman in the black basque, 'You want to cover yourself up?'

Humphrey said, 'I'll, er, get you a . . .' and walked erratically across the living-room to the open bedroom. All the bedroom walls were mirrored, and he could see himself tugging a blanket off the bed as if he were a strange intruder into his own bad dream. Back in the living-room, he handed the blanket to the woman at arm's-length, and tried not to be aware of the way in which she raised herself up to relieve herself of the vibrator.

Bill Bennett had ordered the naked man to sit on a small leather tuffet, where he now perched knock-kneed with his hands clutched between his thighs, looking extremely unhappy.

'You're going to have to tell me your name,' Bill told him. He waved his revolver at the woman and said, 'You too.'

'This is very embarrassing,' the man said.

'Well, of course it's embarrassing,' said Bill. 'But I might have killed you, and *that* would have really been embarrassing.'

'You have no rights,' the woman suddenly said, in her strong Swedish accent. 'What are you, robbers?'

'I want to know your names,' insisted Bill.

Humphrey cleared his throat, and said, 'It really would be better if you told him.' He smiled nervously at the woman, who didn't smile back.

The naked man said, 'This is an outrage. An absolute outrage.'

'All right, it's an outrage,' Bill agreed. 'But I have the gun and you don't, and I want you tell me your name.'

The man closed his eyes for a moment, either in anger or prayer. Then he said, 'My name is Vojtech Mňačko. I am the Czech commercial deputy. This woman is Birgitta Gillsäter, from the St Eriksplan Theatre Group.'

'Neither of you is called Rangström?'

'No,' said Mňačko.

'This apartment is registered in the name of Rangström.'

'Yes.'

'So what are you doing here?' Bill demanded.

'I would have thought that was quite obvious,' said Mňačko. 'Miss Gillsäter and I have been friends for many years. You have interrupted one of our rare opportunities to spend an evening together in private.'

'If this is Mr Rangström's apartment, where is Mr Rangström?' asked Bill.

'You mean *Miss* Rangström,' put in Birgitta Gillsäter, sharply.

'I do? *Miss* Rangström?'

'Miss Angelika Rangström; she also is a member of the St Eriksplan Theatre Group. If you knew anything about Stockholm, of course, you would have been aware of that already. She is considered to be one of Sweden's most talented actresses. Last season her *Hedda Gabler* won her the Valhalla Award.'

'Miss Rangström's man friend,' said Humphrey.

'What about him?' asked Mňačko.

But Birgitta Gallsäter said, 'She has no man friend. She used to, but no longer.'

Bill reached into his inside pocket and produced an artist's sketch of Klaus Hermann. Humphrey leaned forward and looked at it himself; and although the artist

92

had assumed that Hermann would have lost his hair after 40 years, it was a remarkably accurate impression.

'Is this the man?' Bill asked Birgitta Gillsäter.

'She has no man friend.'

'Look at the picture.'

Reluctantly, Birgitta Gillsäter lowered her eyes and examined the drawing. But then she slowly shook her head. 'I don't know this man. I never saw him before. He is a stranger.'

Bill showed the picture to Vojtech Mňačko. 'You know this man? Ever seen him before?'

Mňačko defiantly raised his head and refused even to look at it.

Bill tucked the picture away again. 'I have to tell you that you people have created a serious difficulty, being here tonight.'

'I think it is you who has created the difficulty,' replied Mňačko.

Bill thought for a while, without saying anything, and the other members of this incongruous evening get-together sat and watched him. Humphrey nodded towards Birgitta Gillsäter as if to reassure her that everything would be all right, but the actress looked away from him coldly. It seemed remarkable to Humphrey that a woman whom he had caught out in such an intimate and peculiar sexual act should be able to treat him so haughtily. No shame at all. But, of course, this was Sweden, the home of legalized pornography, and Humphrey supposed that it must have some effect on the manners and morals of the native Swedes.

He hadn't yet plucked up the nerve to look at any pornography himself. He wasn't sure that he would enjoy what he would see: either because it was so unrepentantly vulgar, or because it would disturb feelings in him which he usually did his best to keep under rather a tight management.

Mňačko said, 'What will you do now? We can't sit here all night.'

'Well, I'm trying to decide,' said Bill. 'I think on the whole the best thing for me to do is to tie you up.'

'Tie us up? What is the use of that?' Mňačko demanded.

'Let me decide what the use of it is. Let's do it in the bedroom, we can tear up some sheets.'

'You can't do that,' Birgitta Gillsäter protested. 'This is not our apartment. Angelika will be furious.'

Bill Bennett raised the revolver. 'The gun says I can do what I want. Primitive, I know. Just what you'd expect from an American. But there we are.'

He prodded Mňačko up from the tuffet, and prodded him into the open bedroom door. 'Go lie face down on the floor,' he ordered. Then he beckoned to Birgitta Gillsäter to follow him into the bedroom too. 'Take off the blanket,' he ordered her.

'Bill, that's not absolutely necessary,' said Humphrey.

Bill turned and smiled at him. 'Will you keep an eye on the door, please?'

Humphrey hesitated, but there was something about that smile which made him retreat, and say, 'Yes. All right. Very well. The door.'

Once Humphrey had gone to the hallway, Bill closed the bedroom door and locked it. Mňačko was lying face down on the rug with his hands crossed palms upwards over the small of his hairy back. Birgitta Gillsäter was spread out beside him, her wide-spread bottom as white as the off-white walls. Bill put down the revolver on the bedside table, and said, 'I warn you. Any attempt to get up, and I can go for that gun so fast you won't even know what happened. You want to keep your brains inside of your head, do as you're told.'

Using his penknife to cut through the seams, he quickly ripped up two of the bedsheets into thin ribbons. Then, with all the speed and expertise they had taught him in the service, he tugged Mňačko's hands up behind his back and bound his wrists. Mňačko complained, 'That's tight, hey that's too tight,' but Bill didn't even answer him. He took two more lengths of sheeting and lashed together Mňačko's knees and ankles. Finally, he gagged him.

The bedroom door-handle rattled; then there was a knock. Humphrey said, 'Is everything all right in there, Bill?'

'Fine,' Bill called back. His breathing was forced, his pulse-rate was around 100. 'Go back and watch that door, I'm nearly finished here.'

Birgitta Gillsäter looked up from the floor, and stared at him. 'You're going to kill us, aren't you?' she said. Her voice was shocked, sober.

'Yes,' said Bill.

At this, Mňačko tried to raise his head, and make gargling noises, but Bill placed his foot on the back of his neck, and pushed his face down into the rug.

Birgitta Gillsäter stayed where she was. Her lipstick had made a red smear on the white pile of the carpet. She said, suddenly, 'I don't want to die, please, not like this.'

'You don't have any choice.'

'You want to know about Angelika's man-friend?'

Bill stared down at her, expressionless. 'Well?' he asked her.

'If you spare me, I will tell you where he is.'

Bill took out the artist's impression again, and held it only inches away from her nose. 'This man? You know where he is?'

She nodded.

'You can take me to him personally?'

She nodded again.

Bill thought about that, and then said, 'All right. You can take me to him tonight?'

'He is in Uppsala. Only an hour's drive.'

'All right,' Bill repeated, as if he were agreeing to accompany her to a rather uninteresting restaurant.

'What will you do with Vojtech?

'You get yourself dressed. Vojtech and I are going to have a little talk.' He bent forward, and said loudly, 'Isn't that right, Vojtech? A few minutes' relevant conversation.'

'*Grrrgg*,' said Mňačko.

Birgitta Gillsäter collected her salmon-coloured wool suit from where she had first abandoned it by the side of the bed, and Bill unlocked the bedroom door for her and nudged her back out into the living-room. 'Humphrey', he called. 'Miss Gillsäter's getting herself dressed. Keep an eye on her.'

'Yes, very well,' said Humphrey. He looked uncomfortable standing by the door. Bill went through to the kitchen, and switched on the overhead light. He drummed his fingers on the white worktop, and then he reached up and opened one of the wall-cupboards. There were only cups in there. He opened another, then another, and at last he found what he was looking for. Plastic trash bags. He went back into the bedroom without speaking either to Humphrey or to Birgitta Gillsäter. He locked the bedroom door behind him.

Without a word, he opened out the white plastic bag he had brought from the kitchen, and tugged it over Mňačko's head. Mňačko twisted and writhed, but Bill pushed his knee right into the middle of his back. When the bag was right over Mňačko's head, Bill twisted the neck of it, so that it was an airtight fit.

The bag was sucked in against Mňačko's features as he tried to breathe. Through the plastic, Bill could see the contours of his wide-open eyes, the gaping muscles of his cheeks, a living death-mask in white. He checked his watch. Even the fittest human being was unable to hold his breath for very much longer than two minutes. The bag suddenly blew out and then sucked in again.

Mňačko jerked and shuddered, but Bill pressed as heavily on his back as before.

The bag half-inflated again, carbon dioxide; and then the same carbon dioxide was breathed back in. Then again, and again, and again. At last, after four minutes, the bag relaxed, with a soft crackling sound, and Mňačko lay still.

Bill stood up, and put away his revolver. He looked around the bedroom to make sure that everything was arranged the way he wanted it, and then he stepped out and locked the door. Humphrey was waiting for him in the living-room, and Birgitta Gillsäter was now dressed.

'Very fetching,' Bill remarked, of the salmon-coloured wool suit. Miss Gillsäter refused to smile.

'Mňačko's all right?' asked Humphrey.

'Oh, sure,' said Bill. 'Are we ready to go?'

'I cannot say goodbye to Vojtech?' asked Birgitta Gillsäter.

Bill shook his head. 'He's all right. As soon as we've located Miss Rangström's man-friend, you can come back and cut him loose.'

'That sounds like something out of a cowboy film,' Humphrey remarked, although he was unsettled by the unusual deadness in Bill's voice.

The three of them left the apartment and clattered down the stone stairs to the street. A freezing east wind was blowing across Skeppsbron and whistling up Pilogatan like a bevy of malevolent trolls. Humphrey looked up at the window of the apartment, and saw that it was still brightly lit. He felt quite sorry for Vojtech Mňačko, tied-up and helpless on the bedroom rug. What a way to spend an evening, he thought, and it was almost funny. He gave a small, half-suppressed snicker; and Birgitta Gillsäter stared at him over the collar of her sheepskin coat. 'It's not so cold yet,' she said. 'You wait until winter.'

97

SEVEN

Chiffon Trent was on the very brink of orgasm when the doorbell rang. It was a soft, bland chime, Avon calling; but it was enough to destroy the whole afternoon, the lunch at the Oyster Bar, the arm-in-arm walk in the park; the kisses and the champagne. The young slant-eyed man rose from the sheets and said, 'Who is that? Not Shitface. Not *now*.'

Chiffon touched a finger to her lips, and rolled off the bed. At once she reached for her sheer silk dressing-gown with the ruffled collar; she had always thought of herself as a lady, even in the throes of sex. She swirled across the room, and pressed her tangled blonde curls against the door, and called, 'Who is it?'

'Dick Elmwood, Ms Trent. Just to tell you the Senator's downstairs in the Palm Court, and he'll expect you shortly.'

'Is it four already?'

'It's three-forty-five, Ms Trent. The Senator's a little ahead of time. Traffic from the airport was unusually light.'

Chiffon made a face at the young slant-eyed man on the bed, and mimicked Dick Elmwood's nasal intonation, '*Traffic from the airport was unusually light, huh*?' The young man laughed, and lay on his back, dark and narrow and naked.

'Tell the Senator he's going to have to give me a half-hour,' called Chiffon. 'Tell him I had a headache, you know? I'm only just over it.'

'I think he'd appreciate it if you hurried,' said Dick Elmwood. He waited for a reply, and when none came, he noisily cleared his throat.

'All right,' said Chiffon. 'But I have to curl my hair. And my eyes, I have to bathe my eyes. Tell him a kissy-wissy on the tip of the nose, will you? And another kissy-wissy on the bom-bom.'

The young man on the bed snorted hysterically. Chiffon waved at him to keep quiet. 'Did you get that?' she asked Dick Elmwood.

Dick Elmwood chivvied his throat again, like a man trying to start up a Model-A Ford. 'I got it,' he said, flatly. 'I'll go tell him.'

Chiffon giggled, and danced across the room, swirling her silk dressing-gown, pale bare thighs flickering beneath transparent silk, breasts bouncing. She tossed back the nets at the window, and leaned forward on the window-sill with an exaggerated sigh of contentment.

'*Ah*,' she said. 'Isn't life *perfect*?'

The young man said, uneasily, 'You're coming back to bed?'

'I don't think so. I'm going to dress.'

'You're going to leave me lying here? Look at me! I was holding on for you. That's the only reason I was holding on.'

Chiffon turned to him, and smiled, a beatific smile. 'So you should. Gentlemen always finish last.'

'Last, yes. But at least they get to *finish*.'

'Oh, don't be so animalistic,' Chiffon dismissed him. She pressed her nose to the window so that her breath created a misted butterfly on the glass. Seven storeys below her, the taxi-infested traffic crawled slowly back-wards and forwards along Central Park South, and pedestrians hurried along the sidewalks with their hands on their hats and their scarves flapping in desperate semaphore. New York was right on the brink of fall, just as Chiffon had been right on the brink of her climax: the trees in the park were trembling and thrashing, and a snappy north-east wind was whipping up newspapers and candy wrappers across General Motors Plaza. Something exciting was happening: it was time for change.

The young man sulkily climbed off the bed and stood arms akimbo by the other window, his penis still half-aroused, the curls on his stomach still drying. 'You're like a child,' he told her.

'Of course I am. If I wasn't, you wouldn't like me so much.'

'You're going to go down to see him?'

'Of course. He paid for the room. He pays for everything.'

'He's a pig.'

'I didn't say he wasn't, did I? But he's a rich pig. How do you say that in Russian?'

'Richski pigovich.'

Chiffon giggled. She was 23 years old, a Pisces, and unnervingly pretty. Five-feet-four, with wide green eyes, a straight, perfectly-shaped nose, and high cheek-bones that could have been cut by Rodin out of cold butter. And she had skin and a figure to match: skin that glowed pink-on-white, and big buoyant breasts. When Chiffon walked into a restaurant, wearing one of the white pleated décolleté evening gowns that Reynard had bought her from Sabra, the entire restaurant would hush, and men would sit with their knives and forks frozen in their hands and silently rail against the God who could have created a girl who looked like Chiffon without ever giving them a chance to make love to her. She created social waves, cultural eddies, just by being so stunning; and it had been impossible for Reynard to keep his affair with her a secret. Andy Warhol had called Chiffon, 'the face of total today'; and Norman Mailer had once sent her a rose across the Four Seasons, and finger-waved.

She was smart, and she could be funny; but the truth about Chiffon was that she had been born to utterly ordinary parents in Cedar Lake, Indiana, and that she had been nothing at all in school except flirtatious and gum-chewing and bored with class. She had lost her virginity the day before her fourteenth birthday to a sullen boy called Carl, and after that she had been neither particularly good nor particularly bad, either in bed or out of it. A girl called Mavis Twilley had been named 'the girl most likely to succeed' and Mavis Twilley had married a psychopathic landscape gardener who had killed her with a meat-cleaver five days after the nuptials.

By the time Chiffon had been noticed by Reynard at a private party at Studio 54, she had done almost nothing of note except a casual-wear commercial, a walk-on, giggle-off part in *Knight Rider*, and some fashion spreads for *Seventeen*. But her love-affair with Reynard had immediately fizzed up her fortunes, and now she was making regular guest appearances on *The Dukes of Hazzard* and *Quincy*, and featuring on every kind of magazine cover from *Redbook* to *Secrets*. Reynard had scores of sycophantic Hollywood connections, and infinite supplies of money; and everybody in the business knew that if they wanted to make Reynard happy, they had to make Chiffon happy, too. Especially since there was every likelihood that Reynard was going to be elected the 41st President of the United States.

The newspaper reporters and the television anchormen accepted Reynard's affair quite equably as just another one of his passing infatuations. None of them yet knew that Reynard had permanently separated from Greta; and because of that, none of them were aware that Chiffon already saw herself as the next Mrs Kelly, and *ipso facto* the next First Lady. Not even Reynard was aware of it. But she did, despite the fact that he had made it quite clear to her that he never wanted to marry again; and that he would never allow her to wear panties. It didn't strike Chiffon as at all incongruous that the First Lady should be forbidden to wear panties; after all, she hardly ever wore them anyway, and then only those filmy French triangles with a thin stretch of elastic between the cheeks of her (perfect) bottom.

She drank nothing but White Star champagne these days; and never went to sleep before three o'clock in the morning, and as far as she was concerned, life was wonderful. More than wonderful, ecstatic.

The young boy with the slanting eyes said, 'You should tell Shitface what you think of him. Have some courage.'

'Hm,' said Chiffon, haughtily. 'What would *you* know about courage?'

'Courage is being yourself.'

'I *am* myself. I'm the greediest little girl in town; and that's my nature. Any complaints?'

'I don't know.' The boy rubbed his forehead with the back of his hand. 'Maybe I don't like to think of him sleeping with you.'

'You're jealous?' asked Chiffon in disbelief. She let the nets fall back, and they seemed to drop around her in slow-motion, a pale and slightly grimy shroud.

'I don't like to think of him sleeping with you, that's all.'

She came towards him with her arms outstretched. Her breasts bounced rhythmically under the silk of her dressing-gown; pale nipples glimpsed through transparent silk like orchid-petals seen through smoke. She reached for his mouth with her lips, pushing him backwards towards the bed. Then, all silk and soft flesh, she straddled him, and kissed him, and nipped at him with her teeth.

'Jealousy is a *sin*,' she giggled.

They tussled, and struggled, but at last she grew bored, and rolled away, and got up from the bed and began to dress. He watched her sullenly as she dropped her cream pleated dress around her like a parachute;

and turned his face away when she leaned forward to kiss him.

'Sulking is a sin, too,' she said, less amused.

'All Russians have black moods,' he told her. 'It's in our nature. The vastness of our country weighs around our shoulders like a great heavy cloak which we may never unfasten.'

'Mm?' she said, stretching her mouth in the mirror as she put on her lip liner.

'Well, you wouldn't understand,' he said.

'I'm not at all sure that I'd want to. In any case, you know I have to go see him. I *like* him. And he's my meal-ticket.'

'*Meal-ticket*,' said the boy, disdainfully.

'Listen,' said Chiffon, when she was ready to leave. 'I'll meet you at the Russian Tea Rooms at seven sharp, and I'll fill that sensual mouth of yours with best caviare and finest vodka; and then we'll come back here and finish what we didn't manage to finish this afternoon. So don't say "meal-ticket" down your nose like you're suffering from some kind of allergy.'

'I have to rehearse this evening,' the boy sulked. 'The big love scene, where Natasha finally surrenders.'

'The big love scene, where Natasha finally surrenders,' Chiffon mocked him. 'Skip rehearsal. I'll see you at seven.'

The boy said nothing, but propped himself up on his elbows and stared at the padded bed-head as if he had just thrown a tantrum with Nurse. Chiffon blew him four or five kisses, and left the room, closing the door noisily behind her.

The boy continued to stare at the bed-head, pouting, until he was quite sure that Chiffon had gone; and that she wouldn't come back to apologize, or kiss him, or collect the lipstick which she had left on the dressing-table. Then he got up, and sat on the edge of the bed, and lit a Winston, blowing out the smoke through his nostrils.

In a minor way, the boy was quite famous in his own right. His name was Piotr Lissitzky, and two years ago he had defected to the United States during a tour by the Moscow-Youth Theatre Ensemble. A rainy afternoon in Pittsburgh, a spontaneous escape down the back-stairs of the Carlton House Hotel, a confused appeal at the local police station for political asylum. For one moment, he had been so irritated by the desk sergeant, who had been far more interested in discussing last night's football game with his colleagues than a stuttering young Russian, that he had almost walked back to the hotel again. But at last he had made them understand; and then his life had become a carousel of news reporters, intensive interrogations, and endless visits by gimlet-eyed officials from the State Department. George Rosenbaum had offered him a part in *Days of Sadness* at the Shubert. The official Soviet comment had been, 'Lissitzky is no loss: he was nothing more than a theatrical hoodlum, a *stilyagi* of the boards.' Clive Barnes had said of Piotr's opening night on Broadway, 'Lissitzky's theatrical credentials appear to be that he once saw a James Dean picture.'

Piotr was still acting: mostly in off-Broadway Chekhov revivals and television commercials that required somebody with a thick foreign accent. But these days he was more of a gigolo than anything else: moodily escorting minor starlets in and out of fashionable nightclubs, shopping with wealthy and frustrated widows, swimming, posing. His affair with Chiffon Trent was just eleven days old. Sometimes, like now, as he sat on the edge of this wide expensive bed in the Plaza Hotel, smoking, he felt impotent and old before his time.

He thought of his childhood in Moscow. The concrete apartment block, the yard where he used to play ball.

He thought of the family he had left behind him that teeming day when he had crossed the street in Pittsburgh, and entered the police station. His mother, lively and smiling; his tired father; his two sisters. He hadn't realized that when you defect from one ideology to another, you leave everything behind, including your own history. These days, he felt as if he were nobody at all.

'Natasha,' he said, quoting from the play in which he was about to appear, 'you are nothing but a reflection in a mirror, in an empty room.'

Downstairs, in the Palm Court, Reynard was sitting at his usual table as far away from the piano as possible. He liked piano music but disliked musicians leering at him as they played; music, as far as he was concerned, was a very private experience, like sex. He was dressed in black, with a black-and-white spotted necktie, and gleaming black shoes. He was flying back to Washington on the 7:00 flight, and there was an important late-night meeting with the Burns Committee at 10.

He drank lemon tea, and played with the spoon in his saucer. All around him, the Palm Court bustled with brittle tea-time conversation, and a constant stream of guests and visitors flowed around its perimeter. Reynard was beginning to wish that he had chosen somewhere more private to meet: a white-haired woman in a garish suit of rainbow-coloured silk had already waved saucily to him, and several peple had murmured, *'Reynard Kelly,'* to each other as they had passed. *'You see there . . . don't look . . . you know who that is? Reynard Kelly.'*

Dick Elmwood was standing just outside the entrance to the Palm Court, accompanied by one of Reynard's private security men, a tall cultured-looking man called Pollock. Reynard turned around in his chair and grimaced at Dick, but all Dick could do was tap his wristwatch and shrug.

Fuck it, thought Reynard, I'm not waiting for this girl very much longer. One minute, no more.

But almost as he thought it, he could see Chiffon's curly blonde hair, and the jiggle of her walk, and within a moment she was being escorted over to his table, delicious and tasty-looking as one of the Plaza's cream-cakes, soft and fragrant and still irresistible.

She kissed his cheek. He felt her breast against his wrist. He felt a sudden urge of rampancy, and that annoyed him still more; because he would have to sit down and talk to her, and pretend to be polite, even though he felt like nothing else but taking her upstairs to her room and humping her.

'You look tired,' she told him, opening up her pocket-book and checking her lipstick in her mirror.

'Thank you. You look terrific.'

She closed her pocketbook with a snap and gave him a bright mouth-closed smile as if she hadn't heard him.

'How was Washington?' she asked.

'Cold. Argumentative.'

'Did you miss me?'

'Don't I always?' said Reynard.

The waiter came up and asked Chiffon what she would like. 'A cup of hot water,' she told him. 'And do you have any of those plain crackers? The crackers without the salt.'

Reynard gave her a lopsided smile. 'I don't know why you don't just suck your napkin. It's probably more nutritious.'

'You want me fat?'

'Is that all you think about? Your weight?'

'No,' she said coyly. 'Sometimes I think about you.'

He re-crossed his legs, and looked down at his cup of tea, and started playing with the spoon in his saucer again.

Chiffon said, 'What time are we flying back to Washington tomorrow?'

Reynard continued to play with his spoon. 'Well,' he said, 'that's one of the things I want to talk to you about.'

'What do you mean?'

'I mean – I'm going back to Washington this evening.'

'This evening? But the whole point of me staying in New York was for us to have lunch with Bergel tomorrow. I mean, that's the only reason I'm still here. What about that part? You know how much I want to do that part.'

Reynard glanced up at her, and then back down at his cup. 'The lunch with Bergel is cancelled.'

'Cancelled? Or postponed? Reynard, you *promised* me!'

'There'll be other parts, all right? It's just that, right now, I have to draw in my personal and political horns a little. Everything's set up, I'm going to be running for the nomination in earnest. That means that I have to be careful of any kind of irregularity. Any kind of suggestion that I might be fixing things. And that includes parts in movies for my close friends.'

Chiffon's cheeks were pink. 'You're really serious? You're really going to run?'

'I'm really going to run,' he nodded. 'But don't say it too loud. It isn't official yet.'

All her irritation had evaporated. She glowed. 'Reynard, that's *marvellous*. I forgive you about the part. Just imagine it, Reynard Kelly, President of the United States. And Mrs Kelly, First Lady. Really, I forgive you about the part. It was only some tacky street-crime movie anyway. Oh, I wish I could kiss you.'

Reynard put down his spoon, and laced both his hands together tightly. It was a gesture of self-defence, but it also expressed the difficulty he was having in telling Chiffon what was on his mind.

'Reynard,' smiled Chiffon, and reached out and held his locked-together hands in hers. 'Reynard, you're amazing. There are millions of men half your age who aren't anything like as positive, *or* as good-looking, *or* as virile as you are. You're just *numero uno*, and that's all.'

Reynard opened his mouth, and then closed it again. 'Thank you,' he said, a little more breathily than he'd meant to. Then, 'Chiffon – '

'You don't have to say anything. I love you. That's all that counts.'

The waiter brought Chiffon's hot water, and a plate of plain crackers, with a decoration of cucumber slices and cottage cheese.

Reynard stared at her cucumbers as if he had expected it to be a message of reprieve. Then he said, 'The, er, process of drawing in my horns . . . you know what I'm talking about? The, er, *care* I now have to take to regulate my private and my public life in order to reassure the Democratic Party and the electorate at large that I am a suitable candidate for the Presidency of the United States . . . I mean, I have to regulate my gambling activities . . .'

'Reynard,' said Chiffon, 'I'm a woman, not a Senate hearing on ground-nut planting. *Talk* to me.'

His cheek-muscles tightened, and his chin bunched. 'I *am* talking to you, damn it, if you'd only listen to what I'm saying. Do you understand at all what I'm saying? Is the message getting through?'

Chiffon sat back in her chair and frowned at him. '*No*,' she said, 'it isn't.'

'Well,' he said, 'it's like this. I want you to know here and now, right here, that I think a hell of a lot of you. Without question you're the most understanding girl I ever met in my life. You're also one hell of a lover. One hell. But, when a man decides to put himself up for the nation's highest office, as I have, he has to observe certain proprieties, at least until he's elected. So what I'm saying is, while the media may turn something of a blind eye to a senator who's seen around with a beautiful girl on his arm; they certainly wouldn't afford the same courtesy to a Presidential nominee.'

'Therefore?' said Chiffon, filling in the conjunction for him, her eyes wide, her face flushed.

'Therefore . . . we have to *de-activate* our relationship for a while. I'm sorry. I'll make sure that you have plenty of funds to see you through . . . but the deal I've had to do in order to make sure that I have a fighting chance of winning the Presidency . . . well, I'm very regretful that the deal can't include you.'

Chiffon's eyes filled with tears; more out of rage than out of unhappiness. '*De-activate*?' she snapped at him. 'De-activate? You're not de-activating anything, you're throwing me over. Isn't that it? Come on, you're supposed to be a politician, talk straight, for Christ's sake.'

'Keep your voice down,' Reynard ordered her. 'Will you keep your voice down?'

'Why the hell should I? De-activate, for Christ's sake. You promised me that one day you would be President, and you told me that when you were, I'd be your First Lady. Didn't you say that?'

'Chiffon, something I might have said in bed after a pretty wild party . . .'

'Reynard, you *promised* me. One day, you said, we're going to be standing on the White House lawn, and the whole world's going to be looking at us, and it's going to be like the movies. Mrs Chiffon Kelly, you said, First Lady of the United States of America.'

Reynard beckoned to the waiter to bring him the cheque. 'Listen, Chiffon,' he said, quietly, 'I'm not going to sit here and discuss a few fantastic things I might have said to you in bed; nor am I going to argue with you in public about the future of our relationship.

I told you how I feel. I'm very fond of you, in fact I adore you. But I have a duty to my country as well as a duty to myself, and I thought you'd understand that, and accept it like a lady.'

'You rat,' said Chiffon, with such vehemence that the elderly ladies on the next table turned around in astonishment. 'Do you think I would have stayed with you for one minute if you hadn't promised that I was going to be First Lady? Do you think I wanted *you*? Your *body*? You dried-up old geriatric! Why do you think a girl who looks like me spent her time with a man who looks like you? Did you think I was *crazy* or something?'

'Chiffon – ' said Reynard.

'Don't you say another word,' rapped Chiffon. 'Don't you say one more word. I'm going to scream if you say another word.'

'There isn't any need to get yourself hysterical,' Reynard insisted. 'We only need to break up temporarily, just until the election's over. Meanwhile, you'll be living a life of complete luxury. Anything you want, just name it. If it's money – cars – you name it.'

'I want what you promised me. The White House.'

'What are you so het up about? Being First Lady is all work. You'd hate it. You have to spend all of your time at charity dinners, visiting the handicapped, talking to the wives of African visitors, smiling your ass off. You'd hate it.'

'You promised me the White House,' Chiffon repeated, and her expression was masklike; a face by Norman Norell out of Nō theatre.

'What did she say?' whispered one of the elderly ladies at the next table. 'He promised her *what*?'

Chiffon said, in a voice blind with disappointment and rage, 'Do you know what I'm going to do? I'm going to walk out of here now. But let me tell you something, if I don't hear by this time tomorrow that

110

you've changed your mind, then I'm going to go straight to the media. Television, newspapers, I'm going to show you up for what you are.'

Reynard said, 'If I were you, darling I wouldn't do anything rash.'

'*Darling*,' she spat at him. 'You can make it sound like an insult.'

'If I'd only known that you thought I was going to take you to the White House with me . . . I didn't realize for a moment that you took it so seriously. It just can't be, Chiffon. I adore you, and I'd love to keep you around, but Greta – '

'Greta? What does Greta have to do with it?'

'Well, obviously, if I'm going to be running for the Democratic nomination, I have to do it as a family man. I'm not going to be running on my own, I have to have a wife beside me.'

Chiffon stared at him. 'After everything you said about Greta. What a bitch she was. How she never understood your deepest ambitions. How bad she was in bed. You liar. I don't think I ever met anybody in my whole life so *unprincipled*.'

The waiter brought the cheque. Reynard signed it with his firm, familiar squiggle, and gave the man a $10 tip.

'Thank *you*, Senator,' said the waiter, looking uncertainly at Chiffon.

The two of them walked out of the Palm Court amidst an unusual hush. Heads turned, Reynard found himself obliged to nod to two or three people that he knew; including Ken Gibbs of Standard Oil, who was smirking like a schoolboy.

'Don't bother to see me up to my room,' said Chiffon, and stalked off across the wide patterned carpet.

Dick Elmwood straightened his tie. 'She looked upset.'

'She was upset. I misjudged her.'

111

'What was she so mad about? Didn't she understand that *you* were upset, too?'

Reynard took a breath. 'She thought that when I ran for President, I'd be taking her along with me. She was under the impression that she was going to be First Lady.'

'Are you joking?' asked Dick Elmwood. 'But you never told her that, did you?'

'I might have done, one night when I was feeling drunk and happy. But I never believed for a single moment that she'd take it so seriously. I mean, it's more important to her than money, or anything. She's really sore about it.'

'Hm,' said Dick Elmwood. 'That could be embarrassing, to say the least. If she takes it into her head to talk to the media – '

'She's already taken it into her head to talk to the media. She says if I don't change my mind by this time tomorrow, it's blow-the-whistle time.'

Dick Elmwood chewed at his lip and looked reflectively at Pollock. Pollock stood with his hands neatly parked in front of his genitals and didn't say a word. He only spoke when spoken to; and then monosyllabically.

'What do you want to do?' Dick Elmwood asked Reynard.

'I don't think there's much that we can do,' said Reynard.

'She won't be persuaded? Bought off?'

'I don't believe so,' Reynard told him.

Dick Elmwood thought for a while. Then he said, 'I think you'd better leave her to me, sir.'

Reynard waved and smiled at a passing acquaintance. Still with the smile fixed on his face, he said to Dick Elmwood, 'All right, then, if you think that's the only way. But I don't want to know anything about it whatsoever, do you hear? Don't even mention it to me again, ever.'

'Pollock?' said Dick Elmwood. 'You understand what's going on here?'

'Yes, sir,' said Pollock. He was very handsome, but there was something missing in his expression; a terrible deadness which somehow made him seem asexual and utterly without emotion. He had been hit in the neck by a VC bullet at Cape Batangan; and the only picture in his apartment was a LIFE spread of himself, smothered in blood, being stretchered out by medics. The only ornament was a crucifix.

'Well, then,' said Reynard, uncomfortably. 'I'll freshen up, and see you a little later.'

EIGHT

Edmond was having lunch with Dr John Metcalf at B. Mae Denny's when Oscar Ford came over and laid a hand on his shoulder and said, 'You spare a moment? Hi, J.M. Sorry to interrupt.'

'Can it wait?' asked Edmond. He was halfway through his steak. Besides that, Dr Metcalf was a difficult man to persuade to come out to lunch, and Edmond had been trying for almost two months now to talk to him about improved screening equipment at the clinic.

'I'm too pushed, I'm afraid,' said Oscar, checking his watch. 'Besides . . .' he said, and flapped a blue-foldered autopsy report as if it were the final and conclusive proof that men were descended from chimpanzees.

'That's the Osman autopsy?'

Oscar nodded. 'And believe me, you have to see it.'

Edmond looked across the table at Dr Metcalf. White-haired, elegantly spoken, Dr Metcalf was still chewing his brochette of steak tips and had sipped only a little

113

of his dry white wine. Dr Metcalf's face remained mild and unreadable, as if he refused to give Edmond any clues whatsoever whether or not he would be spoiling his chances of being allocated better equipment by leaving the table now and talking to Oscar.

Oscar pulled a reddened grimace at Edmond, and said, 'Believe me, this is 200% crucial.'

'Dr Metcalf? Could you give me a moment, please?' asked Edmond.

Dr Metcalf closed and re-opened his eyes in the subtlest of acknowledgements. Edmond pushed back his chair, and followed Oscar across the restaurant.

'I hope this isn't a put-on,' said Edmond, as they made their way between the trees and plants which made B. Mae Denny's into a lunchtime jungle. Oscar said nothing, but sniffed, and waved the autopsy report again and ushered Edmond outside to the glass-enclosed balcony. It was brilliantly sunny and oppressively hot out there, but at least it was quiet; away from the laughter and the clatter of knives and forks and that restaurant sound which Arabelle had always called 'the babbling gossip of the air,' after a line in *Twelfth Night*.

'I'll give you a full copy of the autopsy later,' said Oscar. 'But what you have to know right now is that whatever killed Michael Osman, it wasn't polio.'

'If it wasn't, I'd sure as hell like to know what it was,' said Edmond. He wiped his mouth with his handkerchief; steak sauce. He had almost forgotten the Osman autopsy in the past two days, what with a sudden outbreak of measles at the Concord Union School on Rumford Street; and two cases of suspected malnutrition out near Snap Town. Malnutrition, in rural New Hampshire. They'd be having the Black Death next.

Oscar licked his thumb, and leafed his way through the autopsy protocols until he came to the virologist's report. 'It was a virus, all right. But it sure wasn't poliomyelitis, even though it had an exactly similar effect to poliomyelitis.

'Here, let me read it. "A microscopic examination of the tissue sample from the intercostal muscles has revealed the presence of a virus which so far defies identification, although it has evidently been wholly or largely responsible for a polio-like paralysis of the respiratory system. The virus is not unusual in structure, consisting of the usual nucleic acid genome surrounded by a proteinaceous coating. It measures 80 micrometres in diameter. A series of electron microscope pictures of the virus have been taken for the purpose of further identification and study." '

Edmond peered at the report. 'Who did this? Wilson?'

'No, Corning; and you know how goddamned unimaginative *he* is.'

'What's he say down at the bottom there?'

'Ah,' said Oscar, raising a finger. 'This is where we come to it. He adds a footnote to the effect that – here we are, "early tests on this virus under limited conditions suggest that it has an unusual and dramatic rate of growth and replication. In common with many other coated viruses it obtains the lipid for its coating from the host cell during the maturation of the replicative process . . ." well, it gets very technical here, but then he says, "whereas viral infectivity can usually be destroyed by lipid solvents like ether or by ionizing X-Rays or non-ionizing ultra violet . . ." blah, blah . . . now, here it is, "the infectivity of this particular virus appears to be not only unaffected by lipid solvents and radiation, but actually to become more vigorous when attacked. Most viruses are readily destroyed by heat . . . but this virus measurably trebled its replicative process at high temperatures, and in common with other viruses preserved its infectivity even at very low temperatures ($-70°C$)." '

Oscar stopped reading, and stared at Edmond

steadily. It seemed to be even hotter out here on the balcony than before, and there were clear beads of sweat on Oscar's nose.

Edmond said, 'Let me understand this. Corning's saying you can't *kill* this virus?'

'That's what he's saying.'

'Not only that, but it spreads like wildfire?'

Oscar nodded.

Edmond shaded his eyes, and looked out through the dazzling glass window towards the parking-lot, and beyond, to the sun-dancing curve of the Merrimack River. A virus that replicated itself at high speed, and which couldn't be destroyed by conventional means. It was a doctor's nightmare, the kind of unnerving vertiginous dream that woke Edmond up sweating in the small hours of the morning. That, and his endlessly recurring dream of what had happened to Arabelle. It seemed ridiculous, impossible, especially on a bright day in early fall like this one; with people talking and laughing and eating all around them. And yet here it was in Dr Corning's preliminary virology report; and here was the plain ugly fact that Oscar was standing in front of him sweating and red and so worried that he couldn't even joke any more.

'It's a – it could mean an epidemic,' said Edmond. His mouth was dry.

'Well, so far, Michael Osman is the only reported victim,' said Oscar. 'But, you know, we haven't yet found out where this came from – and what's worse, we don't know how it's carried. If it's anything like polio, it could be carried even by people who have been vaccinated against it.'

Edmond licked his lips. 'How long before Corning finishes his full tests?'

'He didn't say. He's sending some samples to Berkley.'

Edmond took a step sideways, so that he could glance

116

back through the restaurant and make sure that Dr Metcalf wasn't growing too impatient.

Oscar said, 'Did you check up on Michael Osman's friend?'

'Young Bernie? Yes. I saw him the same night. Clean as a whistle.'

'No reports since?'

'No.'

'Well, then, maybe it's a freak,' Oscar suggested. 'Maybe, for some reason, this one boy just happened to react to a regular polio virus in such a way that the virus mutated.'

'Do you really believe that?' asked Edmond.

'No, I don't. To tell you the truth, I don't know *what* to believe. I'm just running every goddamned flag that I can think of up the flagpole to see if it flies. I mean, look at it this way – there's a possibility that this virus is only pathogenic to particular types of people, and Michael Osman just happened to be unlucky. It's so virulent that I can't imagine why his friend Bernie didn't pick it up, especially since the two of them spent almost the whole day together, every day. You know what kids are, sharing candy, sharing cans of Coke, not washing their hands after they've taken a leak. There was every opportunity for that virus to be passed on to Bernie, and yet it wasn't.'

Edmond took out his handkerchief, and patted sweat from his forehead. 'I'm going to have to get back to Dr Metcalf,' he said. 'But give me some time to think this over. Have you told Bryce?'

'Not yet. You're the first, apart from the other guys in the lab.'

'You don't think that Bryce is going to like it?'

'Do *you* like it?'

'That's not what I meant.'

'I know what you meant,' said Oscar. Dr Bryce was the medical referee for Merrimack County: a stiffnecked, conservative, hickory-hewn New Hampshire man. He was on the committee of the Sons of the American Revolution, a one-time president of the New Hampshire Hospital Association, the chief consultant for the New Hampshire Heart Association, a major of the Penacook Post of the American Legion, and busily active in about a dozen other local organizations. His family had settled in Concord way back in the days of Nathaniel B. Baker, and as far as he was concerned, Concord was the only righteous and upstanding city in the United States. 'If it hadn't have been for the Concord coach,' he used to say, staring at his staff through intense little wire-rimmed spectacles, 'there never would have been an American West. Even today. Perhaps we should never have built it.'

Both Edmond and Oscar knew that Dr Bryce would receive the autopsy on Michael Osman with more than his usual scepticism and querulous hostility. He regarded every violent or unnatural death in the Concord district as a personal slight, a deliberate and ill-bred slur on our fine community. Oscar used to say that if Dr Bryce had his way, every resident who hadn't been courteous enough to die in his sleep with a smile on his face would be smuggled by night over the Belknap county line, and dumped.

'You're going to have to tell someone else, apart from Bryce,' said Edmond. 'If you leave it up to him, he'll file it under 'Review Next Year' and forget about it. By that time, half the population of Merrimack County could be wiped out.'

'Who do you suggest?' asked Oscar.

'Well, there's always Harold Bunyan.'

'Is he your guardian angel on the Board of Health? H.B.? I thought he might be. He's about the only doctor on the board who's anything like your style.'

'I did Harold a favour a long time ago, in Manhattan,' Edmond explained. 'His son was convicted on a dope-dealing charge; he was a heavy user, too. I managed to get the boy sprung on medical grounds.'

Oscar's bright-red face remained expressionless. It was obvious that he was waiting for Edmond to explain how an ordinary doctor, no matter how wealthy and well-connected, could have saved a drugs dealer from serving his mandatory minimum sentence.

'I was a very close friend of someone who was very close to the Assistant District Attorney,' Edmond added.

Then, when Oscar still remained unmoved, Edmond said, 'His wife.'

'All right,' said Oscar. 'I'll file the report with Bryce, then I'll go tell Harold Bunyan.'

'Can you get me a copy of the autopsy, too?' asked Edmond. 'Then, when Harold's had a chance to read it, I can go over it with him and fill him in with any other details he needs to know, personal case notes, stuff like that.'

Oscar said, 'I just hope this thing doesn't backfire on us, that's all. If Bryce finds out that Harold Bunyan got hold of the autopsy report at the same time he did . . . well, you know what he's like about protocol. Apart from the fact that he can't stand the sight of Harold Bunyan's face.'

Edmond said, 'I'd better get back. Dr Metcalf looks like he's about to get up and walk out on me.'

'Okay,' said Oscar. 'I'll call you this evening, and tell you what Bryce had to say about the virology report. He'll probably say "a freak, Dr Ford, an aberration." But I'll give it my best shot.'

Edmond gripped his hand, and turned to walk back to his table. But as he went, Oscar said, 'One more thing, E.C.'

'What is it?'

Oscar half-lifted the autopsy report in a gesture of

apology. 'I'm sorry about the surprise party, you know?'

Edmond shook his head. 'Don't be. I think you've saved me a visit from my brother.'

'You don't get along with your brother?'

'One day I'll tell you about it. But listen – I'll catch you later.'

Dr Metcalf was distinctly unamused by Edmond's extended absence. He had finished his brochette and was now sitting drumming his fingers on the table and checking his watch.

'I'm sorry,' said Edmond, as he sat down again. 'Dr Ford had something of a crisis on his hands.'

'I see,' said Dr Metcalf. 'Well, I'm afraid it hasn't left us with very much time to talk about screening equipment, has it? I have to be back at the hospital by two.'

'Dr Metcalf, do I really have to sell this equipment to you?' asked Edmond. 'You know yourself how vital it is; and if they reduced next year's building budget by just one per cent they could allocate us all the money we need.'

'Unfortunately, you're not the only consultant who wants to take one per cent of the building budget,' replied Dr Metcalf. 'Dr Abrahams wants a new therapy unit; Dr Krassner wants beds; Dr Wollinsky needs a whole range of laboratory equipment. If I give *you* one per cent, what am I going to say to *them*?'

The waitress came over and said, 'Would either of you two gentlemen care for applie pie? Or we have some terrific Baked Alaska.'

Dr Metcalf looked up at her, and then Edmond. 'I think I'll pass,' he said. 'And I'm afraid I'm going to have to say the same about your screening equipment, Dr Chandler. Talk to me next year; maybe we'll have a little more money then.'

Edmond didn't even try to smile.

Bernie had cried when they told him that Michael was dead. For days afterwards, he had been pale and withdrawn, hardly eating, not speaking to anyone; sitting alone in his bedroom watching television, or cycling out to the fields and sitting with his arms folded tightly as if he were trying to protect himself from the cold wind of knowing that his best friend would soon be buried.

Edmond had explained to Bernie's parents that there would be weeks of grief; and that Bernie should be allowed to feel unhappy and abandoned. Part of his grief was the irrational feeling that his dead friend had somehow betrayed him; slipped away without saying where he was going; not even leaving a note.

Bernie's parents had been terrified to begin with that Bernie might already have contracted the virus which had so quickly killed Michael. But Edmond had examined him closely, and taken samples of blood and spinal fluid, and it was soon clear that he had miraculously remained free of infection.

'But if there's anything . . . even the trace of a sore throat, or stiffness of the joints . . . call me immediately,' Edmond had warned.

On the same afternoon that Edmond was having lunch with Dr Metcalf, Bernie was sitting in his bedroom with the leather case on his desk in front of him. He opened and closed it and then opened it again. Then took out all six of the clear glass bottles, and set them up in a line.

To Bernie the case was a complete mystery. Michael would never have hidden anything in their secret hiding-place without telling him; Bernie couldn't think of a single time when Michael had kept any discovery secret, especially a discovery as momentous as this one. And if Michael hadn't told him about it on the morning before Bernie had gone to his piano lesson, then he must have come across it some time that afternoon, and had been planning to tell him about it when he came back. Only he hadn't been able to, of course. He had died.

Bernie had already examined the leather case over and over again. It seemed pretty old and musty; and there was even mould inside it. Five of the bottles were sealed with some kind of dried-up wax, although the sixth bottle had been opened. By Michael? Bernie didn't know. He had opened the bottle himself, and sniffed at it, but it didn't seem to smell like anything at all. Maybe it was just water.

Bernie had wondered if he ought to show the case to his parents, but he had decided against it, at least for the time being. He and Michael had only ever hidden things in the garage wall if they were top secret, for their eyes only; and Bernie felt that if he showed the case around, he would be letting Michael down. He felt that the case had somehow been entrusted to him, Michael's last cryptic bequest, and until he understood what it was, and why Michael had hidden it, he wanted to keep it to himself.

Mrs Osman had said that Michael had gone out on his bicycle that afternoon. He hadn't gone to any of his schoolfriends' homes; and he hadn't gone to the Winant Mall to find her. He might have gone to Turtle Pond, but usually they rode their bicycles through the mud around the pond's perimeter, and Bernie hadn't noticed any mud on Michael's bicycle. He might have gone to Sugar Ball, to see old Mr Keeler, who used to be their class teacher, but that was unlikely. It was a long ride, and usually they went together, and told their parents where they were going.

He might have gone to Conant's Acre, but how could he have picked up a disease at Conant's Acre? And where could he have discovered this leather case? Right in the middle of the fields?

Bernie slipped all the bottles back into the case and

closed it. Then carefully, he lifted it up on to his top shelf, next to his model airplanes and his Star Wars figures, and hid it behind a row of annuals. Maybe he should bicycle down to Conant's Acre and take a look around. After all, it was the most likely place for Michael to have gone. It wasn't too far away, and they had still been in the process of exploring it; so it had still held some fear and excitement for them.

Apart from that, Bernie felt like being alone.

His mother waved to him from the kitchen window as he cycled off down the road. It was a bright, sunny afternoon, but a sharp wind was blowing from the north-east, and Bernie had put on his green-and-yellow windbreaker and his yellow baseball cap. Old Mrs Rogers called from her front lawn, 'Hi, Bernie!' and he called back in his polite throaty young boy's voice, 'Hi, Mrs Rogers!'

He had to cycle around Webster Crescent on his way to Conant's Acre; past Michael's house. The house looked strange and forlorn; the downstairs drapes were drawn, and there was a plain wreath on the front door. It was weird to think that he would never play in that house again. It was double-weird to think that Michael was dead, lying with his eyes closed in his coffin, all ready for Thursday's funeral. This time last week, they had been playing dirt bikes together out on Appleton Street.

He reached Conant's Acre and dismounted, propping his bike up against the split-rail fence. He looked around for any signs that Michael might have been here, but there was only the usual tangle of weeds and Coke cans and torn-up pages of *TV Guide*. The wind blew across Conant's Acre and made a soft thundering sound in his ear, the way it does with microphones. He sniffed, and climbed over the fence, pausing for a moment on the top rail to shade his eyes and look around. Try to pretend you're Michael, he thought.

You're on your own and you're playing a game. Try to think what Michael would have done.

Across the field, in the distance, were the woods. Would Michael have gone to explore the woods? It didn't seem likely. They were both scared of the woods: Bernie more than he ever cared to admit. They reminded him of the woods in *Dracula*: the sort of woods in which vampires moved like tall grey shadows, and out of whose leafy soil zombies might rise, with wriggling red meat-worms dangling out of their eye-sockets.

There were times when Bernie wished that he hadn't read quite so many horror stories. Even here, a few yards from the split-rail fence, the silence of that windy afternoon was frightening.

He heard a scurrying behind him, and turned around in shock. It was nothing but a rabbit, staring at him bulgy-eyed out of the weeds alongside the fence. He said, 'Here, rabbit; c'mon, rabbit,' but the rabbit loped away up the field, and disappeared into the hedgerow.

Maybe Michael had just found the leather case lying on the ground. Maybe somebody had dropped it, and he was planning to take it down to the police station as lost property, after he had shown it to Bernie. Yet, why hadn't he shown it to his parents? Had he stolen it? That didn't seem very likely; and, besides where would he have stolen it from? There were no second-hand stores anywhere around, not for miles; and even though it was old, the leather case didn't look like the kind of thing that you would find in any of Concord's smart and selective antique shops. So maybe it had come from someplace special; someplace that Michael hadn't wanted his parents to know about, either because he shouldn't really have been there, or because it was a great and secret discovery. Maybe Michael had at last found a hideout. He and Bernie had been looking for a good hideout ever since Bernie's father had caught them lighting matches in the summer-house at the end of Bernie's back yard and forbidden them from using it as a camp. They had tried a pup-tent, but it hadn't been the same, and they had lost most of the pegs.

Bernie walked halfway across the field, and then paused, his hands on his hips, looking at the woods ahead of him. Surely Michael hadn't actually gone as far as the treeline? Not on his own, it was too scary. The woods were rustling and whispering as if they were alive; and even on a bright day like this they were shadowy and dark; a small forest of unexpressed fears.

Bernie turned around, and began plodding back towards the split-rail fence. But after only a few paces, he hesitated, and looked at the woods again. They were scary, yes, but he almost felt as if they were beckoning him. If he had been Michael, alone on that windy day, would *he* have gone into the woods? There was a chance that maybe he might. Think what he could have said to Bernie when he got back; think how he could have boasted that alone he had dared to penetrate the one place where neither of them had dared to go before. He and Michael had argued about which of them was the braver only two or three days before; and Bernie had forced Michael to admit that because he was ten and Michael was only nine, he was a year braver just by virtue of natural human development. As you grew older, you grew braver, and that was it.

Bernie began to head for the woods again. He told himself that there was no danger, not in the daytime, because vampires and loogaroos only come out at night. The trouble was, it might be dark enough inside the woods to qualify as night, and then what? Perhaps Michael had met a vampire, and been bitten, and that was why he had died of disease. Infected blood.

He had almost reached the edge of the woods when he heard a whistling. He looked up the field to his left, and saw a man walking towards him, dressed in a

125

tweed Norfolk jacket and rubbers, and a soft tweed hat. The man took his time, but at last he came up to Bernie and stood there with his hands in his pockets, half-grinning and half-grimacing at him.

'What's your name, son?' the man asked him.

'Bernie,' said Bernie.

'Hm,' said the man, and took out one hand to wipe his nose. 'You know this is private land here, Bernie? Private woods.'

'No, sir?' Of course Bernie knew that it was.

'Well, I'm afraid that it is,' the man explained. 'All of Conant's Acre, all of these woods, right down as far as the Loudun Road.'

'Aren't people allowed to walk here?' asked Bernie.

The man slowly shook his head. 'Question of insurance. Supposing you fell over on this land, broke your ankle or something. Mr Kelly doesn't want anybody suing him for negligence, or nothing like that. He doesn't mean any offence, doesn't want to lose any friends. But he's a wealthy man, and wealthy men have to be careful. Three times he's had children and winos rolling in front of his car, just for the settlement money. You could be up to the same kind of trick. Not saying you necessarily *are*. But you could be.'

In actual fact, Bernie was quite relieved to be turned away from the woods. Now he could retreat without feeling cowardly.

'You get along there,' said the man. 'And tell your friends, too. Mr Kelly's a good man, a good neighbour, but he asks you not to wander around his property.'

Bernie took one last look at the woods; at the tangled briars and the nodding branches; and it was then that he glimpsed on one of the tree-trunks a more-than-familiar mark. It was the secret blaze which he and Michael had devised between them: a triangle, with a circle in the centre of it. He felt his heart bump, and he glanced up at the man to make sure that he hadn't

126

noticed what he was looking at. Michael *had* been here: his guess had been right.

He ran quickly back across the field, his cheeks alight with excitement. He swung over the fence, collected his bicycle, and began to pedal his way home. He was right, he was *right*. There was a mystery, and one of the clues was the leather case with the bottles in it. Somewhere in the woods, he would find the answer, and it was even possible that he would solve the riddle of Michael's death. The first thing he would have to do would be to go home and work out a plan. A plan was essential. Then he would have to find a way of slipping into the woods undetected, and tracing Michael's trail.

It was a stiff pedal up Webster Crescent, and after a few yards he dismounted, and pushed his bicycle beside him. He was still on foot when he passed Michael's home; and he stood outside it for a moment, and stared at it, and suddenly all the excitement of finding out what had happened to Michael seemed to evaporate. All he really wanted was Michael himself, his friend lost for ever. His throat choked up and his eyes filled with tears, even though he didn't want them to.

'Don't ever be ashamed to cry,' Dr Chandler had told him, and remembering those words made him weep all the more.

He took out a crumpled Kleenex, and wiped his eyes. Then he started walking up the crescent again. But as he did so, he saw the most extraordinary thing. In the front upstairs window of Michael's house, there was a tongue-like flicker of orange, almost up to the ceiling. Bright curling orange, as if someone had thrown a vivi-dly-coloured bedspread up into the air. He paused, and he saw it again. But this time it was quite clear that it wasn't a bedspread: it was a flicker of fire. And before he could even think of shouting out to anybody, he

127

saw the bedroom drapes catch alight, and burn at the windows like the draperies of hell.

'Fire!' he shouted.

A man washing his car two houses away raised his head and stared at him. He pointed towards the Osman's bedroom and shouted again. 'Fire! The house is on fire!'

It was Edmond's afternoon off. He needed it, after that lunch with Dr Metcalf. But he and Christy had only just started a game of backgammon when the telephone rang. He picked it up and said, 'Dr Chandler.' Then, to Christy, 'Go ahead, you can throw if you like.'

It was Oscar. His voice sounded faded and blurry, because he was patched through from the mobile phone in his car. He said, 'I'm out at the Osman place on Webster Crescent.'

'What are you doing there?'

'There's been a fire. A real bad one. The fire department have only just gotten it under control. The whole house is a shell.'

'Jesus. What about the Osmans? Was anybody hurt?'

'They're both dead. They were up in the front bedroom where the fire broke out.'

'You want me to get down there?'

'I think you'd better. Wear something warm. It's Goddamned perishing out here.'

'Give me ten minutes, okay?' said Edmond, and put down the phone.

Christy said, 'What's wrong?'

'The Osmans, the parents of that boy who died of poliomyelitis. They both got burned in a fire.'

'Oh, my God.'

Edmond went into the hall, opened the cupboard, and took down the fur-lined anorak he usually wore when he went fishing. 'Don't wait for me,' he said.

'Oscar's down there, and I'm not sure how long I'm going to be.'

Christy kissed him. 'You want a flask of coffee to take with you? It's almost perked.'

He shook his head. 'Jobs like that are better on an empty stomach.'

He drove out to Webster Crescent with the radio playing Vivaldi's Four Seasons, very loud. Arabelle had adored Vivaldi. She had listened to the Four Seasons with her head back and her eyes closed, and one finger tracing and re-tracing the veins on the back of his hand, so gently that it had made him shiver. He could remember the room, the day, the time, the place. He could even remember the way she had smelled, as he buried his face in her hair.

Webster Crescent was crowded with firetrucks, ambulances, rescue cars and pale-faced onlookers. Edmond was waved through by a police patrolman and he parked right behind Oscar's station wagon. Oscar was standing there with Dean Conran, the Fire Chief, and the Assistant Commissioner of the Department of Safety, Tom Simoneau.

'House went up like a torch,' said Oscar. 'They didn't stand a chance.'

Dean Conran said dryly, 'It was one of those upper-storey fires that build up to super-heat. The downstairs windows were open, so that plenty of air was drawn into the lower part of the building and up the stairwell. The bedroom door was open, too, so there was nothing to keep the fire bottled up. The hotter it got, the more air it drew in, and the hotter it got. The heat actually fused the victim's bones to their bedsprings.'

'Any ideas how it started?' asked Edmond.

'Hard to say. They were both upstairs in the bedroom, lying on the bed, so one of them might have been smoking. Maybe there was an electrical fault. It's impossible to tell until we go over the whole building with a crab-comb.'

'Anything left of the bodies?' Edmond asked Oscar. 'I mean, anything worth autopsying?'

'Come see for yourself,' said Oscar. 'We haven't moved them yet because the safety people haven't finished taking pictures.'

They crossed the road, which was running with sooty water. Edmond wished he had worn his rubbers, instead of his light suede golfing shoes. They stepped over a tangle of hoses, and then they were treading over the deep black crunchy ashes of the Osman house, past a skeletal couch that looked like an incinerated horse, a half-melted television set, and a strange array of surrealistically-twisted candlesticks and cutlery.

The bedroom floor had collapsed into the living-room, bringing with it the Osman's fiery bed and what remained of the Osmans. Two bland young men in ash-smeared safety helmets were taking photographs, and making notes. They treated the bizarre spectacle in front of them as if it were nothing more shocking than a modern sculpture at the Penacook Gallery; or an interesting tourist attraction.

The burned-out bed lay at an angle of 45°, its foot propped up in the air by a scaffold of charred flooring. The Osman's bodies still clung to the mattresses, however, because the red-hot springs had literally welded themselves to their flesh and their bones; and so they were suspended like dead flies on a screen door.

Mr Osman's body had been burned far more badly than that of his wife. He was tight and black and tiny, half the size he had been when Edmond had met him a few days ago; more like a shrivelled-up mummy than a man. His club-like hands were held up to his chest, and his legs were drawn into the air: the effect of intense heat on his bodily sinews. His face was stretched into an expression which reminded Edmond of one of those tortured monkeys at a vivisection laboratory.

Mrs Osman had been protected from the worst of the flames by a wardrobe door falling across her. She had already been dead when this had happened, of course; but while her legs had both been burned down to the bones, her torso had been scorched raw but kept reasonably intact. Her face was smashed tomatoes, and Edmond couldn't even look at her.

Oscar said, 'At least I'll have some internal organs to work on. *Cooked* internal organs, but internal organs all the same.'

They trod back through the ashes. The Fire Chief said, 'What do you think, doc? Not a pretty sight, hunh? And people tell you to mind your own business when you warn them against smoking in bed. The deaths I've seen, I can tell you.'

Edmond took Oscar across the road. He bent over and tried to brush some of the clinging wet ash off his shoes, while Oscar stood beside him with his hands in his pockets staring at the burned-out house. Edmond said, 'There's one thing that doesn't seem to ring true.'

Oscar nodded. 'I thought that. What were they doing in bed at four o'clock in the afternoon?'

'Unlikely they were making love, especially so soon after Michael's death.'

'Resting?' suggested Oscar.

'Possibly,' said Edmond. 'But if they were resting, would they have fallen to sleep so soundly that they didn't wake up when the room caught fire? They obviously didn't make any effort to escape.'

'Maybe they were poisoned by toxic gas from their burning mattress,' said Oscar. 'Maybe they were overcome by smoke before they managed to wake up.'

Both of them were silent. An ambulance from the New Hampshire Hospital backed up to the sidewalk, and three medics climbed out of the back carrying body bags. One of them raised a hand in greeting to Oscar, and called, 'Kind of late in the year for a barbecue.'

'That Johnson has the sickest sense of humour,' said Oscar.

Edmond said, 'You know what I'm thinking, don't you?'

Oscar cleared his throat. 'I feel like I had smoke for breakfast, smoke for lunch, and smoke sandwiches for supper.' He paused; then he said, 'Yes. I know what you're thinking. But we won't know for sure until I've run some tests.'

'Did you see Bryce this afternoon?'

'I left the autopsy on his desk. He was stuck in some committee meeting.'

'And Harold?'

'He's out of town until tomorrow afternoon.'

Edmond said, 'On the face of it, it makes a lot of sense, doesn't it? They didn't make any attempt to escape the fire because they were dead or almost dead already.'

Oscar shrugged, and looked away. 'We'll see,' he said.

The early-evening wind blew ashes across the road.

NINE

Bill Bennett insisted that they drive to Uppsala at once, even though Humphrey protested that he was very tired, not as young as he used to be, and that after all he *was* supposed to be on his holidays. What responsibility did *he* have to find Klaus Hermann?

'Your responsibility is, you're the person best qualified to make a positive identification,' said Bill Bennett. They were driving around the monumental modern fountain at Sergels Torg, before heading north-west up Sveavägen to join the E4 motorway which led out towards Arlanda airport and beyond, to Uppsala Län. Bill Bennett drove the Grand Prix at a steady, unrelenting 50 mph, as if the car had no brakes. The worndown tyres protested like hungry piglets as they swerved around the square at the end of Sveavägen and dived under the railroad bridge at Norrtull.

Birgitta Gillsäter sat silently in the back seat, her face intermittently lit up by the passing sodium lamps, smoking a cigarette. She appeared to be strangely resigned to this kidnapping, and even when Humphrey turned around in his seat to ask if she was all right, she did nothing more than shrug one shoulder, and blow smoke out of her nostrils. Humphrey disliked cigarette smoke, and opened his window an inch or two, until the wind grew too chilly.

Bill Bennett felt calmer now. He always felt calmer once an operation started to tick over. He didn't particulary mind the waiting beforehand: after all, he had been trained to wait. But when you were waiting, you had time to think of all the things that might go wrong, some of them petty, some of them inconvenient, some of them disastrous. Some of them, particularly in an operation like this one, potentially fatal.

Dealing with old-time Nazi war criminals wasn't at all like dealing with modern-day spies. Most of the Nazis who had successfully escaped at the end of the war had been able to do so because they had already been well-connected; so they had been given all the necessary facilities to disguise themselves behind layers of aliases and false credentials. It had been nearly 40 years since the end of the war, too, and in those 40 years they had been able to establish themselves in highly influential positions – positions from which it could be diplomatically and economically impossible to remove them. How could American agents arrest and

133

capture Hans von Trenck when he had financed and organized a major offshore oil survey in Mexico, and was one of the most powerful figures in Mexican politics? The capture of Klaus Barbie, with which Bill himself had been directly involved, had caused explosive ructions in the United States; and two other unnamed Nazis who had been captured along with Barbie had been secretly released.

It was sometimes possible for Nazi-hunters to exact vengeance on war criminals and get away with it. Martin Bormann had been the classic example. He had worked for years after the war as chief executive of the Brasilia Mineral Corporation AG, under the name of Walter von Ischl. But he had been abducted one morning in 1971 by Israeli agents, killed at once, and his body returned to Berlin. It had been 'distressed' by forensic experts as if were a piece of reproduction furniture, to give it the appearance of age. Then later, it had been formally identified and the 'mystery' of what had happened to Bormann had been officially cleared up. The Brazilian government had been unable to protest. After all, how could they protest at the abduction of a man who had apparently never been to Brazil, but had been lying dead in Berlin for 35 years?

Only a few agents, Bill included, were aware that the Israelis had been helped to net Bormann in this way by the CIA; as part of a larger foreign-policy bargain in which Israel was to curtail a plan to invade parts of Egypt across the Red Sea.

Sometimes Bill was convinced that the influence of the Third Reich really would endure for a thousand years, just as Hitler had promised.

They drove through the dark pine-forested landscape. On either side, lakes appeared in the blackness like secret mirrors. It was so cold outside that Bill had to keep on using the defroster to keep the car's windows clear of their breath. Birgitta Gillsäter stared out at nothing; Humphrey tried to doze, but kept dreaming about his old headmaster, and confusing him with Major Milner.

When he opened his eyes, he wasn't immediately sure where he was, or even what year it was. Was the war still going on? It looked so dark outside, like the blackout. He glanced across at Bill, whose face was illuminated green by the dials on the instrument panel; and then twisted around to look at Birgitta.

'Where are we?' he asked, in a dry-mouthed voice.

'We just passed Rosersberg. In a minute, we'll be driving past the airport. There, you can see the lights. Over to your right.'

'How much further to Uppsala?'

'The airport's a little better than halfway.'

'I could do with a cup of tea, you know.'

Bill looked at him, and smiled. 'Didn't you know that apart from anything else, the Swedes make even worse tea than the Americans?'

'I've found that out already. However, I'm not particularly fussy at the moment. I just wish I hadn't come. I just wish I hadn't seen Klaus Hermann.'

They drove in silence for another few kilometres, past the airport, up towards Knivsta. Several Saabs and Volvos overtook them at very high speed. A little further on, they had to slow down for a bad car wreck, emergency lights flashing, traffic policemen in white caps waving them on. There was blood and broken glass; and a woman in a blue quilted anorak, sitting by the side of the road, weeping. The first fine flakes of snow began to fall through the night. Humphrey couldn't help thinking of Christmas. How could anybody live in this peculiar land, where it was nearly always Christmas?

After another ten minutes, Birgitta leaned forward from the back seat and abruptly said, 'Why are you looking for Klaus? Has he done something?'

Bill said, 'Nothing too serious. It's a tax matter.'

'For tax, you drive out to find him in the night? I don't believe you. Anyway, you are American. Why does an American want to talk to a German in Sweden about tax?'

'Let's just say that we were involved in a little business together,' said Bill.

'You're not thinking of doing anything . . .' she couldn't think of the word at first, but at last she said, 'wyolent?'

'Of course not. Do we look the wyolent type?'

Humphrey tried to look at Birgitta reassuringly; but the trouble was that he wasn't at all happy about this business himself. If British and American intelligence really wanted to arrest Hermann and deport him, why hadn't they sent a proper security team, instead of this one man? He didn't like the idea of Bill's gun, either. He had never been comfortable when guns were around: he even gave Swedish policemen a wide berth, whenever he could. The only offensive weapon he had ever owned had been a catapult, when he was eleven. His trusty catty.

Bill was aware that Humphrey was uncomfortable, but there was nothing he could do about it. Hermann had to be fingered, and fingered accurately mainly because Bill couldn't risk the legal and diplomatic rows that would follow if he made a mistake; and also because his career wouldn't stand it. If he performed this particular operation smoothly and efficiently, it could be his passport back to headquarters in the United States, and the end of all that sweaty field-work in South America. But if he failed, they would probably send him out indefinitely to Argentina, or Chile, or even worse, Australia. There were only five major Nazi war criminals in Australia, and two of those were running an extremely popular local bakery in Melbourne.

Birgitta said, 'Is it because Klaus lives in the Soviet Union?'

'Is *what* because Klaus lives in the Soviet Union?' asked Bill, deliberately obtuse.

'Are you looking for him because of that? You think perhaps he's a spy?'

'A spy?' scoffed Bill. 'Just because he happens to live in Russia, that doesn't make him a spy. No, no; we were in business together, that's all. A little import-export.'

'He never mentioned you.'

'Why should he?'

'I don't know,' said Birgitta. 'Klaus is a very open man. He is not the sort of person who has secrets. They respect him in the Soviet Union, you know. He lives in Cerepovec for most of the year, a beautiful house on the Rybinskoje Vodochranilisce. Did you know that?'

'Of course. He talks about it often. He even invited me to spend the summer with him once.'

'Then you are lying,' said Birgitta, flatly. 'Klaus lives in Leningrad, and if you knew him at all you would have known that.'

Bill looked up at his driving mirror. His eyes appeared to be suspended above the windshield like the eyes of a creature in a 1950s science-fiction movie. 'You just be careful with me, lady,' he said. 'I didn't fly all the way here to freeze off my ass and have someone like you make a fool out of me.'

'You should let me free,' said Birgitta.

'You think so?'

'You have no right to hold me any longer.'

Without a word, Bill drew the Grand Prix over to the side of the road. He unlocked the doors, then reached behind him and opened Birgitta's door. A freezing wind blew into the car like a bucketful of razor-blades and brine. A few snowflakes whirled around them, although they vanished as soon as they were touched by the warmth of the heater.

'You want to go, go,' Bill told Birgitta.

There were no other cars on the highway, either behind them or ahead of them. The night was howling and dark, and all around them the pine trees thrashed and screamed in the wind. Birgitta hesitated for a moment, then reached out and held Humphrey's shoulder.

'I don't understand what you want,' she said.

'You don't have to understand,' said Bill. 'We're using you to help us for a specific operation. All you have to know is that we're going to require you to perform certain actions for us; and that we'll be mortally upset if you don't. Why we're doing this doesn't concern you. So all I suggest you do is close the car door, keep your mouth closed, and consider yourself quite lucky that we're not looking for *you*.'

Humphrey said, 'I do think we're rather overstepping ourselves, Bill. I mean, we don't actually have any right – '

'*Right?*' asked Bill. 'You're talking about Klaus Hermann here, and you think we don't have the *right*? Did Klaus Hermann think about rights, back at Herbstwald?'

'Herbstwald?' asked Birgitta, frowning. 'That was a concentration camp, surely? Like Auschwitz and Bergen-Belsen. Surely Klaus wasn't anything to do with that?'

'Let me tell you the truth,' said Bill. 'Klaus Hermann was the camp doctor at Herbstwald between 1941 and 1943. He was a close friend of Dr Josef Mengele, whose name may be more familiar to you. Hermann was a specialist in medical virology. The best of his day; and still one of the best in the world.'

Birgitta said, 'I *know* Klaus. I know him well; ever

138

since he first met Angelika. How could any of this be true? Why are you telling me this lie?'

'It's not a lie, my dear,' put in Humphrey. 'Klaus Hermann was indeed responsible for the deaths of more than three thousand men, women, and children during the war. He used them for medical experiments: to develop new strains of virus, and also to find antidotes for existing viral infections. If you were to be completely cold-blooded, I suppose you could say that he was a great man. A *very* great man. Certainly one of the greatest research biologists of his time. But, unfortunately, he cared only for science, and research; and he ignored the terrible suffering he inflicted on thousands of innocent people.'

Birgitta looked from Humphrey to Bill and then back again. 'This is a trick,' she said, her voice desperate. 'How can this be? Klaus has always treated Angelika so well. He is such a gentleman.'

Bill said, 'Are you getting out, or what? My ears are just about to drop off.'

Birgitta hesitated, and then slammed the car door shut. 'I will stay. I do not trust you at all.'

'You're going to have to do what you're told,' said Bill.

'I will do what I have to.'

Bill glanced in his mirror, and then pulled the Grand Prix back on to the highway. The snow began to fall more thickly now, and he was obliged to switch on the wipers. The wipers cleared the snow into fluffy little triangles, which were then whipped off the edge of the windshield by the bone-cold wind.

'Nice country you have here,' said Bill. 'Remind me to stay in Uruguay next fall.'

Humphrey said cautiously to Bill, 'This won't change anything, will it?'

Bill said, 'I don't know. It might.'

'I mean, her knowing about Hermann,' Humphrey

persisted, nodding towards Birgitta. It won't . . . jeopardize her in any way?'

'Why should it?' asked Bill.

'I'm not sure. But it seems to me already that knowing about Hermann is a great personal responsibility.'

'*Jag vet inte var mina skyldigheter börjar och slutar,*' said Birgitta, bitterly.

Bill looked up in his rear-view mirror again. 'Well, neither do I, sweetie,' he told her. 'But that doesn't prevent me from doing my job.'

Birgitta directed them off the E4 just before they drove into Uppsala itself; and on to the 282 east towards Funbo. The snow had died away, although the road was still wet, and the tyres made a sizzling noise on the pavement. It was nearly eleven o'clock now, and it was all that Humphrey could do to stay awake, particularly since it was his normal defence procedure to any situation which he wasn't enjoying to fall asleep. If his sister argued with him, he fell asleep. He quite often fell asleep at dinner parties, and beetle drives.

'It's here,' said Birgitta, just as Humphrey was falling off another precipice.

Bill turned the car sharply off to the right, down a corduroy road made of logs. The car bucked and swayed, and the suspension sounded like spanners being dropped into a trashcan. On both sides, the pine trees closed in, until they were scraping and squeaking at the windows, and scratching the fenders. Humphrey woke up sharply now, and sat upright, staring into the dark tunnel ahead of them. He very badly needed a pee after their long drive, but he was too frightened to ask.

'I hope this is on the level,' said Bill. 'If this track winds up in a lake, or a quarry, I warn you, you've had it. And I mean *had* it.'

But after two or three minutes the trees widened out,

and the corduroy road abruptly gave way to a mud track; and they found themselves driving out in the open, across a nightblown field, under a frigid sky that was magnificent with northern stars.

'Please, turn off the lights,' said Birgitta. 'They will see us, otherwise. The little house is over there now, to the left, behind those two rows of trees. You see the light? You see the logpile?'

Bill steered the car into the shadow of a clump of pines, and switched off the engine.

'Aren't you going to drive all the way up to the house?' asked Humphrey.

Bill shook his head. 'We're going to walk the rest of the way. And we're going to walk there quietly. You understand me? You too, Ms Gillsäter. Any funny business, and somebody's going to get hurt. And we don't want that to happen, do we? We want everybody to come out of this smiling and cheerful. *Glada som lärkor.*'

'I will do as you ask,' said Birgitta, haughtily. 'I have already agreed, because of Angelika.'

'Quite so,' said Humphrey, and then cleared his throat and looked away when Bill stared at him disapprovingly.

Bill reached into his coat and took out his .38 revolver. Then he matter-of-factly fumbled in his jacket pocket, and produced a silencer, which he screwed quickly on to the end of the muzzle. He did all this without taking his eyes off the house, which gave Humphrey the feeling that he had certainly done this kind of thing more than once.

Humphrey said, 'The gun . . . it is only a precaution?'

'Oh, the gun?' asked Bill. He held it up and looked at it as if this was the first time he had ever seen it. 'Oh, sure, a precaution. I mean, you never know, Hermann might get a little jumpy; and just about everybody around this neck of the woods has a hunting-rifle.'

'I'd rather there weren't any shooting,' said Humphrey.

'*You'd* rather there weren't any shooting?' Bill retorted. It was then that they both realized for an instant what disparate characters they were; and for both of them to be wandering around a field in the middle of the night near a place called Funbo seemed incongruous to the point of madness.

Birgitta climbed out of the car first, and Bill promptly followed her. Humphrey eased himself stiffly out of the passenger seat, and said, 'Is it all right if I spend a penny? The cold, don't you know.'

Bill waved his gun impatiently out at the night. 'There's the whole of Sweden out there. Go piss on it.'

As he stood a little way away, embarrassed by the clattering and the steam, Humphrey wondered if it might not be a good idea simply to go walking off into the woods, leaving Bill to cope with Hermann on his own. The only trouble with *that*, however, was that Humphrey was older than he used to be, and felt the chill, and didn't have a clue where he was. They would probably find his snow-covered body three weeks later, and the Reverend Johnson would have yet another opportunity to talk about death being 'a mist of darkness forever'.

'Are you ready?' Bill demanded impatiently, as Humphrey buttoned himself up.

'Quite ready, thank you. Well – as ready as I'm ever going to be, I suppose.'

They set off across the field, dried bracken and tangled weeds. Birgitta walked in front, Bill a few steps behind and a little way off to Birgitta's right. Humphrey puffed along behind them, wishing very much that he'd remembered to bring his scarf. They skirted a diagonal stand of pines, and now the house came into clear view, a small wooden cottage made of varnished pine with a verandah, an upstairs balcony, and a stone chimney which was smoking furiously as if the fire had only recently been lit. The shutters were closed against the cold, but bright chinks of light shone out, and above the low fluting of the wind, they could hear the sound of Bach, the sarabande from his *Partita in B-minor*.

'You can never fault these old Nazis for taste,' whispered Bill. 'They like art, they like music, they like wine.'

Humphrey said, 'I don't think we should forget that they rather enjoyed killing people, as well.'

Bill didn't answer, but ordered, 'Come on,' and the three of them circled the right-hand side of the cottage, until at last they crouched down behind a clump of bracken only 20 yards away from the front door. Both Humphrey and Birgitta were shivering by now, but Bill seemed to be impervious.

'What do you actually plan to do?' asked Humphrey.

'Very simple. I kick the door in, you point Hermann out to me, and I hit him. Not more than 15 seconds' work from start to finish.'

'Yes, but what are we going to do with him afterwards?' Humphrey wanted to know. 'We haven't got anything to tie him up with.'

Bill looked puzzled. 'What do you want to tie him up for?'

'Well . . .' said Humphrey, blushing a little. 'Supposing he tries to make a run for it? Or are you trying to tell me that you don't think he will? He is rather past it, I suppose.' He snickered, then stopped when he realized that wasn't at all funny. In fact, it was bewildering.

Bill said slowly, 'He won't . . . "make a run for it." '

'As long as you're confident,' said Humphrey, sobered.

'Of course he is confident,' put in Birgitta. 'Hermann will not try to escape because your American friend

143

here intends to shoot him. Did you not understand that?'

Humphrey stared at Bill through the darkness. His teeth were chattering. 'You're going to *shoot* him? Is that true?'

'Come on,' said Bill. 'You know who he is. You know what he's done.'

'But he hasn't had a trial. Even Eichmann had a trial.'

'There are plenty of Nazis who didn't. Let me tell you something, Humphrey: shooting is almost too good for this sadist. But it's what I've been told to do.'

'I won't allow it!' Humphrey hissed.

'I'm afraid you don't have any choice in the matter.'

'I refuse to identify him. You can't shoot him unless I identify him.'

'In that case, I'll shoot him anyway, and see what you think about having an innocent man's death on your conscience.'

Humphrey screamed: 'You're mad!'

'For Christ's sake, keep your voice down,' Bill told him. 'Do you want him to hear you?'

'It wouldn't be a bad idea,' said Humphrey.

'Well, make up your mind up,' Bill told him, roughly. 'Are you going to point him out for me, or what? If you don't, I'm going to blow away whoever happens to be in there, so you'd better think about it quick.'

Birgitta held on to Humphrey's sleeve. 'Don't listen to him. He won't shoot anybody. He simply wants you to give this man away. But don't do it! Let him handle his own dirty work. I know this man you are calling Klaus Hermann, and he is not the man you want. How could he be? He is a gentleman!'

Humphrey turned to Bill. 'Well,' he demanded, hotly. He could feel his heart bumping painfully under his ribs. 'What have you got to say about that?'

Bill gave him a quick, emotionless stare, then looked down at his wristwatch, and said, 'We're hitting the front door in ten seconds from now. Make up your mind.'

Humphrey said, 'Really, Bill, I – '

But as he said that, behind him, Birgitta turned, and rose to her feet, and began to run. He heard her legs whipping through the long grass before he had the presence of mind to turn around; when he did so, he was startled how far away she already was, almost to the trees. Because he turned to watch her, he failed to see Bill raising his .38 revolver, his left forearm lifted to act as a support; and he failed to understand how Bill could possibly stop her until he heard that peculiar sharp sneezing noise right next to his ear, and Birgitta began to roll over and over as if she were turning cartwheels.

For one second, he thought: what an amazing woman, how acrobatic. But then he understood that Bill had actually shot her, and that she was tumbling away from him because the impact of the bullet had sent her flying forward, and because she was dead.

He stared at Bill open-mouthed, feeling as if a building had just been demolished inside of his head.

He said, 'You've shot her.'

There was a lengthy silence. Birgitta fell into the grass by the trees with a soft clothy thud. The wind blew, making the bracken whistle like unruly Pan pipes.

Bill said, 'You have to know something, Humphrey. I was going to take her out right from the very beginning, sooner or later. I would have preferred later.'

'But you've *killed* her.'

'I was told to kill anyone involved. It's very important that nobody knows about this.'

'But what about me?' asked Humphrey. 'I know about it. I know *all* about it. In fact, I know more than you. Are you going to kill me, too?'

'Of course not.'

'But supposing I threaten to call the police? Supposing I refuse to identify Hermann?'

'You won't do either of those things.'

'But if I do?'

'You won't.'

Humphrey looked at Bill through the darkness. It was almost impossible to make out the lines of his face. Only his eyes seemed to glitter, like beads from a funeral necklace.

'I think I rather wish that I had never telephoned Major Milner,' he said.

'I don't know why,'' Bill told him. 'They'll probably give you a medal for this, when it's over.'

'As long as it's not posthumous. My sister wouldn't care for that at all. She never liked medals. Only jugs.'

'Jugs?' asked Bill, perplexed.

They heard a sigh and a rustle from the direction of the trees. Humphrey said, 'Listen! Do you think she's still alive?'

Bill shook his head.

'But I heard a noise. I distinctly heard a noise.'

'Come on, Humphrey. If she *is* still alive, she won't be for long. I took most of the side of her head off.'

Humphrey swallowed. 'I think I'm going to go back to the car. I think I've had enough of this for one night.'

'Oh, no, Humphrey. We're going on. We have some urgent business with Herr Hermann, remember?'

'But you've killed her! She was quite innocent, and you've killed her! I won't stand for it!' For the first time, the shock of what had happened actually penetrated Humphrey's consciousness. This wasn't a play; the autumn production of the Baslow Dramatic Society. A girl had actually been shot down and killed in front of his eyes. But the unreal calmness of the event, the matter-of-fact way in which Bill Bennett had turned and aimed and fired at her; the promptness with which she had dropped into the grass; all this had deceived

Humphrey's cortex into believing up until now that her sudden death had been quite an ordinary occurrence.

Bill Bennett snapped, 'For Christ's sake!'

'I'm going,' said Humphrey. He clambered to his feet.

'If you go, I'll kill you,' Bill told him.

'Like her? Just shoot me down, like a dog?'

Bill's eyes glittered. He raised his revolver, and he wasn't smiling.

'You're a murderer,' said Humphrey.

'Don't be so damned stupid,' Bill retorted.

'You're a murderer, I saw you murder that girl. Birgitta. You just – shot her – for your own convenience.'

'Will you pipe down?'

'I'll speak as loudly as I like. And as truthfully as I like. I won't have it. I didn't come along to help you for this.'

'What did you come along for? To add to your sister's jug collection?'

There was a moment of shared exasperation. Then, Humphrey, promptly losing his rage and his energy, sat down again, and protested, 'That was most unfair.'

'Did I say that I was going to be fair?' Bill demanded.

'No, but . . . well, it was most unfair, all the same.' Humphrey looked in the direction in which Birgitta had fallen. There was no movement now, no sound. She had probably died at once, if Bill really had shot most of her head off; and that noise he had heard before had probably been nothing more than a rabbit, or a startled bird.

'This isn't easy, any of it,' said Bill. He kept his eyes fixed like studs on to the verandah of the small wooden cottage. 'It isn't easy physically, and it isn't easy psychologically, and it isn't *morally* easy, either. The overriding principle they teach us is that of the Greater Good. That was why I killed that girl instead of letting her go. More people's lives would have been harmed by letting her go than by killing her. On balance I was serving the Greater Good.'

'The Greater Good?' said Humphrey. He could hardly believe it. He began to feel that he had wandered into some peculiar parallel existence in which all of the commonplace values of life had been turned upside-down, like the time his sister had tried to make Summer Pudding and all the fruit had mysteriously risen to the top, against all the laws of domestic science and specific gravity. He said, 'You're going to shoot Hermann too, I suppose? Is that it? Is that why they sent you here? And that's why you have to have him so positively identified; in case you kill the wrong man.'

'Hermann is a murderer, Humphrey,' said Bill. 'A fanatical, cold-blooded murderer. He also happens, despite his age, to be helping the Soviets to build up the most comprehensive arsenal of plagues and diseases you can imagine.'

'So you *are* going to shoot him?'

'If you must know, yes.'

'Without a trial?'

'We already know that he's the right man, don't we?'

'But even at Nuremberg – '

Bill let out a sharp, tight breath. 'Humphrey,' he said, 'I'm not here to argue the rights and wrongs of killing war criminals without a trial. I'm here to do a job. You're going to help me do it, and that's all there is to it. Now, will you keep quiet?'

At that moment, one of the shutters on the left of the cottage was opened, and a rhomboid of yellow lamplight fell across the verandah. Bill reached out and pressed Humphrey down, right into the grass, and said, 'Quiet, for Christ's sake.'

They heard a casement rattling; and the sound of voices talking in German. A man's voice said, '*Nein. Es war nur eine optische Täuschung. Das licht hat mir einen Streich gespielt.*'

148

Then the casement closed again, with a bang, and the shutter, too.

Humphrey whispered, 'What were they saying?'

'Something about an optical illusion. Maybe they saw us, or thought they did. We've got to be quick.'

He stood up, and beckoned Humphrey to follow him. Humphrey hesitated at first, but then Bill turned and hissed at him, 'Come on, will you? We don't have all night,' and reluctantly Humphrey stood up and traipsed through the bracken like a child who doesn't want to go shopping.

Bill said, 'Will you try to make a little less noise? I mean, would you mind? I mean, try *stalking*, like you did in the Boy Scouts.'

'I didn't join the Scouts,' said Humphrey. 'My chest.'

'Well, just try to walk more quietly. We have to hit them by surprise.'

They went on, carefully approaching the cottage in a half-circle, Bill keeping his revolver raised high in both hands, crouching a little; Humphrey stepping high-footed behind him. They were fewer than ten feet away from the verandah when the shutter suddenly banged open again and they found themselves face-to-face with an astonished-looking young man with a blond moustache.

Bill shouted to Humphrey, 'Drop!' and as Humphrey awkwardly got down on to his knees, Bill fired two shots in quick succession towards the window. Two quick sneezes. The young man dropped out of sight. Bill seized Humphrey's sleeve, and dragged him sideways out of the light with such force that Humphrey heard the lining of his jacket tear.

'My God!' said Humphrey.

'Down!' Bill shouted at him.

There was a rattling noise from the open window; and grass and dirt were kicked up all around the front of the cottage. Bill aimed, but didn't fire again. 'Come on,' he told Humphrey. 'Let's see if we can't hit 'em from around the side.'

'This is quite ridiculous!' shouted Humphrey. His heart felt as if it had expanded inside his ribs like a red hot-water bag blown up by a gas-station air-pump. He gasped, and stumbled; and then there was another burst of rattling, and the grass and stones were torn up all around his feet, and something bit him sharply in the ankle. He cried out loud, and his cry was met by a third rattle, and the air hummed and twanged and whistled all around his ears.

Bill left him now. A liability to the Greater Good, Humphrey supposed. Running at a crouch, Bill skirted around the far end of the cottage, and disappeared.

There was silence for a while. Humphrey lay flat on his face on the ground, his eyes wide, panting, unable to move. He prayed that the people inside the cottage would understand that he was a non-combatant, that he was not involved in this grisly affair out of choice. His shoe felt as if it had been ripped open at the back, and he could feel wet on his heel. He was quite sure that he had been shot. He found that he was reciting under his breath that line in The Ancient Mariner which goes, 'The Nightmare Life-in-Death was she, that thicks man's blood with cold.' It did after all seem quite possible, even *likely*, that he would die tonight; that his predictable life in Derbyshire would come to an abrupt and unpredictable finish in a freezing-cold field in Uppsala. If they were ever to draw a graph of his life, it would be one long tedious line, with an odd hiccup in the end.

'Oh, God,' he prayed.

There was another rattle of sub-machine gun fire. It sounded hollower this time, as if the gun were being fired indoors. There was a short silence, and then a scream, a woman's scream, and a lot of shouting in

150

German. *'Das dürfen Sie nicht tun! Aufhören! Nicht schiessen!'*

The front door of the cottage was thrown open as if somebody were trying to wrench it right off its hinges. Two men hurtled out, crouching as low as Bill had done; one of them in blue pyjamas, the other wearing a white raincoat. The one with the white raincoat was obviously the younger of the two, because he grasped his companion's arm and dragged him at full pelt away across the field, towards the trees where Birgitta had fallen; and the one in pyjamas kept shouting to him hoarsely to slow down.

Humphrey rolled over in the bracken and rose unsteadily to his feet, just as Bill came hurtling through the door, too, shouting: 'Freeze, you bastards!' and raising his revolver.

'Bill!' shouted Humphrey, and limped rapidly up to the house, up the verandah steps, and threw himself heavily on to Bill as if he were embracing him after a long sea-voyage. Both men teetered for a moment, staggered, then fell on to the verandah with a bruising thud.

'Jesus Christ!' Bill screamed at Humphrey. 'You stupid bastard! I could have hit him!'

Humphrey got up on to his hands and knees, panting. 'I didn't *want* you to hit him.'

'That was Hermann, you stupid bastard! I had him and you let him get away!'

'I *wanted* him to get away.'

'Are you crazy? Are you absolutely 108% certifiably *crazy*? That was Klaus Hermann!'

'I know,' said Humphrey, trying to get his breath back. 'But even the Vampire of Herbstwald deserves a trial. If we don't allow him a trial, then we're just as bestial as he is.'

Bill stood up, and smacked his hand against one of the verandah posts in frustration. 'Jesus,' he repeated.

'We won't even *get* him to trial now. We won't ever see him again. He'll be back in Russia before you can whistle The Red Flag.'

Humphrey said, 'I'm sorry. But I have to do what I believe is right and proper, that's all.'

'You meddling old bastard,' snapped Bill. He looked away, so that the only visible clue which Humphrey had to his high-voltage professional tension was the extreme tightness of his grip on the verandah railing. After a few moments, however, Bill turned around again, and said, 'I'm sorry. I apologize. I shouldn't have called you that. You'd better come along inside and see what we've got.'

'I think a bullet hit my heel,' said Humphrey.

Bill looked down, then crouched beside Humphrey and raised his left trouser-leg. The back of Humphrey's shoe had been shot off, and his green Wolsey sock was sticky with blood, but it was only a superficial graze, and it had congealed already.

'You were lucky,' said Bill, standing up again, 'Couple of inches further and you might have lost your foot. Peg-leg Humphrey Browne.'

Humphrey twisted around to look at his heel, and then gave Bill a self-deprecatory little smirk. 'Wounded in the course of action,' he said. 'I expect it will leave something of a scar.'

'Oh yes, I'm sure,' said Bill. 'Now, let's get inside. There's something I want to show you.'

Angelika Rangström was sitting by the blue-and-white enamelled stove, wrapped up tightly in a red dressing-gown, smoking a cigarette with quick, anxious puffs. Humphrey recognized her at once as the woman who had been sitting with Klaus Hermann at the outdoor restaurant; a rather tired-looking middle-aged blonde with pale blue eyes and perfect Swedish bone structure. Years ago, she must have been ravishing, and she still had an extraordinary femininity about her which made Humphrey feel quite clumsy.

Bill Bennett leaned towards her, his nickel-plated revolver hanging loose from his hand, and said, 'Your boyfriend got away. You can thank Mr Browne here. Mr Browne believes in trial by jury.'

Fru Rangström glanced up at him, and then looked away again. 'You can believe about him whatever you like,' she said, in an English accent that was as cold as marble.

'We know who he is, Fru Rangström. It's no good trying to pretend.'

'He is not what you think,' she retorted.

Bill gave Humphrey a wink and a smile. 'Gutsy, isn't she? Well, she must be, to be able to sleep with an ageing old butcher like Klaus Hermann. Just think about it, lying next to a man who *personally* murdered three thousand people. Kissing a fellow who slaughtered innocent children in their hundreds. Very gutsy indeed.'

Humphrey said, 'I don't think I really understand.' Then, 'Do you mind if I sit down? My foot hurts.'

'Help yourself,' said Bill. He dragged over a painted wooden chair, and offered it up to Humphrey's descending bottom. Most of the furniture in the cottage was painted, and it was furnished and decorated in the style of Carl Larsson – carved tables, wooden walls of eggshell white with painted blue borders, rows of potted fuchsias on the window-sills, and the Gothic-lettered words *Guds Fred* over the lintel.

Bill said to Angelika Rangström: 'I suppose you did know who Klaus actually was, when you first met him?'

She dragged at her cigarette, and then she said, 'You have no authority here. How can you ask me such questions?'

'Your friend Birgitta is dead,' said Bill. He raised one

153

eyebrow and stared at her very hard to show that he meant it.

Angelika Rangström raised her head as if she were acting. Humphrey found himself watching her like a theatregoer; wondering what she was going to say.

'Are you trying to tell me that you have killed her?'

Bill said, 'She didn't co-operate.'

'Co-operate? Co-operate with whom? With *you*? With this man here, with his bleeding foot? And now Klaus has had to run for his life. You understand that I may never see him again. That is what you have done to me. I don't think threats of death mean very much after this. Here,' she said, and bent her head forward so that her blonde hair parted from the white mole-patterned nape of her neck, 'Shoot me if you wish. What difference does it make?'

Bill sniffed. 'There's a dead man in the kitchen.'

'That was poor Vassili,' she said, without lifting her head.

'Were both of them Russian?'

'Yes. They met us here. Klaus was talking to Bendix – when was it, two days ago – something like that – because he was afraid he had been recognized. Bendix told us to come here, at least until he could be sure that there was no longer any danger. But, of course there was. I told Klaus to go straight back to Leningrad. I told him over and over. What is a few weeks lost, compared with a lifetime. But he wouldn't listen. Such a stubborn man. And look what has happened.'

Bill walked around the room, his sneakers squeaking on the polished boards. He peered at a painted plate as if he were a connoisseur. Then he turned around and stood over Angelika Rangström and said, 'Klaus talked to Bendix?'

'Who is Bendix?' Humphrey wanted to know.

'A code-name for the Soviet officer who deals with all the imports and exports which go through Stockholm,' said Bill. '*Human* imports and exports that is. It's not a secret. I think there was an article about him in *Time* magazine. He deals with defections, that kind of thing.'

'He will not allow Klaus to return,' said Angelika Rangström. 'Not after this.' She looked up now, her pale eyes sharp with tears. 'I will never see Klaus again, because of you.'

'Listen, Fru Rangström, there were thousands of Jewish women who never got to see their husbands and lovers again because of your boyfriend,' said Bill. 'So don't get too sentimental about it.'

'You killed Birgitta,' Angelika Rangström said. Her voice was completely expressionless. Humphrey thought she was probably suffering from shock. He knew that *he* was. He said, 'I must have a drink of water,' and limped across the room and into the hallway.

The dead Russian agent was crumpled up in a corner. Bill's bullet had hit him smack on the bridge of the nose, and the wound was soggy and dark, so large you could have probed your fingers inside it and touched his naked brain. The wall above him was decorated with loops and squiggles of blood. Humphrey's mouth felt very dry, and he gave the body as wide a berth as he could manage, pressing himself against the opposite wall.

He stood in the darkened kitchen, and drank a large glass of very cold water, one hand still resting on the pump-handle as he drank.

When he returned to the living-room, Angelika Rangström had left her chair, and was standing on the far side of the room, smoking a fresh cigarette. She held the pack in the palm of her hand, some Swedish brand called Solna. The smoke in the room was bright blue and very pungent. She was saying, 'I suppose it fascinated me at first, what Klaus had done. I was going

155

through a very strange period of my life then. My first husband had been very cruel to me – very physically cruel. What he did to me, I cannot describe to you, but believe me no man has ever humiliated a woman in the ways that he did. Night after night, week after week, month after month, until I was completely subjugated. And still I had to pretend each day when I went to the theatre that I was normal, happy and bright. I dreaded the nights at first; but then I grew to accept them. My family believed we were such a contented pair. Well, sometimes I think that my father suspected. There was a look in his eyes whenever we met. But that was all. The experience changed me forever. I took drugs for a long time. I was still taking drugs when I met Klaus.'

Humphrey was about to say something, baffled at this unexpected confession, but Bill shot him a quick look to silence him.

Angelika Rangström touched the back rail of the chair on which Humphrey had been sitting, and said, 'How we poor mortals become caught up in larger events; swept along, thinking we control our own destiny. I never would have met Klaus if it hadn't have been for the war.'

Bill and Humphrey watched her without saying a word. Gradually, as she spoke, Humphrey began to realize what she was doing. She was acting out the part of the woman who has taken as her lover one of the most terrible butchers of all time, and who for years has suffered a secret guilt that her lovemaking has somehow implicated her in each of the murders which he committed. How many times, looking at her face in her dressing-table mirror, had she imagined she heard the voices of those three thousand crying from their mass graves? How many times had she promised herself that she would never see Klaus again? Yet, the fascination of his soft, manicured hands . . . the barbaric culture hiding in his eyes . . .

'I met him in Prague,' she said, 'In 1951.'

'Yes,' said Bill.

'Prague is my favourite city . . . do you know that it was once occupied by the Swedes? In the middle of the seventeenth century, I think. I was on tour there, with the theatre company. We were performing *A Doll's House*. 'In that moment it burst upon me that I had been living here those eight years with a strange man, and had borne him three children.' Do you know *A Doll's House*?'

'Yes,' said Bill.

'Not exactly,' said Humphrey.

'There was a party,' said Angelika Rangström, as if she hadn't heard either of them. 'And Klaus appeared . . . materialized out of the crowd . . . smiling . . . he never told me why he was there. And, well, I suppose I saw in him the total masculinity which my first husband had exhibited, yet combined with courtesy and understanding. We went to bed together that same evening, and who can blame us?'

There was a long and difficult silence in the room. Angelika Rangström finished her cigarette, and crushed it out impatiently in a small blue-and-white dish. Bill said nothing, but leaned back against the wall with his arms folded. Humphrey felt that he had a hundred questions to ask, but didn't dare break the atmosphere.

As a coda, Angelika Rangström said, 'Klaus took me for a long walk through Prague. It was late afternoon, in summer, the shadows were very long. He had visited Prague during the war, because he used to be a friend of Heydrich. Such parties, he used to say! Wine, and roasted game, and women. All gone, when the Third Reich collapsed. He took me to see the cathedral of St Vitus, where all the kings of Bohemia were crowned; and then to the royal palace on Hradčany hill. You cannot imagine a more beautiful place to fall in love, with the Vltava river flowing beneath us . . .'

157

Another long silence. Bill sniffed, and looked around the room; and Humphrey sat on a chair and nursed his foot. It hadn't been as badly cut as he had first imagined, and he was quite concerned that he wouldn't even have a scar to show for his trouble.

Bill said, 'They won't be able to get him back to the Soviet Union, you know. Not straight away.'

Angelika Rangström said, 'I don't understand.'

'Well, the ports and the airports are all being watched, as well as the major highways. Nynashamn, Oxelosund, Saltsjobaden . . . I made sure that every one of them was alerted before we came out tonight. As well as Bromma and Arlanda airports. Bendix will know that he can't get him back to Leningrad, not yet.'

Angelika Rangström took out another cigarette. 'You must want Klaus very badly,' she said, almost with pride.

'We want him, yes,' said Bill. Humphrey, in an effort to show his neutrality, gave a spastic shrug.

'Well, I can tell you where Bendix will probably take him,' said Angelika. 'But I will only do this on the absolute understanding that you will not try to kill him. You will have to arrest him, won't you? But I do not want him shot. He is not a beast, whatever you may think. He is not to be exterminated. And, I want your guarantee that I will be able to see him whenever I want.'

'You want conjugal rights?' asked Bill.

Angelika Rangström shook her head. 'Don't you think we're both a little too old for that? A little too dignified?'

Unexpectedly Bill said, 'What do you think, Humphrey? Think we should play along? We don't have to. We could always let Hermann go. After all, what has he ever done to us? Only problem is, we'll have to take care of Angelika here, can't have her squealing to the Swedish police.'

'You're bluffing,' said Humphrey, in a disgruntled voice.

'Well, you think so?' asked Bill.

'You mean you're going to shoot her?' Humphrey replied. 'Right here, right in front of my eyes?'

'If necessary,' said Bill. Then, without warning, he held up his revolver and fired off four shots, one after the other, four silenced sneezes; and two plates on the wall shattered into shards, and the cuckoo clock burst apart; and a window dropped out of its frame. Bill smiled. The room was full of flat, powdery-smelling smoke.

Angelika Rangström said, bravely, 'Why don't you stop play-acting? You knew from the beginning that I would help you.'

'Yes,' said Bill. 'I did.'

'Well, then,' said Angelika Rangström, 'they will probably take Klaus to Lingslätö. It's a little village on the Baltic coast south of Grisslehamn, I've only been there once. They call it their 'safe house'. You know, in case of emergency.'

Bill flipped open the cylinder of his .38 and reloaded it with fresh shells. Then he tucked the revolver away into his windcheater. 'All right,' he smiled. 'Lingslätö it is. How's your foot, Humphrey?'

Humphrey pressed his thumb and his index finger to his eyelids. He felt shocked, and old, and impossibly tired. 'How far is it?' he asked.

'Sixty kilometres,' said Angelika Rangström. 'It won't take long.'

'You'd better get dressed, then,' Bill advised her.

When Angelika Rangström had gone into the bedroom to find her clothes Humphrey said to Bill, dully, 'I never imagined it was going to be like this.'

'I know,' said Bill. 'I guess I ought to say that I'm sorry.'

'Sorry? Well, a little late for that now. Two people dead already.'

'Klaus Hermann has to be caught, Humphrey. I have to tell you that. A whole lot of people in the United States and Britain want him silenced, believe me. Important people, know what I mean?'

Humphrey didn't answer, but closed his eyes and leaned back against the panelled wall. He felt as if the inside of his head were a *carceri d'invenzione*, an imaginary prison, from which even the most sensible of actions would not be able to release him. Who were these people in the United States and Britain who wanted Klaus Hermann silenced? Was their need so urgent that he had to stay up all night in Uppsala Län, tired beyond belief, with a neurotic Swedish actress and a trigger-happy young American who seemed to have been taking etiquette lessons from George C. Scott?

He was due to fly back to England the day after tomorrow. Manchester Airport, rain, grey skies, and the soft green curves of the Derbyshire Dales. They all seemed so ordinary, and yet beyond achievement. Something had died inside of him, here in Sweden, and perhaps it was simply his faith in human nature, and in the sanctity of human life.

He said to Bill, 'Why did she tell you where Hermann might be?'

Bill looked surprised. 'Didn't you think she would?'

'But they're . . . *lovers*,' said Humphrey.

Bill shook his head. 'She's been dying to confess to this for years. All she needed was the opportunity. You wait. She'll spend the whole 60 kilometre ride to Lingslätö telling us the full gory story of what they did together, and how often she felt like calling up Simon Wiesenthal. Women are all the same.'

'If you say so,' said Humphrey. He thought of his sister. He thought of the Reverend Johnson. He closed his eyes, and thought of his heel.

TEN

Reynard flew back to Concord that weekend to make the announcement that he intended to run for the Democratic nomination against John Glenn and Walter Mondale. Already, the newspapers were heatedly speculating KELLY TO DECLARE? and re-hashing the old Winnipesaukee scandal, as well as publishing saucy photographs of Ellen Wangerin, his one-time gangster girlfriend. Reynard pretended to find the Press reports irritating, and as far as his campaign was concerned, they were. But he had always privately thought of himself as a swashbuckler, a man with red-blooded desires, both carnal and political, and secretly he found his notoriety exciting. Especially since Greta would be standing by his side when he sought election, forgiving and loving and every single inch a First Lady.

The LearJet circled over the Soucook River and made its approach to Concord Airport from the south-east, whistling low over the scattered lights of Pembroke. Next to him, Dick Elmwood began to gather his papers together and screw the caps on to his variously-coloured pens. Reynard said, 'This is it, hey, Dick?'

'Yes, sir,' said Dick, with a smile about as appealing as a plateful of ground oats.

Reynard said, 'I want you to understand that Mrs Kelly has to be treated just as respectfully and just as warmly as if everything were normal. I don't want any sharp remarks, if you understand what I mean. I want warmth.'

'Yes, sir.'

'Is Dean Farber coming up tomorrow?'

'Oh, I expect he'll be here tonight, sir. He has a lot of preparation to do.'

'Good. He's keen, isn't he, Dean? Better than Frank Margolies.'

'That's the impression he gives me, senator. But I think I'm going to wait and see. I suppose I'm naturally conservative.'

'Hm,' said Reynard. 'Once in a while, Dick, you ought to let yourself go. It's bad for the spirit, too much reserve. Once in a while, you ought to get smashed and find yourself an accommodating broad.'

The LearJet nudged the runway, then touched down, and roared its engines in reverse thrust. The amber marking lamps of a limousine detached themselves from the clustering lights around the airport terminal, and moved swiftly towards them as they taxied around to park. Dick said, a little too brightly, 'I get all the satisfaction I need out of my work, sir. Can you believe that?'

Reynard grunted. 'If you say so, Dick. But don't let me catch you with any of those Kelly-for-President girls. Otherwise I'll start thinking you're getting tired of your job.'

They held on to their hats as they crossed the windy tarmac and climbed into the long black Cadillac limousine. Then they were swept almost silently out of the airport, and out on to the Loudon Road towards the Kelly estate, and The Colonnades.

Reynard said, for no particular reason, 'I always feel wary at this time of year. I always get the feeling that something or somebody is going to die. Unsettling, isn't it? I always get the feeling that not all of us are going to survive the winter.'

'Pre-declaration nerves,' suggested Dick Elmwood.

Reynard shrugged, and grunted, but secretly he thought: what a damned vapid thing to say.

Greta's red Ferrari was already drawn up in front of

the house when they arrived. The limousine's head-lights swept across the shingled driveway, and transformed the twin rows of bay trees on either side of the entrance into giant lime-green suckers. Two of Reynard's house staff came forward as soon as the limousine crunched to a halt, and opened the door for him.

'Welcome home, senator.'

'Good to have you back so soon, sir.'

They escorted Reynard up the steps and into the domed hallway. There, he was greeted by Len Gieves and Natalia Vanspronsen, his leading publicity agents. Len was a snappy, aggressive man with gingery hair and a wild moustache; Natalia came from the efficient-immaculate division of the women's movement, beaut-iful and bespectacled and faultlessly groomed, and poli-tically serious as all hell.

'I see my wife's arrived,' said Reynard, handing his hat and his coat to Eunice, and his working papers to Dick Elmwood. 'What kind of a mood is she in?'

'Wavering between sardonic and acidulous,' Natalia Vanspronsen replied. She, for one, had not been particularly enthused about the idea of promoting Reynard and Greta's family togetherness as a number-one campaign sales point; even though she was unaware that, up until now, the two of them had decided to part permanently. Natalia had even argued at one meeting that Reynard should promise, if elected, to abolish the traditional title of 'First Lady', since it imposed an overwhelming political-social stereotype on the female partner in the nation's most prominent marriage. 'If the *President* treats his wife as a secondary human being, what is every other man in the country going to think?' Nevertheless, Reynard liked her. She turned him on. She was a very sharp operator, and she always wore classic silk blouses through which in most lights he was able to admire her dark pink nipples.

Len Gieves said, 'There's something you ought to know, sir. Doctor Walt Seabrook's here, too.'

'That ape? Who invited him? Well, of course, my wife did. Shit.'

'He appears to be keeping a comparatively low profile, sir.'

'The only comparatively low thing about Walt Seabrook is his brow,' said Reynard. 'I hope you searched him for dope before you let him in. We're going to have enough problems with Winnipesaukee and that Wangerin business, without playing host to coke-snorting simians with degrees in self-lobotomy.'

'Don't worry,' said Len Gieves. 'I'll have a quiet word with him.'

'Make sure it doesn't have too many syllables,' said Reynard. 'I do want him to understand what you're saying.'

'Dean Farber called,' put in Natalia. 'He'll be here at ten. I'll send the limousine for him if I may.'

Eunice said, 'Your bath is ready for you, sir.'

'I'll be right up. Dick, will you call Senator Hampton and ask him if he still has those papers on Green Mountain. That's one of the issues I want to raise tomorrow.'

'We have some new material on that,' said Len Gieves. 'Maybe we can run through it later.'

'I had Jack Pope from *Congress Special* on the phone, too,' said Natalia. 'I think he's quite interested in a background piece on your whole conservation ethic.'

'Do I have a conservation ethic?' asked Reynard. 'I thought I just wanted to stop people turning New Hampshire's forests into paperback books.'

'You *have* a conservation ethic,' insisted Natalia, unmoved by Reynard's attempt at humour. 'Your conservation programme is one of the most important planks in your platform. Along with your Medicare ethic, that is; and your defence ethic.'

Reynard said, 'I think I'll go take my bath, if you don't mind.'

'We have a presentation meeting at ten,' said Len.

'Provided I've had my dinner, and finished with Greta, then I'll be there,' said Reynard. 'Natalia, give Greta my compliments, will you, and make sure that Doctor Seabrook has enough to drink. I'd hate him to be intelligible when I come down.'

'Yes, senator,' said Len, and propelled Natalia back to the living-room, in spite of her obvious wrath. Reynard heard him saying, 'You want to keep your job or don't you? Calm down, for Christ's sake.'

Reynard went upstairs, and across the wide landing to his private suite of rooms. There were portraits and landscapes on every wall: views of Rum Hill and Apple Town, and dour portrayals of Kellys and Bloods and Houghs. Reynard liked to be reminded of his dignity and his roots. He saluted out of habit the portrait of his father, John H. Kelly, and then walked through the double oak doors of his sitting-room, and stripped off his jacket.

His private rooms were uncompromisingly masculine: furnished in button-backed leather and lined with books. One wall of the sitting-room was clustered with signed photographs of Reynard shaking hands with ten presidents from Hoover to Reagan. On the other wall, there were scores of gilt-framed advertisements from old-time newspapers, like 'Pioneer Baking Powder, Put Up In Pails'. Reynard unbuttoned his vest and called, 'Eunice?'

Eunice was waiting for him in the old-fashioned white-tiled bathroom. She had changed out of her maid's uniform into a white towelling bathrobe, tied right around her waist. She came out and helped Reynard to loosen his necktie, unfasten his shirt, and unlace his shoes.

'Are you tired?' she asked him. 'You look tired.'

165

'I feel tired all the time,' he told her. 'Sometimes I think I ought to quit politics altogether and raise horses for a living.'

'You'll feel better after your bath,' she told him. That was one of the reasons why he had employed her: she was the only person who spoke to him as if he were an ordinary man, with ordinary problems, and ordinary weaknesses. She never once called him 'senator', and she never talked about politics. Either she didn't understand it, or she wasn't interested. But that was the way Reynard preferred her.

She unfastened his pants, and slipped off his long white undershorts. 'You know something?' he asked her. 'If I could believe for one moment that I would be satisfied rearing bloodstock, then I'd resign from the Senate tomorrow.'

'You won't quit politics until you've been President,' said Eunice, gently ushering him into the bathroom. It was very steamy in there, and smelled of English Leather. 'Now, easy into the tub,' she warned him. 'It's hot. Just what you need to soak all of those worries out of your system.'

He stepped carefully into the bath, wincing at the heat. Eunice made him lie right down in it, despite the fact that his face was already maroon, and he was puffing.

'You're going to kill me, one of these days,' he warned her. She smiled, and began to spread a little shampoo on the sandy-coloured palms of her hands. Then she rubbed the shampoo into his hair, humming as she did so.

'What do you think of me, really?' he asked her, as she used the shower fixture to rinse the soap out of his hair.

'You've asked me that question before,' she reminded him. 'You're always asking me.'

'That's because you never tell me the answer.'

'I'm here. Isn't that enough of an answer?'

'But you're prepared to be my slave, virtually; and I don't understand that. I wouldn't serve anyone.'

Eunice smiled, her eyes dreamily half-closed, as if she were already thinking about something else, and someplace else, somewhere that Reynard would never be able to comprehend.

'I'm not your slave,' she said, simply, reaching for a towel to dry his hair. 'You pay me $800 a month, so I can't be.'

'I still don't understand you.'

'Maybe that's why you'll never be President.'

'You don't think I will be?'

'Only you can decide that. Now, stand up.'

Reynard grasped the gold handles at the sides of the tub and pulled himself up. Eunice soaped his back, his stomach, and thrust her hand in between his buttocks. His cock half-rose as she soaped it, but she handled it in such a matter-of-fact way that he simply felt pampered rather than aroused. She rubbed it vigorously up and down a few times, to tease him, and then she told him to sit down and rinse himself. He lay back in the water, watching his toes at the far end. Eunice went to unfold his towels.

'Eunice,' he called after her. 'Do you believe in destiny?'

'Destiny?' she asked him, opening out a pale turquoise bath sheet, thick Turkish cotton. On one corner the initials RK were embroidered in darker blue. 'No, I don't believe in destiny.'

'Why not?' he asked her. He wiped sweat away from his forehead.

'Do you believe in magic?' she retorted.

'No.'

'Well, then, the reason why you don't believe in magic is the reason why I don't believe in destiny.'

'That's a riddle.'

She held out the towel for him. 'Come on, step out,' she coaxed him. 'Your wife is waiting for you, and it's too late for games.'

He lowered his head, and looked down at the soapy bathwater eddying around his chest. He felt monstrously old, gigantically tired, enormously ugly; but at last he rose out of the water and stood in the middle of the bathroom while Eunice dried him.

'You know what someone once said about politics?' he asked, keeping his eyes fixed on his own face in the bathroom mirror. Such an *old* face, like a worn-out pigskin briefcase that somebody had left at an abandoned railroad terminal.

'What did someone once say about politics?' asked Eunice, rubbing his back and giving him a quick, practical kiss between the shoulder-blades.

'They said that politics will only survive as long as there are men who can't find anything better to do.'

'Now, who said a thing like that?' Eunice demanded, kneeling down to give his thighs a quick *frisson* with the towel.

Reynard saw his face in the mirror refuse to smile. 'I did,' he said. Then he looked down at Eunice, and said, much more gently, 'I did.'

Greta was in fine sharp fettle; and Walt Seabrook had already helped himself to an over-generous glassful of Reynard's 1927 cognac. The fire in the drawing-room was lit, and crackling, and Reynard's Great Dane lay on the rug by the fire-irons, looking as if it were sadly contemplating the rising price of Gravy Train. Reynard walked in red-faced from his bath, smelling of Floris cologne, and bowed like Edmond Purdom making an entrance in *The Student Prince*.

'Well, well,' said Greta. 'Nice of you to come.'

'Hullo, Greta,' Reynard nodded, and walked across to kiss her hand. Then he turned to Walt Seabrook, and looked him up and down. 'Less hairy than usual, Dr Seabrook. What happened to the beard?'

'I donated it to medical science,' said Walt Seabrook. 'How are you keeping, Reynard?'

'I'm keeping my peace and I'm keeping my temper, and I'm keeping them well,' Reynard told him. 'You shouldn't have come up here today, Dr Seabrook, you weren't invited. And if there's one kind of animal I dislike worse than a gloater, it's an uninvited gloater.'

'What do I have to gloat about?' asked Walt Seabrook. 'Besides, I *was* invited. Greta invited me.'

'This is no longer Greta's house.'

'Well, for your sake, I just hope the Press aren't going to get wind of that,' Walt Seabrook retaliated.

Reynard said, 'You know something? My mother once told me that some matches are made in heaven. All these years I didn't believe her. Until now, looking at you two. The bitch and the blusterer.'

'I hope we're not going to have a fight here,' said Walt Seabrook. 'I didn't come up here to start a scrap.'

'I don't care why you came,' Reynard told him. 'This is my house and if I want to tell you what I think of you, I will.'

'Reynard, for God's sake pour yourself a drink,' said Greta. 'Walt's been anxious enough about meeting you face-to-face as it is; without you actually living up to all of his anxieties.'

Reynard looked at Walt Seabrook keenly, and then nodded, and walked over to the drinks table, where he selected the bottle of Jack Daniel's, and poured himself a very small glassful.

'So,' he said, 'Dr Seabrook's anxious, is he?'

'Of course he is,' said Greta. 'He's a very sensitive person indeed.'

'Oh,' said Reynard. 'Sensitive. Well, that's something I never was. Acute, sometimes. Understanding, occasionally. But never sensitive. I congratulate you, Greta, on having found yourself somebody sensitive, at last.'

He came right up close to Walt Seabrook with the sourest of smiles on his face, and added, 'You're not *too* sensitive, though, right? I mean, anyone with real sensitivity couldn't stand Greta for more than a half-hour. Forty-five minutes, at the outside.'

Walt Seabrook said, 'I'd prefer it if you'd take that back.'

'Why?' Reynard demanded. 'Because I'm talking about "the woman you love"?'

'If you want to put it that way, yes.'

'You know what you are?' Reynard told him, and this time he was heated, and he was serious. 'You, Dr Seabrook, are an opportunist; and the worst possible kind of opportunist, a medical opportunist. You see Greta as a way of getting rich, and setting yourself up as a big cheese in the medical profession. Well, let me tell you something, straight from the shoulder. I'm going to appoint you Assistant Secretary for Health, because that's part of my deal with Greta. But the deal stops there. The job is all you get. Don't expect me to be nice to you, or generous to you, or polite to you; because I won't be.'

Reynard tipped back a little whiskey, and then looked at Walt Seabrook as if he pitied him.

'Sensitive,' he mocked. 'I've seen blocks of Barre granite more sensitive.'

Greta watched Reynard as he walked across to the window, and then came back and sat down. 'You're a sore loser, you know that?' she told him. 'I just wonder what kind of a *winner* you're going to be.'

Reynard smiled, and shrugged. It was almost unnatural to see them together, Greta and Dr Seabrook. Greta after all was so elegant, in her suede Polly Edwards tunic with handpainted fleur-de-lis, her nails painted like claws, her gold jewellery and her flawless

170

skin; whereas Dr Seabrook seemed so blunt and unkempt. He was a heavily-built man, Dr Seabrook, on the late side of 45, with thick dark hair through which his scalp was beginning to gleam, and that kind of rounded, round-nosed face which Reynard could never take totally seriously. Reynard found it extremely difficult to imagine them in bed together. Who usually climbed on top? Samson or Delilah?

Dr Seabrook said, 'It seems to me, sir, that we have to work out some kind of *modus vivendi*.'

'It seems to *you*,' Reynard retorted.

Greta interrupted, 'Are you two boys going to spend the whole afternoon squabbling?'

'You shouldn't have brought him,' said Reynard. 'And you can tell him something else. We don't have to work out any kind of *modus vivendi* because I don't have any intention at all of vivending with him. I don't ever want to have anything to do with him. When I'm President, and he's Assistant Secretary for Health, God forbid, he's going to be answerable to the Secretary for HEW, and that's it; and if he ever comes within a half-mile of the White House, I'll have him exterminated.'

'Reynard,' said Greta, 'you're not being rational.'

'Rational? With this Neanderthal?'

'Let's have less of the names, please, sir?' said Walt Seabrook.

Reynard pointed a finger at him. 'Listen, Dr Seabrook, you learn something and you learn something now. You're getting this appointment because Greta fixed it for you. No other reason. I'm already having your medical background checked to make sure that you're clean; and I warn you now that if you give me any aggravation at all, you're out, deal or no deal.'

'I think I'm aggravating you already,' said Walt Seabrook.

'Well, you think what you like. What you think is of no interest, as far as I'm concerned.'

'I think I'm aggravating you because you're jealous,' Walt Seabrook persisted. 'Isn't that it? You can't stand the thought of me going to bed with Greta. You can't stand it.'

Greta laughed, high and bright, like a mad nun throwing a carillon of bells out of a convent window.

Both men looked at her in involuntary surprise. Then Reynard said, quite soberly, 'Perhaps you're right.'

Greta said, '*Reynard*?'

'No, no,' said Reynard. 'Perhaps Dr Seabrook's right. Perhaps I *am* jealous. I'm not afraid to admit it. Jealousy only gets poisonous when people are afraid to admit it. I am going to be President, remember. I have to be completely honest with myself. Perhaps I *am* jealous, thinking of you going to bed with this ape.

There was a very long pause. The Great Dane snuffled by the fire, and rolled over. Reynard swilled his brandy around in his glass.

'Perhaps, on the other hand,' said Reynard. 'I've grown out of jealousy. Grown up, *altogether*. Perhaps I'm old enough and cold-blooded enough to be seeking the Presidency because it's a job that I know I can handle, and handle exceptionally well. And perhaps I'm occasionally prepared to put up with clowns like you, Dr Seabrook, because you're going to help me win. But I don't want any illusions about it. I made a deal with Greta whereby you will be appointed as Assistant Secretary for Health when I get elected President; and that deal doesn't entitle you to be arrogant, or intrusive, or to show your face where it isn't wanted, which includes here.'

Walt Seabrook put down his brandy. 'I'm very sorry to hear you say that,' he replied, in the quietest of voices.

'Well, I'm glad,' said Reynard. 'Because anything that brings you sorrow brings me joy.'

Greta said, 'Reynard, you're behaving like a savage.'

172

'It's a savage world,' said Reynard.

Walt Seabrook picked up his glass again, and finished off his brandy.

'You know what that was?' Reynard asked him, as he finished it.

'Sure. Very old cognac. Late 1920s, something like that?'

'As long as you were aware of that, when you drained it like a pig.'

Walt Seabrook stood up, and said. 'Listen, I'd better go. Otherwise we're going to fight like this all night, and it's bad for Greta's nerves.'

'Oh,' said Reynard, 'you're an expert on Greta's nerves, now?'

'I've been treating Greta. I know what's wrong with her.'

'Nothing that a good fuck can't put right, hm?' challenged Reynard.

Walt Seabrook looked unhappy. 'I'd better go. Really. It would be better for all of us.'

'It would certainly be better for me,' put in Reynard.

Greta said, 'Don't go, Walt, darling. Don't let him get to you.'

Walt Seabrook shook his head, and then gave Greta a quick dismissive smile. 'I think I know what the problem is. I'll go, okay? I don't mind. Senator Kelly here is feeling crowded, and maybe a little inferior, too; quite apart from the fact that he doesn't happen to like my breed of doctor. All right, I accept that. But he has to accept in return that I very much want that job with HEW, and that I'll do anything at all to get it. Let's face it, it's the ultimate Government health job; and suddenly I'm going to find all those surgeons and neurologists who snubbed me on the golf course are going to start crawling on their hands and knees in front of me, just to make sure they get a few extra bucks allocation. Well, I can live with Reynard Kelly for that, all things being equal. I'll keep my mouth shut and I'll enjoy my job. But let me just say one thing: I won't take any insults towards Greta, any bad treatment. She may be your phony First Lady but I'm the guy who takes care of her; *really* takes care of her, and I want that understood.'

Reynard could think of a dozen cutting things to say. But the soap-opera quality of Walt Seabrook's speech had quite tickled him; and instead he lifted his glass, and said, 'You're a stout man, Dr Seabrook, in every sense of the word. Greta, I congratulate you. A stout man. Though, of course, sensitive.'

'And *you're* running for President,' said Greta, in disgust.

'Oh, I'm not just running,' said Reynard. 'This time, I'm going to win.'

At that moment, there was a knock at the living-room door. It was Eunice, in her evening uniform: a long back dress with small triangular sleeves, and a buttoned bodice. Greta looked sharply at Reynard, but Reynard ignored her, and said, 'Come in, Eunice.'

'There's a telephone call for you, sir,' she said. She looked back at Greta, and quelled Greta's stare as effectively as if she had thrown a damp blanket on a fire. 'It's urgent, so the gentleman says, and private.'

'Do we know who it is?'

'Mr Eldridge, sir. Commissioner of Health and Welfare.'

'Hm,' said Reynard. He finished his bourbon. Then he said, 'Greta, Dr Seabrook; perhaps you'll excuse me for a minute or two.'

'I'm sure you're excused,' said Greta.

Reynard went through to the library, closed the door tightly behind him, and picked up the phone.

'Hello?' he said. 'Reynard Kelly speaking.'

'Senator Kelly? I'm very sorry to trouble you, sir, at

this time of the evening. This is Jim Eldridge, New Hampshire Commissioner of Health and Welfare.'

'How do you do, Mr Eldridge. Do you want to tell me what your problem is? I'm a little pushed for time right now.'

'Well, sir, I've just received a call from Carol Bryce, he's the Medical Referee for Merrimack County and an old friend of mine. Been to every one of my daughters' weddings, six in all. You wouldn't credit six daughters, would you?'

'Have we met at all?' asked Reynard, patiently.

'Oh, yes, sir. Two or three times. We met at the Douglas Everett Ice Arena, five years ago, when they held that gala; and we sat four places away from each other at the Kidney Foundation dinner last fall.'

'Ah, yes,' lied Reynard. 'Now I remember you. The dignified-looking gentleman.'

'Well, good of you to say so, senator. That's what my wife always says, but I guess it's just the grey hair.'

'What's on your mind?' Reynard asked him. He sometimes wondered, probably blasphemously, whether Jesus had ever felt as bored when people came to Him with sores, and madness and twisted limbs.

'Well, senator, Carol Bryce said that he was given the autopsy protocols on a boy who died in East Concord last week; and it appears from some of the early tests they did that he was killed by some kind of a virus. Just like poliomyelitis, that's what Dr Bryce said, only it's much quicker, the way it acts.'

'Yes?' asked Reynard.

Mr Eldridge was hesitant. 'It's difficult to come to any conclusions, senator; but it seems like we might have the makings of an epidemic on our hands. That's what Dr Bryce said. You see, the trouble with this virus is that it doesn't respond to any of the usual treatments.'

'You're talking about a polio epidemic?'

'That's right, senator. And quite a bad one.'

175

'Can't you organize a vaccination programme? How much would that cost?

'Senator, I'm trying to explain to you. This virus doesn't respond to any of the usual treatments.'

Reynard frowned. 'It's what, it's polio?'

'Kind of. Only much more virulent.'

'How many people have caught it already?'

'As far as Dr Bryce can make out, just the one sir.'

'Well, one person, and you're predicating an epidemic? That doesn't make too much sense, does it?'

Mr Eldridge was silent for a moment. Then he said, 'Dr Bryce is an extremely conservative man, senator. I have never known him to call me up the way he has today and raise the alarm. I have to tell you that he's *very* worried. He's seen the virology report, and some early cultures; and he's *very* worried.'

'Er, how, I mean, where – ' said Reynard. 'I mean, where did this boy pick this virus up? I mean, he must have caught it from somewhere. Are we talking about some kind of health hazard here?'

'We don't know, sir. There are very few available facts, apart from the autopsy protocols. The boy seemed to live a completely normal life. Up until the afternoon he died, he showed no symptoms of any illness, and during the afternoon he met none of his friends, or anybody that we can find who might have passed on polio.'

Reynard slowly rubbed his eyes. There was a knock at the library door, and Dick Elmwood put his head around and mouthed something, but Reynard waved him away.

He said to Mr Eldridge, 'Listen – does anyone know where the boy lived?'

'East Concord, sir. Right on Webster Crescent, next to Conant's Acre.

'So, presumably, he picked it up somewhere around his home locality?'

176

'Well, presumably,' agreed Mr Eldridge.

Reynard was silent again. But a dark voice inside of his head recited, *'What have you done? The voice of your brother's blood is crying to Me from the ground. And now you are cursed from the ground, which has opened its mouth to receive your brother's blood from your hand.'*

Mr Eldridge said, 'Senator Kelly? I did think you ought to know. We might meet some resistance here, because of local interests, I don't think the Commissioner of the Department of Safety is going to be too happy. In fact, I believe that he's going to be downright hostile. And the Department of Resources and Economic Development are probably going to fight us all the way.'

Reynard said, 'Well . . . we need to know some more facts, don't we? One boy dying of a freak virus . . .'

Mr Eldridge said, 'I had hoped for a more positive response, Senator Kelly. The way to stop epidemics is to nip them in the bud.'

'You have to understand that I can't do anything officially,' said Reynard. 'Apart from that, I don't want to cause any unnecessary panic. The effects of panic might be more dangerous than the effects of the virus itself.'

Mr Eldridge took a deep breath. He was obviously a reserved man, unused to expressing himself forcibly in public, let alone fighting his senior state senator one-to-one.

But, he said quietly, 'I wouldn't have troubled you with any of this, senator, not unless I'd believed it was serious. We're still waiting for some more virology tests, from Berkeley and Santa Fé. Even so, Dr Bryce thinks that it's serious, a very serious threat; and if Dr Bryce thinks it's serious, then I do, too. Believe me, senator, there are a lot of very old people in Merrimack County who daren't die at all in case Dr Bryce thinks that they're letting him down. Yet today he called me on the phone and he said something which I've never heard him say before, he said, "Jim, we've got trouble." And believe me, senator, when Dr Bryce says you've got trouble – well, by jiminy, you've got trouble. Well, I'm sorry to say anything so antiquated as "by jiminy".'

Reynard heard that voice in his head recite, 'And now you are cursed from the ground . . . which has opened its mouth to receive your brother's blood . . .' And aloud, he said to himself, 'Condor.'

'I beg your pardon?' asked Mr Eldridge. 'I'm counting on you, senator. I really am. Do you think we could meet, you know, and maybe talk about it some more? See what we can do?'

'Give me your number,' said Reynard, abstractedly.

'Well, sure thing. 271–4334. But you'll call me soon?'

'What? Oh, yes. Yes, I'll call you tomorrow. Thank you very much for letting me know, Mr . . .'

'Eldridge, senator. Jim Eldridge.'

'Fine. Sure – Jim Eldridge. Fine, thank you. And Rice, that's the name of the Medical Referee?'

'Bryce, sir.'

'Right. Bryce with a 'B'. Very good, thank you. Good night.'

A hesitant pause. Anxiety on the other end of the line that the call had failed, that the senator hadn't been infused with the right degree of urgency. But, without saying anything else, Reynard put down the receiver, and sat tapping his teeth with the note-card on which he had written Jim Eldridge's number, deeply preoccupied. Surely, after all these years . . . surely it wasn't possible. Yet the words from the Bible kept on sternly repeating themselves in his mind, like the chimes of some terrible clock; and the name with which his deepest sin had been identified kept on forming itself on his lips.

'Condor.'

It was polio, wasn't it? A virulent kind of polio, just

as they had told him. And the boy had contracted it near Conant's Acre. God, there was a frightening kind of natural vengefulness about it which was far greater than the usual course of human justice. Reynard felt as if he had been suddenly and belatedly judged by God; and found guilty.

Dick Elmwood poked his head through the library doorway again. 'I'm sorry to interrupt you, senator. But Dean Farber's here. Do you want to come say hello?'

Reynard stared at him as if he didn't know who he was. Then he said, blurrily, 'Whatever happened to Chiffon?'

Dick Elmwood lowered his eyes. 'You told me never to answer that question, senator.'

'Well, I didn't expect you to,' said Reynard. 'The question was what – rhetorical. But – there was no difficulty, was there?'

Dick Elmwood said nothing. At last, Reynard got up from his desk, and looked around; and then said, 'Winter, that's all it is. Winter's coming. You can always tell, here in New Hampshire. You get a sense of fear.'

'Yes, sir,' said Dick Elmwood, after a pause.

Much later, Reynard excused himself from his meeting with Dean Farber, and went upstairs to his bedroom. There, on his personal line, he put in a telephone call to a number in Anama City, in West Florida. The number rang and rang and rang, but Reynard was patient. He knew that the man he was calling was very old, and that he would probably take quite a time getting to the phone.

At last, a croaky voice said, 'Hello? Ted Peale here. Who's this?'

'Ted? It's Reynard.'

'Reynard? My God almighty.'

'Ted,' said Reynard, urgently. 'I'm sorry to call you so late, but I have to talk to you.'

'Well, shoot. I was only having a drink out on the verandah, prior to turning in. It's a real warm night; although I guess it isn't where you are.'

'Ted, can you get up to New Hampshire? I have to speak to you in person.'

There was a sucking sound at the other end of the phone, as if Ted Peale had taken his dentures out. 'Well, now,' he said, 'I really don't get around too much any more. Thrombosis in the right leg, doc says it could finish me off any time at all, without a warning. Have to rest up most of the time.'

'Ted, it's about Condor. Something's happened.'

'Condor? Come on, Reynard, I thought that was all dead and buried.'

'So did I. But something's happened. A young boy up here in Concord has contracted poliomyelitis.'

There was a crackling silence. Then Ted Peale said, 'Aw, come on, Rey-nard. That's nothing to worry about. Kids are catching poliomyelitis 19 to the dozen. That doesn't mean nothing.'

'This isn't just ordinary poliomyelitis, Ted. I've just had the New Hampshire Commissioner for Health and Welfare on the line. The Merrimack county Medical Referee says that it's something different, something special. Everybody's worried to hell about it.'

Ted Peale was silent for a while. Then he said, 'I really don't see how this could be anything to do with Condor, Reynard. I mean, we don't even know where that thing came down; or even if it came down at all.'

'It must have come down. You know that.'

'We never heard it come down.'

'You couldn't have heard anything in that electric storm,' Reynard retorted.

'*I* would have heard it come down. Leastways, I believe so.'

Reynard said, 'I want you up here, Ted. I want to talk this over in a lot more detail.'

'I don't think I'm going to be able to make it, Reynard. I'd like to help out, really, but it's a long way to New Hampshire; and besides that, it's cold, and I'm not sure my heart's going to be able to take the cold, not at my time of life, and the way it's been playing up lately.'

'Ted, do you want me to send someone down to get you? I want you here, Ted.'

Another silence, longer. Then – 'I don't want to go back over those days, Reynard. Let sleeping dogs lie, that's what I say. We were all younger then. Different ideals. Different ways of looking at things. It was a different world then, Reynard. America wasn't the same as she is now. You know that, you're a politician. Things are different.'

'Ted – '

'I don't have anything useful to tell you, Reynard. I never saw it come down. Never heard it and never saw it. Maybe it overshot, who knows. It could have wound up anywhere from Turtle Town to Mast Yard forest. Who knows?'

Reynard let out a sharp, exasperated breath. 'You heard them on the radio, though, didn't you? And Michael did, too. You heard them saying they were in trouble.'

'That's what Michael told me. But, who knows what he heard? And anyway he's dead now. Dead these six years, at least.'

'I know. Hilda wrote and told me.'

At last, Ted Peale said, 'There's no good in digging up old ghosts, Reynard. Best to leave them lie. Really, that's my advice. And I'm not coming up, not to New Hampshire. Lynn Haven is about the most I can manage these days.'

Reynard thought: he hasn't changed. Still the same old tight-minded Ted. Ignorant, prejudiced, and stubborn as a constipated mule. In those early days, in the 1940s, Ted's dogmatic approach to life had seemed like strength, and certainty, especially at a time when everything was uncertain, and nobody seemed strong. But the passing years had shown him up for what he really was. A redneck of the reddest hue. A tedious, small-minded, self-centred bigot.

'Well, Ted,' said Reynard, 'I want you to think about what happened that night. I want you to go over the whole thing, in your mind. I want you to *think*. Is there anything you might have left out? The slightest detail could help us. Is there anything you saw, or heard; or thought you might have seen?'

'Well, I'll think,' said Ted. 'I don't object to thinking.' He sounded as if he didn't actually know what 'thinking' was, but was too embarrassed to ask.

Reynard wished there were something more he could say, but there wasn't.

'Okay, Ted,' he said. 'I'm sorry I troubled you.'

'It's been 40 years, nigh on,' said Ted.

'Yes,' said Reynard, although hearing Ted's voice, he felt as if it hadn't been very much longer than 40 minutes. Ted was one of those people who could make Reynard believe that time was collapsible, a dull series of inconsequential pictures in a folding travelogue, only half-seen and less than half understood. Goose-stepping marchers in Germany; the Japanese surrender on USS *Missouri*; Ike and Dulles and the raging days of Nikita Khruschev; Senator McCarthy and those 'points of order'; Kent State, and flowers being pushed into National Guard rifle barrels; LBJ hefting up his beagles by their ears; Watergate. Nothing more than a collection of images from some far-off land called America's Past.

All these things had happened since Condor. Some people had lived whole lifetimes since that night in 1944. Born, grown up, married, and died. But it had never gone away. Reynard had always harboured the terrible feeling that one day it would rise up from the ground again to haunt him. Every now and then he had woken up sweating, thinking of Condor and what he had done. And the worst thing had been that he had never known what had happened to it, or where it was. It had vanished, in that September storm, and nobody had ever discovered how, or where.

Ted had always maintained that it had lost its bearings, and gone down in Winnipesaukee Lake; and that was why the Winnipesaukee scandal which had forced Reynard to withdraw from the 1972 elections had been so ironic. He had felt cursed, and he still felt cursed, even today. Condor had thrown a cloaklike shadow over his life from which he had never been able to escape.

Mind you, there was another memory. A sweeter, more fragile memory. These days, it scarcely ever entered his conscious thoughts; and he was almost afraid to let it, in case, like a delicate piece of tapestry, it grew faded from constant exposure.

It was because of that memory that he had first gone to Germany in the late 1930s, as a very young and very dashing young man. It was because of that memory that he had first met some of the most high-ranking Nazis, and grown attracted to their cause.

The memory was Ilse von Soltau, the Berlin actress, with her blonde plaits and her grey eyes and her face as cold and Germanic and adamantly beautiful as a Rhine-goddess. Reynard had met her when she was on tour in New York, then sailed on the *Berengaria* to see her in Germany. There had been dinners, parties, walks under the linden-trees. There had been music, and love-making.

After his return to the United States, she had written to him saying that she was expecting his baby. He had written back, pledging his love, and begging her to come to America to join him.

Three weeks later, Hitler had invaded Poland, and he had never heard from her again. But he had never forgotten her, ever; even though he had no picture of her, nothing at all to remind him of the fiercest and the sweetest passion that he had ever experienced.

Perhaps, in Condor, he had seen the possibility of his pre-war romance returning to him; like the tearful ending to a Marlene Dietrich movie. But life wasn't like the movies, ever; and Reynard had been left with nothing but regret.

He switched off the lights in the library and went back through to the games room to rejoin Dean Farber and the others. A large board had been laid over the pool table and now it was spread with maps and diagrams and flow-charts. Dean Farber was an election specialist, and probably the most efficient and technically-experienced campaign manager that Reynard had ever had. As Reynard walked into the room, his hands in his pockets, Dean Farber had just finished explaining to Jeremy Ruyton just how they were going to tackle the problem of white bitterness against the democrats in Chicago.

Natalia Vanspronsen was sitting perched on the edge of a leather Chesterfield on the far side of the room, wreathed in smoke from the small cigar she was lighting. She looked up, and across at Reynard; and the low-hung Tiffany lamp over the pool table shone through her pale pink blouse and softly revealed her bare breasts. Reynard eyed her, unabashed, and then slowly and quite deliberately looked away.

Dean Farber raised his head, too; and the lamplight illuminated the prickles of his blond, close-cut hair. He had the milk-white face of a technocrat, and the slightly protuberant eyes of a man who probably spends too much time in front of a PTS 600.

'I have to tell you, Reynard, that on almost every count you have the positive edge. We've had some excellent responses from Democrats who voted for Carter in 1976 but abstained in 1980 because they didn't feel that he had the strength or the statesmanlike quality they expected in a President. They see that strength and that statesmanlike quality in you. You're older, more experienced, more *comforting*. They know you've been involved in one or two scandals in the past, but at this distance in time they're not only prepared to forgive you, they're actually willing to see your involvement in those scandals as an asset. The voting public goes for a man who knows what he's doing; a man of the world.'

Dean Farber looked around the table, one hand clasped on top of the other hand in a curious gesture that reminded Reynard of a small boy who is too shy to ask for the bathroom. 'That's the way I propose we present you in this campaign; as a politician of experience and acumen. As a candidate seasoned by time and experience, who not only cares for the welfare of the American people in every respect, financially, medically, and socially; but who is strong enough and mature enough to deal with the Soviets nose-to-nose.'

'You make me sound like an ancient relic,' said Reynard, dryly.

'Not at all, senator,' said Dean Farber. 'Not in the slightest. An ancient relic you're certainly not. Reagan may be, but not you. *You*, senator – ' and here he seized a sheet of paper with a dramatic flourish and unrolled it in front of everybody in the room. 'You, senator, are A Man of the World.'

Reynard looked for a long time at the blown-up photograph of himself with his hand resting possessively on his library globe. He had to admit it was one of the more flattering pictures he had seen lately; but he wondered if the symbolism wasn't a little too obvious.

And he sharply found himself thinking of that *Laugh-In* parody of the Nazi dictator. 'Today . . . America. Tomorrow . . . *Die Welt.*'

He said, 'I don't like it, Dean.'

185

'I beg your pardon?' blinked Dean Farber.

'I said, I don't *like* it. Don't you understand English?'

Dean Farber glanced from left to right as if he were reassuring himself where he was; that he was still in New Hampshire, campaign manager for Reynard Kelly; that it was still the 1980s. Then he looked back at Reynard, and said, 'You will, senator. Believe me. You will.'

ELEVEN

Chiffon Trent opened one eye and tried to think what that unfamiliar triangle of sunlight on the opposite wall could be. The sunlight never came into her bedroom, not first thing in the morning. So maybe she had overslept; or drunk too much champagne and crashed out on the living-room sofa. She found it difficult to focus, and her brain felt like a large bath-sponge filled with tepid water.

She opened the other eye. She was lying on a pillow, so she must be in bed. But why had she slept so late? She couldn't seem to remember what had happened yesterday, or why she felt so weird. She hadn't been free-basing, had she? Piotr had brought over three ounces of really good coke yesterday (if it *was* yesterday) but she had never had a downer like this before.

She tried to turn over, and discovered that she couldn't. Her wrists and ankles felt as if they were tied up; not with ropes but with bedsheets or scarves. She struggled and twisted, and managed to raise her head, but whoever had tied her up had made a tight professional job of it. Both of her wrists were knotted with red silk scarves to the brass head of the bed, and presumably both of her ankles were similarly tied to the foot, although it was impossible for her to see.

A feeling of deep, dark panic surged up inside her. Her fear was made all the more wrenching because she couldn't even start to remember how she had come to be here. She didn't scream: but she uttered a queer, suppressed little honking sound, like a child who is too frightened even to articulate. She struggled again, more desperately this time, but she succeeded only in tightening the scarves even more.

She lay still: her panic subsided. She said to herself, think, think what happened, think why you're here. But her memory wouldn't, or couldn't function. Jigsaws can't be put together without any pieces, and there was no picture in her mind, not even a disassembled picture.

She began to feel cold. It hadn't really struck her before, since she always slept in the nude, but she was naked. Bound and naked in a room she had never seen before, with no memory of how she had got here.

Maybe it had been the coke. Maybe her brain had dysfunctioned, and she was lying in a mental hospital. But why would a mental hospital be furnished with this strange tatty-rococo type of bedroom furniture, white bureaux with gilt handles and plastic curlicues? And there was another feeling, too, which Chiffon couldn't quite define. A feeling of being *elsewhere*; as if she wasn't in New York, or Los Angeles, or any of the places she knew.

There was a different, elsewhere kind of sound outside her window. A distant swish of traffic, the sound of an airplane circling very high up, a radio playing country and western.

'If I should leave you in the rain in Klamath County . . .
If I should walk away and leave our love behind . . .'

Chiffon thought of Reynard. She remembered Reynard, saying that they would have to stop seeing each other. She remembered the Palm Court at the

Plaza, the piano music, the scraping violin. She remembered the faces of Reynard's henchmen as she walked away across the broad patterned carpet. But that was all. After that, silence, invisibility, emptiness.

The triangle of sunlight moved across the wall. Chiffon closed her eyes, tried to get back inside of herself, to persuade herself that she was really Chiffon Trent, and not a dream, or a character in a movie. If she was lost, or sick, or mad, then surely somebody would come looking for her? Where was Piotr? He had been waiting for her in her hotel room. Surely he must have missed her.

Where was Reynard? Where was anybody? She had been lying here for hours, and she hadn't seen or heard anything that might have suggested that there was anybody else in the building. Only that ceaseless noise of traffic, and that endless twanging country and western music. But if there was music, *somebody* must be listening to it.

Hours went by. The sun faded. It grew colder, and the country and western music was switched off. Chiffon tried struggling at her bonds again, but her wrists and ankles were sore and swollen now, and so she gave up. She was bursting to pee, but she hung on and refused to wet the bed because somehow that would have meant that she no longer had any chance of being released, or returning to that life which she believed to be real.

When it grew dark, she dozed; and when she dozed, the door of her room opened with a subtle clicking of lock-levers. She became aware that there was somebody standing by the bed only when a hand touched her bare back, very gently, like the hand of an alien touching a human being for the very first time.

She opened her eyes, and said, 'Wha – ?' but a whispery voice immediately said, 'Sh, you don't have to get yourself excited.'

She looked up, shivering. Her visitor was a large, bulky-shouldered man in a light grey three-piece that looked as if it had been bought at an auction of old Victor Mature suits. He had chestnut-brown hair, waved in the style of a 1950s movie idol, and a wide, bland face that was surprisingly young.

'Well, I'm sorry I couldn't get back to see you earlier,' he smiled. 'Unfortunately, I had an errand to run. You know, errands. Always take longer than you think they're going to.'

'Where the *hell* am I?' Chiffon demanded, in a rush of fury. How could this man be so nonchalant when she had been tied up all day in this bedroom, without a word of explanation, without food or water or even a chance to go to the bathroom? The whole situation was crazy, and insulting, and frightening, too, and this pale imitation of Robert Taylor needn't think that he was going to get away with it.

'Calm down,' said the man. He took one hand out of his jacket pocket and examined his fingernails. 'You're lucky you're alive.'

'What is that supposed to mean? And you untie these damned knots, for beginners!'

'I *said*,' the man repeated, more quietly, but with greater insistence, 'that you're lucky to be alive. I mean, it's lucky for you that I recognized who you were. Otherwise, if you'd just been some dumb broad that somebody wanted disposed of . . .'

Chiffon stared at him. 'What are you talking about?' she demanded. 'Will you please untie me. *Please*. I have to go to the bathroom.'

'Well, I expect you do,' said the man. He pushed his hand back into his pocket, and stared towards the window absent-mindedly. In profile, he looked even more like Robert Taylor. 'It's really only natural.'

'You're crazy,' said Chiffon. 'Listen, I want you to

untie me. I'll make it worth your while. I have money. I'll pay you anything you want. But please untie me.'

The man smiled, without looking at her. 'Do you remember how you got here yet?' he asked her.

She was silent for a moment. Then, in a hushed voice, she said, 'No. I don't.'

'It's the sodium pentathol,' said the man. 'It sometimes gives you a temporary loss of memory. But, you'll remember. Most of them don't, of course. Most of them never wake up. But it's lucky that I recognized who you were.'

Chiffon said, 'I want you to tell me what's happened. Why am I here? What is this place? And who are you?'

The man took out a cigarette, tapped it on his thumbnail, and lit it in a curiously old-fashioned way, with a match. He blew out the match without taking the cigarette out of his mouth. 'My name's Denzil Forbes,' he said. 'You probably wouldn't have heard of me, not unless you were in at the dirty end of politics. But I come highly recommended, usually, as an entrepreneur. Jobs done, messages passed on, goods and services supplied, no questions asked, cash on the barrelhead. *You*, you see – I was asked to deal with you. Senator Kelly's right-hand man asked me. Deal with this lady for me, he said, and make sure she's dealt with good. In other words, accidental demise, no embarrassing questions to be asked.'

Chiffon felt even colder. 'Reynard wanted you to *kill* me?' she asked Denzil Forbes. 'He actually hired you to – ?'

Denzil Forbes smiled amiably. 'Lucky I recognized who you were. When they brought you in, I took one quick look at you; and then I said, my gosh, Denzil – I was talking to myself, you understand – my gosh, Denzil, that is the well-known Chiffon Trent. I, uh, take a lot of interest in the movies, you understand. I always liked you a lot, especially in that made-for-TV movie, what was it, don't tell me, *Night Wind*. Was it *Night Wind*?'

Chiffon lowered her head back on to the pillow. She closed her eyes. She could hear Denzil Forbes talking as if he were a television programme in the room above. A chatty, unperturbed commentary on the way in which Reynard had tried to get rid of her. Actually have her *murdered*, so that she wouldn't cause him any more fuss.

'Fortunately for you, I just happened to be in New York. I could have been anywhere, then the boys would have done what they were told to do, and that would have been the end of it. But when Dick called us up from the Plaza, I decided to stay around, see what the boys brought in, and it was you, which was good luck for me, wasn't it? And for you, because you didn't wind up burning.'

'Is that what you were going to do to me?'

'Aha,' said Denzil Forbes. 'That is what we have *already* done to you. Officially, of course. Look at this.'

He walked around the bed, out of Chiffon's vision, and came back with a copy of the New York *Daily News*. On page three, there was a photograph of a black, gutted sports car, and underneath, the headline, *Starlet Chiffon Trent Dies In Auto Blaze.*

'You see that?' Denzil asked her, waving the paper in front of her nose. 'You're dead. Charred to a crisp. But, you know the way you used to drive. You never should have crossed that intersection on a red light. Especially with that half-empty gas truck coming the other way. The truck driver was real lucky, he survived. In fact, he got scorched trying to pull you out of the wreck. He recognized your face at the window of the car, wasn't that fortunate? Here – do you know what it says here – "right in front of my eyes that beautiful girl was burned into raw meat – it was like watching it on television – except that I knew it was real." '

Denzil Forbes tossed the paper aside. 'Everybody has different realities, of course. And reality can always be adjusted to suit your convenience. Wouldn't you say that? You're a movie actress, of course, you know that. Make-up, trick camera-work. Stand-ins.'

Chiffon said, 'Who *was* that?'

'I'm sorry, who was who?'

'Who was that in my car?'

'Who *died*, you mean? Oh, nobody you need to worry about. Just another girl that nobody had much use for. You know how it is. There are always plenty of girls around who know too much. It's not a very healthy thing, knowing too much. But now I'm beginning to sound like an Edward G. Robinson picture.'

'Another girl died in my place?' insisted Chiffon.

'That's it. Right on the button.'

'You burned another girl, *alive*?'

Denzil looked a little uncomfortable. 'She was well drugged. She wouldn't have felt anything. Besides, there was a whole lot of gasoline around. The heat, you know . . . You don't last for long in a situation like that.'

Chiffon felt numb. She tried to relax, but gradually the fragments of memory were beginning to come together again in her mind, stray multi-coloured pieces. And there were snatches of conversation, too; and faces; and glimpses of street scenes. She could remember Piotr at the door, opening the door and turning back to look at her, and saying, 'I'll see you at the Russian Tea Rooms . . .' and then opening the door again and turning back to look at her again, like a video loop that kept running over and over and over. 'I'll see you at the Russian Tea Rooms.'

Then almost immediately afterwards, a knock at the door. Piotr coming back, she thought. Must have forgotten something. But then the door slamming right back and two men in fright masks jostling their way into the room and twisting her arm around and forcing her face-down on the bed.

Reynard, she thought. My God, what a bastard. Reynard who said he loved me and cherished me and would have given me anything at all in the whole world. Reynard who said he would die for me, if I asked him. Reynard had actually taken out a contract on my *life*.

Chiffon said, 'I have to go to the bathroom, you know.'

'Yes,' said Denzil. It was more of a question than a proper response. Chiffon wondered if he were tripping on something. His attention kept wandering, in and out of the doors of his eyes; as if he were leading three or four simultaneous and parallel lives. He seemed to be much more complicated than he looked, Denzil Forbes.

'I have to go,' insisted Chiffon.

Denzil Forbes went to the door and Chiffon heard him unlocking it. There must have been someone standing right outside, because no words were spoken, and the next thing Chiffon knew, someone was untying the scarves around her ankles. A woman, Chiffon guessed, by the coolness and dexterity of her fingers. And when her wrists were untied, Chiffon looked up and saw that her guess had been right.

A blonde girl, in her mid-twenties, with heavy make-up and a tight turquoise-blue mini-dress. The kind of girl you only saw on Hollywood Boulevard, or Lexington Avenue, or occasionally (not whores at all, but quite innocently anachronistic) in small towns in Kansas. Some places in America still live in the 1960s, the Kennedy years in perspex, and Chiffon sometimes used to think that Reynard's mind was one of those places. Now she was sure of it.

The girl lisped, 'My name's Mae-Beth. I'll be taking care of you. Chiffon, that's a beautiful name. I always wanted a name like Chiffon. You know my mom was called Cleopatra? Isn't that a beautiful name? My grandfather got it from a book.'

Mae-Beth wrapped the bedcover over Chiffon's shoulders, and then helped her out of the bedroom door and along the landing to the bathroom. The landing was bare, decorated with brown-and-yellow floral wallpaper which looked as if it hadn't been changed since 1955. A skylight at the far end was open, and let in the chill night air, and the sound of traffic.

Chiffon said, 'Where am I? I don't even know where I am.'

Mae-Beth gave her an affectionate squeeze. 'No place terrific, darling.'

'But where? What city? This isn't New York, is it? Are we outside of New York? White Plains?'

'Unh-hunh. I'm not s'posed to tell you nothing. But, there was a beer which made this place famous, and it kind of rhymes with . . . I don't know, bits. Or *tits*, I guess.'

Mae-Beth giggled. Chiffon stared at her, and said, 'Milwaukee?

We're in *Milwaukee*?'

'Don't say I told you. You're not supposed to know that.'

'But what am I doing in Milwaukee?' protested Chiffon. 'I never went to Milwaukee in my life.'

'The toilet's here,' said Mae-Beth, and opened the door for her.

The bathroom was small, cold, white-tiled.

'I have to watch you,' said Mae-Beth. 'They don't want you going out the window.'

Chiffon was too relieved to worry. She sat and shivered while Mae-Beth primped her hair in the measly mirror over the washbasin. Mae-Beth said, 'Denzil's in a funny kind of a mood today, don't you think? He has his moods. But I think he likes you. He's a pretty good-hearted kind of a guy, usually. Very neat, that's what

194

I like in a man. I'm not into that dirty-fingernail scene. Ugh-ee.'

Chiffon said, 'Who is he? I mean, what is he keeping me here for?'

'Oh, well, hasn't he told you? He's quite famous in his own field. He makes movies.'

'In Milwaukee?'

'I don't know. I never saw anything wrong with Milwaukee. Kind of blue collar, I suppose. But you can't have everything.'

Chiffon stood up, and flushed the handle. 'I don't understand. Denzil makes movies? What kind of movies? For advertising, or something?'

'He'll tell you,' said Mae-Beth, pouting at herself. She turned to Chiffon and smiled. 'At least he likes you. God, if he didn't *like* you.'

'He burned a girl alive,' said Chiffon.

'Well, that's right,' agreed Mae-Beth.

'Doesn't that *scare* you?' Chiffon asked.

'Well of course it does. Denzil's a very scary person. But don't you think he has wonderful charisma? When you're around him, you know, it's the scariness that makes him so attractive. Then there's the Baszczewski Brothers. They're pretty scary too, but they're professional, you know. Billy Baszczewski, he does the cameras and the lights, Nat Baszczewski does the rest of it, the sound and everything.'

'Two guys, that's all Denzil has?'

'Well, yes, I guess.'

'How does he make movies with just two guys?' Chiffon wanted to know.

'They're only skin movies,' said Mae-Beth. 'They're not epics, or anything like that.'

'Skin movies? You have to be kidding. Denzil wants to put me in a skin movie? Who the hell does he think he is?'

'He was very pleased to get you. I mean, a skin movie

with the name of Chiffon Trent on it has got to be worth a lot of money. He told me how pleased he was.'

'I don't *believe* this,' said Chiffon; but at that moment the bedroom door opened, further down the landing, and Denzil appeared, smoking a cigarette.

'Aren't you girls through dolling yourselves up yet?' he asked. 'I have to go see Dan Berman before nine.'

Mae-Beth whispered to Chiffon, 'For your own sake, please, don't say nothing. For mine, too. He'll flay me.'

Chiffon glanced at her and saw at once that she meant it. She was tempted to push her away, and make a run for it down the stairs, but she guessed that if Denzil had taken the precaution of tying her to the bed, he had probably made sure that all the doors were locked, too. And where was she going to go, at this time of night, in Milwaukee, with no clothes on? She would probably wind up raped.

'Come on, will you, for Pete's sake,' urged Denzil; and so they came.

Piotr stepped out of the stage door of the O'Connor Theatre, two French loaves under one arm, and a scruffy script under the other. It was a cold, blustery day, three days after Chiffon Trent had died in that auto accident on 93rd Street. Piotr felt depressed and a little drunk. He had finished half a bottle of Wodka Wyborowa with his breakfast that morning; not so much because Chiffon had died, but simply because it didn't seem to matter any more whether he was drunk or sober, and so he might as well be drunk.

He hated the play which he was rehearsing, and he particularly loathed his leading lady, who was French, and smelled of Brie, and never shaved her armpits. This morning's love scene between them had been a war of two overpowering flavours of halitosis.

He crossed Sixth Avenue with the collar of his leather jacket turned up against the wind. Moscow could be perishing; but only New York could scour your face with that particular mixture of grit and fumes and freezing-cold wind; that smell of bagels and subways and domestic cigars. He made his way along 36th Street, sniffing from time to time. His self-esteem had never been lower. After all the glamorous pictures that had appeared in *People* and *The National Enquirer* when he had dated Lois Brace, the actress wife of oil magnate George Brace III, to be walking unknown and hungover through Manhattan on a chilly Wednesday morning was very far from uplifting.

He had almost reached the corner of Fifth Avenue when a shabby blue Buick Electra drew into the gutter beside him, and one of the windows was rolled down. A sallow-faced man with heavy eyebrows and a grey hat leaned out of the window and said, 'Hey, Piotr Lissitzky, isn't it?'

Piotr ignored him, and kept on walking. The Buick crept along beside him, its tyres crushing discarded 7-Up cans, yogurt cartons, and a scattering of broken pizza.

The man said, 'I heard from your mother.'

Piotr stopped where he was. 'What do you want this time?' he asked, sharply. This must be the sixth or seventh time that the Russians had approached him with 'messages from his family' or 'kind greetings from the people of the Soviet Socialist Republics'. It was all pressure; anything to prevent him from feeling that he had broken his ties with his mother country for good. Anything to make him feel uncomfortable and alien. Because in spite of what *Pravda* had said about him, his defection had irritated the Russians a very great deal, especially since he had by chance chosen a moment to defect when the Soviet Ambassador had been making a public announcement that freedom of movement and freedom of speech within the Soviet Union were 'cherished and valued by all Russians'.

'I have a message from your mother, that's all,' said the man in the Buick.

Piotr glanced right and left, in case he had to make a quick escape. But he was only 20 feet away from Fifth Avenue, and there were plenty of people around, so he didn't feel that he was in too much danger of a sudden abduction.

'What's the message?' he asked.

'Get in the car, I'll tell you about it.'

'You tell me right here and now.'

The man turned away, and said something to the driver. Then he leaned out of the window again, and said, 'Look, it's personal. If you don't want to get in the car, let's talk in that coffee shop right across the street. How about that? We're not trying to kidnap you.'

Piotr hesitated, frowning across Fifth Avenue at the Mucho Mocha. It looked as if it was pretty full, so the man in the hat and his unseen companion would have trouble trying anything smart. There were two cops on the corner, too, talking to Con-Ed workers who were repairing cables. It seemed to be safe enough.

'Okay,' said Piotr. 'I'll meet you there.' And with that, he walked briskly away, crossing Fifth Avenue, and pushing his way straight through the doors of the coffee-shop. He found a plastic-covered seat opposite the cashier, disconcertingly close to a large rubber-plant.

After a minute or two, the man came in, carrying his hat in his hands. He was almost bald, but his remaining hairs had been meticulously combed across his scalp. There was no sign of his companion. He sat down, unbuttoning the top button of his overcoat, and setting his hat on the table.

'I must introduce myself,' he said. His Russian accent was much more marked now than it had been outside in the street. 'Ilia Cerenkov. I work for Mr Tamm, first deputy.'

'What do you want?' Piotr asked him, aggressively.

'It is what *you* want that we must concern ourselves with.'

'From you, I want nothing,' Piotr told him.

'Well, it's your mother,' said Cerenkov. The waitress came across with an absurdly huge bow in her hair, and he raised his hand and said, 'Tea, please,' then looked to Piotr and said, 'for two?'

'Coffee, black,' said Piotr. He couldn't find anywhere to put his French bread, so finally he propped it up in the one free chair, next to him.

'I don't really think that I'm going to believe anything you tell me,' said Piotr.

'This time, I think you can,' said Cerenkov. 'Your mother sends you a message, or rather we are sending you a message on your mother's behalf. And, you know that we always do what we say.'

'Go on.'

Cerenkov took out a handkerchief and blew his nose. 'The warmth, after coming in from the cold,' he explained. He folded the handkerchief away, shifted his chair forward a little, and then said earnestly, 'Your mother is about to be very ill.'

'*About* to be?'

'Well, we both know that she is not particularly strong, don't we? Her heart has never been good. And if she is sent to Galic, or Buj . . . it is a fairly safe assumption that she is about to be very ill.'

'Why should she be sent to Galic or Buj? What has she done?'

'Ah, now, that's it,' said Cerenkov. He rummaged around in one of his pockets, and at last produced a crumpled letter. He held it up, and on the front it was clearly marked for the attention of Piotr Lissitzky, c/o U.S. Embassy, Helsinki. 'This is a letter from your mother to you, which fortunately was intercepted by a loyal Soviet citizen before it could reach its destination.'

199

'Fortunately?' asked Piotr, dully.

'Of course, because it contains all manner of lies and defamatory statements about the Soviet Union, and it would have been most unfortunate if those had fallen into the hands of those who could and *would* have made propaganda out of them.'

'Let me see that,' snapped Piotr, and tried to snatch the letter.

'Aha, I'm afraid not,' said Cerenkov. 'Because of its scurrilous content, the letter is now a prime exhibit in your mother's forthcoming trial. You know of course that it is an offence to defame the Soviet Union. You also know that the punishments can be severe.'

Piotr said, 'I don't believe any of this.'

'That, of course, is your privilege,' said Cerenkov. 'You have, after all, washed your hands of your mother country, and washed your hands of your parents as well. I assure you, however, that your mother will be arrested and brought to trial; and I can also assure you that the result of that trial is something of a foregone conclusion.'

Cerenkov opened up the letter, and peered down at it as if he usually wore reading-glasses. 'Here,' he said, 'here she says that "Life in Moscow is worse than you can imagine . . . the food shortages are chronic, and we haven't tasted fresh meat in three weeks." Well now, you and I both know what a slander that is, don't we, Piotr? Your mother is simply pandering to the prejudice of the Western media. What a story the American papers would make of this! "Defected Actor's Mother Says She Is Starving In Moscow Food Shortage!" '

Piotr said, 'My mother didn't write that letter. My mother would never write anything like that. Whatever she is, whatever she was, she's not a fool.'

Cerenkov tucked the letter back in his pocket, and shrugged. 'A State handwriting expert will conclusively prove that the script was hers.'

The waitress brought their tea and their coffee. Piotr said, as an afterthought, 'Bring me a blueberry muffin.'

'You have become very Americanized,' Cerenkov remarked, sipping his tea.

'At least nobody threatens me, in America, the way people are threatened in the Soviet Union.'

'It is up to the people to support the State. The State is the people; anyone who slanders or betrays it, slanders or betrays their fellow citizens. You don't think such a crime should be punished?'

'I want to know what this is all about,' said Piotr. 'Come on, Cerenkov, without the flannel, and the phony evidence. The truth.'

'The truth?' asked Cerenkov, raising his shaggy eyebrows. 'Now you're asking for more than most people ever get in a lifetime. And over coffee, you want it, in New York? But, wait, I will tell you what we require, and that is almost as important as the truth.'

'Well?' asked Piotr.

Cerenkov leaned forward confidentially. 'Something a little embarrassing is about to happen in Afghanistan. Well, I shouldn't tell you this, but it may help you to understand how serious we are about all this; and it won't alter what you have to do. When this event occurs, many people in the West will, quite naturally, misunderstand the actions that the Soviet Union will be obliged to take. We will, in all probability, get a very bad Press.'

'So what does that have to do with me?'

'It has everything to do with you. At the moment this event occurs, it will be announced that you have turned your back on the American way of life, and that you are gladly and freely returning to live in the Soviet Union. You will talk about the corrupt, misguided values of capitalism; and the laxness and immorality of the American people. You will divert media attention

201

away from Afghanistan, and give us coverage that is both entertaining, popular, and supportive.'

Piotr poured Sweet'n'Lo in his coffee and stirred it over and over and over. Cerenkov watched him, smiling.

'And, of course, if I don't agree . . .' said Piotr, at last.

'We won't have any choice,' nodded Cerenkov. 'I'm sorry about her heart but . . . as Turgenev said, "every man who prays, prays for a miracle." Dear God, please grant me that twice two be not four!'

'Don't talk to me of God and of prayers,' said Piotr. 'Not you. Not on this rat's errand. You want me to come back to the Soviet Union, and you're threatening to murder my mother if I don't. That's the beginning and the end of it, isn't it?'

'Do you want me to deny it?' asked Cerenkov.

'Should I call the police?' Piotr retorted.

An old white-haired man came over and pointed to the chair on which Piotr's French bread was propped up.

'Do you mind moving your groceries so that an old man can sit down?' he asked.

'That seat is taken,' said Cerenkov, with a humourless smile.

'Two loaves of bread should occupy a seat?'

'Somebody's joining us,' said Piotr, as kindly as he could.

The old man shuffled off, grumbling. Cerenkov said, 'You have plenty of time to think this over. But we would like to know within a day or so whether you're willing in principle to come back to the Soviet Union. You will be treated like a hero, you know, especially if you tell the Western media that you are tired of capitalism, tired of the emptiness of American greed, and that you long for real red-blooded Soviet life. You were brave to leave, we know that. But you will be even braver if you admit your mistake and come back.'

Piotr said, 'I have to tell you this. I'm not coming back.'

'I don't think that's very reasonable. Do you?'

'Cerenkov, you know New York. Would you go back, if you had any choice at all?'

Cerenkov shrugged, smiled, stirred his tea. 'The question doesn't arise. But none of this will help your mother. And I'm afraid they're serious about it. If you don't come back, they will try her; and almost certainly find her guilty.'

Piotr covered his eyes with his hand and was silent for a long time. Cerenkov placidly sat and watched him, occasionally clearing his throat, and once saying to a black woman, 'I'm sorry. That seat's occupied.'

Piotr looked up. 'Do you think there's any chance of a deal?' he asked Cerenkov.

'A *deal*? I shouldn't think so. What kind of a deal?'

'Well, the thing is, I have some quite interesting information. If you'd lay off my mother, and lay off me; then maybe I could tell you.'

'Well . . . that doesn't sound a very attractive proposition,' said Cerenkov. 'I'm supposed to bring you back alive. You know? Big game hunt.'

Piotr said, 'You know that I used to date Chiffon Trent? That actress who died three days ago?'

'Yes, that was very tragic,' said Cerenkov. 'You have my condolences. But from what the newspaper said, she was always a very impetuous driver. Not a girl to stop for red lights.'

'She was the mistress of Senator Reynard Kelly,' said Piotr. 'When she was dating me, she was two-timing him. And, she told me *all* about him. Very interesting information, some of it. And one piece of information in particular. Well, that was dynamite.'

'Hm,' said Cerenkov.

'Come on, Cerenkov, don't be coy,' said Piotr. 'You know as well as I do that Reynard Kelly stands every chance of being the next President of the United States . . . and if you have a really scandalous piece of inside information about him, well, wouldn't that help your masters in Moscow? Wouldn't that be worth something? Destroying that letter of yours, maybe?'

'I don't think I have the authority . . .' Cerenkov pouted.

Piotr beckoned Cerenkov closer to him. Cerenkov hesitated at first, but eventually leaned his elbow on the table and bent his heavy head forward.

Piotr said, 'If I tell you that I have information which links Senator Reynard Kelly directly with Adolf Hitler . . . now, what would you think about that?'

Cerenkov sat back. 'You're bluffing.'

Piotr shook his head.

Cerenkov folded his arms. 'You're bluffing.'

'Why should I bluff?' asked Piotr. 'During the war, Reynard Kelly had direct dealings with the Nazis. He told Chiffon all about it, I don't know why. He told her that he'd never said a word about it to anyone else. Maybe he told her because he felt guilty. Maybe he was just trying to impress her. But whatever the reason, he told her, and *she* told me.'

Cerenkov leaned back, and eyed Piotr coldly. 'I still don't believe you. Why should I believe you?'

'There were plenty of American politicians who didn't want to fight against the Germans, weren't there?'

'*Da.*'

'And there were plenty of American industrialists, too, who didn't approve of the war?'

'*Da.*'

'So . . . Reynard Kelly was a young politician in those days, in the 1940s, with a father who had made billions and billions of dollars out of trading with Europe, particularly with Krupps, and Junkers, and Horst . . .

and he had been brought up as a boy with the sons and daughters of German industrialists and politicians . . . don't you think perhaps it was natural for him to think quite kindly of Adolf Hitler, and to consider that Germany was a better ally for the United States than Britain? Squalid, arrogant, cantankerous Britain? And Hitler all the time being so reasonable? And not only reasonable but successful, too.'

Cerenkov beckoned the waitress to bring him some more tea. 'How do you know so much about this?' he asked Piotr. 'All these things about Krupps, and Junkers?'

'When Chiffon told me, I went to the public library and looked it all up.'

'Why?'

'Because . . I don't know, I suppose I was interested, and I didn't have anything else better to do. And I suppose, in a way, I wanted to know something more about this man whose mistress I was taking to bed.'

'Jealous?'

'There's no point in that now, is there? She's dead.'

'And you're grieving?' asked Cerenkov. 'You don't look like a man who's grieving.'

'I don't know what to think,' said Piotr. 'Now, I'm not so sure what I felt about her. Whether I loved her or not.'

'No woman should be so unlucky as to have you for a lover,' commented Cerenkov. 'But still, tell me about this connection between Senator Kelly and Adolf Hitler.'

'I can't tell you any more until you guarantee that my mother won't be arrested,' said Piotr. 'And you must also guarantee that you won't make any more attempts to get me back to the Soviet Union, and that from now on you will leave me alone.'

Cerenkov thought about that, and then slowly shook his head. 'I can't make you any guarantees like that.'

'Then you don't get the information, and that's it.'

'Well . . . I shall certainly have to talk to my superiors.'

'Then talk to your superiors. You know where to find me.'

'You say Reynard Kelly had a direct connection with Adolf Hitler?'

'Direct,' nodded Piotr. 'They spoke to each other several times, just before the war, and Chiffon said that Reynard was quite sentimental about him.'

Cerenkov thought for a while, drumming his fingers on the table so that his tea-glass rattled in its holder. 'It's hard to believe, all this story of yours. I could have thought of five or six American politicians who might have sympathized with Hitler . . . but not one of them would have been a Democrat, and I certainly wouldn't have counted Reynard Kelly's name amongst them.'

'Times change, Comrade Cerenkov, and people with them.'

'Obviously. You, too, have changed. You are not just one of the *stilyagi* any more.'

'The women of famous men always know secrets,' said Piotr. 'I learned that in Hollywood. I also learned that, the more secrets you know, the more influence you have. But most of the secrets I learned in Hollywood were simply who was going to bed with whom. Who was smoking dope, who was homosexual, who had money and who didn't. But this secret that Chiffon Trent told me about Senator Reynard Kelly, that was a truly influential secret. An American politician, making deals with the Nazis?'

'He made deals?' asked Cerenkov, quickly.

Piotr shook his head. 'I'm not going to say any more until you guarantee my mother's safety; and my right to stay in the United States unmolested.'

Cerenkov sipped his tea and scalded the roof of his

mouth. He took out his handkerchief and dabbed at his lips. 'Let me call you at home,' he said.

'Of course. You know the number,' said Piotr. 'I expect you have it tapped, too.'

Cerenkov gave a non-committal wave of his hand. 'You know how things are, comrade.'

Piotr picked up his French bread, and his script, and stood up. 'I'm not your comrade any longer, comrade. You ought to remember that. I'll wait to hear from you. *Da skorigh vstyrichi.*'

He left the Mucho Mocha, and walked out into the street. Suddenly he realized that he liked New York very much, whether he was famous or not. Suddenly he realized that he would give up anything, and betray almost anyone, not to have to go back to the Soviet Union.

He began to walk uptown, against the wind. Cerenkov stood outside the coffee shop, blowing his nose and watching Piotr go.

TWELVE

The epidemic broke out abruptly and unpredictably, and within the space of four hours on Wednesday afternoon, Edmond had driven around to seven fatalities amongst his own patients; and heard from Oscar and one of the county paramedics that other local doctors had attended five more.

Officially, of course, it still wasn't an epidemic. Just eleven unrelated domestic deaths caused by apparent asphyxiation. But on the three occasions when Edmond and Oscar met each other during the course of the afternoon, they exchanged looks of mutual understanding; and arranged to meet again later to discuss their fears in private.

'You heard from Bryce?' Edmond asked Oscar, as they stood outside a small house on North Curtisville Road, and watched three sheeted figures being wheeled out to a waiting ambulance. Oscar wiped his forehead with the back of his arm, and shook his head.

'Doesn't anybody understand what's *happening* here?' Edmond asked him, 50 minutes later, at a neat little house on Frost Road.

'It's not co-related yet,' said Oscar, with audible irony. 'No matter how many people die, it isn't an epidemic until all their deaths have been co-related. Even the Black Death wasn't anything but 25 million individual fatalities. Or it might have been, if the New Hampshire Health and Welfare Department had had anything to do with it.'

The deaths at Frost Road – the fifth, sixth, and seventh of the day – were the first to make Edmond feel frightened. Suddenly, something was happening which was beyond his control. And not only his patients were at high risk, *he* was, too.

The family had still been lying on the sofa when he went into the house: a young couple in their mid-thirties with their eight-year-old daughter between them. The television had been tuned to *General Hospital*. They could have been asleep, all of them, except that they were dead. A neighbour had looked in with a promised recipe for apple pandowdy, and found them there.

'I saw them only this morning,' she had said. 'They were fine this morning, right as rain.'

Edmond had given the neighbour an injection of Sabin-type vaccine, which was probably useless, a placebo for both of them. But it was all that he could think of. His real fears now were that the virus would begin to spread quickly out of control, and also that he would contract it himself. He had already seen how inexorably it brought on paralysis of the respiratory system; and the thought of struggling for breath and knowing as he struggled that his condition was incurable was another of those medical nightmares which he found mentally hard to handle.

He thought of slicing Arabelle's throat, and couldn't keep the image out of his mind. The scarlet blood, the desperate struggle for breath. Perhaps this epidemic was God's revenge on him: so that he would have to die just as Arabelle had died, gasping for air.

He called Christy at home, and asked her if she had heard anything on the television news about deaths in Merrimack County, but she said no. There was nothing in the *Concord Herald*, either; nor on WKXL. He began to feel that he and Oscar were fighting against a disease which didn't even exist. A dream disease, which haunted failed paediatricians and overworked medical examiners. An infectious treadmill, to punish them for having dared to set themselves up as medical gods.

'I had a call from Malcolm,' Christy told him. 'He said he might come up later this evening.'

'I thought the party wasn't until Friday. Why does he have to come up tonight?'

'Because he's your brother. Besides, he's getting a ride from a friend of his, who lives in Portland.'

'I didn't think Malcolm had any friends.'

'Darling, he's your *brother*.'

'That's how I know what a 100% bastard he is.'

He met up with Oscar about eight o'clock in the evening at the Cat'N'Fiddle on Manchester Street. He was drowning his fatigue and sterilizing his imaginary contagions in vodka and tonic, and wondering whether he ought to send Christy to stay with her friends in New York until the epidemic was under control. Or at least until his birthday party was over. Oscar walked into the bar with his coat slung over his shoulder, saying hi to everyone he knew; and then he pulled out a stool and sat next to Edmond and beckoned to the barkeep to bring him his usual, three fingers of Jack Daniel's, on the rocks.

'Well,' said Edmond.

'Well?' asked Oscar. 'They can't say we didn't warn them.'

'Still no word from Bryce?'

'Nothing. I tried to discuss it with him this afternoon, after the first two fatalities, that couple at Bow Mills. But all he could say was that he was trying to get some action out of Eldridge. Well, you know what *that's* like, trying to get some action out of Eldridge. You might just as well try to get dogshit to dance the fandango.'

'Did you get the autopsy report on the Osmans?'

'That was what I wanted to see you about,' said Oscar. His drink was served up, and he drank it down in four larynx-bobbing gulps. He banged the glass on to the counter and ordered another. 'And another one here for my friend, the quack,' he told the barkeep. 'Vodka, forget the tonic.'

Edmond said, 'It's serious, isn't it? I mean, for no apparent reason at all, it seems to have broken out all over.'

'Which is not at all usual in epidemics of poliomyelitis,' put in Oscar. 'Poliomyelitis is generally transmitted hand to mouth. But this bug . . . well, it seems to have spread all over the locality without any particular pattern. In some cases there might have been contact; but in others there wasn't any at all.'

The barkeep set them up two more drinks; but Edmond called him back and asked him to top up his glass with White Rock. Edmond was apprehensive about the epidemic, and frightened of catching the virus himself – but he wasn't yet ready to drink himself into total unconsciousness.

Oscar opened up a brown manila envelope and produced a sheaf of blurrily-Xeroxed autopsy protocols.

'The mayor will talk to Harold Bunyan, and Harold Bunyan will tell him that he's keeping a watch on the situation, and not to panic. The mayor will then unquestionably decide to sit on his hands and smile. The winter tourist season is about to start. The last thing the mayor wants is to scare off half of the tourist trade.'

'Jesus, this sounds like *Jaws*,' said Edmond. 'A couple of guys discover a shark and nobody will admit that it's there, let alone dangerous, just in case it hurts the tourist trade. We've got exactly the same situation here in Concord, with this Goddamned virus.'

'You've got to face it,' Oscar told him. 'We're just the dogfaces in the field, the medical infantry. And no general likes to take advice from his infantrymen. Not when it comes to strategy.'

'Then let's talk to the media,' said Edmond. 'Let's talk to the newspapers, and the television people. Tell them we think there's an epidemic on the way. Then Eldridge will *have* to act.'

'I'm not sure,' said Oscar. He waved to the barkeep to bring him another drink. 'Give me 24 hours to see what I can get out of Bryce myself. The point is, if we go straight to the media, we're going to antagonize everybody: Bryce, Eldridge, the mayor. And Harold Bunyan will *definitely* disown us. We're going to need their help, that's the trouble, and if we go straight to the television, they're going to spend a whole lot of time and energy trying to show that we're over-reacting, that we're just a couple of local troublemakers. In fact, they're probably going to spend more time doing that than they are coping with the epidemic.'

Edmond pressed his fingertips to his forehead. He had the dull beginnings of a headache. 'Twenty-four hours, hmh?' he asked.

'Well, sooner if I can, of course,' put in Oscar.

'Oscar, I saw seven people dead today, in four hours alone. You saw a dozen. And if you're sure about this virus becoming stronger and more infective each time it replicates itself . . .'

'I'm as sure as I can be. At least, Dr Corning's as sure as he can be. He still has a whole lot of work to do on it. But what he says is, the virus shows some incredibly unusual twist in the way that its ribonucleic acid dictates the synthesis of new viral proteins. Instead of the RNA being exactly replicated, time after time, it alters each time to improve itself, so that each time it's much more active, much more infective, and much more resistant to heat or solvents.'

'So it's rare, and it's highly contagious, and it's becoming more dangerous every time somebody passes it on. And you don't want to tell the media?'

'Not yet, E.C. What Dr Corning is saying is so far out on a virological limb that Eldridge could easily produce another expert virologist who could legitimately say that it's all wild-eyed nonsense, and that no virus can possibly alter its genome, and that Dr Corning must have cracked. All of which would hold us up even longer. E.C., listen, I'm as wound up about this as you are, but the name of the game is politics, and we're not going to get ourselves any official help unless we play the situation *their* way.'

Edmond said, 'Meanwhile, another twelve of my patients die. Maybe more.'

Oscar laid his hand on his shoulder. 'E.C., I know it. But there's no other way. I've upset Byrce too many times already, and this time it's got to be done by the book. The chain of command, that's one of Bryce's favourite phrases. "Follow the chain of command, Dr Ford." '

'I still think we ought to bring in the media,' said Edmond. 'God, at least I'll feel as if we're *doing* something!'

'You go to the media, E.C.,' said Oscar, in his harshest voice, 'and they'll ruin you. I mean that.

They'll dump everything on you – everything – including the blame for the epidemic. You won't even practise again.'

'Maybe that wouldn't be such a bad thing.'

'Let me tell you something,' Oscar confided in him. 'There was a young surgeon practising under Dr McLellan at the Penacook Gynecological Clinic. This was, what, five years ago now. Harris, his name was, or Henry, I forget which. He wasn't around long enough to make himself very memorable. Dr McLellan bungled a hysterectomy, and the woman died. Dr Bryce said it was death as a result of post-operative complications, including pneumonia. But young Harris or Henry or whatever his name was went to Eldridge and said that McLellan had fouled the operation up, and that the death was a direct result of incompetence in the operation theatre.'

'And?' asked Edmond.

'And', said Oscar, 'Eldridge ignored him, of course. So young Harris or Henry went to the media, and complained of a cover-up. He was promptly sacked, sued for defamation, and eventually struck from the medical register. And *he* didn't even have a murky past, like you do. I warn you, E.C., you're in the country now, and the country is run by country boys; especially the medical profession. This isn't New York. Here, the doctors are tight as termites with the local politicians and even tighter with the local chamber of commerce, and everybody massages everybody else's ass. How do you think they managed to finance the White Park Clinic? Well, I won't tell you: I don't want to depress you more than I have already.'

Edmond said, 'Oscar, for Christ's sake, people's *lives* are at stake here. People are going to die.'

'Don't you think I know that? But there's nothing else we can do.'

Edmond ordered another drink. He was halfway

215

drunk already, he didn't think another one was going to make very much difference. The barkeep winked at him, and said, 'Problems, huh?'

'Some,' said Oscar. 'Including a bartender who doesn't seem to be able to mind his own business.'

'Just trying to be sociable,' said the barkeep.

'Sociability is a disease,' Oscar retorted. 'Set me up another drink.'

Edmond stirred the ice in his glass. For some reason he couldn't quite pin down, he was beginning to feel very alone, very defeated.

'Do any other doctors feel the way that I do?' he asked Oscar. 'Dr Redman had two patients die today, didn't he? And how about Dr Krauss?'

'Well, they're being cautious,' said Oscar. 'They agree that we seem to have a form of poliomyelitis on our hands, but until they've seen the autopsy reports, they're not prepared to commit themselves too far.'

'Not prepared to commit themselves, huh?'

'E.C., this whole epidemic could fizzle out into nothing. The virus could well be so fierce that it burns itself out after a couple of days.'

'You don't believe that, do you?'

'No, not personally. But it's the way that Dr Redman and Dr Krauss feel about it, and Dr Clements, too. They don't want to start flapping around like headless chickens until they can be sure of their ground. We've sent tissue and spinal-fluid samples from all of their fatalities down to Dr Corning, and all we can do is pray that he's quick.'

Edmond said, 'I've been trying to analyse the way this infection has been spreading. At least, among my own patients, and let's face it, I've got the lion's share, at least so far. But, you know, you're right – there doesn't seem to be any *pattern* to it. None of the people who died today were acquainted with the Osmans; although one of the families, the Perrins, were quite good friends of the Mayers, whose son Bernie was Michael Osman's best pal.'

'You've checked on the Mayers in the past 24 hours?'

'I checked them about an hour ago, before I left the hospital. They're all fine, fit, and healthy, and showing no signs of any stiffening of the muscles or any aches and pains at all.'

'Maybe Bernie was simply a carrier,' suggested Oscar. 'It's quite possible that some people might naturally have an immunity to this virus, and Bernie could be one of them. It happens with poliomyelitis: children can be vaccinated, and not catch polio themselves, but quite freely pass it on to others.'

'I don't know,' said Edmond. 'I'm still going to leave all the avenues open. But both Bernie and Michael were vaccinated with a standard Salk preparation, at approximately the same age; and if it didn't protect Michael I can't on the face of it see any particular reason why it should have protected Bernie. It might just have been chance, I don't know. But this virus seems to be so virulent that I don't see how Bernie could have contracted it or carried it without at least showing *some* symptoms.'

'Well, maybe you're right,' said Oscar. 'But Dr Corning's still waiting for the full tests on Michael's virus sample; and I don't suppose we'll see the results of Mrs Osman's virus tests for three or four days, and that's being optimistic. We won't know for sure until then.'

'There must be *some* connection, God damn it,' said Edmond. 'And where did the damn thing come from in the first place? Why did it break out in East Concord, for no apparent reason? We don't have any known environmental health risks there. A few swamps around Turtle Pond, I suppose; and septic-tank sewerage in most of the houses. But nothing that could have been a breeding-ground for a special and unusual

217

kind of poliomyelitis virus. Nothing like this I mean, if Dr Corning's right, and this thing has a way of progressively altering the reproductive information passed on by its RNA – I mean, come on, Oscar, we're talking about a very rare bird here. Not to mention a dangerous one.'

Oscar looked down at his whiskey, thought for a moment, and then tipped it down his throat. 'Listen,' he said, 'I shouldn't be telling you this. I promised Dr Corning that I'd keep it to myself. But he has a strong private opinion about this virus, based on all the years he's been analysing and studying picorna-viruses, like polio, which are his particular speciality. *He* thinks – and I know this sounds crazy – but *he* thinks that this virus was artificially-bred.'

'He thinks *what*?'

'He thinks the virus was artificially bred. Genetically engineered. Developed by some scientist or other for the specific purpose of infecting large numbers of people at an accelerating rate. Germ warfare, if that's what you want to call it.'

Edmond stared at Oscar's boiled-red face in disbelief. 'What are you trying to tell me?' he asked. His voice sounded as hollow as an emptying wash-basin. 'You're trying to tell me this was the *Russians* or something? Or some kind of a leak from a germ warfare factory?'

'I'm telling you what Dr Corning thinks, that's all. And you know Dr Corning. The world's driest and most unimaginative virologist. And let's face it, *all* virologists are pretty dry and unimaginative.'

'We don't have any germ warfare centres near East Concord, do we?' asked Edmond. 'There's that military area off Greeley Street in Sugar Ball . . . but they're not doing anything like that *there*, are they?'

'I don't think so,' said Oscar. 'But listen, E.C., you mustn't repeat any of this. Dr Corning won't know for sure until he's run about a week's worth of tests, minimum. He's promised to let me know as soon as he comes up with anything. Meanwhile, the best we can do is work on Bryce and Eldridge, convince them that we're looking at an epidemic, and see if we can get Concord quarantined. The whole of Merrimack County, if possible.'

Edmond sat for a long time in silence. Then he said. 'This could be it, couldn't it? It's quite within the bounds of possibility. This could be the start of World War Three.'

Oscar looked at him seriously. 'Not with a bang, with a whimper, huh?'

'Are you afraid?' asked Edmond.

'Afraid?'

'Are you afraid of catching it? Have you seen how quickly it kills you? Suffocates you. You and I, we could pick it up at any time, just like that. We may have contracted it already.'

Oscar beckoned to the barkeep for another drink, 'You haven't lost your professional nerve, have you, E.C.?'

'I don't know. Maybe. I'm just beginning to think that if I have to die, I'd at least like to know what it was that killed me.'

Just then, the 'L'il Bugger' in Oscar's pocket started beeping. He left his drink, and went to the telephone at the end of the bar and dialled the county coroner's office.

When he came back, he said tersely, 'Another family, out on Sawmill Road, near St Paul's school. Five of them, father, mother, three daughters. Looks like a long, long night.'

'In that case,' said Edmond, 'let *me* call Bryce.'

Oscar finished up his drink, and laid $12 flat-handed on the bar. 'All right,' he said. 'But for the love of this world in which we live, don't upset him.'

'Take care, Oscar,' said Edmond, as Oscar left the bar; and meant it.

Bernie spent the evening at home, carefully putting together a new plastic-model kit of a Turbo Mustang. The model had cost him $6.85, partly financed by his pocket-money, and partly financed by his sale at school of his 'secret obedience potion' – six glass phials of a clear, sugary-tasting liquid, guaranteed when dropped into your parents' coffee or cocktails to make them obey your demands to let you stay up as late as you wanted, and to eat as many cookies as took your fancy. Each phial, 80 cents.

At first, he had thought of keeping the phials. But the truth was that he didn't understand them, he didn't understand why Michael had hidden them in the garage wall, and the more he took them out and looked at them the more they irritated him. They didn't even *do* anything. They were nothing more than phials of water, in a leather case. If they were filled up with magic potion, that would be something. At least if they were filled up with magic potion he could get some money for them. And that was how he had thought of selling them as 'secret obedience potion', and succeeded in disposing of the entire six phials for $4.80.

His interest in finding out what had happened to Michael had met another setback when he had cycled down to Conant's Acre on Monday after school and found that the fence had been recently wound around with barbed wire. Now it was almost impossible for anyone to trespass across the field, no matter how innocently. He had stood by the wire, looking across at the woods, and the sky above him had been a jigsaw of white cloud. Well, supposing Michael *had* managed to get as far as the woods, and blaze his mark there? He couldn't have gone very far. Michael had never equalled Bernie's craft in tracking, and hunting; and he had never been as courageous as Bernie. A good sidekick, Michael. A good Tonto to Bernie's Lone Ranger. But that was all. That mark that Bernie had seen on the tree was probably the only mark that Michael had been brave enough to cut.

He carefully glued the suspension of his model Mustang together, his tongue protruding slightly as he did so. He heard the telephone ring downstairs, and his mother answer it. The instruction said: *Glue wheel hub (23a) to wheel drum (27b) and leave to dry before affixing to axle (10).* His mother's footsteps came upstairs, and his bedroom door opened.

'Bernie.'

He looked up. In the light from his desklamp, his mother's face looked oddly pale, a mother's mask.

'Bernie, something terrible's happened.'

He didn't move, the model car still held in his hands. Grown-ups' idea of terrible wasn't always *his* idea of terrible; and so he waited to hear what it was that had brought his mother upstairs, looking so white. Once, in tears, she had told him that his Uncle Walter had died, and he had never been able to understand her grief. Uncle Walter, who smelled of tobacco and garlic, and spat in the street? Why had his mother cried? And now she was saying that something terrible had happened.

'Jane Wyman died this afternoon. And her parents, all of them. They're all dead, the whole family.'

Bernie stared at her and didn't realise that he was as white and cold as she was. 'What?' he asked, but he wasn't conscious of asking it. Jane Wyman was one of his classmates, two rows in front, two to the left. He had seen her this morning, only this morning, with the sun shining through the classroom window and lighting up her bright auburn hair. Jane Wyman, one of the few girls he actually liked. But *dead*?

'They all caught some disease. That's what Mrs

Downing told me. They found them all on the couch, in front of the television. Oh, Bernie, I'm so sorry.'

And it was then, straight away, with the plastic parts of his car still in his hand, that Bernie connected the glass phials of 'secret-obedience potion' with the way in which Michael had died, and with Jane. Because Jane had bought one of his 'secret obedience potions' the day before yesterday, Monday. And Jane had promised that she would try out the potion on her father when he came home from his business trip to Cleveland on Wednesday, which was today. She had wanted her father to let her stay up all evening, and have late-night dinner. But instead she had died, and both of her parents had died with her.

Bernie put down his model. His mother said, 'Would you like something to drink? Your father brought root-beer. Maybe some root-beer, and a pizza?'

'No,' said Bernie. Then, remembering his manners, 'No, thanks, mom.'

His mother said: 'I hope you're not too upset, honey. But I had to tell you. I didn't want you to go to school tomorrow and find out by accident. I didn't want you to have a shock. You know what shocks are. Are you sure you don't want a root-beer? Your father brought it specially for you, wasn't that kind?'

Talking brought the colour back to Mrs Mayer's cheeks. After all, she hadn't actually *known* the Wymans; and since Bernie didn't seem to be desperately upset, maybe it wasn't such a tragedy after all; not as far as they were concerned, was what she meant. It has obviously been quite a tragedy for the Wymans, all of them dead like that on the couch, side by side, the whole family taken in one fell swoop. But then, worse things had happened in the Bible, hadn't they? The first-born had died like flies, and the second-born hadn't had a particularly easy time of it, either.

Bernie sat and looked at his unfinished model. How

could he finish it now – now that he knew how much it had really cost? The water in those phials must have been polluted, and Michael had drunk some and died; and then Jane Wyman had dripped it into her parents' food and they had died, too; and she had probably tasted it as well. All dead. God. What was he going to do? He had sold every one of those six phials at school, and that meant that five other families were still at risk. For all he knew, they might already be dead. It might already be too late to call and save them.

His mother left the room, leaving his door slightly ajar. God, he thought. Double-God. What am I going to do now? If I don't tell someone that all of those glass phials are poison, if I don't warn them, then think of all the people who could die. Dennis Murphy, Clark Kounas, Theresa Natti . . . He could already picture his classmates in his mind's eye, laid out in caskets, their white-faced families all around them, a company of corpses. God, I have to warn them! But then they would find out that it was me who killed the Wyman family. I killed an entire family. I *killed* them. For 80 cents, I killed Jane Wyman and her mother and father. They're going to lock me up in jail for *ever*. Maybe they'll even send me to the chair.

He sat there holding his plastic construction kit, and the tears sprang to his eyes. He felt so rotten and mean and selfish. Those stupid glass phials. That stupid Michael. Now he had ruined his whole life for ever. It was going to be reformatory, or prison, or worse. All for $4.80. God, even Judas had gotten more than that.

Slowly, agonizingly, he crushed the model Mustang to pieces, snapping the suspension and twisting the roof and bending the windshield. Then he buried his face in his hands and sobbed until his throat ached.

Edmond crossed the parking-lot, climbed into his Camaro, and started up the engine. But he didn't pull away immediately. Instead, he sat where he was, his head lowered; feeling emotionally and physically shattered. Doctors should be inured to death, he thought to himself. Old ladies, taken by cancer. Middle-aged men, stricken by heart disease. But this epidemic seemed to be more significant. It seemed to be a challenge not only to his medical competence but to his ability to survive as a practising doctor. He had only just managed to survive the consequences of Arabelle's death. Now it looked as if he was faced with a crisis that was even more difficult, and even more challenging to his personal and professional honour.

He picked up his mobile telephone, and called Lara, his receptionist at the Merrimack Clinic.

'Lara? Dr Chandler here. Any more emergencies?'

'Not so far, doctor. A couple of minors. Sore throats, chills; and one accidentally ingested Batman.'

'Can Dr Colgan cope? I'd like to take a couple of hours off.'

'Dr Colgan's out at Pembroke. But I guess Dr Wang can manage. Can I call you if things get too busy?'

'Just squeeze me a couple of hours, will you?'

A short silence. Then a quiet, sympathetic, 'Okay.' Lara knew what her doctors had to go through, each and every day. She also knew that Edmond had attended seven deaths that afternoon; seven people he had liked and cared for. Even the hardest of doctors found death difficult. They were frightened of it not so much because of the pain and the bereavement it brought, but because (unless it was dignified and natural) it represented failure, their personal failure. Death was a constant reminder that the medical profession was neither magic nor infallible.

Edmond drove home. There was a single soft lamp shining in the living-room window; and upstairs he saw Christy's shadow move across the blind. He eased himself wearily out of his car and walked to the front

224

door jingling his keys. The vodka had done nothing but give him a pounding hangover, and a feeling of nausea in the pit of his stomach. He opened the door and called, 'Christy?'

There was no answer at first. He called, 'Christy?' again, and began to mount the stairs. Christy appeared on the upstairs landing, flushed, her hair awry, tying up the belt of her turquoise silk negligée. She had an extraordinary expression on her face which he had never seen before: fright, almost. Her eyes were wide and yet she didn't seem to be looking at him at all.

'Christy?' he asked her.

'You came back so early,' she said, flustered. 'I wasn't expecting you back till nine or ten.'

'Is everything all right?' he said.

'Well, sure, of course everything's all right. I was just taking a shower, that's all. I thought you were a burglar or something. You scared me.'

He came a little way further up the stairs. Christy stayed where she was, by the half-open bedroom door.

'Has anybody else died since you called me?' she said.

'I haven't heard. Death seems to have allowed me the evening off. I had a few drinks with Oscar, you know? My head's thumping like a Cuban nightclub. I'm just going to get myself a couple of Alka-Seltzer.'

'Well, no,' said Christy. 'Why don't you go downstairs, stretch out on the couch, and I'll bring them down to you.'

He came up to the landing and stood over her. She seemed ridiculously agitated; off-balance and upset. He held her shoulder, and through the thin slippery silk of the negligée, he could feel her trembling.

'What's the matter, are you *cold*?' he asked her.

'It's nothing. I don't know. I don't know what it is. Just let me get you the Alka-Seltzer. I'll be okay. Go on, go downstairs and put your feet up.'

'Christy, I'm quite capable of fixing my own Alka-Seltzer. Remember I'm a doctor.'

'For once, let me pamper you,' she said. She was trying to be coaxing, trying to sound warm and sweet, but the words came out all angular and dismembered, like an early Picasso.

Edmond glanced towards the half-open bedroom door. The nausea and the weariness rose up inside him again, unbidden, and he could hardly believe the question that he asked Christy next, even when he heard it in his own ears. It seemed like a line from some stilted stage-play.

'Is there somebody in there? In the bedroom?'

Christy didn't answer: didn't have to. But for the first time she raised her head and looked him directly in the eyes; and for the first time there was a challenge in her face, as well as guilt.

Edmond pushed her aside and went towards the bedroom. Christy shrilled, '*Edmond*!' and for a second he hesitated.

'Edmond,' she said, trembling. 'Please don't.'

'I think I have to,' he told her.

She turned her face away. 'You couldn't expect me to do anything else,' she said. 'Not after everything you've done to me. Not after all the women that *you've* had.'

He looked at the half-open door. 'Well, well,' he said. 'I thought all that was over and done with. I thought we'd left that kind of thinking behind in New York. It looks like I was being naïve, doesn't it?'

'Edmond, don't go in there. Just take yourself out for a drive, ten minutes, half an hour. Go round the block. When you come back, he won't be here any more. You can just pretend that it never happened.'

'A total stranger just screwed my wife; in my own bed; and I'm supposed to pretend that it never *happened*?

Just *pretend*? Christy, what the hell is going on inside your head? I mean, what the *hell* is going on?'

'Edmond – '

But his anger and his sickness were unstoppable now, and Edmond threw back the bedroom door so that it collided with the edge of the bureau and juddered back again. The bedroom was softly lamp-lit. The white woven bedspread was twisted and crumpled, the heaps of pillows in disarray. There was a smell of heat and perfume and sex in the air. Sitting up in bed, his attempt at a smile distorted like a puppet-face by fear and tension but also by the weird relief of the found-out, was Edmond's brother Malcolm. Darker-skinned, more plumply built, hairier, younger; the one man in the entire cosmos whom Edmond would never be able to forgive Christy for taking as a lover.

Malcolm said, 'I guess you don't want me to come to your party now. Well, *c'est la vie.*' He let out a nervous and irrelevant chuckle, and pulled the sheets a little tighter and more protectively up beneath his shaggy armpits.

Edmond stood for a long time staring at Malcolm in utter explosive disbelief. Christy stood behind him, looking from one brother to the other, twisting the belt of her negligée around and around her hands.

'Aren't you going to *say* something?' asked Malcolm. 'Even if it's nothing more than "get the hell out of my bed"?'

Edmond opened his mouth but at first no words came out. Then he said hoarsely, 'How long has this been going on?'

'Oh, come *on*, now,' said Malcolm. 'Of all the clichés. Don't we deserve better than that?'

'I want to know,' insisted Edmond.

'So that you can judge how hard to hit me?' Malcolm asked. 'Go on, hit me. Get it over with.'

But Christy whispered. 'Since New York.'

Edmond stared at her. 'Since New York? Since New *York*?'

'Since Arabelle, if you want to know the truth. Since the very beginning of you and Arabelle. You thought I didn't know, didn't you? All those late-night business meetings, all those medical conventions. Five conventions in a single month? And the whole time you were walking around as if there were flowers twined in your hair and birds singing around the top of your head.'

She paused for a moment, and then she looked with great gentleness towards Malcolm, and said, 'Malcolm helped me then. He didn't push himself. He genuinely helped me. If it hadn't been for Malcolm, I don't think I would have survived. You never thought about anything that *I* was going through, did you? Not once. But Malcolm helped me to stay alive, at a time when you were slowly killing me.'

'At the expense of his own marriage, I suppose,' said Edmond. 'Not exactly the behaviour of a great moralist.'

'You know all about Dolores,' Malcolm bit back. 'Drunken, hysterical, falling to pieces.'

'Not worth saving, then?' asked Edmond, coldly. 'Trash, garbage. Unfit for a debonair man like you.'

The atmosphere in the bedroom was charged with the overwhelming voltage of family rivalry. Christy moved back almost as if she expected a devastating discharge of power to leap from one brother to the other. She had never in her life seen such total naked hatred. She had never seen two men look at each other with nothing else on their faces but the total need to destroy each other. At that moment, both men frightened her beyond excitement, beyond any kind of desire. The emotion hummed and crackled within them as if they were both sacrificing themselves on the electric chairs of their own fury. As if they would rather burn than forgive.

Christy said, 'Please, Edmond. This isn't the way.'

'You don't want to face up to what you've done, is

that it?' Edmond demanded. 'You screwed my brother. God help you, you screwed my repulsive fat toad of a brother. And you can stand there and tell me this isn't the way. Well, the way to me is crystal clear, my dear. The way is divorce, on the grounds of your fornication with something that should have been aborted at eleven weeks. Of course, there's still the small matter of Dolores, but what do either of you care for Dolores?'

'What did you ever care for *me*?' Christy screamed at him.

'I cared the whole damned world for you once, before you started judging my ethics. I made too much money in Manhattan, remember?'

'God, Edmond, it wasn't the money you made, it was the way that you made it.'

'Arabelle never cared about that.'

'She should have done. She might still be alive today.'

Edmond had swung out at Christy before he realized what he was doing. But she must have half-expected him to hit her, because she instinctively flinched away, and his hand caught her shoulder-blade, and sent her stumbling back against the bedroom chair.

'You touch her again, you quack!' shouted Malcolm, and tugged back the bedcovers, jumping naked out of the bed in protective rage.

Edmond raised a hand to him, palm forwards warningly. 'Get back, Malcolm. I don't want to have to knock you down.'

'You bastard.'

Edmond lowered his hand, and then turned away from his brother with his teeth clenched in a huge effort of self-control. He should have ripped Malcolm to pieces. He should have screamed and roared and torn the whole bedroom apart. He should have smashed mirrors, splattered make up around, wrecked everything which this softly-lit bedroom represented. Jesus Christ, Malcolm and Christy had been fornicating

229

together since *New York*. Three years of clandestine fucking, three years in which his brother had been anointing his wife's vagina with just as much enthusiasm as he had. The thought of it turned his stomach. He had always disliked Malcolm, even as a small boy. And as he had grown older, he had found Malcolm increasingly self-satisfied and obnoxious, an opinionated boor without a single original idea between one fat temple and the other.

What made it worse, he had always found Malcolm bodily unpleasant. Rounded, round face, round shoulders, round thighs, as if he wore a coat of subcutaneous fat. Cold-handed, too, from poor circulation. Other brothers embraced, rolled together, played together. Edmond used to sit beside the tub watching Malcolm wash himself, and revel in the disgust he felt for Malcolm's white hairy skin, his chubby breasts, and the pendulous girdle of fat around his stomach. Malcolm, physically, had inherited the weakest of their parents' features. His mother's plumpness, his father's lack of grace. At grade school his classmates had called him Porpoise, and Edmond had led the taunting.

Maybe, after all these years, this was Malcolm's revenge. Edmond, irrationally, had always believed in destiny, or at least in divine justice. Maybe his marriage to Christy had never been the strong and handsome bond he had thought it to be. Maybe it had been nothing more than a subplot in some Shakespearean tragedy; Edmond and Christy, or What You Will; in which the despised younger brother cuckolds his older sibling in order to pay him back for years of childhood misery.

His marriage may not have been fierce any more; it may have been flawed, and at times uncertain. But as far as he was concerned, even after Arabelle, it had been one of his major hopes for the future.

If only he had known, these past three years, how

empty that hope had been. Eaten away from inside, so that only the shell remained.

Christy said, 'Believe me, Edmond, I didn't want things to turn out like this. I tried so hard.'

'Put some clothes on,' Edmond told Malcolm. 'You look disgusting.'

'Not to Christy, old buddy.'

'Christy never had too much taste,' Edmond snapped.

'Oh, I see. Was that why she stuck with you?'

'Right now, I don't know why the hell she stuck with me. Now, get your clothes on, and get the hell out of here.'

Malcolm sat down on the edge of the bed. Edmond looked away from the thick black hair which grew out of the cleft of his buttocks. Puffing a little, Malcolm pulled on a pair of Hawaiian-style undershorts, all sunsets and cocoanut palms, and then a pair of pale-blue locknit pants.

'I've got to tell you,' he said, rummaging around under the bed for his socks. 'I'm not leaving unless I'm sure that Christy's going to be safe. I'm telling you that now.'

Christy said, 'Edmond, please. Come downstairs. Let's at least try to talk about it.'

'What the hell is there to talk about?' Edmond wanted to know. 'You've been screwing my brother. That's it. There's nothing to talk about.'

'Now, let's be reasonable here, Eddie,' Malcolm began. But he didn't get the chance to finish his sentence. Edmond stalked forward, angry and jealous beyond any kind of control, seized Malcolm's hair, and punched him hard in the face. Malcolm said, 'Eh,' and fell backwards on to the bed, his nose spattering blood all over the white woven bedspread.

'Edmond, for God's sake!' screamed Christy.

'Forget it,' Edmond screeched back at her. His voice

was so high and so angry that he felt as if he had ripped all the flesh away from the inside of his throat. 'I'm leaving, you can keep him. Keep him, fuck him all you like! Do what the hell you want!'

He stalked across to the bureau. On the bed, Malcolm was holding his nose and mumbling. Edmond opened the top two drawers, took out his spare watch, his insurance certificates, his cufflinks. Then, losing the last shreds of patience and self-discipline that had been holding him together he heaved out all of the drawers, one by one, and threw them across the room, scattering handkerchiefs, underwear, socks, and shirts.

'Edmond! You're a stupid, insensitive *bastard*!' Malcolm shouted; and blood sprayed out of his nose all down his chest.

Edmond looked around the bedroom. There had been scenes of love here, or so he had thought; shared emotions; shared ambitions. But he would never come back here again. Whatever he and Christy might have had together, and it must have been something, it was all gone for good.

He walked out of the room with the suddenness of a cartoon robot, summoned from another planet. He ran quickly down the stairs, across the hall, and opened the front door. Before he knew it, he was driving at speed back towards Concord. Without thinking, he checked his own pulse-rate. Too fast, too angry, too crazy. But Christy, with Malcolm? He felt like driving straight off the Frederic E. Everett Highway into the Merrimack River. Doctor Drowns in Death Plunge. But at least it would blot out the thought of that fat white belly on top of Christy, all these years. At least he wouldn't have to think about Christy's fingers, interlaced with that thick black body-hair.

As he passed the Fort Eddy cloverleaf, there was a discreet beep from his mobile phone. He left it until it beeped again; then he picked it up and said, 'Dr Chandler here.'

'Dr Chandler? This is Lara. You've had another emergency call, out on Hazen Drive. The Flanders family, number 1196.'

Edmond didn't answer at first, and Lara said, 'Dr Chandler? Can you hear me?'

'I hear you. I'll be on my way.'

'Are you all right, Dr Chandler? I called your home first, and Mrs Chandler said she didn't know where you were.'

'That's right, Lara,' said Edmond. 'She doesn't.'

Very much later that evening, only twenty minutes before midnight, Edmond sat in his room at the Brick Tower Motor Inn, on South Main Street, and telephoned Dr Bryce at his home number. The Brick Tower's restaurant closed at 8.15, but the captain had brought him a club sandwich, nuts, and two cans of Schlitz. In the corner of the room, the television flickered silently.

The phone rang for a long time before Dr Bryce answered, and when he did he sounded sleepy and irritable.

'Dr Bryce? This is Dr Edmond Chandler, from the Merrimack Clinic.'

'Kind of late, isn't it, Dr Chandler? Can't you call me back in the morning?'

'I'm sorry, sir I'm afraid not. It's about this polio virus. I've been working with Dr Oscar Ford, and it really seems as if – '

'I'm sorry, Dr Chandler,' Dr Bryce interrupted him. 'But I've done everything necessary and everything possible as far as this particular incident is concerned, and I don't want to discuss it any further, not right now.'

'What about Mr Eldridge? What did he say?'

233

'Mr Eldridge made a full report to the Health and Welfare Department, to the governor's office, and to Senator Reynard Kelly. He expressed some concern at the outbreak, just like I did, and he made specific requests for a county-wide quarantine, and certain other measures, including vaccination and blood-tests.'

'And?'

'I told you I didn't want to discuss it right now,' Dr Bryce insisted. 'Now, if you don't mind – '

'But what are you all going to do about it?' Edmond demanded. 'You might have discussed it, you might have agreed it's a problem; but what are you actually going to *do*?'

'For the time being, nothing,' said Dr Bryce. 'Watch and wait.'

'Listen,' said Edmond. 'I have just come back from 1196 Hazen Drive. The Flanders family, four of them, all patients of mine. They're all dead, and the indications are that they were killed by this virus.'

'I'm very sorry to hear that,' said Dr Bryce. 'Believe me, I'm doing everything I can.'

'It's not enough, Dr Bryce,' Edmond insisted. 'We've lost sixteen people, men, women, and children, in less than a day. Tomorrow, it's going to get worse. By the end of the week, half of New Hampshire could be wiped out.'

'I think you're exaggerating a little, don't you, Dr Chandler? I'm sure that we can keep this business under control.'

'It's not under control now. Haven't you seen the autopsy reports? The virus grows stronger every time it replicates itself.'

'That's simply Dr Corning's personal opinion.'

'Well, what's *your* personal opinion?' Edmond demanded. 'That we should let half of the population suffocate to death, because of paralysed respiratory muscles? Is that what you think we should do?'

234

Dr Bryce retaliated, 'Dr Chandler, it's late and I'm tired and I have no wish to discuss this now. I'm doing as much as I can, but my hands are tied by the Department of Safety and the Department of Health and Welfare; not to mention the wishes of Senator Reynard Kelly.'

'Oh, yes? And what does Senator Reynard Kelly have to say about it?'

Dr Bryce paused, and then he said, more quietly, and in an unusually confiding tone, 'Mr Eldridge spoke to Senator Kelly, on three occasions. Each time, Senator Kelly made it clear that the interests of New Hampshire could best be served by maintaining a low profile on this virus. Contain it, identify it, and eradicate it, without making people hysterical.'

'And what do you think?' asked Edmond, carefully.

'What do *I* think? In this particular case, at this particular time, I'm reserving my judgement.'

'Dr Bryce – '

'Listen, Dr Chandler. I know you, and I know something about your record. If I were you, just at this moment, I'd back off. There's a whole lot more to this outbreak than meets the eye.'

'Like what?' Edmond demanded.

But Dr Bryce refused to be drawn. 'I've told you everything I'm going to, just at the moment. My advice is to back off. Whatever Dr Ford says, I'm not insensitive to what he's been saying; and I appreciate that this outbreak could get very much worse. But we're talking about political reality here as well as medicine; and one has to go in hand with the other.'

'So I've learned,' said Edmond, bitterly.

'Well, you've learned something, then,' said Dr Bryce, and put down the phone.

Edmond didn't sleep that night. He was still looking out of the window at the Boston & Maine Railroad yard when the sky began to leak away its darkness, like ink washed out of a linen cloth, and daylight appeared. At 6.30, he showered, and shaved; and by 7 he was sitting in the motel restaurant, waiting for his breakfast, and reading the *Concord Journal*.

On page 3, on the left-hand side, there was a story about 'Hazen Drive Family Found Dead.'

Edmond read it twice, then folded up the newspaper and drank his coffee.

THIRTEEN

It was snowing in Raggarön, when they arrived there. Thick blurry clots of white that whirled and danced and then instantly dissolved into the sea. On their left, the Baltic was dark, and greeny-grey, and visibility was down to less than a hundred feet. Humphrey felt as if they were now very close to Valhalla, the dominion of the Norse gods; or at least to the palace of the Snow Queen. In the past three days he had completely lost touch with any kind of reality. Derbyshire seemed like a memory, and nothing more. He had already missed his flight home by 72 hours, and he expected that by now his sister would have called the police. Unless, of course, Bill Bennett had somehow arranged for him to disappear, without any questions being asked. And from what he had already seen of Bill Bennett, that wouldn't have surprised him in the slightest.

He had said to Bill Bennett only yesterday morning, as they sat over a breakfast of ham and beer at a farm-house near Edebo, 'What if we *never* find him? What are we going to do then?'

But Bill Bennett had only smiled, and cut himself more Emmenthal cheese, as if this whole expedition

236

were nothing more than a game which he had made up for his own amusement.

They had missed Klaus Hermann at Lingslätö. At first, Bill hadn't believed Angelika that he had ever been there, but after a thorough search of the small fishing-cottage which Angelika had said was a Soviet 'safe-house', they had found traces of cigarette ash, and the white plastic cap of a tube of cream which Hermann used to ease the irritation of piles. Humphrey had waited outside while Bill searched the cottage. It had been a misty, mystical morning, and the ocean had beaten a drab message against the seashore. He had wondered whether it was worth trying to make a run for it; but then he had imagined himself stumbling across the rocks and the shingle, panting in his heavy overcoat, and Bill Bennett slowly raising his .38, and dropping him as he ran; and so he had remained where he was, his hands clasped together in their grey knitted gloves, his polished shoes scuffed and dull after walking across the beach, and he had accepted his age and his weakness with as much dignity as he could manage.

Bill had emerged from the cottage and called, 'He's been here, but he's gone. Angelika says he might be trying to get away further up the coast.'

Behind him, Angelika Rangström had looked white and exhausted and cold. But Bill had taken her arm, and led her back towards the car as warmly and as quickly if she were a willing friend. Humphrey had followed them, at a distance, but close enough not to alert Bill's suspicions. It was possible that an opportunity for escape would present itself, sooner or later, and when it did, Humphrey wanted it to be a complete surprise, like something out of Alfred Hitchcock.

At the moment, he very much wanted Bill to trust him.

They had driven north-west at first, on 76; then sharp east to the small fishing-port of Hargshamn, then north-west again to Osthammär. Bill had driven down every single side-street, through every narrow lane, and into every muddy farmyard, asking questions in Swedish, handing out cigarettes and money, smiling, chatting, laying his arm around the shoulders of plump blonde fishwives and grizzled toothless farmers. And always the same question, 'Have you seen two men, one old, white-haired, one younger?' And all the time the weather had blown north-westerly from Gavleborgs Län, and grown thicker, and colder, and more congealed.

Bill Bennett had assured Humphrey that Hermann was cornered: that the Swedish coastguard would be watching every possible port. It was just a question of scouring the local countryside and finding out where Hermann was hiding. Angelika had sat in the back of the car humming tunes by Abba. Humphrey had stared at the endlessly wooded landscape. It had been like a dream. Trees, wooden houses, dark serrated horizons. And now, as they drove into Raggarön, the snow.

They drew up outside a wooden fishing-cottage with a carved verandah. Bill said, 'Stay here,' and twisted around in his seat to pick up his hat from the back. Now that the windshield wipers had stopped, the snow began to collect on the glass, and Humphrey began to feel that they were being entombed alive. Angelika lit a cigarette, and smoked it with her usual exaggerated gestures.

Bill opened up the car door and the wind blew in with the ferocity of smashed glass. Humphrey and Angelika watched him struggle across to the fishing-cottage, his head bowed against the snow. As usual, he had remembered to take the ignition keys with him. Humphrey knew that it was possible to 'hot-wire' a car, but he didn't have the faintest idea how to do it. The few snowflakes which Bill had admitted into the interior of the car melted on the vinyl upholstery.

Angelika said, 'We are chasing a wild goose, don't you think?'

Humphrey shrugged.

'All this, for one old man,' she said. 'And what use will he be when we find him?'

'Do you think we actually will?'

'Your friend Mr Bennett seems to be determined to succeed.'

'Determination isn't everything.'

'No,' said Angelika. 'But he is also very ruthless, in a courteous way.'

'Well, that's the American secret service for you. Always polite. But too trigger-happy for my liking.'

'I haven't forgotten that he killed my friend,' said Angelika, flatly.

Humphrey looked at her, and then sympathetically patted her hand. 'I know. That was a dreadful thing to do. Completely unnecessary, not called for at all. Don't you worry, he's going to have to account for that, one day soon.'

There was a lengthy period of silence between them. The snow softly built up on the car's windows until they could no longer see out. Angelika crushed out her cigarette and then began to rummage in her purse.

'Do you have a penknife?' she asked Humphrey. 'I left some loose thread in my purse and now it's all tangled up.'

Humphrey reached into his inside pocket, and produced a razor-blade in a chrome holder. 'This will probably do, won't it? I use it for cutting fishing-line.'

'Thank you,' she said.

They waited for nearly five minutes more. Then the door of the car abruptly opened, and Bill swung himself into the driver's seat, his hat clotted with white, his shoulders soaking.

'Didn't even ask me inside,' he complained, peeling off his gloves and taking out his keys. 'I guess he

239

thought the weather was pretty mild, for the time of year. Thought I was enjoying it, out there.'

'Any joy?' asked Humphrey.

Bill started up the engine. 'As it happens, yes. Three hours ago, two strangers came past in a blue Volvo and drove out to the far side of the island. There's a kind of an inlet there, apparently.'

'Three hours ago?' asked Humphrey. 'Most probably they've been taken off by now, if there was a boat waiting for them. We must have lost them.'

'Let's go take a look, shall we?' Bill suggested, and swung the Grand Prix sideways across the street, the tyres whinnying and skating on the freshly-fallen snow. 'In this weather, it would have been pretty difficult to bring a boat in through the islands, especially with the coastguard at Ellan on the alert. You never know your luck.'

They drove between tightly-shuttered weatherboard cottages, most of them deserted. The snow squeaked under their wheels like felt. They reached the end of the road, where an outcropping of reddish rock reared out of the sea. Bill cut the engine, and the Grand Prix rolled to a silent stop. 'Come on,' he said, 'let's get out and take a look around on foot.'

'Not me,' said Angelika. 'I am too tired.'

Bill hesitated for a second, and then said, 'Okay. But no funny business, you got it? You stay here and you keep quiet.'

'*Ich verstande, mein führer,*' Angelika nodded, sarcastically.

Humphrey said, 'I'd really rather not go, either. This cold is far too much for me.'

'You're coming, and that's all there is to it,' said Bill. He smiled. 'You're the only one of us who can independently put the finger on Hermann, remember? I can't trust Fru Rangström here, much as I'd like to.'

Humphrey started to protest, but Angelika touched his arm and said, 'Go. It is necessary, you know that.'

'Very well,' said Humphrey. 'But I don't like any of this one bit, and I don't mind saying so.'

He heaved himself out of the car, and into the snow. He almost slid and fell, but he managed awkwardly to seize hold of the open car door, and regain his balance. All the same, he painfully wrenched his shoulder.

'I'm not cut out for this kind of thing, you know,' he told Bill, blinking against the snowflakes.

'Don't give me that, you're a pro,' said Bill. 'Come on, let's take a look over those rocks.'

The north-west wind blew the teeming snow out towards the Baltic, where it was swallowed up. The ocean itself was so dark that it was almost invisible; and unless Humphrey had heard the chilly splashing of waves against the rocks, he would almost have thought that this was the brink of the world, and that there was nothing out there but blackness, and hopelessly-lost souls, and wind-sculptured memorials to long-forgotten scenes of Nordic carnage.

'This way,' Bill ordered him. 'And will you *please* try to keep it as silent as possible?'

'Well, I'll do my best,' said Humphrey, climbing up a large stratified slab. 'Oh, damn it. I've scraped my hand.'

They made their way uphill and a little way inland, eventually managing to reach a large rock which over-hung the inlet. Bill reached the edge first, and peered over, shielding his eyes against the snow with his hand. Almost immediately, he thrust his hand inside his over-coat and tugged out his gun, and waved at Humphrey to keep well back.

'Are they there?' panted Humphrey.

'Get down,' Bill instructed him, irritably. 'If they see you, they'll run. For Christ's sake, get your head down. Your *head*.'

241

Humphrey uncomfortably crouched on the rock. He felt as if he were playing bears. Bill lay flat on the ground, and shouldered his way back to the edge of the rock, and then beckoned Humphrey forward with his gun.

'There,' said Bill. '*Now* tell me that Hermann isn't important.'

Humphrey strained his eyes against the gloom and the dancing snow. On the shoreline, which was distinguishable only because of a faint and broken pattern of foam, he could just make out two men, both of them huddled with cold and tiredness. On the left, parked at an angle, was a bright blue Volvo, its marker lights still shining. The snow slanted over the whole scene like an endlessly falling curtain, and gave it a peculiar feeling of theatricality.

'Look towards the inlet,' said Bill. 'Now – what can you see there?'

Humphrey said, 'In the sea, you mean?'

'That's right. Look, you can just make it out.'

Humphrey took out his handkerchief and wiped the wet from his face. Then he looked even more intently out to sea, and at last managed to make out an extraordinary dark shape, five or six hundred feet away from the shoreline, like the fin of a whale. Between this fin and the shoreline, a small black rubber dinghy was bobbling up and down on the water, making its way infinitely slowly towards the rocks.

'The wind's against them, that's good,' said Bill. He cocked his .38 and lifted its barrel as if he were preparing himself for some heavy-duty shooting.

'You're not going to kill him,' Humphrey insisted.

'We'll have to see what happens.'

'I shall report you, you know, if you start firing indiscriminately.'

'Humphrey,' said Bill. 'I'm *never* indiscriminate.'

'Well, that's what *you* say, but – '

'*Never*. You understand me?'

Humphrey looked away, the snow stinging his cheeks. He felt annoyed and resentful, but at the same time curiously excited. This was the first time in his whole life in which he had been involved in anything real. It was hard to believe he was here, on this snowy night in eastern Sweden, lying on the ground beside a man with a loaded revolver. It was even harder to believe that he and Bill could actually succeed in capturing the men who were huddled on the shore.

'Submarine, I suppose,' said Humphrey, nodding towards the distant fin.

'That's right. Soviet *Serpuchov*-class diesel vessel. Just like the Russians to name a submarine after a city that lies two hundred miles inland, in any direction.'

'What are you going to do?' asked Humphrey. Despite his dislike of Bill's methods, he was extremely reluctant to see Hermann taken off by dinghy, and transmitted safely back by submarine to the Soviet Union. Hermann was, after all, a Nazi war criminal; and he had been working against the West for nearly 40 years, helping to build up Russia's stocks of noxious and infective chemicals, for use in war. Humphrey could still remember his father sitting in that brown brocade armchair by the parlour window at No. 49 Cavendish Street, talking about the gas attacks on the Ypres salient in 1915. 'That gas shrivelled everything it touched, men and vegetation both. I heard my old school chum Ronald screaming, with a burned throat, and burned-up lungs.'

Bill said, 'Follow me. But please, Humphrey, keep quiet. We don't want to alert them before we have to.'

Quickly, moving crabwise, knees bent and head lowered, Bill led the way down the left-hand side of the rocks, and then skirted around until he was no more than twenty or thirty feet away from the two men standing on the shore. Humphrey came after him with as much agility as he could manage, but he barked his shins twice on the rocks, and tore his trousers, and by the time he reached the inlet's uneven beach, he felt sore and bruised and ready to give up.

From their new vantage point, the rubber dinghy looked very much closer to the shore, although it was only making slow progress against the wind; and the Russian submarine's fin seemed to loom far higher over the snow-spotted ocean. Bill said, 'Is that Hermann? The one on the left? For Christ's sake, Humphrey, look at him. Tell me that's Hermann.'

Humphrey cleared his throat. 'It's very hard to be sure.'

'*Look* at him, for Christ's sake. Is that Hermann or isn't it?'

Humphrey knew. He knew it was Hermann. He could tell by the shape of the head, he could tell by the stance. He had memorized so many pictures of Hermann during the war, sketches by prisoners who had been in and out of Herbstwald, photographs by Jewish resistance workers, and student portraits from Heidelberg University before the war. Each of these pictures had helped him to form in his mind a holographic illusion of what Hermann actually looked like; and apart from underestimating Hermann's height, and the exaggerated squareness of his jaw, that illusion had been startlingly accurate.

'Yes,' said Humphrey. 'I believe that's Hermann.'

Bill lifted up his revolver in both hands. But before he aimed it, he said to Humphrey, 'If you push me, or touch me, or try to put me off my shot, then by God I'm going to shoot you, too. So be warned.'

The snow pelted down between them. Bill held the revolver steady, squinting along the sights, for what seemed like forever. Then he fired twice, in quick succession, deafeningly loud shots. A man dropped from the rubber dinghy into the sea, quickly followed by another.

Hermann and his Russian bodyguard crouched down to the ground immediately. But Bill quickly backed away, keeping himself doubled-up, and detoured around the rocks until he was very close to the shoreline on Humphrey's left, completely concealed by the darkness and the snow. Humphrey felt very lonely and confused, with the snow settling all around him, and slowly he began to retreat, making sure that he kept his head out of the firing-line. God, he thought, a holiday in Sweden. What a holiday.

He waited for three or four minutes, huddled up behind a jutting rock. Then he heard Bill calling, 'Hermann! Klaus Hermann! My name's Bennett! I'm an agent of the United States government! I know where you are! Come on out of there with your hands on top of your head! Otherwise, you've got five, and then I start shooting.'

There was a very long silence. Then a German-accented voice called back, 'You're making a mistake, Mr Bennett!'

'No mistake, Hermann,' Bill called back. 'You've been identified!'

'I deny completely that I am Klaus Hermann.'

'Angelika seems to disagree with you.'

'*Angelika*?'

'We have her here, Hermann. She's sitting in the car, waiting for you. Better give yourself up, don't you think. That's if you want to see her again.'

'You're mistaken,' Hermann repeated. His voice was off-key with cold and exhaustion. 'You have the wrong fellow.'

Just then, there was a loud knocking sound from out at sea, like somebody hitting a radiator with a wrench. Sparkling lights winked amidst the snow, and the next thing that Humphrey knew, a burst of heavy machine-gun fire from the Russian submarine was howling and rattling around the rocks and moaning off into the night.

'Oh, my God,' Humphrey said to himself, louder than he had meant to.

'Don't get upset!' Bill called over. 'They can't bring the submarine any closer in to shore. They're firing blind.'

'It doesn't matter *how* they're firing, if they hit us,' Humphrey protested.

Without a word, Bill raised himself up, and fired off a single shot into the darkness. Humphrey heard the light crack of a retaliatory pistol shot; then another; then Bill fired a second time, and there was silence.

Bill strained forward, wiping the snow from his face so that he could see better. At last he called, 'I got him, I think. I can see Hermann, he's down by the shore.'

Humphrey waited for a moment, and then clambered over the rocks to join Bill closer to the shore.

'He may not be Hermann,' said Humphrey.

'Of course he's Hermann, for God's sake.'

'Well, if you're so sure about it, why did you want me to come along?'

Bill deftly reloaded his .38. The snow fell all around him like a Christmas card. Apart from the gun in his hand, he was kneeling in exactly the same pose as one of the adoring Magi.

Humphrey said, 'I suppose you're going to kill him now.'

'It depends.'

'Well, I wash my hands of all this,' said Humphrey.

'Down,' said Bill.

Humphrey immediately dropped his head down; and as he did so a searchlight beam from the submarine's fin swept across the shoreline, and then probed up into the rocks.

It was then that they heard Hermann crying, *'Na pomahsch! Na pomahsch! Eedyeeti syuda!'*

Bill gave Humphrey a broad, self-satisfied wink. 'He's calling for help. Sad, isn't it? They can't get near him.'

Humphrey cautiously raised his head. 'He's not trying to swim for it, is he?'

Bill looked quickly back towards the shoreline. 'I hope not. Jesus, that water's freezing. An old guy like him won't last longer than two or three minutes.'

But, sure enough, Hermann was already knee-deep in the icy surf, and wading out towards the Russian submarine. He was still wearing his heavy overcoat, and his arms were raised in supplication. The searchlight from the submarine's fin abruptly lanced over and illuminated him, and his white hair shone like a crown.

From the submarine, an amplified voice bellowed, *'Stoy! Stoy! Ahpahsnah!'*

Bill said to Humphrey, 'Wait here,' and vaulted over the rocks. Humphrey could see him silhouetted against the floodlight as he ran across the beach, shoulders ducked down, and straight into the water. The Russians didn't fire at him; but then of course they were afraid of hitting Hermann. They kept their searchlight on them both, however, as Bill plunged waist-deep through the waves, and football-tackled Hermann just as he was about to launch himself into the breast-stroke.

'Na pomahsch!' shrieked Hermann, but Bill seized his coat-collar, and dragged him around and back towards the shore. There was a brief flurry of spray and fists, as Hermann struck out at his assailant. But then Bill twisted the old man's arm around his back, and half-shoved him, half-carried him back to the rocks.

Humphrey stayed where he was. He didn't want the Russians picking *him* off, out of pique. After a minute or two, however, Bill and Hermann came panting and struggling around the outcropping, and collapsed side by side both of them noisily shivering, and soaked.

'I will make a formal protest to the American Embassy about this,' said Hermann.

'You're lucky you weren't killed,' Humphrey retorted, petulantly. 'If this fellow hadn't have shot you, then you certainly would have drowned.'

'I see,' said Hermann. His face was luminously white, and his teeth were chattering. 'I'm supposed to thank you both, for saving my life.'

'You're supposed to keep quiet and do what you're told,' said Bill. He looked up over the rocks, to make sure that the Russians hadn't dispatched another dinghy. 'I want to get you back to Stockholm as fast as possible, before any of your Russian friends really understand what's going on.'

'I hope you realize that you are making a grotesque mistake,' said Hermann.

Bill tucked away his gun, and sniffed seawater out of his nose. 'What do you think, Humphrey?' he wanted to know. 'Is this our man, or isn't it? Because if it isn't, I think I'm going to blow his head off, and then bill him for dry-cleaning my coat.'

Humphrey scrutinized the German closely. There was no question about it; never had been, as far as Humphrey was concerned. The nose, the skull, the set of the jaw. They were Hermann's; as distinctive an identification as if he had been wearing a badge saying 'Klaus Hermann, Nazi War Criminals Convention.'

Unhappily, he said, 'This is Klaus Hermann. No mistake. But, I must insist that you don't shoot him.'

'He was trying to escape,' said Bill, with a smile.

'I insist,' Humphrey repeated. 'He may have behaved like a monster, but he must have a trial.'

'I don't really think that's going to be possible. There are too many influential people in the United States who would rather that didn't happen.'

'So, for the sake of those influential people, you're

going to execute a man in cold blood? I shall report you, you know.'

'In that case, I'll have to dispose of you too,' said Bill.

'You wouldn't dare,' Humphrey challenged him.

'You don't think so?'

'No,' said Humphrey slowly. 'I don't think so. There's been enough of a disturbance here, without a British national being shot. Especially since Major Milner knows what's going on.'

Hermann put in, 'Gentlemen, I'm very cold. If you have a car, as you say, perhaps we can then go back to it.'

Bill Bennett glanced back towards the seashore. Then he said, 'Okay. I think I'm going to have to take some advice on this. Let's make our way back. Up the rock there, and along the overhang. The Russians will still be watching us.'

Hermann said to Humphrey, stretching out his hand, 'Will you help me, please? I am very cold.'

Humphrey looked at Bill, and then back at Hermann. 'No,' he said, simply. Then he began to climb unsteadily up and away through the thick of the snowstorm, catching his hands on the rocks, feeling tired and dull and sick with everything that history did to people, and people did to themselves. Behind him, he heard Bill and Hermann speaking to each other quickly in German; and as he reached the ledge he saw Hermann unsteadily scaling the rocks behind him, with Bill pushing him on.

They were almost out of sight of the inlet when they heard a loud flackering sound. Humphrey turned around, bewildered. He had thought for a moment that the Russian submarine was shooting at them again. But then Bill waved towards the north, through the slanting snow; and from the direction of the Ormön inlet, Humphrey saw a helicopter approaching, shining a dazzling white floodlight on the ocean below it. It was an SH-2 Seasprite of the Swedish Navy, and it was quickly followed by another, and another. The three helicopters gathered around the Russian submarine, illuminating it so brightly that it looked as if it were a model, constructed for a stage-set, and the entire inlet around it became theatrically bright.

'What you are now witnessing is an international incident in the making,' smiled Bill. 'And all thanks to young Hermann here.'

'I am not Hermann,' insisted the old man. 'Now, please. I am dying from cold.'

Humphrey said, 'What will they do?'

'The Swedes?' asked Bill. 'It's up to them. But this is the second submarine incursion into Swedish waters in four weeks.'

They continued on their way back to the car as the Seasprites danced and wove around the surfaced submarine. Then, suddenly, there was a deafening roaring noise, as if a huge furnace door had been opened up; and a Sidewinder missile curved downwards from one of the helicopters and struck the Russian submarine directly on the side of its fin.

'Time we left,' said Bill, and hurried them on; until they were out of sight of the inlet, and almost back to the car.

Behind them, there was a shattering explosion. Humphrey felt it on the back of his head, a wall of compressed air; and then a wave of heat. Bill said, 'Come on,' but Humphrey had to turn around and look, and what he saw were chunks of fiery metal turning and turning in the air, amidst the snow, and gouts of flame; and then a sharp abrasive crackle as hundreds of rounds of machine-gun ammunition went off.

'Tomorrow's headlines,' said Bill. 'Come on, Humphrey, let's hustle. I want us out of here as quick as we possibly can.'

The helicopters were still waltzing and roaring

around as Bill swerved the Grand Prix away from the shoreline and drove at high speed back through Raggarön. Bill had pushed Hermann into the front passenger seat, next to him, while Humphrey had clambered into the back with Angelika.

'This is *ein Alpdrücken*,' Hermann garbled. 'I am not the man.'

The sky was still lit with orange fire as they drove across the causeway to the island of Tvärnö. Angelika must have fallen asleep, for she nodded and bounced against Humphrey with every jolt in the pavement. The darkness closed in again; and soon they could see nothing through the windshield but snow, and the white curves of the road, a chaotic pillow-fight. But Bill drove through the tumbling flakes with his foot hard down on the floor, and skated the car through bends and turns, and over the last blinded bridge to the mainland.

They sped southwards on 76 towards Norrtälje; where they would link up with E3, the main motorway back to Stockholm.

Humphrey sat back, feeling oddly deflated that their search for Hermann was over. Now, looking back on it, it had held for him an extraordinary wild excitement, a dangerous expedition in a strange land. He felt an urge to go on to Gavleborgs Län, and Västernorrlands Län, and eventually to Lapland.

He had imagined a last melodramatic confrontation, like the denouement of *Women in Love*, in which Gerald had collapsed in his hollow basin of snow. But now they were driving back through the night; a boring three-hour motor-car journey with a silent American and an elderly German and a Swedish actress who was determinedly asleep.

The helicopter attack had been exciting. But excitement seemed to be so quick. The missiles, and the explosions, they had all been over in a matter of seconds. Humphrey could scarcely believe that it had actually happened.

'*Ein Alpdrücken*,' Hermann repeated.

'What does that mean?' asked Humphrey.

'A nightmare,' Bill translated.

'Ah. How long before we get back to Stockholm?'

'Two, two-and-a-half hours. It depends on the weather.'

Humphrey looked out of the window. Nothing but the night; snowy fields and dark rows of trees.

'Do you think they sunk that submarine?' he asked.

'I doubt it. Damaged, more like. Just enough to keep it on the surface while they make an official complaint to the Soviet ambassador.'

'I see. It looked very dramatic.'

'It was dramatic. It was probably the beginning of World War Three.'

Hermann shifted around in his seat and looked first at Angelika and then at Humphrey.

'She's asleep?' he asked.

'She's exhausted,' said Humphrey.

'Well, it is my fault,' said Hermann. 'I have put her through hell.'

'Seems to be your vocation in life,' commented Bill.

They drove through Brollsta. Hermann dozed for a while, his heavy head resting on his chest. Humphrey found it impossible to rest; his mind felt as if it were tumbling over and over like a child's kaleidoscope.

'You know, I don't understand you at all,' he said to Bill.

'Do you find it necessary to understand me?' asked Bill.

'I don't know. I'm half-afraid of what I might discover if I did.'

'I'm a professional cleaner-upper, that's all,' said Bill. 'An international janitor.'

'No, you're not that at all. I can't make out whether

252

you enjoy what you're doing or not. I keep thinking to myself, if you're so good at what you do, why are you doing it? You seem to be intelligent; almost witty at times. Yet you shoot people as if they were flies.'

Bill said nothing for a few miles. Then he said, 'You forget that I went through Vietnam.'

'Was it really that bad?'

'For some. But it had an effect on almost all of us. It introduced us to our own innate brutality. The trouble is,' and here his eyes flicked up to the rear-view mirror and regarded Humphrey steadily, 'once you've discovered that Mr Hyde inside of you, he refuses to go back into concealment.'

'I'm not sure what you mean.'

'I was trained to kill people, and I actually killed them, all in the line of military duty, that's what I mean. But killing people is one of those strange things that you can get a taste for. That's one of the reasons I do this job. If the urge comes over me; then at least I'll be killing with official permission. Better a Soviet agent than an innocent bystander.'

'You don't think that woman Birgitta was an innocent bystander?' Humphrey demanded.

'She was involved.'

'And was that sufficient justification for killing her?'

Bill's eyes returned to the road. 'Just be thankful I haven't climbed up any tall buildings and started picking people off at random.'

'*Thankful*?' Humphrey, being English, found Bill's psychology completely impossible to follow.

'Killing's a drug,' Bill commented. 'Unfortunately, I happen to be an addict.'

At that moment, Angelika Rangström slid sideways and her head struck Humphrey's knee. Humphrey attempted to raise her up again, but then he realized that she was very cold and very heavy. He struggled to push her into a sitting position, and as he did so he found that his hands were becoming smothered in something cold and sticky and dark.

'My God,' he said.

'What's up?' asked Bill.

'For God's sake, she's dead.'

'What do you mean, she's dead?'

'For God's sake, stop the car, she's dead. She's cut her wrists. The whole car's full of blood.'

Bill steered the Grand Prix into the side of the highway and switched off the engine. Hermann woke up, and lifted his head. *Was ist los?* he asked. He looked quizzically at Bill, and then turned around in his seat to stare at Humphrey. Humphrey was holding up both his hands and they were treacly and crimson with blood, as if he were wearing a pair of melted red rubber gloves.

'Seine Händer,' frowned Hermann. *'Sie haben roten Händer.'*

'It's Fru Rangström,' said Humphrey, desperately upset. 'I'm afraid there's been an accident.'

There was no option now but to call the police. They stayed by the side of the highway with their hazard lights flashing, and the snow tumbling down all around them. They laid Angelika Rangström on a piece of carpet in the snow, and Klaus Hermann stood over her, weeping freely, and every now and then letting out a shivering sob.

Bill paced up and down, quite patient, quite resigned. He had learned years and years ago that this was far from a perfect world.

FOURTEEN

Natalia Vanspronsen was typing up her notes for next week's media campaign in Connecticut when the telephone rang. She picked up the receiver and tucked it under her chin, and carried on typing.

'I wanted to speak to Senator Reynard Kelly,' said a man's voice.

'I'm sorry, Senator Kelly isn't here right now. This is Natalia Vanspronsen, I'm his media assistant. Can I help you at all?'

'Well, I don't think so. I have to speak to the senator personally. Do you knew where I could get hold of him?'

'He and Mrs Kelly are on their way back to Washington right now. You could try his office at the Senate. Do you have the number?'

'Damn it,' said the man. Then, 'I'm sorry, I apologize, I had hoped to speak to him face-to-face.'

'He's real busy right now. You know he's declared himself a candidate for Presidential nomination?'

'I read it in the paper. Listen – does he have an assistant, somebody I can discuss a serious problem with?'

Natalia stopped typing. She took the telephone out from under her chin and held it in her hand. 'It depends what kind of problem,' she said. Something in the man's voice had alerted her seventh sense for trouble. 'Can you tell me who you are? Perhaps I can do something to help.'

'Dr Edmond Chandler. I'm a paediatrician at the Merrimack Clinic. The point is I believe we have the beginnings of a polio epidemic here in Concord, and

255

yet it seems as if there's been some kind of cover-up going on. Well, when I say cover-up, I don't exactly mean Watergate; but the impression I get is that for some reason Senator Kelly has directed that everybody should keep it under wraps.'

Natalia looked towards the window. Outside there was autumn sunlight, and a view of The Colonnades' fruit orchards; the pear trees naked now, and pruned for winter. 'I, er, I'd like to know who gave you that impression,' she said. Then, 'A *polio* epidemic? I haven't heard anything about it on the news. And nothing's come on to the senator's desk.'

'Believe me, the senator knows about it. The Medical Referee has sent him a note, and so has the Commissioner for Health and Welfare.'

'Well, how serious is it?'

'As of right now, we've had nineteen deaths. Is that serious enough? I attended one about an hour ago, and that's why I'm calling. If I can't talk to the senator and find out what's going on here, I'm going to go straight to the media.'

'Have you talked to the Medical Referee?' asked Natalia. Quickly, worriedly, she jotted down notes on her pad.

'No response at all. He says he's aware of the situation, but intends to keep a watch on it, and that's as far as he's prepared to go. I can tell you something, that isn't enough. There's a cover-up here, of some sort, and if I can't get anything done about it, then I intend to blow the whistle.'

'Dr Chandler,' said Natalia, in her softest and most persuasive voice, 'can I please ask you not to contact the media until we've had a chance to check this out? I can't believe for a moment that anything as serious as a polio epidemic would be covered up; especially not by Senator Kelly. As you know he's a strong advocate of public medicine.'

'I'm not going to wait all day,' said Edmond. 'My patients are dying and I want something done.'

'But, please, don't go to the media just yet. Not until I've had a word with the senator himself. There could well be a very good reason why this outbreak is being kept discreet, and if you go to the media without consultation – well, it could have a very negative effect. Panic, for instance, or people leaving the county and spreading it around uncontrolled.'

Edmond said testily, 'I don't think I need a media assistant to tell me the consequences of letting this epidemic get out of control. Now, how long are you going to be?'

'I'm going to contact the senator right now.'

'And then what?'

'Well – where can I reach you?'

'Either at the Merrimack Clinic or my private office in East Concord on the Brick Tower Motor Inn. I'm at the clinic right now.'

'The Brick Tower Motor Inn?' asked Natalia, raising an eyebrow.

'That's what I said. South Main Street, 224–9565.'

'I'll be right back.'

Natalia put down the phone and immediately punched out Len Gieves' number. It rang and rang, but Len Gieves didn't answer. He must have left for Stamford already. She tried Dick Elmwood's phone, but he had gone, too. She tossed back her hair tensely, and opened up her telephone book to find Reynard's number in Washington.

It was while she was punching out this number that there was a rap at her door, and Walt Seabrook put his head in. 'Hi. Oh, I'm sorry. I didn't realize you were on the phone.'

'That's okay. Come in.'

Walt Seabrook went to the window and looked out

over the orchard. 'Some place here, isn't it? It would make a terrific country club.'

Natalia got through to Washington. The nasal voice of Reynard's personal secretary said, 'I'm sorry, the senator hasn't arrived at the office yet.'

'Could you tell him it's Natalia Vanspronsen and it's a crisis.'

'A crisis?' asked Walt Seabrook, as Natalia put down the phone.

Natalia sat back, biting her lip.

'Hey, that's a very serious expression you're wearing right there,' Walt Seabrook chided her. 'I hope this isn't a *real* crisis.'

'It could be,' said Natalia, standing up. 'I'm not really sure yet. Listen, Walt, you're a doctor. Do you know anything at all about a polio epidemic in Concord?'

'A polio epidemic?' Walt frowned. 'Not a thing. You're not serious are you? Oh, come on, we haven't had a polio epidemic in the continental United States since 1954. Polio doesn't even rate as a percentile cause of death these days, not in the selective mortality statistics. It comes under "all other diseases".'

'I've had a doctor on the phone and he says there's the beginnings of a polio epidemic in Concord. He says nineteen people have already died. Worse than that, he's kind of suggesting that Reynard already knows about it and has been trying to keep it quiet.'

Walt stared at Natalia in bewilderment. 'Reynard knows about an epidemic and hasn't told anybody?'

'That's what he's saying.'

'Well, who is he?'

'Dr Edmond Chandler, a paediatrician at the Merrimack Clinic.'

Walt Seabrook said, 'Listen, we'd better talk to this man. If I'm going to be Assistant Secretary for Health, the last thing I want to have on my record is a covered-up epidemic.'

'I think we'd better talk to Reynard first.'

'Reynard won't get to Washington for another three or four hours yet. We've got to talk to this joker before he starts making any more accusations.'

Natalia thought for a second, and then said, 'Okay. I'll get my jacket.'

'A polio epidemic,' Walt repeated. 'Listen, it's got to be a put-on.

'It didn't sound like it,' said Natalia. She took out her pale grey tweed jacket and put it on over her white silk blouse. She tucked her spectacles into her hair, and packed her notebook into her purse.

'He hasn't talked to the media yet?' asked Walt.

'Not so far. But he will, unless we do something positive.'

'This is all I need,' said Walt. 'I was going to play golf with the hospital superintendent today. We haven't played together in six years. This is just my luck, you know that?'

'You're worried about golf? If this turns out as bad as I think it's going to turn out, you're going to be worrying about the future of the whole world.'

They walked side by side along the decoratively-carpeted landing, and then down the wide sweeping staircase. Walt said testily, 'Greta's right, you know. He's incapable of doing anything straight. He's a natural twister. He wouldn't know the truth if it came up to him and punched him on the nose.'

Eunice was walking across the hallway as they came downstairs, and said, 'You're going out, Ms Vanspronsen? Dr Seabrook?'

'We shouldn't be much longer than an hour or so.'

'Can I say where you are, if anybody calls?'

'The Merrimack Clinic, okay? Talking to Dr Chandler.'

They crossed the driveway to the old white-painted stables, where all the cars were garaged. The day was sharp and sunny, and as far as Natalia could see, the hills and fields were bright with the colours of fall, red maples, and yellow larches, and birches like showers of coins. They climbed into Natalia's silver BMW, and drove out towards Concord.

Walt Seabrook said, as they passed through the gates of The Colonnades, 'You know something? I have a very bad feeling about this.'

Denzil Forbes was seated at a corner table in the bar of the Marquette Hotel in Wauwatosa when the red-jacketed waitress came over with a telephone, and said, 'You're Mr Hope?'

'That's right. Thanks,' said Denzil, and reached into his inside pocket for his billfold, to tip the girl a dollar. Then he picked up the phone and said, 'Mr Hope here.'

The voice on the other end of the line sounded small and far away; and there was a long-distance twanging on the line. Most of the black vinyl-covered banquettes around Denzil were empty; it was almost midnight, after all; but the jukebox was still playing and he had to put his finger in his ear to squash out the sound of the Bee Gees.

'I got your message,' said the voice. 'I've talked to the principals involved, and they're very interested. They're not sure about the price though. The price you're asking is very steep.'

'They think so? Well, that's too bad.'

'They want to see the finished product first, before they put up any money.

'I'm sorry, Mr Billings. It's cash up front or nothing. This isn't something I can do twice, after all.'

There was a pause on the other end of the line. Then the voice said, 'You won't come down from 1.1 million?'

'That's the price. Come on, Mr Billings; this is Chiffon Trent we're talking about. You've seen the Polaroids, you know this is on the level.'

'There's a lot of risk involved.'

'Are you telling *me*? Listen – either you want in to the movie or else I go to the Chinaman. You want me to go to the Chinaman?'

'Of course not, Mr Hope. But this is a lot of lettuce we're talking about here, and supposing you skip? That's what the principals are worried about. With that much lettuce, you could disappear and never resurface.'

Denzil beckoned to the waitress to bring him another drink. Into the phone, he said, 'Are they stupid or something? I've got a 15 per cent royalty in perpetuity. That's going to make me a million-one fifty times over. Why should I skip?'

Another pause, then, 'Okay . . . but they want to know how you're going to do it. You haven't even sent down an outline.'

'You think we're making *Snow White and the Seven Dwarfs*?'

'Listen, Mr Hope, they're probably willing to put up the money but they want to know how you're going to do it.'

'All right,' Denzil agreed, impatiently. 'Roughly what we're going to do is this. Make six regular one-hour videos, over the next three days, then bring in four or five guys for the final torture scenario.'

'The principals don't want phony.'

'They won't get phony. They'll get whatever they want. Pliers, broomhandles, whatever they want.'

There was an even longer pause. 'This is an open line, right?'

'Don't worry about it. I'm in a bar. I never been here before and I'll never come here again.'

'You're not taping any of this?'

'Listen, Mr Billings, do you want me to put down the phone on you?'

'We're careful, that's all. It doesn't seem to us like *you're* being too careful.'

'I'm as careful as I need to be. You want me to wear a mask, and speak through a handkerchief? Just remember this girl's already officially dead and buried. It's not like there's anybody looking for her.'

'All right,' said the voice, reluctantly. There was a moment's conversation on the other end of the phone with somebody else. Then, 'They just want to know how you're going to do it. You know, the *dénouement*.'

'They've got a choice. The straightforward shot through the head in mid-hump; or strangling, some of them like; although we did a burning once and that was good. Seems kind of appropriate, in the circumstances.'

Two or three minutes' silence. Denzil waited patiently, examining his very clean fingernails and smiling at the waitress when she brought him a fresh frozen daiquiri. 'Business, business, business,' he told her, and she smiled back at him.

Eventually, the voice on the other end of the line said, 'They like the burning. What are we talking about, gasoline?'

'I have a warehouse where I can do it.'

'Okay, then. They'll put the money where you asked for it, no later than tomorrow afternoon.'

'Sooner if you can. I'm not shooting one single inch of tape until it's there.'

'All right, Mr Hope. I think we understand where you're coming from. My principals just want to say that for 1.1 million they expect the best, you understand me?'

'They'll get their money's worth. Not a cent more, not a cent less.'

'Good evening, Mr Hope.'

'Same to you, Mr Billings.'

Denzil sat for a long time finishing his drink. The Bee Gees sang '*Ah – ah – ah – ah – staying alive, staying alive.*' Then Denzil beckoned to the waitress and said, 'What's your name, honey?'

'Sally, sir. Why?'

A noisy impromptu party was already in progress at the Georgetown apartment of Reynard's younger brother Lincoln when Reynard and Greta arrived from the airport. There was Dom Perignon champagne and Iranian caviare, and five or six of those stunning toothy girls who always seem to hover around Lincoln like a cloud of butterflies. His 'cheer-leaders', he called them. His wife called them his 'ego-masseuses'.

Senator Willard Pearson of Alabama was there; the fat and powerful chairman of the committee for Banking, Housing, and Urban Affairs; so was Senator Pete Kolaski, the hard-headed northern Democrat whom Reynard was considering as his Attorney-General designate. And the noisiness of the crowd was doubled by Robert Trump, the liberal novelist; and Phil Weston, the young movie actor who had made *All Of Our Days*, the controversial film about the Vietnam generation.

Lincoln came over and hugged Reynard and slapped him on the back; and most of the party cheered.

'What a declaration speech!' Lincoln enthused. 'That was a declaration speech with *everything*: timing, relevance, dignity, and warmth. Did you see what John Glenn had to say about it?'

Reynard smiled, a little cagily. 'You can't blame him, I suppose.'

'And *Greta*, how are you, it seems like forever,' said Lincoln, kissing her on both cheeks. Greta was looking cuttingly stylish in a grey suit by Bill Blass, and a diamond spray brooch the size of a small laurelbush. Lincoln took her arm and led her into his white, white-carpeted apartment, where politicians and campaign supporters and newspeople now sprawled on the white-leather furniture, or sat on the white-railed stairs, or tangled in the white-cushioned conversation pit.

Reynard shook a few hands, and accepted a few congratulations, and spent a few minutes talking to Senator Pearson about campaign finance; but then he excused himself and called Lincoln across to the side of the room. 'Listen,' he said, 'something's come up. Sort of a hiccup.'

'A hiccup?' asked Lincoln. He smiled and raised his champagne glass to a passing acquaintance. He was leaner and sharper-looking than Reynard, although his hair was whiter, and his face was always dark orange, from too much sunlamping. He looked closely at Reynard, and said, 'What do you mean by a *hiccup*?'

'Come into the study,' said Reynard.

'And leave the party?'

'Just for a minute,' Reynard insisted.

'Well, okay. But don't you just adore that redhead in the corner? The one in blue? I found her in Macon, Georgia, of all places. She votes with her tits.'

Reynard impatiently took Lincoln through to the study, which was equally stark and equally white, with Italian stainless-steel lamps and leather chairs that looked like enormous white catcher's mitts.

'I thought everything was grody to the max,' said Lincoln. 'Dick Elmwood was on the phone this morning and he said that you were almost certain to clean up in New England, especially since New Hampshire is your home turf, and New Hampshire votes first.'

'Something's happened, something's come up,' said Reynard, edgily. 'It's an epidemic, of sorts.'

'An *epidemic*? You mean a political epidemic or a disease-type epidemic?'

'A disease. A kind of polio.'

'*Where*? I haven't heard anything about it.'

'In Concord. So far, I don't know, fifteen or twenty people have died.

Lincoln drained his champagne and went across to

the icebox to find another bottle. 'I thought more or less everybody was vaccinated against polio.'

'Not against this polio, they're not. It's very swift, very fast-breeding, and it can kill you in a couple of hours. Apparently, it – suffocates you, by paralysing your respiratory system.'

Lincoln eased the cork out of the narrow neck of the Dom Perignon bottle. 'I don't really see why you're so worried. I mean, you could actually make some capital out of it, couldn't you? Presidential candidate urges epidemic relief. They could take some shots of you weeping by some poor kid's bedside. You think you can manage some real tears?'

The cork came out with a satisfying *pssh*, and Lincoln poured them both another glassful. He looked at Reynard intently as he was doing so, and said, 'Show the media you know how to cope in a crisis. Come January, you'll be off and running, and not even Walter Mondale will be able to catch you.'

'You're not listening to me, Linc,' said Reynard. 'This epidemic is very, very serious. The virus is virtually unstoppable. By next week, the whole of Merrimack County could be dead or dying. The virus gains strength with every regeneration. By next month, there may not be anybody left in New England to vote for me, come January.'

Lincoln said nothing at first, but then he sat down in one of the catcher's-mitt chairs, and crossed his legs, and stared at Reynard acutely. 'There's *more* to this, too, isn't there? Am I right? It's not just the epidemic you're worried about.'

'No, you're right. The point is, the disease spread from *my* land. It came from my estate. So in a way I'm partly responsible. In fact, a great many people may say later that I'm wholly responsible.'

'The disease spread from your land? How? What are you talking about?'

'I can't explain any more than that, Linc. But take it from me, if any of this comes out, we're finished.'

'*We're* finished?'

Reynard turned around and jabbed a finger at his brother with all the abruptness of a street-fighter. 'Don't forget who you are and why you're so successful in politics, that's all.'

'Are you threatening me, or what?' Lincoln demanded. 'First of all you come out with some half-assed story about an epidemic – '

'There's nothing half-assed about this particular epidemic, I can assure you,' Reynard interrupted him. 'It comes from something that we were doing on the estates during the war. That's all I can tell you.'

'What was it, some kind of experiment? Nobody ever told *me*.' Jesus, *Reynard*.

'You were too young. You wouldn't have understood. Besides, it had to be kept a total secret.'

'Look, you're asking me for help and yet you won't tell me what's going on. Well, Reynard, you listen to this, unless you explain *exactly* what it is that you're so damn worried about; unless you fill me in completely; then you can *forget* any help, now or ever. I've had just about enough of this big-brother "I-know-better-than-you" stuff, ever since I was knee high.'

Reynard was about to bark something; but then he pressed his mouth shut and took a deep flaring breath through his nostrils to control himself. The truth was that he was in a state of completely unprecedented panic. He had managed to keep Eldridge quiet, at least, for the time being, but he knew that Eldridge was a determined and responsible man, and wouldn't be silenced for very long; not unless Reynard could come up with some real boiler-plate reasons why. He also knew that any one of the doctors or pathologists in Concord who were having to deal with the epidemic – might take it into his head to contact the newspapers or the television channels at any moment. The only lever he had was a mucky little piece of political scandal which he could use against the state's Attorney General, but if he stooped to using that, he would gain himself nothing more than a day or two, or maybe only an hour or two; and in return he would certainly lose for ever the support of some of New Hampshire's key government executives.

Usually, Reynard had an unerring talent for formulating a comprehensive political game-plan to deal with almost any crisis which came his way. He had survived Winnipesaukee by playing off the Water Resources Board against the Department of Resources and Economic Development, until everybody was blaming everybody else, but nobody was blaming him. He had secured massive support for his Presidential candidacy by bribing Greta and Walter Seabrook.

Now, however, he felt as if he were in a devastating spin. If he tried to keep the polio epidemic under wraps for very much longer, he would almost certainly be accused of deliberately playing down a vicious sickness for the sake of protecting the business interests of his home city. If, on the other hand, he publicly announced that there was a polio outbreak, there would be confusion and recrimination and mass chaos, and he would be held responsible for all of it.

Even worse, the Health and Welfare Department would quickly send in trained medical researchers, and how long would it be before one of them was able to trace the virus back to its source? And when *that* happened . . .

Reynard felt as if everything for which he had worked during forty years of politics, everything for which he had lived his life, was teetering beneath him on the very edge of collapse.

He remembered that night in 1944 as if it were the night before last. To establish his personal alibi, he had been dining and dancing that night at the PeeWee Club in Manhattan with Lydia Jennings, the beautiful wife of Congressman Richard Jennings. It was typical of Reynard's lateral thinking that he had chosen to create an alibi which itself was slightly scandalous. If he said he was dating another man's wife, why, he *must* be telling the truth. Anybody else would have said that they were visiting their mother, or going to confession, or reading to the sick at Havenwood.

The barman had called him over to the telephone. Ted Peale's voice had said, croakily, 'Is it storming down there in New York?'

'I don't think so,' Reynard had told him. 'I haven't been outside in three hours. Why, is it storming up there?'

'It's Hades up here. Let me tell you. Absolute Hades.'

'And?'

'Well, we think it came in.'

'You *think* it came in? What do you mean, you *think* it came in?'

'I don't know. Maybe we heard it and maybe we didn't. Michael swore it came right overhead. But, I don't know. We don't have any radio contact now. Lost that totally. I'd say that it's probably gone down over Snap Town, or Penacook.'

'You mean crashed?'

'That's about the size of it.'

'Jesus Christ.'

And then dancing the rest of the evening with Lydia Jennings, cheek-to-cheek, trying not to sweat, trying not to show that he was worried, waiting all the time for that phone call which never came, that phone call which would have told him that everything was all right, that Condor was down, that he didn't have to worry any longer.

And the band playing *Blue Baby*:

'*Blue baby, don't say you're sad,*

Tell me that you'll always stick around . . .'

Lincoln said, more soberly, 'If this really is serious, Reynard . . .'

Reynard went to the window and looked out over the grey curve of the Potomac, and the dim outline of Theodore Roosevelt Island. 'You know something,' he said, 'the world changes and the public mood changes every couple of months, and if you really believe in something, consistently, strongly – well, you can get caught out. You know – taken by surprise. During the war, things were different. Oh, sure, we tell the revised version these days. How everybody supported the war effort, how we all wanted to crush Hitler . . . But that wasn't the way it was, not at all. In 1943, in 1944, there were still millions of Americans who believed in what Germany was doing. A strong, unified Europe would have given us a powerful counterbalance to the U.S. economy; helped us to get over the hill. We would have had none of this recession, none of this NATO business, none of this weakness in the face of the Soviets.'

'What are you trying to tell me, Reynard?' Lincoln asked him. 'Hitler, NATO, what are you saying? I don't understand.'

'Well, I don't understand it, either, not now. History turned out different. But it needn't have done. Just imagine what the world would have been like now, if Hitler had been allowed to stay in charge of Europe. Well, that all seems pretty old-fashioned now, doesn't it? But in those days, there were plenty of young American politicians who believed in what Hitler was doing.'

'In Auschwitz? And Belsen? You believed in that?'

'We didn't *know*, Linc. We just didn't know. And if Hitler had been allowed to stay in charge, well, who can say? The whole problem would have sorted itself out in time. A lot of people died in that war, Linc. Nearly three hundred thousand Americans died in battle. It was a war, the whole result of an economic and social turmoil. The world develops, changes, people become casualties. But go ahead – you ask anybody today if they would trade the world they have now for the world they had in 1942; and I guarantee to you that not one of them would say yes.'

'Reynard,' Lincoln chided him, quite gently. 'Reynard, you're rambling. I don't know what this is all about, but you're rambling.'

'I'm trying to *explain*, Linc. I'm trying to make you understand why we did it.'

'Did *what*, Reynard? I mean – is this something to do with this virus? You cooked up this virus in 1944? I mean, for what? What did you do? I can't help you unless you tell me.'

Reynard sat down, and slowly washed his face with his hands. 'You're going to judge me, Lincoln. You're going to weigh me in the scales and you're going to find me wanting.'

He looked up. 'I'm a hero, do you know that? One of the great hero-figures of the 20th century. When they come to write the political history of the 1970s and the 1980s, my name's going to be up there along with the best of them. Reynard Kelly. The man who carried the work of Jack Kennedy and LBJ into the 1980s, and beyond . . . the one man who kept the faith.'

He was silent for a long moment, and then he said, pleadingly, 'The thing is, you're going to have to help me, Linc. Otherwise this administration is going to be stillborn even before it gets itself embedded in the womb. I have everything it takes to be President, Linc, but you must help me.'

Lincoln poured himself some more champagne. This was his sixth glass; but although his face had turned even more violently orange, he was still extremely sober. He had never seen his brother like this before, and he had certainly never heard him talk this way, even at his drunkest.

Reynard said, 'I've had to carry this cross now for forty years. Forty years, just coming up to our ruby anniversary. How about a toast, forty years, my cross and me. *Skol*!'

'Reynard – ' said Lincoln.

'No, no, no. Don't "Reynard" me, Linc, whatever you do. Let me tell you something. In the spring of 1944, after I'd been out boating with a girl called Frances Couderay on Lake Massebesic, I was approached by a man who said his name was Johnson. I could pick him out today, if you showed him to me. Small spectacles, big nose, and a ridiculous laugh. Ridiculous, for a man. Frances Couderay said he sounded like a hyena. Well, anyway, this man Johnson said I could help to end the war, if I wanted to; and so naturally I listened to what he had to say.'

'A man came up to you after a boating trip and said you could help to end the war? And you believed him?'

Reynard raised a hand. 'Those were much more innocent times, let me tell you. People took more on face value than they do today. A man's expression was his guarantee, and for most people that was enough.'

'Must have been *great* times,' said Lincoln, sarcastically.

'You can mock, but they were,' retorted Reynard. 'Did you ever know what it was like, driving through Mine La Motte, Missouri, in a ragtop Chrysler Saratoga . . . two years old, of course, because we stopped car production in 1942 . . . but do you know what that *felt* like? You were a kid in those days. But they were great days.'

'Reynard,' said Lincoln, worriedly. 'Reynard, why don't I get you some coffee? Come on, Reynard; you're not making too much sense here. Really.'

Reynard stared at the floor for a long time. Then he

said, 'God Linc, I don't know what to do. This one, I can't work out how to handle. We've got to talk this over, get it all straightened out before the media get their hands on it – and there's twenty people dead already. Twenty. And all of those bodies are laid at my door, Linc. All of those were people were my responsibility.'

'So some virus escaped from your property? Or somebody stole it? Is that it, somebody stole it? Was it in a test-tube or something? How can you blame yourself? How can *anybody* blame you? It wasn't your fault; we can produce patent proof of that.'

Reynard said dully, 'They'll find out how old the virus is; that's for sure; and how it was developed. Have you seen the forensic equipment they use these days? I've already read the preliminary virology reports, from HEW. Well, half of the stuff I couldn't understand, but the virologist made it quite clear that he believed the virus had been artificially developed, and that it was growing stronger every time it infected someone, and that as yet there was no known antidote.'

Lincoln said, 'You'd better tell me the whole story, Reynard. This way, I can't help you at all.'

Reynard finished his champagne, and looked down into the bottom of his glass. 'I'm not drunk, you know,' he told his brother.

'I know. But carry on. Tell me what happened.'

'Well,' said Reynard, wearily, 'you may or may not know it, but during the war, the Germans had one airplane that was capable of flying the Atlantic nonstop. It was the Focke-Wulf 200, and it was mostly used to harass the merchant fleets that supplied Britain with food and armaments after Dunkirk. Tremendous airplane, way ahead of its time. Churchill called it the 'scourge of the Atlantic.' It went out of active service in 1944, because it was actually designed as nothing more than an airliner, and eventually it couldn't stand up to the rigours of combat duty, or attacks by British fighter patrols. But Hitler several times considered sending one of these airplanes to drop bombs on New York, as a show of strength, and one of them flew the Atlantic and actually dropped a bomb on Glace Bay, Nova Scotia, just to prove to Hitler and Göring that an attack on New York was feasible.'

Lincoln said nothing. By now, however, he was quite convinced that the strain of preparing and declaring his candidacy had tired his brother to the point of semi-breakdown, and that he was going to have to usher everybody discreetly out of the party and call for Dr Lansing.

But Reynard was too preoccupied to be aware of Lincoln's reservations about his sanity, and he continued to drink, and pace up and down, and relate disjointedly the story behind the six glass phials which Michael Osman had found in the woods at Conant's Acre.

'This man Johnson met me at the old Parkway Motel on Manchester Street, and told me that Hitler had already drawn up outline plans for the invasion of the United States. Hitler had decided apparently that a full-scale military assault was out of the question. At that stage of war, he had neither the finance nor the resources to meet the United States head-on. Apart from that, he knew that he already had millions of sympathizers within the United States, and that it would probably take only a single strong move to force a United States truce. Six Wall Street banks had already pledged him support if he could pull it off; and the list of major industrialists who said they would go along with him would be worth a fortune if you could find it today.'

Lincoln said, a little testily, 'You believed all this?'

'Johnson showed me his credentials. Papers, copies of letters, notes from American financiers. But what

273

really convinced me was when he showed me a letter from Henry Weidman, and I recognized Weidman's initials.'

'But you weren't a Nazi,' said Lincoln. 'Why did you even listen to this man Johnson?'

'You're looking at this thing with modern eyes,' Reynard told him. 'In those days, before we knew what the outcome of the war was going to be, there were still plenty of people within the United States who felt that by fighting against Germany we were fighting our friends. And what did we care about some power-struggle in Europe? Much better to let the best country win and leave it at that. Americans weren't very internationally-minded then, Linc. Besides, whatever you say, we didn't know anything about Auschwitz, or Ravensbruck. We just didn't *know*.'

'But you weren't *politically* a Nazi.'

'I was a nationalist; and I still am. I sympathized with many of the Nazi ideals. Lots of us did. I've changed since those days, of course. The war, and the bomb, and the 1950s, they changed us all. It was finding out about the Holocaust that changed me, more than anything. I could understand persecution, particularly at a time when Germany was struggling for its survival. But I could never understand that.

'So where does this airplane fit in?' asked Lincoln. 'This Focke-Wulf 200 or whatever you call it? Reynard, you're not making any sense whatsoever. And what does this epidemic have to do with it?'

Reynard said, 'You have to help me, Linc.'

'I'll help you.'

'Then don't ask me any more.'

'Reynard, you have to tell me what's going on.'

'Don't ask me, okay? Just help me. You're my brother.'

Lincoln sat back in his chair in exasperation. 'If any of this is true, we're in deep, deep trouble. Now, what is all this about this airplane? Come on, Reynard, if I don't know, then I'm working in the dark. Were you involved in some kind of German bombing raid, or what?'

Reynard at last sat down. He loosened his necktie with his finger, and then he said, 'Don't judge me, all right? Remember the times were different, more uncertain. I was thinking of the family's future. I never guessed – well, I never guessed, let's leave it at that.'

'More champagne?' asked Lincoln, but Reynard ignored him.

Slowly, precisely, in a much more collected voice, Reynard said, 'I met Johnson three times. On the third occasion he made it clear that in any kind of treaty between Germany and the United States, I would play a powerful political rôle. I suppose I actually believed that I was doing something great; something of international importance. Anyway, the plan was that the Germans should fly into the United States six phials of a newly-developed virus – a very potent piece of microbiological warfare which one of their leading doctors had developed in the 1930s. The airplane was supposed to land at The Colonnades, which was well within the limits of its range if it took off from Paris. Johnson and his agents would take the virus and distribute five phials of it around the United States, at military centres in San Francisco, Fort Mead, Fort Rucker, and a couple of other places I forget.'

'You were going to spread an epidemic amongst the U.S. Forces?' asked Lincoln, incredulously.

Reynard shook his head. 'There was no serious intention of actually releasing the virus. Once the phials were distributed, we were simply going to communicate with President Roosevelt and his cabinet, and tell him that Adolf Hitler was very interested in a truce between our two nations; and that it would be much more reasonable of the President to comply than to carry on fighting. The

Focke-Wulf airplane would be shown to the President as proof that the mission had actually been carried out, and the one remaining phial of virus would be given to the Pentagon for analysis, so that they would understand fully the pressure they were under.'

'You were prepared to blackmail the entire country? Your own country to which you had pledged complete loyalty and allegiance? You were actually prepared to act like a traitor? Jesus God, Reynard, what the hell were you *thinking* about?'

'I keep telling you, things were different then,' Reynard growled at him. 'If everything had gone according to plan, this family could have been the wealthiest and most influential dynasty in America. Don't you believe in the Kellys even that much?'

'I don't know what the hell to believe in.'

'Anyway,' said Reynard, breathing heavily, 'the question doesn't arise. The airplane arrived at New Hampshire in a heavy electric storm, and just before landing we lost contact with it. It crashed somewhere, we searched but we never found out where. Well, you know how thick some of the woods are. Even an airplane that size could have vanished; and of course I didn't dare to send out anybody to look for it who wasn't involved in the plan.'

'How many people knew about it?' asked Lincoln. 'More pertinently, how many of these people are still alive today?'

'Only three people knew, including myself; and the Germans, of course. Michael Rearden, our groundsman, and Ted Peale. Michael Rearden's dead now, but Ted Peale's still alive. He lives in Florida.'

'Do you think there's any chance of him talking?'

Reynard gave Lincoln an odd sideways look which Lincoln couldn't quite understand. 'I don't think so,' said Reynard.

'And you never told anybody else, before me?'

Reynard shook his head. 'I once told Chiffon that I'd had contact with the Nazis during the war.'

'What the hell did you do that for?'

'I don't know. There was a television programme on CBS about Hitler, and she wanted to know something about it. She was so young, you know, none of the old wartime figures seemed like real people to her. She was amazed that I'd actually met Churchill. Then she asked me if I'd ever met any real Nazis. I don't know why I told her; I'd never told anyone else. But it doesn't really matter too much now, does it? Not now she's dead.'

Lincoln said, 'Let's pray that she didn't pass the information on to anyone else.'

'Chiffon?' For a moment, Reynard looked almost wistful. Then he took a mouthful of Dom Perignon, and shook his head, and said, 'No. Not Chiffon. She was too loyal. She wouldn't have talked.'

'Okay,' said Lincoln, 'if only Ted Peale and you know where this virus came from, what are you so worried about?'

'They'll track it down, Linc. You know that as well as I do. If that virus has gotten loose, that means that somebody's found the six glass phials, and if they've found the glass phials they'll find the airplane, or whatever's left of it. I daren't set up a search myself, it'll cause too much suspicion; and supposing the health department finds the airplane first and knows that I've been searching? Instant incrimination.'

Lincoln said, 'Well, well. The Nazi skeleton in good old Reynard's closet. And I thought that Winnipesaukee was a scandal.'

'You have to help me, Linc. You have to think of some way out of this.

'To begin with,' said Lincoln, 'you simply have to deny all knowledge of it; that's if they *do* find the airplane.'

'But meanwhile all these people are dying. The longer

277

I keep quiet about all this, the more people are going to die. There are *children* dying, Linc. And what do you think's going to happen to me if they eventually discover what I did, after several thousand people have already been wiped out? I've got twenty on my conscience already.'

'You never had too much of a conscience ever before.'

'Don't be crass.'

'Well, Jesus, Reynard, what the hell do you *expect* me to say? Either you're going to be ruthless or you're not. If you can't be ruthless then you're not fit to be President. We can't have a man in the White House who's going to hesitate to push the nuclear button because he's worried about all the people he's going to have on his conscience.'

Reynard raged, 'Nuclear war is fantasy, theory. These people are real and they're already dead.'

'What do you mean nuclear war is fantasy?'

'Well, do you seriously believe that if we were truly capable of grasping what would actually happen if we used those weapons, what it would do to us, do you think we ever would have built them?'

'Reynard,' said Lincoln, 'I think I'd better get you a doctor.'

'I don't *need* a doctor.'

'Reynard, you're going out of your mind! First you tell me all this Nazi stuff, and then you start sounding off like a peace-freak!'

'I've killed people, Linc. Can't you understand that? New Hampshire people. Concord people. And something worse than that.'

Reynard raised his head, and there were tears in his eyes. Not genuine tears of grief, he was incapable of those; but tears of sentimental regret, and bitterness at himself for being what he was.

'I killed Chiffon, too.'

Lincoln stared at his older brother for a long time.

Then he picked up the phone, and said, 'Dean? I need you in here, right now. That's it. The library. Something's come up.'

Dean Farber came in, holding a glass of orange-juice, his white face as innocent as a child's blancmange. There was a brief burble of laughter and conversation from the living room as he opened and closed the door.

Reynard was sitting with his head in his hands. Lincoln had his back to the door. Dean Farber's smile gradually diminished. 'Is anything *wrong*?' he asked, cautiously.

'Yes,' said Lincoln. 'Reynard's announcing his withdrawal from the Presidential race, as of now. His doctor's just told him that to continue would be detrimental to his health.'

'Doctor?' asked Dean Farber, in astonishment. 'What doctor?'

'Doctor Death,' said Reynard, in a harsh voice. 'Linc - pour me some more champagne.'

Later that morning, near Anama City, Florida, Ted Peale was sitting on the boarded verandah of his retirement home, cleaning and repairing his fishing-tackle, when his wife called, 'Ted! There's a telephone call for you!'

Ted laid down his tackle, and slopped slowly into the house in his loud Hawaiian shirt and his droopy-assed Bermudas and his plastic flip-flops. His wife had been baking, and there was a smell of apple-pie in the house. He picked up the phone and scratched his stomach and said, 'Yes, who is it?'

'A friend, Mr Peale,' whispered a hoarse Chicano voice. 'Somebody from New Hampshire sent me.'

'Well, I told my friend I couldn't make it up to New Hampshire. I'm sorry.'

'Your friend understands that. But your friend says that he should maybe pay you a little something, to make sure that you say nothing to anybody about the little business you had together.'

Ted Peale sniffed. 'He wants to pay me money?'

'Just a little something, for your trouble.'

'Well, he can do that if he wants to.'

'Unfortunately, not at your house, Mr Peale. Too suspicious. But come down to the intersection of George and St Andrews in fifteen minutes' time, and park behind a green Chevy you'll see there, Florida plates. Get into the back seat of the Chevy, and I'll be there to pay you the cash.'

'How much cash?' asked Ted Peale, suspiciously.

'I think twenty-five.'

'Twenty-five *thousand*?'

'I think.'

'I'll see you in fifteen minutes.'

Under a glaring noonday sun, Ted Peale backed his '66 Impala out of the creeper-lined parking space at the back of his bungalow; giving his wife a toot on the horn goodbye. She had asked him to bring back some cinnamon since he was going out. He had put on his green eyeshade against the glare. He could have been any other old Florida geriatric, trundling down to the market for groceries, gives the old boys something to do, running a few errands for the wife.

He parked, badly, behind the rusting green Chevrolet. Leaving the engine of his own car running, he flip-flopped along the sidewalk and bent down so that he could see who was inside. Two young Chicanos, both with mirror sunglasses and greased-back quiffs. One of them was sitting in the driver's seat, smiling, a thin wrist with a ritzy gold wristwatch resting casually on the steering-wheel; the other was sitting in the back, with a large brown-paper parcel.

'How you going, granpa, get in,' said the one in the back.

'Can't you just pass it to me, out the window?' asked Ted Peale.

'People going to see us,' the boy insisted.

'Well, okay,' said Ted Peale, and opened up the rear door of the car with a complaining *skronk*, and eased himself on to the sticky green vinyl seat.

'You don't have to worry about nothing,' grinned the boy. 'It's all here, twenty-five g's.'

'How come my friend sent you two?' asked Ted Peale. 'You don't look like his usual style.'

'Different jobs, different styles,' said the youth in the driver's seat. 'For this job, he wanted somebody real glamorous.' And he gave out a high-pitched giggle.

'Like your shirt, man,' said the other boy, fingering the sleeve of Ted Peale's Hawaiian top. 'That would suit me, something with pineapples on.' And both of them giggled even more.

Ted Peale gave an uneasy nod. 'You don't want a receipt or nothing?' he asked. 'Then I guess I'll just take the money and go.'

'Oh – wait a second, man,' said the boy sitting next to him, and plunged a foot-long double-edged bayonet right up to the handle into Ted Peale's stomach.

Ted Peale gasped with shock as the cold steel went right into his intestines. He stared at the boy; then down at the bayonet-handle; then back at the boy again. 'What you do that for?' he asked.

'Yes, man, what you do that for?' mimicked the boy in the driver's seat. 'You just ruin the fucking shirt.'

Ted Peale was about to open his mouth and scream, but the shock had already been too much for him. His heart stopped, and he died within less than a minute, blue in the face, gasping.

'Let's go,' said the boy in the back seat.

'Old man Freiburg ready for him?'

'You bet.'

The Chevrolet lurched away from the curb, and began

281

the long trip to Bonita Springs, in Lee County, Florida, just west of the Corkscrew Swamp Sanctuary. There, at Freiburg's Marvel Gardens & Alligator Farm, Ted Peale's body, like so many others before him, would be roughly dismembered with a chain saw, and fed in pieces to old man Freiburg's thirty fully-grown alligators; although some of his neighbours could never understand how he prospered so well on the proceeds of $2.50 entrance tickets, popcorn, soda, and plastic alligator souvenirs.

'What a way to end up, unh?' said one of the Chicano boys rhetorically, as they joined highway 10 near Cottondale. 'Alligator shit.' He nudged Ted Peale's body, and said, 'You hear that, granpa? Alligator shit.'

FIFTEEN

Piotr was changing into his jockstrap and tights at the O'Connor Theatre when Billy Manzanetti walked in, carrying a large grocery bag full of sausages and cheeses and fresh fruit, and smoking a smelly French cigarette. Piotr had worked with Billy in an off-off-Broadway satire which had mostly involved jokes about herpes and baring their asses to the sparse and unenthusiastic audience.

'How are you doing, Rasputin?' Billy asked him.

'Billy, hi. I'm doing fine, as a matter of fact. Well, at least I'm working. How are you doing?'

'Oh, bad, good; here, there; up, down. You know how it is. You want an apple?'

'Thanks.'

'You want a sausage? Bologna, they're the best.'

'Mm, no thanks. My whole childhood was sausages, remember. A sea of sausages. How's Trixi?'

'Pixi? Oh, good, bad. You know. Actually as a matter of fact pretty indifferent.'

Piotr bit into the apple. 'You got something on your mind?' he asked Billy.

Billy nodded. Smoke dangled up the left side of his face, and he coughed out of the right side of his mouth.

'You remember I told you I knew some guy who was big in porno movies?

Piotr looked at him suspiciously. 'I remember.'

'Well, apparently, and I got this from Jack Bigelow himself, you know the guy they called the Mighty Salami, apparently there's a real big picture going down. One of the classics of all time, that's what the word is, and they're paying big big money for the right guys. Guys who can screw like mules and keep their mouths shut. But I mean big money.'

Piotr tugged up his tights, and shovelled his genitals into them as if he were making pizza dough. 'What are you telling *me* for?' he wanted to know.

'Well, this could be your big chance to break into the skin business. A famous young exile like you. They're offering twenty grand for each of the male parts, and I say parts advisedly.'

'Billy,' Piotr protested, 'I'm a serious actor.'

'A lot of actors are serious actors, but they still do porno. Come on, it's just money for old rope. Or young ropes, should I say. What have you got to lose? Twenty big ones, all in cash; IRS exempt.'

'You sound like you're recruiting,' said Piotr.

'Well, I guess I am, really. I'm supposed to come up with five guys. And they're all supposed to be exceptional. I get an extra 10 per cent commission.'

'Hm,' said Piotr. Twenty thousand dollars sounded extremely tempting, he had to admit. The theatre production hadn't paid him a salary cheque for two weeks now, and he was a month behind with his rent. To a Russian mind, pornography seemed anathema,

283

the lowest of the low; but he was a free citizen now, wasn't he? If he wanted to act in a sex movie, who was to stop him? And his agent didn't have to know about it; nor would he ever be likely to find out, a respectable man like Daniel Fish.

'You want to give me some details?' Piotr asked, trying to sound offhanded.

'They start shooting on Monday; a selection of videos. Then a big s-and-m production.'

'S-and-m?'

'Spaghetti and meatballs.'

'What?'

'I'm kidding. It means sado-masochism. You know, tying the girl up, pretending to rape her, that kind of thing. You'll love it.'

'They won't put the movie on general release?'

'Oh, no, nothing like that. It's for private distribution only. Clubs, private parties, mail-order sales. Nobody who sees it is even going to know that it's you; and even if they guess, I don't think they're going to worry, as long as you keep it up.'

'I don't know,' said Piotr, reluctantly.

'Well, make your mind up by tomorrow. Then call me. Here – don't use my home number, call me on this one. You have to make up your mind by tomorrow because the filming's out of town, and I have to book tickets.'

'How much out of town?' asked Piotr. 'Not New Jersey? I went there once; and never again.'

Billy pinched the stub of his cigarette out from between his lips, and spat a shred of tobacco. 'Unh-hunh. You ever heard of Wisconsin?'

'Wisconsin? But that's not out of town. That's the mid-West!'

Billy winked. 'I knew you'd like the idea. Call me tomorrow. And remember. Twenty big ones, all for you.'

Piotr sat in the dressing-room for five or ten minutes after Billy had gone. He had to admit that the idea of appearing in a sex movie quite aroused him. To make love to a girl in front of other people, and to be paid for it, too. And maybe if the first movie was good, there might be others; and he could earn himself a steady income to enable him to hold out for bigger and more satisfying rôles on the stage.

'It makes sense,' he told himself. 'And what, after all, is immoral about it, if the girl is getting paid, too?'

Edmond took Natalia and Walt Seabrook out of the Merrimack clinic to the Hot Cookie Coffee Shop across the street. The day had grown suddenly dull, and a chilly wind had risen from the north-west, scattering red and yellow leaves across the sidewalks. They found a corner table and ordered coffee. Edmond asked for a lemon Danish, because he hadn't yet eaten breakfast.

'I might as well tell you why I'm living at the Brick Tower,' he said. 'My wife and I just parted.'

'I'm sorry,' said Natalia.'

'Don't worry,' put in Walt. 'You're better off without her. I left my wife on our sixth anniversary. I told her, "For six years I've been listening to you talking about things you know nothing about. For six years I've been wondering whether I ought to tell you that your face gives me chronic dyspepsia. That's it. Now I'm going to live a life of silence and certainty, with a settled stomach." '

They laughed. But they soon grew serious again. For all of them, the epidemic and its consequences were crucial.

'I haven't had any further reports of hyper-polio since earlier this morning,' said Edmond. 'But I don't have any doubt at all that it's going to spread. In the last few cases we've attended, death was very rapid indeed, and although we haven't yet been able to work out how the epidemic started, or why, we're now beginning to be able to trace chains of contact from one family to another. The most alarming part about it, though, is that each time it seems to take the virus less time to infect its new hosts. In other words, the rate of new infection is accelerating, as well as the speed with which the virus kills its host.'

Natalia said, 'I don't want to change the subject, Dr Chandler, but have you any idea why Senator Kelly might have wanted to keep the spread of this epidemic under wraps? Is there any medical reason?'

'I thought you were on his staff. I was expecting you to tell *me* the answer to that,' said Edmond.

Walt Seabrook gave a lemony little smile. 'Well . . . Dr Chandler . . . a politician like Senator Kelly doesn't always take everybody into his confidence. All we're trying to discover here is how serious this epidemic might be; and what you consider might be the most effective way of dealing with it.'

Edmond glanced from Natalia to Walt and back again. He felt fresher and more collected this morning. Surprisingly, he had slept better at the motel than he had slept in years; and he had debated with his reflection as he shaved that morning whether his marriage to Christy hadn't been giving way piece by piece from the moment they had walked out of Stamford Episcopal Church. He had thought at various times that he had loved her overwhelmingly, but he had decided this morning that he really loved only those women who were just beyond his reach. Now that he had left her, he felt a deep sense of relief and purpose. It may have been nothing more substantial than the euphoria that follows any kind of important break in our lives. As a doctor, he was realistic enough to recognize that. But he felt it was more. He felt that for years he may well have been pretending to be someone else; just because Christy wanted him that way.

'There is no medical reason that I can think of for suppressing the news of this epidemic,' he told Natalia. 'There may be an *administrative* reason. It may be that Senator Kelly is concerned that there may be widespread panic, and that more people may be killed or injured as a result of a wholesale exodus. After all, we have 35,000 people here in Concord, and if they were all to try and leave the area at once . . .'

Walt Seabrook nodded towards the file of reports that Edmond had laid on the table. 'Those are the autopsy protocols?'

'That's right. Take a look, if you want to. Dr Corning is quite emphatic. We have a fast-regenerating, highly infective polio-type virus here with certain unusual characteristics in the way that its RNA acts as a genome. It's very dangerous; and I for one would have gone to the media a couple of days ago, although not all of my colleagues agree with me. Some of them say that it hasn't technically reached epidemic proportions yet, and that we still have a massive amount of detailed research to do, and that if we break up the community by stampeding everybody, we may jeopardize our chances of discovering how the virus spreads.'

'And what's your argument against that?' asked Natalia, looking at Edmond steadily. Despite the gravity of the problem, she was conscious that she found him attractive, and that she liked talking to him.

Edmond said, 'My argument against that is simple. Every time the virus spreads, it kills somebody. If we fail to alert the community, then we're guilty of treating people as human guinea-pigs. We may even be guilty of something worse than that.'

Walt Seabrook said, 'What does Carol Bryce think?'

'You know Dr Bryce?'

'Sure, we play golf. What's his view? I mean, I'll speak to him later, but first of all I want to find out what kind of response you guys in the field are getting from HQ.'

'Well . . . ambiguous,' said Edmond. 'I get the feeling that Dr Bryce is very anxious about the situation. At the same time I get the feeling that he's doing what he's told. He's a stickler for protocol, as you know, and he's not likely to go against direct instructions from the Department of Health and Welfare, or the Attorney-General'

'Or from Senator Kelly?' Walt Seabrook suggested.

'Senator Kelly may well be President next year,' Edmond pointed out.

'Precisely,' said Natalia.

At that moment, Edmond's beeper sounded. He said, 'Excuse me,' and went to the coffee-shop telephone. He came back and said, 'Another one. A family out at Swenson Avenue. I'm afraid I'm going to have to leave you. Would you mind picking up the cheque for the coffee?'

'You go right ahead,' said Walt Seabrook.

When Edmond had gone, Natalia and Walt Seabrook sat and looked at each other.

'Something doesn't fit here,' said Natalia. 'There's something about this epidemic that smells and it doesn't just smell of dead bodies.'

'My view exactly,' agreed Walt. 'One of the first procedures in the outbreak of any dangerous infection is immediately to inform the local populace through the media. It's been almost a week since the first case of hyper-polio, and so far there's hardly been a squeak. Dr Chandler is prepared to speak out, but I get the feeling that he's a little reserved. Maybe he's got a skeleton in his closet. Carol Bryce is usually outspoken, and I certainly would have thought that *he* would have said something official by now. Then there's Eldridge at the New Hampshire Department of Health and Welfare. Why doesn't *he* make any announcements?'

'Reynard asked them not to. Well, more than asked them, I shouldn't wonder. Coerced them. But why?'

'Natalia,' said Walt, 'if Reynard finds it expedient to cover up the existence of an epidemic, then there's only one reason why. In some way, he must be responsible for it.'

'But how could he be? A *disease*?'

'They don't know where it came from yet, do they? But supposing the cattle on Reynard's land are diseased, and they've been giving contaminated milk, simply because Reynard has ignored proper pasteurizing procedures. Or supposing a sewer on Reynard's property has cracked, and raw sewage has been leaking into Concord's drinking-water. That's highly likely, especially when you consider that polio viruses are usually passed from excrement to mouth.'

'But how can we find out?'

'We can ask Reynard.'

'But supposing it *is* something like that . . . diseased cattle or something? That's going to be disastrous for his candidacy. Nineteen people dead, and all because he couldn't be bothered to keep his property or his livestock in good condition.'

Walt Seabrook paid the cheque and the two of them walked out on to Pleasant Street. The wind blew Natalia's hair. Walt Seabrook said, 'I don't know about you, Natalia, but it means a very great deal to me, Reynard Kelly being elected President.'

Natalia looked at him narrowly.

'I'm an excellent administrative doctor,' he said. 'I'm chairman of the hospital committee, senior gynecological consultant, and I go to more health service finance and administrative meetings than there are days in the week. I'm supporting Reynard because I'm what you might call a friend of the family. But, more important, I'm supporting him because I want to be Assistant Secretary for Health. I'll never get another chance. It's my medical and political goal in life. I want to make an impression on this country's health services, and with Reynard's help I can do it.'

They had reached Natalia's Porsche. Natalia took her keys out of her purse and opened the doors.

'And you?' Walt Seabrook asked her. 'What's your reason for being here?'

'I'm here because it's my job,' she said. She didn't look at him. 'I'm here because I was asked to be here.'

'Is that all?'

Natalia started up the engine. 'Of course it's not all, damn it. I'm here because opportunities like this only come once in a lifetime, and if you throw them away, you're crazy.'

Natalia had her hand on the gearshift. Walt Seabrook laid his own hand on top of it, and looked at her closely. 'Let's agree that we're both ambitious then, shall we? And let's agree that if Dr Chandler is even halfway right about this epidemic, that Reynard could be in serious trouble. So let's agree to call Reynard and see what we can do.'

Natalia waited without moving or speaking until Walt Seabrook had taken his hand away. Then she violently shifted the Porsche into second, and screeched away from the curb with smoke pouring out from the tyres.

Greta had already expressed her opinion about Reynard's suggested withdrawal from the Presidential race by hurling her champagne glass at the wall.

'I thought you had courage, God damn it! I didn't think you had much else. Maybe a certain brutish charisma. Maybe a kind of macho Blake Carrington cuff-tugging soap-opera masculinity. But certainly *courage*, God damn it.'

Lincoln said defensively, 'We don't have a courage difficulty here, Greta. We have an historical political problem which is threatening to bring this whole family crashing into ruin, you included.'

'I can hardly believe it,' snapped Greta. 'You did some grubby little deal with the Germans in 1944, some ridiculous comic-opera arrangement for which you didn't even get paid . . .'

'You're wrong about that,' Reynard interrupted.

'What do you mean? The Germans *paid* you?' asked Dean Farber. He looked whiter than ever, as if he had been dusted with flour.

Reynard nodded. 'Six million dollars in gold bullion. Well, I only got half of it. The rest was due on completion.'

Lincoln pressed his knuckles to his forehead and let out a sigh of total resignation. 'This is it,' he said. 'This is the absolute finish. The Nazis paid you three million dollars in gold for blackmailing FDR? And you accepted it? You *banked* it?'

'It was all banked in Switzerland. It was still there after the war. Just how do you think this family remained so prosperous, when everybody else was feeling the pinch? How do you think we were able to keep The Colonnades up to such a high standard of excellence?'

Lincoln said, 'Did father know about any of this?'

'No. I told him the money came from a deal I'd done in South America.

'Well, thank God for small mercies. At least he went to his grave still believing you were decent.'

Greta snapped her fingers at Dean Farber. 'Find me some more champagne, will you? I can't even begin to think about any of this without a drink. And let's stop moaning and moralizing, shall we, Lincoln? What on earth does it matter if your father knew or not? The most important thing we can do now is decide how we're going to manoeuvre our way out of all this. We have several important points in our favour: and the strongest of those is that nobody has yet connected the epidemic with those glass phials of yours – even supposing that anybody has found them. It's more than likely that they've been thrown away by now.

'The second point is that even if the outbreak *is* connected with your estates, and the medical people start searching for a possible cause, what do you seriously think they're going to come up with? You're panicking, Reynard. If *you* haven't come across that airplane in forty years, do you honestly believe for one moment that a few off-duty policemen are going to stumble into it?'

'But the plane must be *somewhere* there,' Reynard told her. 'The first few victims of the epidemic all lived around the southern part of the estate, Conant's Acre and the Middle Meadow. Logically, that must have been where the phials were found. I've had the place wired off, and I've taken a cursory look around there myself, but the trouble is that I wouldn't trust either of my groundsmen to keep quiet if they actually found it.'

'Good God, Reynard, you can plead complete ignorance of the whole thing,' put in Greta.

'While more and more people die of this hyper-polio, I can pretend that I don't know anything about it? Is that what you're suggesting?'

'You were in New York when the plane came in, weren't you?' Greta insisted. 'And you've told us already that only two other people knew about it, and one of those is dead. The other man could be paid off, couldn't he? or, I don't know, faced with a little friendly persuasion? Even if the health people *do* trace the phials, and *do* find the airplane, all you have to do is act completely surprised.'

Reynard stood up, and went to pour himself another drink. Lincoln moved forward to stop him, but Reynard lowered his head in that way that Lincoln recognized from boyhood as a signal that he was completely adamant.

'Maybe you're right, Greta,' said Reynard, with studied graciousness. 'Maybe I *did* panic, to begin with. But I think you all know what this bid for the Presidency means to me, and what it means to this family; and it has to be 100 per cent. This is my last possible shot at the White House, and if anything goes wrong, or if anything is likely to go wrong, then I'd rather back off. We have the name of Kelly to think about, too.

'You say that the likelihood of anyone tracing those phials or connecting them with me is remote. Well, that may be the case, but we don't know for sure; and believe me as this epidemic gets worse, which it will, then the Health Department's efforts to discover where it came from are going to grow increasingly intensive and increasingly thorough. If that plane is there to be found, which I believe it must be, then in the end they'll find it.'

'But, for God's sake, all you have to do is stare at it as if you've never seen it before,' Greta protested.

'Greta,' said Reynard, gently, 'you're living in an unreal world. What do you think would happen if a 1944 Focke-Wulf Condor were to be discovered on the New Hampshire estate of one of the leading candidates for the Democratic presidential nomination? It would be one of the sensations of the century – politically, historically, aeronautically. That airplane would be stripped down to the last bolt, re-assembled, photographed, identified, and every research historian in the whole world with the slightest interest in World War Two would want to know what it was doing there. Eventually – in weeks or maybe months they'd find out. The Germans kept meticulous logs of all their Condor flights – you don't think that a special flight like this one would have gone unrecorded? I was worried enough when they dug up those Hitler Diaries, in case there was any mention of Condor. As it turned out, there wasn't, which makes me think those diaries were a fake. But there's bound to be a memorandum about it somewhere, believe me.'

The telephone rang. Dean Farber picked it up, said, 'Congressman Kelly's home.' Then, 'You wanted *Senator* Kelly? Okay, just hold one moment and I'll see if he's still here. What's that? I see. Okay, well, hold on, please.'

He covered the receiver with his hand, and said to Reynard, 'It's Mr Eldridge, from the New Hampshire Health & Welfare Department. He wants to talk to you.'

'Of course he wants to talk to me. What does he want to say?'

'He wants to say that twenty-six more cases of hyper-polio have been identified in the past two hours and that he intends to declare Merrimack County a quarantine area, regardless of any personal consequences.'

Reynard said, 'Give me the phone.'

Mr Eldridge sounded calm. He said, 'Your aide gave you the message, I gather. From right now, what we have here is officially an epidemic.'

'Mr Eldridge,' said Reynard. 'I specifically asked you to keep this under wraps, didn't I? For the sake of the people of New Hampshire, remember?'

'I also remember that you threatened me.'

'Mr Eldridge, this outbreak still hasn't reached epidemic proportions, has it? You're creating a public panic here, Mr Eldridge, without any justifiable cause.'

'That's my responsibility,' replied Mr Eldridge, severely. 'If I'm wrong, I'm prepared to take the blame. I've carried quite a few cans back in my time; I'm not frightened to do it now. People are dying here, senator, and I have to say that I'm surprised at your attitude. You won't be getting any vote from me, I can assure you of that.'

Reynard could think of all kinds of absurdly

browbeating things to say, like 'I'll break you, Eldridge,' or 'You'll never work in government again,' but as it was he simply said, 'All right, Mr Eldridge, if that's the way you want to do it,' and put the phone down.

They were all watching him as he did so, their faces serious. Greta, Lincoln, Dean Farber – they could have been mourners at a premature baby's funeral.

'That's it,' said Reynard. 'Lincoln's right. I'm going to have to withdraw. There's no other way in which we're going to get out of this with our reputation in one piece; and even then we're going to have a whole lot of difficult questions to answer.'

'You will *not* withdraw,' said Greta. 'You'll stay in the race, and you'll win it.'

'Greta, it's too risky. Too many people have died already, you have to call a halt somewhere. Besides, think of the international repercussions of this if it's discovered *after* I'm elected President.'

'Think of the repercussions if I announce to the media that we've been living apart for the past few months, and that you bribed me to pretend that we were still happily married.'

Lincoln and Dean Farber raised their heads simultaneously, like Hope and Crosby, and stared at each other.

'Is this *true*?' asked Lincoln. 'I knew you two hadn't been seeing too much of each other; but that happens to all congressmen. Reynard, is Greta telling me what I think she's telling me?'

'We had a temporary marital glitch, that's all,' said Reynard, dismissively. 'We've settled it now.

'Let me tell you how temporary it was,' put in Greta, with a sharp-cut smile on her face. 'All of my clothes have been moved down to Newport. Reynard is paying me a separate allowance. And I have a new man in my life who makes Reynard seem like Attila the Hun. Oh

– I beg your pardon, I forgot that it was bad taste to mention Germans around here.'

Lincoln raised both hands. 'Now I've heard everything,' he said. 'Jesus, Reynard, do you know much money we've invested in this campaign, how hard people have been working to arrange tours and media appearances and rallies? And all the time you have a Nazi warplane in your back-garden and a fortune founded on Nazi gold and a First Lady-to-be who doesn't even *like* you, let alone live with you.'

Reynard cleared his throat. He drummed his fingers on the back of one of the catcher's-mitt chairs. 'It seems as if I've miscalculated, doesn't it?'

'I think "miscalculated" is the understatement of all time,' said Lincoln. 'Do you know something, Reynard, I always thought you were strong. I always thought you were self-confident. But all of that strength, all of that self-confidence, do you know what that was? Nothing more than the dining-out suit of a character completely devoid of any kind of moral judgement whatever.'

He paused, and then he said, 'If it's any consolation, I think you're ideal Presidential material.'

Dean Farber had been making notes on his clipboard. He raised his hand as if he were in class, and then he said, 'Excuse me, I think we're all forgetting something here. Something essential. What I'm talking about is the epidemic.'

'What about it?' barked Reynard. There's nothing more we can do now. Eldridge is going to declare a state of quarantine.'

'But you said it was unstoppable. You said it couldn't be cured. That means if nobody finds an antidote, or at least some kind of preventive treatment, the entire population of Merrimack County might die. The last census figure I have here for Merrimack County is 85,265. And in all probability the epidemic will spread even wider than that. Some people may already have carried the virus out of state.'

Reynard looked around the room. 'Well,' he said, at last. 'There *was* a treatment, as far as I know. Johnson said that the doctors who developed the virus had also found a way of keeping it in check. But this was all of forty years ago. The doctors are probably dead by now. It would take months to discover who they were, and whether they'd ever left any notes about it.'

'What I'm trying to say here is that regardless of our political or personal problems, we still have an epidemic on our hands,' said Dean Farber.

'Well, we *know* that,' said Greta, obtusely.

'You're missing my point,' said Dean Farber.

'I wasn't aware that you were making one,' Greta retorted.

Dean Farber set his clipboard down on the desk as if it were a point in itself.

'The point is that whenever you have a disadvantageous political situation, instead of trying to run away from it, or withdraw, or even argue about it, you should *take charge of it*. Senator Kelly by his present actions is only attracting suspicion. What he should do is to call Mr Eldridge, and regardless of the fact that Mr Eldridge has already announced a state of quarantine in Merrimack County, he should *demand* a state of quarantine in Merrimack County; and then he should go to the media and make the official announcement that Concord has been struck by a mystery disease – while – let me finish, please – while at the same time making a pledge to pour thousands of dollars of his own money into setting up an epidemic research laboratory to find out where the virus came from.

'Then, he will not only have gained the political initiative, and all the credit that goes with it; but also total control over any laboratory tests that have to be made. Most important of all, he will have diverted suspicion away from his own estates and his own unfortunate involvement in all of this. Maybe long enough for a few of us to make a fresh search, and come up with that Nazi airplane, and destroy it.'

Reynard looked across the room at Lincoln. 'Where did you find this guy?' he wanted to know. 'He's good.'

Greta said, icily, 'Perhaps he ought to be running for President, instead of you. I think personally I'd feel safer about the future of the world.'

Later that day, it was announced on network television news that an epidemic of a disease called 'hyper-polio' had broken out in Concord, the capital of New Hampshire, and that thirty people had already died from it. The true figure was nearer fifty, but some had yet to be discovered, and others were waiting on slabs at the New Hampshire Hospital for examination by pathologists.

Edmond would always remember it as the day when chaos finally broke loose. After meeting Natalia and Walt Seabrook, he had gone straight to attend a young family who had died in the most Saturday Evening Post of circumstances. Mom in the kitchen, halfway through frosting a chocolate fudge cake. Dad and one of the younger boys lying in the yard, curled up amongst the leaves they had been sweeping. Tragedy in suburbia. And in the bedroom, a little girl of only eighteen months, one hand still clutching the bar of her crib.

A young paramedic who had already seen five other deaths that day had turned away to the window and wept.

During the afternoon and into the evening, the epidemic spread wider and wider, like a forest fire that could leap from the top of one tree to the top of another. But instead of the roaring of fire, there was the rustling undercurrent of fear and anxiety; the whinnying of estate cars starting up, loaded with people and possessions; the banging of shutters as homes were locked up and garage doors were closed, and lawnmowers left abandoned in half-trimmed suburban gardens.

For six or seven hours, the highways from Concord out to Keene, Manchester, and Laconia were blocked solid with lines of red-lighted traffic. Some were bolder, and took complicated side-turnings, but every highway and side-turning and rural lane was barred by police, and the signs were up 'Quarantine Area.' The cars and trucks and vans were jammed so solid that many drivers simply switched off their engines, engaged neutral, and went to sleep where they were, allowing the slow-nudging tide of traffic to bear them along.

The news was out. Senator Reynard Kelly had made an official announcement on television news at five o'clock, serious and drawn, the new Democratic candidate for Presidential nomination who had already upstaged John Glenn and Walter Mondale and a half-dozen more hopefuls.

'This outbreak is both tragic and alarming. I mourn the deaths of those who have already been taken, and grieve alongside the bereaved. We don't know yet what caused this epidemic, what triggered it; but we intend to. And I am personally financing an emergency laboratory to be staffed by some of the finest neurologists and virologists in the country, as well as a team of medical researchers from New Hampshire's Department of Health & Welfare, in a concerted effort to bring this terrible epidemic under control.'

There were fresh cases reported around the nation; in Los Angeles, in Denver, in Seattle, as relatives and acquaintances of people who had recently returned from New Hampshire fell victim to the viruses which their loved ones had unknowingly brought back with them. In Lincoln, Nebraska, fifteen students at the Wesleyan University died at a party in the small hours of the following day. In South Portland, Maine, a family of three were found drowned in their indoor swimming-pool, all of them suffocated by hyper-polio. A couple died at their table at the Sun-Dial revolving restaurant at Atlanta, Georgia.

Outbreaks were still sporadic, however, and because so many cases went unrecognized at first (the couple at the Sun-Dial were thought for over 24 hours to be choke victims) no immediate connection was made between the epidemic in Concord and the sudden asphyxiations all around the country. But coroners and medical examiners and medical referees from Maine to California found that they were working through the night; and it would only be a matter of hours before the Department of Health discovered that what was happening was the beginning of a devastating national epidemic.

Edmond was called to eleven more cases before Thursday dawned. After the panicking exodus of the previous evening, Concord was now unnaturally silent, and most of the cars on the streets were police cars, looking for would-be looters. A large fire was burning over at New Hampshire Technical Institute, by Fort Eddy Pond; huge rolling orange flames, with thick black smoke; and somewhere to the west there was another, fiercer blaze, as if a car or a light aircraft was on fire.

Oscar Ford was already in attendance when Edmond arrived at his tenth case, on Shawmut Avenue, in East Concord. He looked tired and sweaty, and he blew his nose loudly as two paramedics carried the first of the dead family out of the house.

'You know them well?' Oscar asked him.

Edmond nodded. 'Nice family, well-behaved kids.'

'Nice people are going down all over,' said Oscar. 'Nice people, well-behaved kids.'

'Some surprise party, hunh?' said Edmond.

Oscar took his arm, and squeezed it. 'This is what they call a disaster, E.C. You know on television, when they show those movies about fires and earthquakes and stuff like that? Well, this time we're living it, for real.'

'You know that it's going to get one of us next. Or both of us.'

Oscar pulled a face. 'We pathologists don't think about things like that. When you have to spend your working days probing around in half-rotten stiffs, you block out of your mind the inevitability that one day you're going to be a stiff yourself.'

'What's that? Dr Ford's profound thought for today?'

Oscar tapped his forehead with his finger. 'Just a way of staying alive, inside of here.'

The paramedics brought out the last of the family, a boy of six. The red blanket didn't quite cover his tousled hair, and Oscar stepped forward and tugged it over.

'By the way,' he said to Edmond, reaching in his pocket. 'What do you make of this?'

He passed Edmond a glassine envelope containing a clear glass phial, empty. Edmond turned the envelope over in his fingers, and then held it up to the spotlight on top of the ambulance. There was a tiny quantity of colourless liquid clinging to the bottom of the phial, and there were whitish translucent blobs around the neck of it, as if it had once been sealed with wax.

'Where did you find this?' Edmond asked.

'In the house there, down the back of the sofa. I always shove my hand down the backs of sofas, you'd be amazed what you find down there. Force of habit, I guess. I once found a twenty-dollar bill down the back of my mother-in-law's lounger, and I thought that was a small but just recompense for all the bullet-hard cookies of hers I'd ever had to eat. The Dentist's Friend, that's what I call her.'

'This is German,' said Edmond. 'Look, there's a German name engraved on the side of it.'

Oscar leaned over, and frowned at the envelope. 'I don't have my glasses,' he said. 'Here – take it out of the envelope if you want to, but hold it at either end. I want to have it checked for prints when I get back.'

Edmond opened the envelope and carefully extracted the phial. He had a magnifying-glass in his bag, and so he took the phial over to his car to examine it. Oscar waited beside him, his hands in his pockets, sniffing from time to time. 'I bet I caught that stupid Moretti's cold,' he remarked.

'Here, it's quite clear,' said Edmond. 'Oberhausen Glasfabrik, and then a serial number. 77/4AP.'

'Could have contained some kind of drug?' Oscar suggested.

'We can soon find out, can't we? There's enough in the bottom to analyse. I'd be interested to see what it is.'

'Well, I'll pass it over to Lim Kim. He's our mysterious-substance expert. The only analysis that's had him licked so far is the ingredient of my mother-in-law's cookies. We both agreed that the principal constituent was cement, but we're still arguing over the granite and the deadly nightshade.'

Edmond knew that Oscar was only bantering because he was frightened and unhappy. He handed him the glass phial, then gave him a slap on the back, and said, 'I hope I don't see you later, okay?'

'Forty-seven so far,' said Oscar.

'At least Eldridge has ordered a quarantine.'

'Bryce said they should have done it earlier. Much earlier, when we first suggested it.'

'Bryce said that?'

'Bryce may be a stickler for protocol, but he's a good doctor, too.'

They drove off their different ways; Oscar back to the New Hampshire Hospital, Edmond to the Brick Tower Motor Hotel. He was exhausted now, and sticky with sweat, and all he wanted was a hot shower, a cup of coffee, and an hour's sleep. It was almost dawn, and a

302

smear of greyish light was appearing on the horizon from behind the darkened brow of Taylor State Forest. The radio was tuned to the news, but the only mention of the epidemic was a message from the governor which Edmond had heard twice already, appealing to the citizens of Concord and Merrimack County to 'remain calm, don't panic, and observe the quarantine.' The governor then gave five emergency telephone number to call 'should you feel unwell, or experience any untoward difficulty in breathing.' One of the numbers was Edmond's. He expected that Lara was tearing her hair out back at the clinic, trying to answer all the calls. The governor should have given his own damned number.

Edmond had just joined the Frederick E. Everett highway when there was a beep on his car phone. He picked it up, and said, 'How's it going, Lara? Chaotic?'

'I think the switchboard's going to melt,' she told him. 'But I'm not too bad. I've had one of my roommates in to help me. We take it in turns to answer twenty calls each.'

'I'm going to try to catch an hour's sleep and a cup of coffee,' said Edmond. 'We haven't had any more emergencies, have we?'

'Only one, and Dr Pryor's dealing with that.'

'God bless Dr Pryor. Anything else?'

'Well, if you're still anywhere near East Concord, we had a call from the Mayer family – you know, young Bernie Mayer? Apparently Bernie's not feeling too well, although they don't think he's actually contracted hyper-polio.'

Edmond said, 'Tell them to give him a junior aspirin and send him to bed.'

'Okay,' sighed Lara. But supposing young Bernie had caught hyper-polio.

Edmond rubbed his eyes. God, he felt tired. 'On second thoughts, I'll go around there,' he told Lara.

303

'Maybe I'll be able to catch somebody who's only just caught the disease. So far all I've seen is corpses.'

'Whatever you say, doctor.'

He turned off the highway at the Ford Eddy cloverleaf. The fires at the technical institute had died down now, although there was still a pall of heavy black smoke around, through which a tracery of skeletal fires flickered like a prehistoric encampment. A police car was parked halfway across the turn-off ramp to Sugar Ball, and the officer waved him to the side of the road, but as soon as Edmond showed his doctor's ID, the officer told him to carry on.

'We're just watching for looters, you know? We caught a family coming through here with a trunkful of garden furniture. People are dying, you know, and all they can think of is garden furniture.'

Edmond arrived outside the Mayer's house and parked his car. It was light now, and a solitary bird was chirping and fluttering on the small tree in the centre of the lawn. Mrs Mayer opened the front door when Edmond was only halfway up the path, and beckoned him inside.

'I know how busy you are, doctor, what with this epidemic and everything. But Bernie's in a terrible condition. He won't speak to us; he won't eat. He keeps crying all the time. And if we ask him how he's feeling, he tells us we won't understand.'

'Hi, doctor,' said Mr Mayer, coming out of the kitchen in his underpants. 'Sorry to call you out like this, but you know, we're *worried*. Especially after what happened to Michael.'

'Will you put some pants on?' his wife told him.

'You think Dr Chandler never saw anybody in their shorts before? He spends his life looking at people in shorts.'

'Do you always have to argue? I'm worried sick about the boy and all you can do is argue about shorts.'

'*You're* worried sick about the boy?'

Edmond raised a hand. 'Please,' he told the Mayers. 'Can we leave the discussion until later? I'm kind of pushed for time.'

'Would you like some coffee?' asked Mrs Mayer.

'You never said a more enticing word,' Edmond replied.

He went upstairs to Bernie's bedroom. The drapes were still drawn, and Bernie was huddled in the corner in his pyjamas, his face pressed into his hands. Edmond drew up a chair, turned it around, and straddled it. He looked at Bernie for a long time before he spoke.

'Your mom and pop tell me you're not feeling too good.'

Bernie didn't answer.

'They say you're not talking; not eating. They say you keep crying all the time.'

Still no answer. But Bernie opened his fingers just a crack, and Edmond could see one glittering eye examining him carefully.

Edmond ran his fingers through his hair. 'Is it something to do with Michael?' he asked. 'I told you before that you'd have real feelings of sadness for him.'

'No,' Bernie croaked.

'It's not about Michael?'

'It was Michael's fault.'

'What was Michael's fault? That he died, and left you?'

'Unh-hunh. It was Michael's fault that all these people got sick.'

Edmond frowned. 'It wasn't his *fault*, Bernie. He got sick, too. It's just one of those tragic things that happen.'

'It wasn't me. I didn't know what was in them. But now everybody's going to think that it was my fault when it was Michael's. It wasn't me at all. I swear it, swear it hope to die. I didn't know.'

305

Edmond got up from the chair and went to sit over on the end of the bed. He laid a hand on Bernie's knee, and said, 'Listen, Bernie, I'm not sure that I understand any of this. What wasn't your fault?'

Bernie was trembling like a terrified young animal. Although he kept his hands pressed to his face, a single sparkling tear oozed out from between his fingers and ran down to his wrist.

'Bernie,' Edmond urged him, 'I'm a doctor. Do you know what that means? That means that no matter what you say to me, no matter what you've done, I'm not allowed to tell anybody else about it, not unless you want me to. When I became a doctor, I had to take that oath of professional secrecy, and I've never broken it.'

Bernie parted his fingers a little. 'You mean that? You've never told anybody anything? What if I said I was a murderer?'

'Well, I'd probably try to persuade you to give yourself up. But I wouldn't go directly to the cops.'

'It wasn't my fault,' Bernie repeated. 'It really wasn't, honest.'

Edmond was silent for a moment. Then he said, gently, 'Tell me.'

'It must have been the bottles.'

'Bottles?'

Bernie took his hands away from his red, tear-stained face, and held his finger and his thumb about four inches apart. 'Six little glass bottles, in a leather case. I didn't know what they were. I found them in our secret hiding-place in Michael's garage. I didn't know what they were. I got, I don't know, kind of *angry* about them because I didn't know what they were and Michael was dead so he couldn't tell me. In the end I got tired of taking them out and looking at them, so I took them to school and sold them. I told everybody they were secret obedience potion, if you gave it to your mom and dad, they'd do anything you wanted them to.'

Edmond said, in a quiet and controlled voice, 'Can you remember the names of the people you sold them to?'

Bernie nodded.

'Let me tell you who they were,' said Edmond, and recited a list of six family names, ending with the family at Shawmut Avenue whose house he had just left.

Bernie sat and stared at Edmond in amazement. His eyelashes were stuck together with tears.

'How did you know that?' he asked.

'Because all of those families have a child at your school, Bernie; and all of them are dead.'

Bernie looked down at the bedspread. Two more tears ran from his eyes and down his cheeks.

'Will they lock me up?' he asked.

Edmond put his arm around Bernie's shoulder. 'They won't lock you up, Bernie. Maybe you should have come out and said something sooner. But I think everybody will understand why you didn't. It takes a whole lot of courage to admit that you've been wrong, and that you've been foolish, especially when the consequences of what you've done have been really terrible, like they have this time. A whole lot of people who are much older than you have done far less terrible things than this, and been scared to admit they made a mistake.'

Bernie clung to Edmond tightly, and wept. Edmond patted his back, and calmed him down, and then at last said, 'Do you have any idea at all where Michael might have found those bottles? Any idea at all?'

Bernie sniffed, and nodded. 'I think so. When I was out at my music lesson he went to Conant's Acre, you know right by Webster Crescent, and I think he explored the woods on the far side there. I went across myself and I saw Michael's mark on one of the trees, we had a secret trailblazing mark, but I couldn't find

307

out where it went because a man came along and told me to go away.'

Edmond stood up. 'Listen, Bernie,' he said, 'I'm going to use your mom's phone; and while I'm phoning, I want you to get dressed. Jeans and a sweatshirt, something warm. Then I think you ought to take me over to Conant's Acre and show me just where you saw Michael's mark. Do you think you can do that?'

'Yes, sir.'

'Okay, then. Quick as you can, you got it?'

Edmond went downstairs. Mr and Mrs Mayer were waiting for him in the hallway. 'Is he all right?' asked Mrs Mayer. 'He doesn't have that polio, does he?'

Edmond shook his head. 'Physically, he's fine.'

'What are you trying to tell me, mentally he's not?' Mr Mayer asked. He seemed to have been able to find a pair of grey Evvaprest pants.

'Mentally, Mr Mayer, he's just a little worried. But I think we're going to be able to clear up that worry pretty fast. Do you mind if I use your telephone?'

'Go ahead,' said Mr Mayer, obviously bewildered.

Edmond put in a call to New Hampshire Hospital, Dr Oscar Ford. Oscar had only just reached his office, and he sounded tired and irritable.

'Oscar, it's Edmond,' said Edmond. 'Listen – I've had a real breakthrough. I want you to come down to East Concord as fast as you can make it.'

'E.C., that's *impossible*. I've got bodies backed up to the parking-lot. It's seven-thirty, I haven't slept all night, and I've got nine autopsies to finish before I get to bed. *Nine*, E.C. So don't ask me.'

'Oscar, I think I may have found where the virus has been coming from.'

Oscar was silent for a long, ruminative moment. 'You're sure about that?'

'As sure as I can be. That glass phial you found at the Harrington place, that was one of six. Young Bernie

308

Mayer discovered them in a secret hiding-place at Michael Osman's house, after Michael had died. Bernie kept them for a while, then sold them to all of his schoolfriends. And all of his schoolfriends' names tally with the death list.'

'For Christ's sake,' said Oscar. 'Where did Michael get them from?'

'Bernie thinks that Michael might have found them on Conant's Acre someplace. He went up there a couple of days ago, and saw marks that Michael had blazed on the trees. He wasn't able to follow them up because one of Senator Kelly's men told him to clear off, but he seems to be pretty sure that Michael must have found the phials somewhere around there. The two kids were bosom buddies; and always told each other everything. So if Michael had been blazing marks on trees, he must have done it on that one afternoon when Bernie wasn't with him – the afternoon that Michael died. He didn't get a chance to tell Bernie what it was that he found, or exactly where he'd found it, because he died so suddenly.'

Oscar said, 'I've already sent the phial down to Lim Kim for analysis. I don't think he gets into the lab until nine-thirty; but we should have some results by lunchtime.'

'Oscar, just get down here, will you? Let the dead wait for the dead.'

Oscar pressed his hand over the telephone for a moment: Edmond could hear his speaking in a muffled voice to someone else. Then he said, 'All right, E.C. I'll be with you in ten minutes. Give me the address, will you?'

SIXTEEN

At almost the same time, Chiffon Trent was being given her first taste of Denzil's creative movie-making.

He had woken her at first light by screaming at the top of his voice in her ear. She had screamed back at him in terror, and twisted against her bonds. But Denzil had stood back, his hands in his pockets, and laughed at her. He had been smartly dressed in a pearl-grey 1940s-style suit, and a wide tie with a purple palm tree painted on it.

'Scared you, didn't I? It's dawn.'

'Dawn?' she had asked him, blurrily.

'Didn't you know that all great directors get up at dawn? That's when the stars are at their freshest and their most vulnerabubble. You – well, my love, you look especially, *superbly* vulnerabubble.'

'You're not going to – you're not going to make a movie? Not *now*?'

'Now, pronto, *immediat-er-ment*.'

'You're crazy, it's dawn. I'm not going to – '

Denzil had laughed. Not a very humorous laugh, more like the laugh of a carny clown, or a sideshow busker. 'You're dead, remember? Such a tragedy. Even more tragic that once you're dead, you're not entitled to have opinions any more. How can you call me crazy, when you're dead? How can you object to starring in a couple of little movies, when you're dead? You're *dead*, Ms Trent. Deader'n mutton. So if anything should happen to you; you know, if you should start getting ideas about *protesting*, well, just think that nobody's going to come looking for you, and nobody's going to care. You're already beyond care, my love. You're already sitting at the right hand of Mary Magdalene, not to mention a few rather grubby seraphim. Understand me, young lady: if you don't do what you're told, you're going to regret it. And I mean, really regret it.'

He had quickly snapped free the scarves which bound her, and then ushered her naked down the corridor, soft carpet on bare feet; and down a narrow carpeted flight of stairs; and along another corridor lined with framed prints by P. Buckley Moss, spindly people in spindly landscapes, until he suddenly slammed open a door and there it was: the studio. Dazzlingly-lit, a large high-ceilinged room which had originally been a body-shop, but the brick walls of which Denzil had now painted a photographic matt-black, and at the end of which he had erected a three-sided plasterboard wall, decorated with gold-flock wallpaper and hung with mock-Regency paintings, a suitably rococo background for the orgy-sized curlicued bed which stood centre-stage, carefully made, as if by a hotel chambermaid, with plumped-up pillows and neatly turned-down sheets.

It was not the bed which immediately caught Chiffon's attention, however. It was the sight of two naked men who stood on the opposite side of the studio, arms folded, sharing a joint. One was black, one was white. Both of them were well over six feet, and built like football-players, with deep muscular chests and narrow waists, and sinewy thighs like Kentucky hams. They were talking slowly and slurrily, random phrases as if they were standing in line for a job at an Illinois meat-packing plant. Men who had come to service whatever girls had been arranged for them. Did you see the Giants last night? What about that 11-yard rush? That was *bad*.

'Here she is boys,' said Denzil. 'The star of our show.'

The two men glanced at Chiffon quickly, and then turned back to each other. Chiffon had the feeling that they were almost embarrassed to look at her, although she couldn't think why. If they were skin-flick actors, why should they be embarrassed?

'Come on over,' said Denzil. 'Introduce yourselves. You ought to be *introduced*, at least. I'll go see what's happened to Billy.'

Chiffon stood where she was, close to the end of the bed. The two men shrugged to each other, and walked across to her, and then stood either side of her with their muscular arms folded.

The black man was the taller of the two by two or three inches. His scalp was utterly bald, and polished, so that it had the dented sheen of a Washington Red apple. His cock and his balls had been shaved, too, and lightly oiled, so that they looked like some glossy mobile sculpture. He said, 'If you want to call me anything at all, you can call me Pisco. That's what my friends call me.'

The white man was blond, with tangled blond curls and a small blond moustache. He did nothing but grin shyly, and say, 'I'm John. How're you doing?'

Chiffon said, 'I never did anything like this before.'

'Well, sure, everybody has to start somewhere,' said John, with an absent grin. 'You'll probably take to it, you know. It's good money for easy work. Well, I mean, it's easier for a girl than it is for a guy. I mean, a guy has to keep it solid all the time, and that takes a special kind of talent, you know? You have to think about something else, like second-hand auto prices. I'm in second-hand autos, when I'm not doing this. John's High-Class Heaps.'

'Shit, man,' put in Pisco. He sucked at the roach, and then pinched it out with his fingers.

Just then, Denzil came back, with Mae-Beth strutting close behind him in a salmon-pink crochet mini-dress and his cameraman Billy Baszczewski slopping in a few paces after carrying a tripod. Baszczewski wore a red baseball cap and sneakers that sounded as if they were three sizes too large for him. The legend on his sweat-shirt read 'Help Save Whales, Stop Chewing Blubber.' He didn't even look across at Chiffon as he went to set up his video-camera.

Mae-Beth came and put her arm around Chiffon and said, 'Don't worry about this one, honey. This one is nothing at all, just a straight half-hour fuck film.' She smiled, and kissed Chiffon's cheek, and said, 'I know these two guys. They'll treat you good, I promise. Won't you, guys?'

'Sure, Mae-Beth,' said Pisco, laconically. 'Good as gold.'

Denzil coughed into his hand and said, 'Are we going to get this one together, or what? Let's have you people on the bed, all right; Chiffon in the middle. Let's start with lots of foreplay, okay? John, you can start by fond-ling her ass, right, and Pisco, I want to see those black hands squeezing those white tits, you got me? Never let it be said that I'm prejudiced. They should have the NAACP down here to see just what I'm doing to help the cause.'

Pisco shot Denzil a hard look when he said that; but obediently climbed on to the bed with the others. Chiffon lay down between them, smelling the coconut-oil on Pisco, the plain sweat on John, and she shivered because she was half-frightened and half-aroused. It was the feeling that her own free will had been taken away from her which disturbed her the most: that she no longer existed as a person. She was nothing more than a nameless naked woman whom any man could use exactly as he wanted. Because nobody was ever going to come to rescue her; and the only way in which she could survive from day to day was by doing exactly what these men demanded.

'Chiffon, this is going to be a fantasy sequence, right?' said Denzil, strutting in front of the camera with his hands in his pockets. 'Later on, we're going to slot this into a longer movie, you understand me, but we're also going to market it as a short video. You've fallen asleep, you've been having dreams about making it with these two guys; and all of a sudden you believe that you're actually doing it.'

Chiffon was trembling. In a choked voice, she asked Denzil, 'I don't know what to *do*.'

'Just respond, okay? You know how to *respond*, don't you?'

'I don't know whether I can.'

'Well, for Christ's sake, you're going to have to.'

'I don't know, I don't know, I *can't*.'

But then Pisco turned over, and murmured to her, 'Don't panic. You understand me? We're not going to hurt you. Take it easy. Be cool. Just close your eyes and think of somebody you love. You can do that much, can't you?'

Chiffon swallowed, and nodded. She was so frightened that her nipples were tight and stiff, and Pisco reached over and took one of them between his finger and his thumb, and gently rolled it, until it stiffened even more; and then he took hold of as much of her breast as he could contain in the palm of one hand, and squeezed it, black fingers into soft white flesh, and again he murmured to her, 'Don't panic, okay? Just think of somebody you love.'

The lights were angled until they dazzled her. Mae-Beth, somewhere behind the dazzle, put on a tape, soft samba music, the kind of music they play in cocktail lounges at over-expensive hotels. Chiffon lay back with her hair spread across the pillow, feeling Pisco's hands massaging her breasts, sliding down the sides of her body; and then John's hands, different, caressing her back and running up and down the backs of her thighs.

She tried to think of someone she loved, but the only person she could think of was Reynard; and when she thought of Reynard her head seemed to burst with frustration and anger and a feeling of being cheap and cheated. He must have thought she was trash, to have treated her like that. To have ordered her killed when she had once been his special lover.

Now Pisco was squeezing her breasts even harder, tugging at the nipples painfully. She let out an open-mouthed gasp; but all he did was to take her wrist in his powerful fingers and guide her hand downwards, until it touched his huge naked erection. He closed his hand around hers, so that she was obliged to clutch him; and when she tried to let go, he closed his hand even tighter, so that the message was clear.

Chiffon opened her eyes and looked at him. He was smiling reassuringly but there was something in his expression which warned her to do what she was told. 'Stroke me,' he told her; and she eased her hand up and down on the shaft of his cock, which was so distended that she could scarcely close her fingers around it; and all the time she was conscious of Mae-Beth watching her intently, and Denzil, with his hands in his pockets, and the cameraman Baszczewski moving in closer with his Panasonic video-camera. The soft whirr of the video recorder.

Now Pisco raised himself up on the bed, and turned over on to his back, his huge black member rearing upwards. He grasped Chiffon's hair, and forced her head towards his loins, until her closed lips were actually pressed against the dark-purplish head of his penis.

'Eat me, honey,' he said, with a stagey groan of pleasure, but there was no mistaking the command in his voice. Chiffon tentatively parted her lips, and tasted slippery salt and coconut, and then Pisco thrust the whole head right into her mouth, like a swollen plum.

'Come on, *eat* me,' he repeated, massaging her shoulders, and at the same time pushing her closer and closer, so that her whole mouth was filled with his hard black flesh, and she felt his tight crinkled balls against her chin. She almost choked as eight inches was pushed repeatedly into her throat, hard and fast, as if he were actually making love to her, again and again and again, and she held on to his bare slippery shaft only to stop it from thrusting in too far and suffocating her.

And meanwhile, the video camera was only inches away from her, recording in violent colour the sharpest detail of black skin against pink lips.

John climbed up behind her now, she could feel him even if she couldn't see him. He spread apart the cheeks of her bottom; and then, as the cameraman came around and zoomed in close, he seductively worked his fingers up between her legs, the middle finger into her blonde furry vulva, the index finger into the tense pink starfish of her anus.

She gasped as John probed deeper, although her mouth was crammed full, but as he worked his way into the interior of her body she began to feel more and more like a slave, more like a body to be used, and as she accepted her rôle as victim she began to feel increasingly aroused, and increasingly willing to let John and Pisco do what they wanted. It was the loss of her own identity that she was beginning to accept, the fact that she was nobody at all, not Chiffon Trent, not even 'O', but nothing and nobody at all.

Afterwards, she remembered only part of what had happened. She remembered both of them thrusting into her at once, two slick muscular sweaty bodies, one underneath her, one bearing down on her from above. She remembered Pisco buried tightly in her bottom, and John working his entire fist into her sex, so that he could clutch Pisco's erection through the thin membrane of skin that divided back from front. She remembered shrieking in pain and ecstasy, while the camera less coldly observed her from less than six inches away.

Denzil watched all of this without blinking more than

316

twenty or thirty times, smoking a cigarette. He had seen it scores of times before and he would see it scores of times again. Raw, sado-masochistic pornography. The gradual stripping-away of a girl's pride and identity and sense of herself, until she was willing to do anything for anybody and not even care if she was being paid for it, or even if it meant the difference between living and dying. When the final scenes were filmed, the shootings or the stranglings or whatever it was that the client had requested the girls were almost always ready for it; almost glad of it; a final cleansing agony; a sexual martyrdom. Ordinary people didn't understand. It frightened them. But Denzil knew how close this lay beneath the skins of ordinary men and women, and that was why it didn't frighten him at all. Violent orgasm and violent death shared the same basic ingredients.

'Two minutes,' he remarked to Baszczewski watching with complete detachment as Pisco started to climax spectacularly all over Chiffon's red-bruised breasts.

Mae-Beth said, 'It seems like a shame, you know?'

'*Life* is a shame,' replied Denzil.

Rossi stepped back at a three-quarter angle from the bed to record John's climax; then abruptly raised the video-camera and said, 'That's it, that's a wrap.' As suddenly as it had begun, it was all over.

Chiffon lay where she was, staring up at the black-painted ceiling. Mae-Beth went over and sat on the edge of the bed with a box of Kleenex.

'Are you all right, honey?'

Chiffon looked at her, as if she couldn't understand what was happening. Mae-Beth dabbed at her; and then said, 'It's a shame, the whole thing, but what can you do? It's supply and demand, you know? People want something, other people are prepared to pay good money for it. That's it.'

317

'All right, Mae-Beth,' said Denzil, coldly. 'Just get her back to her room, will you?'

Baszczewski the photographer sniffed loudly, and said, 'Where did I put that fucking lens-cap?'

Chiffon was led away by Mae-Beth like a woman hypnotized. Pisco meanwhile pulled on a black leather supporter and opened a can of V-8; John sat naked on the very end of the bed with his knees together and painstakingly began to roll another joint. Denzil went around switching off the lights, so that the studio flicked dimmer, and then dimmer.

A door at the side of the studio opened, and three young men walked awkwardly in. One of them came straight up to Denzil and held out his hand and said, 'Hello, Mr Forbes. How's things?'

'Oh, you,' said Denzil, without shaking hands. 'Who are these bozos?'

'Two of the best studs in the business; actors, too. Professional actors.'

'Any experience?' Denzil asked them.

'Some,' said one of the young men, a tough-looking Hispanic in yellow jeans.

'You?' Denzil asked the other one.

'I am a professional actor, just as Mr Manzanetti said. You want me to do something, and I will do it.'

'What are you, Polish? Last Polack I used, there was nothing but problems. Thought cocks were used for making holes in *ponczki*.'

He laughed, and slapped the young man on the arm. 'Just a joke, unh?'

'Russian,' the young man told him, sharply.

'Russian? Well, well. *Rad pazhnakomitsah*.'

'You speak Russian?' Piotr asked him, warily.

'Oh, boy, I know lots of things,' grinned Denzil. 'As long as you can keep it up for as long as those Soyuz space-stations, we're in business. Did you get a look at that last session we shot? Isn't that girl something?

That's the girl you'll be working with. And she's something.'

Piotr nodded, and tried to smile, but didn't answer. He was still shocked by what he had seen from the studio's upstairs gallery. Chiffon, of all the girls in the world. Chiffon, over whom he had grieved so bitterly. Alive, and provocative as ever, and making sex movies in the Mid-West. He felt such an explosion of emotions over seeing her that he didn't know what to say or even what to think. Relief, at seeing her alive; but revulsion, at seeing her with two strange men, being filmed; and ultimately anger, at having been taken for a dupe. She must have decided to break with him, and break with Reynard, and break with that failing movie-career of hers, and make money as a porno queen. Then what? A new life under a new name? Piotr neither knew nor wanted to care. It had been difficult enough for him to decide to come to Milwaukee and make himself some money as a hired stud. To find that the girl he was most fond of in the whole of the United States was already here, and making sex movies with black men . . . He tasted bile in the back of his mouth, and the hot smell of movie lights and electrical equipment began to make him feel suffocated and bilious.

'I must get some air,' he told Billy Manzanetti.

'You're not sick? You look kind of pallid.'

'I'm okay, just tired.'

'You'd better not be sick. You can't make sex movies when you're sick.'

'I'm not sick, all right? I just need some air.'

Billy Manzanetti reached into his jeans pocket and brought out a set of Avis keys with a red-and-white plastic tag. 'Take the car; go down to that grocery store we saw on the corner and buy us a couple of bottles of Chardonnay. You need some money?'

'I'm okay. I'll be back in ten minutes. I'm tired, that's all.'

Piotr left the large scabby-looking building on West Good Hope Road and walked out to the parking-lot. The white Pinto they had rented at the airport was parked next to Denzil's huge sagging Imperial Le Baron. It was nearly eight o'clock in the morning. The sky was light, with high cloud-cover, and the air was chilly. A typical fall morning close to Lake Michigan. Piotr rubbed his hands together to warm them up, and for some reason felt for the first time in years like a Russian; a compromised stranger in an uncompromising land.

He drove down to the Goodfayre store on the corner, and parked. He climbed out of the car, crossed in front of the store, and picked up one of the telephones outside. He said, breathily, 'I want a collect call to a number in New York, please.'

It took almost three minutes before the call was cleared. Then a sharp voice answered. 'Yes? This is Cerenkov.'

'I'm in Milwaukee,' said Piotr.

'So I understand. I'm paying for this call, remember.'

'Listen, I've found the girl. She's still alive.'

'What girl?'

'Chiffon Trent. It must have been a trick of some kind. Chiffon Trent is still alive and she's here. She can tell you everything you want to know about Reynard Kelly first hand. She knows more than I do.'

'Give me your address.'

'No. First, I want a promise from you that my mother will be left alone.'

'Oh, come on, now, Piotr. You could be making all of this up. It said in the newspaper that the girl was dead; and now you have made her alive again?'

'It's true.'

Cerenkov was silent for a while. Then he said, 'We may be able to come to some arrangement; if it is really her.'

'It really is.'

320

'Well, it's most suspicious.'

'Cerenkov, it's true. I can hardly believe it myself. One minute we were lovers, the next minute she was gone; and then I heard she was killed. Now I come to Milwaukee and by accident find that she is here. But, it is true. She is alive, and she is here.'

'I'm not sure, Piotr. Your mother has been guilty of many serious offences.'

'Leave her alone, Cerenkov, and I will tell you where you can find Chiffon Trent. I won't consider any other arrangement.'

'Hm,' said Cerenkov.

A chilly breeze blew a centre section of *The Milwaukee Journal* across the parking-lot; then the front page. The headline read *Mystery Polio Hits M'kee?*

Cerenkov at last said, 'All right. I think I believe you. I guarantee I will send instructions to Moscow to let your mother go. Now, tell me where you are.

Piotr told him. Then he hung up the phone, and stood in the wind for a while, his arms crossed over his chest as if he were ill, or growing old. At last, he pushed his way into the Goodfayre store, and looked around for the liquor cabinet.

The proprietor said, in a false-teethy voice, 'Kind of snappy this morning, aint it?'

SEVENTEEN

Edmond had borrowed a pair of wire-clippers from Bernie's father, and it took them only three or four minutes to snip away enough of the barbed-wire to clear an access. Oscar said, 'I hope very much that you know what you're doing, E.C. Senator Kelly isn't known for his sense of humour.'

Oscar didn't really mean it: it was nothing more than a way of concealing his nervousness. He was very tired now, he had been up all night, and like everybody at the New Hampshire Hospital; he was frayed and edgy and almost on the point of fritzing out. Edmond tugged away the last length of barbed wire, and said, 'I'm not asking anybody to *laugh*, Oscar. Heaven forbid.'

Bernie stood a little way off with his mother. His father had gone off to work already. He said, 'It's over there, by that big tree there. A triangle, with a circle in the middle.'

Edmond looked at Oscar meaningfully, although Oscar didn't really care or understand why. The triangle with the circle in the middle had been the secret blaze-mark that Bernie and Michael had devised between them, and this was the first time that Bernie had ever divulged it to anyone else. Edmond thought: thank God that people can still keep confidences between each other; that intimate secrets can still be held safe. Poor Bernie. He had suffered so much because of the bond he had had with Michael; even after Michael's death. Edmond hoped that God and whatever guardian angels there were would keep him safe from hyper-polio, and from every other disaster, natural or unnatural.

'We'll go ahead on our own now,' said Edmond. 'I think it's wiser. But we'll tell you straight away if we find anything.'

'Okay,' said Bernie.

'And what do you *say*?' demanded his mother.

'Thank you,' Bernie told Edmond. He was embarrassed, but Edmond could tell that he meant it.

'That's okay,' Edmond acknowledged 'If I'd ever had a boy, I would have wanted that boy to be just like you. You got me? Secret Agent X-17 over and out.'

Bernie joined in the game, and saluted. Oscar pulled a face, and said, 'What is this? The *Gangbusters* fan club?'

'Don't show your age,' said Edmond.

Edmond and Oscar climbed over the fence, and jumped heavily down into the ploughed soil of Conant's Acre. In the distance, over the trees, a flock of crows rose into the early-morning sky like a sprinkling of cloves. It was cold this morning; in New Hampshire, winter wasn't far away. They trudged over the furrows and their shoes made a brittle, crumbling sound in the earth.

'Do you have any idea at all what we're looking for?' asked Oscar, sniffing because of the chill.

'Do you?' asked Edmond. 'Where could a leather case full of virus-infected liquid have come from? The *glass* is made in Germany, but that doesn't mean anything.'

'Lim Kim said the phial looked old-fashioned. He hadn't seen one like that for twenty years.'

'Did he have any preliminary opinions about the liquid?'

'He's going to run every test on it known to man. Do you know what he said, though? There's an old Chinese saying. Truth comes in bottles, but out of old bottles come old truths. Not bad, huh?'

Edmond wiped sweat from his forehead with his handkerchief. 'I don't think I've ever believed in old sayings; except never trust a woman and keep your powder dry.'

They were almost halfway across the field. Oscar said, 'You're still staying away from home, hunh?'

'What would you do, if you found your brother was screwing your wife?'

Oscar took out his handkerchief, and trumpeted his nose. 'I think I'd probably shake him by the hand and nominate him for a Congressional Medal of Honour.'

Edmond smiled wryly, then laughed. 'You're a stupid bastard,' he said, affectionately.

They reached the woods. At first, they couldn't find Michael's blazemarks, and they walked up and down for fifty yards in either direction, north and south. Oscar called, 'I hope young Bernie was telling the truth. I'd hate to think I did all this exercise for nothing.' But then he suddenly said, 'Here it is. Is this it? The triangle with a circle inside it?'

The two of them strode noisily through the undergrowth and examined the blazemark carved into the bark of the tree. Edmond touched it with his fingertips. If only young Michael had known what was in store for him, when he had cut that mark. 'This is it,' he nodded to Oscar, and they trod further into the woods, stepping carefully, and looking out for further marks.

They found another, and another. The fourth one was way off to the right. 'If you ask me, he got scared round about here, didn't want to go too deep,' Oscar commented.

Edmond listened to the silence of the woods. There was a strange eeriness about them. The dry leaves fell without a sound on to the crisp, carpeted floor. Up above, the clouds were as still as a painting of clouds. No wind blew. 'There's another mark here,' said Oscar.

They came across the Condor undramatically, almost expectedly; as if a strange spectre like this was the inevitable source of a malevolent sickness like hyperpolio. The excavation was exactly as Michael had left it when he ran away, except that foxes or squirrels had been there, and the stretched yellow skin had been torn from the skeletal face of the airplane's pilot. Edmond and Oscar approached the airplane in awe; neither of them shocked by the sight of a corpse, because of their gruesome daily work; but both of them silenced by the sight of an entire airliner cockpit buried in the leaves and the loam of a New Hampshire wood.

'Jesus Christ,' said Oscar, hunkering down.

Edmond carefully slid down the side of the diggings and brushed loose soil and leaves from the airplane's roof. He peered inside the broken windows and said,

'There are two other bodies in there. Well, what's left of them.'

'Look at that flying-jacket,' said Oscar. 'This looks like something from the 'fifties, maybe even earlier. Did you ever see a flying-jacket like that?'

Edmond said, 'We must be able to get into that cockpit somehow. Maybe there's a door a little further back along the fuselage.'

'But how did it *get* here?' asked Oscar. 'How does anybody bury an entire airliner in a wood? I can hardly believe what I'm seeing.'

Edmond stood up, and shaded his eyes against the grey brightness of the morning. He pointed to the south-east, and said, 'Supposing it was trying to make an emergency landing on Conant's Acre . . . I mean, Conant's Acre would make quite a reasonable airfield for a large airplane like this.'

'Then what?'

'Well, supposing the pilot misjudged his approach. He could have hit the earth bank on the other side of the woods there, and gone straight in. The ground's very soft and boggy around here, and it's even softer down there.'

'Are you kidding?'

'Not at all. There was an article in the newspaper about six or seven months ago, about this historical society in England that goes around locating and excavating old World War Two fighters and bombers that were shot down during the Battle of Britain. Whole Dornier bombers, buried in fields in Kent. Spitfires and Hurricanes and what have you, complete with the pilot still inside them. Twenty feet deep, some of them. They dug up an entire B–17, too.'

Oscar rested his hands on his hips and looked down at the half-buried cockpit of the Condor. 'But *here*?' he asked, rhetorically.

Edmond said, 'Some of those planes hit the ground

at two or three hundred miles an hour. If the angle was right, and the dirt was soft, they went right in like a knife through butter, and nobody ever knew they were there.'

'So you think this plane hit the bank down at the bottom there, and pushed its way right in under the woods?'

'I don't see how else it could have gotten here. It hasn't been buried deliberately. Look at the way those tree roots are tangled around it, and most of those trees must be a whole lot older than the airplane.'

Oscar said, 'Let's dig back a bit more, see if we can't find a door.'

They found a couple of strong sticks, and began to hack away at the damp, crumbly soil. After five minutes or so, Oscar took off his coat, and rolled up his sleeves. They hardly spoke as they dug. Both of them felt unreal, as if they were participating in an extraordinary nightmare and the stillness of the woods served only to heighten the unreality. A squirrel watched them from high in a nearby tree; and birds chittered excitedly every time they struck the airplane's aluminium frame.

At last, a few feet back from the cockpit windows, they came across the edge of an access door. The aluminium skin of the airliner was corroded and leprous here, and as cold as a metal coffin. With the point of his stick, Edmond cleared the dirt out of the sides of the door, and chivvied a bowl-shaped lump of impacted mud out of the recess which housed the handle.

'There's some lettering here,' said Oscar, wiping the aluminium with his hand.

Edmond took a look. The words were painted in black, scratched and faded, but unmistakable. *Hier öffnen*.

'German,' he said, quietly. 'It's a wartime German bomber.'

'It can't be,' said Oscar.

326

'I don't know whether it can or it can't be, it *is*,' Edmond insisted.

'Did the Nazis have planes that could fly the Atlantic?'

'I don't know. Well – they must have done. Here it is. QED.'

'Maybe it was an airliner from the 1930s, made in Germany,' Oscar suggested.

'There's only one way to tell for sure. Help me get this door open.

'Maybe we should go back and tell someone before we start tampering with it,' said Oscar. 'We don't want to do any damage, mess up any clues or anything.'

'Oscar, we don't have the time. If that virus came from this airplane, I want to know how and I want to know why. The quickest way of identifying it is going to be by discovering who synthesized it. And if we can do that, we may be able to find out how to contain it, and vaccinate people against it.'

'If this is a German bomber, E.C., then the guy who synthesized it is very likely dead by now. Long dead.'

'Let's just get this door open.'

The two of them took turns to wrestle with the corroded handle for over fifteen minutes. They broke three sticks trying to lever it downwards, and they were almost about to give up when Edmond picked up the stone which Michael had used to break open the cockpit windows, and gave the handle six or seven heavy thumps. Gradually, a fraction at a time, the handle budged downwards, until at last Edmond could ease it free by hand. He gave one last pull, and the door of the Condor rattled open.

They cautiously climbed inside. There was a choking smell of earth and decay. A little light strained down the airplane's interior corridor from the broken cockpit windows up at the front, but the main body of the fuselage was pitch dark.

'I want to take a look in the cockpit first,' said Edmond.

They made their way forward between grey aluminium walls dripping with moisture and scaly with corrosion. The first body they came to was that of the navigator, a headless heap of bones in a black flying-jacket hunched over a chart-table. The map in front of him was mildewed and spotted with damp, but there was no mistaking what it was. A chart of New England and Nova Scotia, folded in half, with vectors drawn on Concord New Hampshire. The map was marked Nordöstliche Vereinigte Staaten. (Hamburg, 1942). As Edmond carefully eased the chart out from beneath the navigator's skeletal hand, Oscar shuffled forward a little and dislodged something on the floor which noisily rolled all the way down the dark length of the airplane's body.

'What the hell was that?' Edmond aked him, as the object reached the unseen tail-end of the airplane with a hollow clonk.

'Sorry. The navigator's skull,' said Oscar. 'Guy was careless enough to leave it on the floor. No wonder he flew his buddies into this wood.'

They went forward, into the main body of the cockpit. There was a pilot and co-pilot; the pilot leaning side-ways with his head half-out of the broken window, the co-pilot still sitting stiff and mummified at the controls. Behind the pilot's seat, hunched up into a fetal position as if bracing himself for a crash, was a yellow-skinned semi-skeleton in a green raincoat. He was wearing an old-fashioned trilby hat, and round horn-rimmed spectacles, and amongst the scattered finger-bones of his left hand there was a gold wedding-band.

Edmond distastefully opened the skeleton's raincoat, and reached into its inside-pocket. Between finger and thumb, he carefully drew out a brown leather wallet, and took it over to the navigation table.

Inside the wallet, there were $500 in U.S. bills; a folded receipt for cleaning at Zur Wäscherin, 71 Neukirchstrasse; Minden; a small black-and-white photograph of a plain-looking woman with dark braided hair sitting on a bicycle; two torn-off theatre-ticket stubs, each priced at 2 Reichsmarks; and an ID card issued by the OKW, the German Supreme Command naming the mummy in the trilby hat as Dr Wilhelm Eckhardt. There was a curled-up photograph of a round-faced man with short black hair.

'What do you think?' asked Oscar.

'I don't know. I don't know what to think. But this is a German wartime airplane, all right, and for some reason it was flown here to New Hampshire sometime during the war. Late 1944, I'd say – look at the date on the laundry bill. They obviously *meant* to fly here, to Concord, because it's all worked out on their map. In fact, they meant to land exactly here, on Conant's Acre.'

'*On* it, rather than *in* it,' Oscar commented. 'But what the hell were they doing here?'

'Maybe they were bringing the virus over to infect the population of the United States,' suggested Edmond. 'Maybe they thought they'd never win the war by military force, so they'd try something else, something more subtle.'

'I don't call hyper-polio subtle,' said Oscar, harshly.

They poked around the cockpit, but apart from code books and flying charts, they found nothing else of interest.

'What do we do now?' Oscar asked.

'What we do now is what we should have done way back at the very beginning. We go to the media and tell them what we've discovered. We show them the maps, the wallet, the leather case, and as many of those glass phials as we can find. We put the whole thing in front of the public; and hope that somebody out there will know enough about World War Two to be able to help us, and help us quickly.'

'You're going to upset a whole lot of people, including some of our friends. I misjudged Bryce, you know: he's really been pulling for us on this one. Why don't we take the whole lot to Bryce?'

'Because it's too late for protocol, Oscar; and something else has been rattling around in the back of my mind, too. Why did Senator Kelly really try to keep this epidemic under wraps? Do you think he might have *known* about this airplane, and what was in it?'

Oscar led the way back along the airplane's corridor, and grunted his way out of the open hatch. 'I don't see how he could have known. I mean, if he'd known about it, and wanted to keep it quiet, then all he had to do was destroy it. And the virus, too. If it *is* the virus. We'll have to wait and see what the lab has to say about it.'

Edmond climbed out of the airplane's hatch and scaled the side of their rough excavation, holding on to tree-roots to help himself up. 'What do *you* think it is?'

'I think it's the virus, but I'd prefer to know for sure.'

'How long is that going to take?'

'A couple of hours. They may even know by now.'

Edmond dusted off the maps and the wallet. 'All right. Let's go back to the hospital and wait until the lab can tell us for sure. Then we're going straight to the *Concord Journal* and WKXL.'

They retraced their steps through the woods, and then crossed Conant's Acre until they reached the fence. Edmond twisted some of the barbed-wire back togther again with his pliers so that it wouldn't immediately be obvious that someone had broken through.

Oscar looked back across the field. 'You know something,' he said, 'I almost wish we'd never found that thing.'

'I don't see why. Not if it's going to help us save some lives.'

'Oh, I know that. It's just that I don't think I'm ever going to feel happy about flying again.'

Edmond's car phone was bleeping when he opened the door. He sat sideways on the seat, picked up the receiver, and said, 'Dr Chandler here.'

It was Lara. She said, 'We've had seven more cases reported, doctor. And there's one special one.

'Special? What's special about it?'

There was a long pause, and a crackling on the phone. Then Lara said, in a strained voice, 'It's Mrs Chandler, doctor. Your wife.'

They sat in a bare cream-painted room at the American Embassy in Stockholm's Diplomatstaden; looking out through barred French windows over the embassy courtyard, and beyond to the bright green slope of Ladugards Gardet. It was an unexpectedly bright and sunny afternoon, with the sunshine through the bars casting striped shadows of imprisonment across Klaus Hermann's face and shoulders.

Bill Bennett stood with his arms folded, watching Klaus Hermann proprietorially. He wore sharply-pressed grey slacks and a sweatshirt with *Montana State University Bozeman* printed on it, in red.

Humphrey sat in the corner, on a tubular-steel chair. They had allowed him to go back to his hotel and collect his clothes (which had been crammed untidily into his suitcase and left in the lost-property closet). Now, however, they wanted him to remain in Stockholm for two or three more days in order to complete his formal identification of Klaus Hermann, and to assist with their lengthy investigation into the circumstances of his capture. Several people had died, and the Swedish police and intelligence services were anxious to have all the formalities properly dealt with.

Klaus Hermann himself seemed a little sad, a little tired, but philosophical about his fate. He told Humphrey that 'it was a day of terrible destiny, wasn't it, when I sat in that café next to you?' Humphrey had shrugged, and said, 'Yes, I suppose it was.'

Today, they had been running through Klaus Hermann's version of what he had been doing since 1945. He claimed that he had been working as a clerk for the Vsevolosk chemical factory, nothing more. 'Do you think they would have entrusted a German, a Nazi, with anything more important?' But neither Bill nor Humphrey believed him for a moment; and it was clear from the flat way in which he spoke that he didn't expect them to. He was simply making it clear to them that they would get nothing more out of him.

Bill said, 'Tell me something about Angelika Rangström.'

'What can I tell you? asked Hermann. 'She's dead.'

'All the same.'

'I loved her. She died for me. What else do you need to know?'

'You tell me. Did she ever come to Russia with you? Did she sympathize with the Soviet Union?'

'Sympathize? What kind of a question is that?' asked Hermann. 'How can anyone sympathize with the Soviet Union? The Soviet Union is not a sympathetic nation; it never pretends to be. Sentimental, yes. Gloomy and magnificent. But not sympathetic.'

They sat again in silence. Humphrey wasn't at all sure what the purpose of these sessions actually was, or why Bill Bennett expected him to stay there, too. He had already formally identified Klaus Hermann six times to six different officials, including a taciturn and mealy-faced colonel of the Swedish security services, and a young Israeli lady who smelled of onions. Bill appeared to be making no serious attempt to interrogate

Hermann, and quite often they had sat together without saying a word for more than twenty minutes.

Humphrey said, after a while, 'Do you think we might all have some tea?'

'Tea?' asked Bill. 'Yes, of course.'

Klaus Hermann shifted his position on his chair. 'It was with tea that the British won the war, you know. If there were any secret weapons in 1945, tea was the greatest. Dr Mengele used to say that an Englishman can endure anything, any torture, any privation, as long as you give him nine cups of tea every day, with sugar. He had quite a sense of humour, you know, Josef.'

Bill went out of the room to call the embassy secretary who had been detailed to look after them. He left the door ajar.

Humphrey said, 'This really does seem to be taking an awfully long time, doesn't it?'

Klaus Hermann shrugged. 'It is the way of all great bureaucracies to move with infinite slowness. You will probably find that all manner of complicated negotiations are taking place in order to have me extradited. And of course several different nations will be laying a claim to the right to try me, and hang me. As long as the Israelis don't get me, then I don't think that I really care very much.'

'Aren't you frightened?'

'I don't know. A little, I suppose. Everybody will say that I killed so many innocent people during the war without compunction, that I have no right to be frightened for my own life. But, yes, I am; just as all those unfortunate Jews were.'

Humphrey looked at Hermann for a long time. Then he said, 'Do you still feel guilty about what you did? Have you *ever* felt guilty?'

'It is difficult for me to describe what I feel. Regret was useless; there were so many of them. I felt no regret. But, some time during the 1950s, about ten years

333

after it was all over, I felt strangely *haunted*, as if I had been trailing the ghosts of all those Jews around after me like an invisible cloak; a cloak which grew heavier and heavier as the years went by. I decided that, whether you feel guilty or not, the souls of the people you kill cling to you, and never leave you, like the terrible chain which Marley had to drag behind him in *A Christmas Carol*.'

Humphrey stood up, and walked to the window. The sun had retreated now behind a heavy bank of clouds, and the shadows of the bars had faded. 'I believe in fate,' he said. 'I came here to Sweden because fate dictated it. My first holiday alone for years and years! And I should meet you.'

Klaus Hermann said, 'Well . . .' in a philosophical voice. Then, quite suddenly 'Have you heard the news from America?'

'What?'

'I was listening to the radio this morning. I have a radio in my room upstairs. They say that America has been struck by an epidemic.'

'Yes, so I understand. Quite serious, too. The British government is insisting that all visitors from America have polio vaccinations.'

'Yes, quite so.'

Humphrey turned around. 'What made you think of it?'

'I beg your pardon?'

'Just now. The epidemic. What made you think of it?'

'Well,' said Hermann, rubbing his hands together. 'The open door made me think of it. Or rather, the idea of being able to walk out of the open door.'

'I don't understand.'

'Ah, Mr Browne, then let me make it clearer. This is a delicate matter, you see, I have to phrase it correctly or you might possibly get the wrong idea. You are a fair man, I think. You are rather different from your friend Mr Bennett.'

'He's not my friend, you know. I didn't go with him voluntarily. I'm not here voluntarily, even now.'

'I understand that,' said Hermann. 'But nonetheless Mr Bennett needs you because you lend some legitimacy to what he is doing. He badly wants to see me dead, but he must be careful.'

'What has the epidemic got to do with any of this?'

'I believe . . . although I am not yet completely sure . . . that I am the cause of the epidemic.'

'*You*? How?'

Hermann looked down at the floor. He spoke quickly, and quietly, as if he were reading from a book. 'During the war, I was commissioned to breed a strain of virus which would be capable of decimating the population of the United States. Hitler had spoken again and again of how the wealth and power of the United States would bring about his downfall, unless some way were found either to persuade Roosevelt to withdraw his support for Britain, or if the United States could be so crippled that she would have to withdraw from the conflict out of sheer public fear and revulsion.'

Humphrey said, 'Germ warfare, that was the answer, was it?'

Hermann shrugged. 'We didn't exactly call it that. *Biokrieg* was the phrase we used at the laboratory at Herbstwald. There were twenty-nine of us there, research chemists and bio-physicists and virologists, the best in the country; and I was in charge. They gave us unlimited money, you know, the finest facilities you could dream of. And of course we had all those human guinea-pigs on which to test our various preparations.

'We made huge strides forward in bio-chemistry and bio-physics which were almost absurd, even by the standards of today. We discovered so much that sometimes we used to laugh out loud in the laboratory, as if

335

we were drunk! And then in 1943, one hot summer afternoon, we made the final breakthrough which allowed us to develop a strain of poliomyelitis virus which would be almost completely impervious to the usual methods of immunization and cure. Also, as the virus was passed from one human being to another, it would grow in strength and infectiousness, until it could cut swathes through millions of people in the space of a few weeks.'

Humphrey said, 'I don't know whether to believe you or not. It sounds so dreadful.'

'Dreadful, yes! The very word to describe it! We called it Pest-91, simply because that was the number of the culture in which we first developed it. But dreadful, certainly; and also very difficult to breed and to handle. You know what difficulty Sir Howard Florey had when he tried to manufacture penicillin in large quantities. Pest-91 was far worse. In the end we managed to suspend the virus in a liquid solution which would preserve it, we hoped, for several months. But we were only able to produce six small phials of this liquid in time for Hitler's proposed biological attack on the United States.'

Hermann took out his handkerchief and blew his nose loudly. Then, folding up his handkerchief again, he said, 'The plan was for one of our team to fly to the United States in a Focke-Wulf Condor. That was the only aircraft we had which was capable of crossing the Atlantic without refuelling. There, our man would make contact with some Americans who were sympathetic to the Nazi cause – *now* you can talk about sympathy! – and five of the phials would be distributed to German agents the length and breadth of the United States, in the most populous cities. New York, certainly; Philadelphia, I think; Washington; Los Angeles; and Chicago. The sixth phial would openly be shown to the American government, as would the airplane itself. Roosevelt would be threatened that unless he withdrew immediately from the European theatre of war, the virus would be released, and millions would die.'

'I've never heard a word about this before,' said Humphrey. 'You're inventing it. You're making it up.'

'No, my dear Mr Browne. I regret not. *Now* I can talk about regret! The Condor set off for the United States; but disappeared. Perhaps at sea, we don't know. Our friends in America swore they had heard it pass over the landing-site. But wherever it came down, it vanished completely. And inside it, of course, were the six phials of Pest-91. On the radio, they call it hyper-polio.'

Humphrey said, 'Why are you telling me this? I don't get your drift.

'My drift is this, Mr Browne. You are the only person who can rescue me. You are the only person who will even contemplate helping me to escape.'

'I won't do anything of the kind! Just because I've held all along that even a beggar like you deserves a fair trial – well, good gracious man, that doesn't mean that I'm going to help you get away! You're a mass murderer! You've as much as admitted it! And worse, if this story of yours is true, about the epidemic! Good God, you're still killing people, even today!'

'*Listen,*' insisted Hermann. 'The Americans are determined to silence me. After the war, when I was first working for the Russians, I was involved in a great many business deals between arms manufacturers and drug suppliers both in America and in the Soviet Union. I know far too much for the comfort of far too many American industrialists. You've heard of Mr Walter Ridgefield, of Ridgefield Petroleum? Yes – he is one of those honourable gentlemen who would do anything to have me disposed of. And there are many more. You remember what embarrassment Klaus Barbie caused among the good people of Lyons? I can wreak far more havoc, should I survive. But, of course, your friend Mr Bennett will make sure that I don't.'

'But this virus – '

'This virus, my dear Mr Browne, is my key to freedom. My only key! And the reason for that is that all of my wartime colleagues are now dead; and all of my records are safely stored in the Soviet Union. The only person in the Western hemisphere who knows how to stop that virus from wiping out 60% of the population of the United States by Christmas-time, is me.'

'There *is* an antidote?'

'Oh, yes. But it isn't at all conventional. If any American scientist manages to work out what it is in time to save the last few per cent of his countrymen, then I shall regard it as a miracle.'

'*Now* I understand you,' said Humphrey, outraged. '*Now* I understand what you are. Once a Nazi, always a Nazi!'

Hermann gave a faint and faintly nostalgic smile. 'You are probably quite right, Mr Browne. Hitler instilled in us a deep and everlasting hatred which never completely seems to leave one's mind or one's body. He always used to say that freedom could only be achieved by pride, and willpower, and hate, and hate, and once again hate.'

Humphrey said, 'You'd better tell Mr Bennett what this antidote is, so that he can pass it on to the right authorities.'

'Are you mad, Mr Browne?'

Humphrey flushed. 'You can't let thousands of people die when you know perfectly well how to save them!'

'Oh, I can. Why should I care? I'm old, I will die soon in any event, if Mr Bennett doesn't blow off my head first.'

'This is insane.'

'No, Mr Browne, not insane. It is nothing but the ruthless bargaining of an elderly man who wishes to stay alive. Now, listen to me. They will be taking me away soon, and disposing of me. There can't be many more opportunities remaining for you to help me to escape. You must go and speak to a man called Bendix. He has a house on Ostermalmsgatan. Tell him where I am and what is going to happen to me. Tell him also that you will try to get me out of the embassy, at some time of the day or night; and that he is always to have a man ready to whisk me away.'

'Herr Hermann, this is preposterous. You're under guard! I'll never be able to get you out of here!'

'You don't think so? Well, perhaps it will be difficult. But while you go to speak to Bendix, I will do my best to think of a way.'

'And in return for your freedom, you'll tell Mr Bennett what the antidote to this virus is?'

Hermann shook his head. 'I'll tell *you*. I'll write it down some time today, and when you have managed to get me out of the building, I will give it to you. If I don't keep my part of the bargain, you will have a chance to cry out for help, and I might still be caught. So you see that you have some guarantee.'

'Supposing you just write down something completely worthless? And how do I know that there really *is* an antidote to this virus?'

'Mr Browne, if I escape, I scarcely wish to live on a planet where Pest-91 is loose. You have my word that there is an antidote, and that I will give it to you when I am free.'

Humphrey said, 'I've a good mind to tell Mr Bennett all about this, right away.'

'And what good will that do you? I will deny everything you say. And I can assure you that even under torture I will not reveal the antidote. If you hurt me or kill me, then you will all come to hell with me, you and Mr Bennett and the entire population of the world.'

There was a staring, fanatical look in Klaus Hermann's eyes; and Humphrey involuntarily shivered, as if someone had 'walked over his grave'. Perhaps someone had.

'I'm going to have to think this over,' he said, solemnly. 'I'm not the treacherous type, you know. I worked very hard for the war effort, trying to catch up with chaps like you; and this does rather fly in the face of all that.'

Bill Bennett walked back in again, smoking the last of a cigarette. 'Tea's going to be here in a couple of minutes,' he said, breathing smoke out of his nostrils. He went back to the corner of the room, and stood where he had been standing for most of the morning.

'Perhaps we should have a game of cards,' suggested Hermann.

Bill stared at him without a word.

'Well, it was only an idea. Something to pass the time.'

humphrey said, 'They don't have any biscuits, do they? I'm afraid my stomach's rumbling rather a lot.'

Bill didn't answer. Silence fell between them again. Humphrey went back to his tubular-steel chair and sat down.

He didn't dare look at Hermann; but Hermann's proposition was churning around in his head like cake batter. Nobody had to know that it was he who had released Hermann; he could always pretend that Hermann had forced him – with a knife, perhaps, or a broken bottle. And when he produced the antidote for the virus, think of the fame and the recognition he would receive for that. Fifty times more than any of the credit he would get for having identified an old ex-Nazi. He would be seen as the man who had single-handedly saved the world. He would mix with royalty, and film stars, and heads of state.

Bill said to him, sharply, 'Something on your mind, Humphrey?'

'What? Oh, no. Not particularly. I was just wondering whether I might be allowed out to do some shopping this afternoon.'

'I'm going to need you back here at four. I've got two guys coming over from Finland.'

'Well, of course. I'll be back whenever you need me.'

'That's very co-operative of you, all of a sudden.'

Humphrey attempted a smile. 'We're all on the same side, aren't we? Special relationship, and all that. And, well, now we've caught Hermann there's nothing much else to worry about, is there?'

'If you say not.'

Humphrey let out a peculiar little noise, something like a cough, and then very much wished that he hadn't. 'I say not,' he said, trying to be jovial, and then he wished that he hadn't done that, either.

Malcolm was downstairs in the living-room, already half-drunk. Edmond walked in and stood looking at him without speaking.

'I didn't think that it could be so sudden,' said Malcolm, in a blotchy voice. 'One minute she said she couldn't breathe properly. The next . . .'

Edmond said, 'You realise that you may now be infected, too.'

'Huh,' said Malcolm. 'Yes. It had crossed my mind.'

'As far as we can ascertain, the virus is passed through the digestive tract just like the usual polio virus. Since you and Christy have been having sex, the possibility of a virus having been passed between you is relatively high.'

Malcolm opened his mouth, and then closed it again.

341

Edmond said, 'As yet, we have no way of curing it. If you have contracted hyper-polio, you're going to die.'

'I see,' said Malcolm. He let out an uneven laugh. 'The wrath of God, hunh, for taking my brother's wife in adultery?'

'Maybe.'

'Oh, "maybe." Listen to you, you priggish bastard. You screwed around more than anybody I ever knew. And now *I* get punished for it? Whoever punished *you*?'

'You did,' said Edmond quietly. 'You punished me, when you slept with Christy. The fact of the matter is that I did love her.'

'You don't know the meaning of the word.'

Edmond said, 'Have another drink. You might as well. It won't feel so painful if you're smashed.'

Malcolm swayed, and then suddenly sat down on the arm of the sofa, splashing whiskey over his wrist.

'You're serious?' he said. 'You really don't have any kind of cure for this at all?'

'Have you heard the news? It's broken out all over now, and there's nothing that anybody can do to stop it. They're sending up a special team of bio-physicists from UCLA tomorrow morning, and a whole regiment of assorted specialists from every germ-warfare centre in the country. Eighteen hundred dead already.'

'Edmond, if I really have caught this thing – '

Suddenly, there were tears in Malcolm's eyes.

Edmond said, 'Don't plead with me, Malcolm. If I had a cure, I'd give it to you. But don't plead, because there isn't one. And for God's sake don't tell me you're sorry.'

Malcolm raised both hands in a gesture of helpless despair. Tears ran down both cheeks.

'Go on, finish the bottle,' said Edmond. 'Knowing your luck, you probably haven't caught it anyway.'

He left Malcolm and went upstairs to the bedroom. Christy was lying on the bed, fully-dressed in a turquoise wool suit; and very white in the face. Edmond approached the bed slowly, and stared down at her as if he expected her to open her eyes any moment and smile at him. He felt almost foolish for not saying 'hello'!

So this is where it ends, he thought. All those years together. All those arguments, all those problems; all that loving. For this we met and courted and married. For this we went on vacation to South Carolina. He looked over at the wardrobes with their white louvred doors, and wondered whether it was worth taking her clothes out, and sorting out her jewellery. But then he thought to himself, what's the point? It's finished. All of her possessions are as dead now as she is.

He thought: it's strange, but I don't feel like crying.

There was a soft knock at the door behind him. It was Oscar. He said, 'You okay, E.C.?'

Edmond nodded. 'I think so. Maybe the shock'll hit me later.'

'You still want to go talk to the press?'

'I want to do that right now.'

'I'll drive you down there, hunh? Stacey and Killigan can take care of Christy for you; and I'll make sure that they lock up the house.'

'Don't worry about that. My brother's here.'

'You mean the dark-haired guy who pushed past me in the hallway? No, he's not. He went out of the door and took off like a rabbit.'

Edmond glanced towards Christy. 'He may have contracted hyper-polio.'

Oscar said, 'You told him?'

'Yes.'

'Well, then,' said Oscar. 'You did get your own back on him, after all, didn't you?'

By mid-afternoon, the President had declared a nation-wide state of emergency. The National Guard were mobilized in every state, and contingents of regular

343

soldiers were sent out to guard every hospital and clinic and medical warehouse. All police leave was cancelled, except in Alaska, and a nationwide curfew of seven o'clock was imposed on everybody except those performing essential services.

'I may be accused of over-reacting,' the President said gravely, on network television news. 'But I have to take serious account of the fact that nearly two-and-a-half thousand Americans have already died from the effects of hyper-polio, and that so far the epidemic shows no signs of abating.

'We must do whatever we can to minimize the spread of this deadly and indiscriminate disease. I ask you to remain calm, to avoid travelling away from home whenever possible, and to be constantly vigilant. Be assured that we have already set hundreds of highly-qualified scientists the urgent task of finding a cure for hyper-polio; and that we shall soon be successful. A special government fund is being set up to finance the vaccination of every man, woman and child in the United States as soon as an antidote is discovered, and that will halt hyper-polio in its tracks. We can lick this disease, and lick it promptly, but we need your help. So stay at home. Stay alert. And stay safe.'

It was impossible for the economic survival of the nation for the Administration to impose a total ban on travel; but medical students were drafted in from hospitals and colleges all over the country, and given the job of checking passengers at airports, harbours, bus terminals and railroad stations. They were told to check for redness at the back of the throat, shortness of breath, cramps, stiffness, and shivering.

The nation was unusually calm, and quiet. A newspaper reporter wrote that he drove all the way from Salinas to Ventura and didn't pass a single other car on the road. There were some fragmented outbursts of hysteria. Hundreds of would-be emigrants clashed with

344

Canadian customs officers at the border station of Blaine, Washington; and an elderly man was shot dead when he tried to ram the barrier in his station-wagon. His two-year-old grand-daughter was found crying on the back seat in a chequered pink romper-suit. And at Tijuana, CBS news cameras filmed the jarring spectacle of Mexican police and customs officials using truncheons and rifle-butts to push back scores of screaming Californian refugees, many of whom were brandishing diamond necklaces and hundred-dollar-bills, and even paintings, just to be allowed to escape from the United States and make their way south to Brazil and Uruguay.

A family of five were shot dead as they walked across the border at Sasabe, Arizona; and they lay in the sun for three hours with their blood drying in the dust before U.S. officials were allowed to come across and take them away.

But, mostly, there was an extraordinary quiet over America, from the shoreline of Kill Devil Hills to the beach at Punta Gorda; through the suburbs of Baltimore and Chicago, to the Creole quarter of New Orleans. Silence and anticipation, as if the whole nation was afraid to draw a breath in case the air was infected.

Reynard Kelly sat in his colonial house at English Village, Maryland, and watched the President's announcement with a stony expression. Then he pressed the Off button on his remote control, and sat back in his large buttoned armchair, one hand clasping a large glass goblet of white wine the other masking the lower part of his face.

He had been thinking all afternoon of his pre-war days in Germany. Daydreaming of Ilse, and those dances where the only way in which it had been possible to tell the men from the women was that the men were often prettier. Strange, heady, perverse days; as alluring in his memory as they had been in reality.

And he could almost hear, even today, the moist soft click of Ilse's lips parting to kiss him.

He had been in love then. Yet his love had come back to destroy him. Perhaps men who sought political greatness should never fall in love, he thought to himself. And he remembered with terrible vividness the way Goebbels had shook his hand, and nodded his head, and said, 'You have the face of a dreamer, Mr Kelly.'

On the far side of the room, Natalia Vanspronsen observed him with care and anticipation. She wore sharply-creased white slacks, and a dark blue linen blouse. She was reflected in the highly-burnished oak flooring; a white and immaculate image of professional femininity. She smelled of Joy.

'Well?' she asked.

Reynard didn't even look at her. For some reason, he had decided since her arrival in Washington that he didn't like her any more. Perhaps it was because she made it quite obvious that she wouldn't go to bed with him; not just to him, but to everybody around them. He couldn't even intimate that they were lovers. Everybody could see that they patently weren't. That, for Reynard, was something of a small defeat.

'Well,' he said, clearing his throat, 'they'll find an antidote, that's for sure. They must do. Dozens of the best scientists in the United States working on it, how long can it take? A week, maybe two weeks, not longer.'

'Do you think that will absolve you?' she asked.

'Absolve me? From what?' Now he shifted around to look at her.

'From guilt. From responsibility. It was you who had brought the virus into the country, after all. Everyone of those two thousand deaths is your responsibility, in the final analysis. Or don't you think so?'

'Do I pay you to provoke me?' asked Reynard.

'You don't pay me at all. My fees are met by the Democrats for Reynard Kelly.'

'But *I'm* Reynard Kelly.'

'Yes. And right at this moment, I expect you wish that you weren't.'

Reynard drank wine. He looked at Natalia, at her well-boned face, at the dark but obvious nipples that showed through her blouse. 'You're a bitch, of any kind,' he told her.

'That's why I was chosen to represent you. Or didn't you know that?'

'You and that wife of mine, both bitches.'

'Well, we're both Aries, if that's got anything to do with it.'

'I'm a Virgo,' said Reynard, gloomily.

'Well, in *that* case,' said Natalia, airy and dismissive.

'What was your suggestion again?' said Reynard, abruptly changing the subject. He didn't feel in the mood for sword-fencing on a personal level especially with a woman whose mind was as sharp as her looks. He could cope with women who were fuckable: women who cooed and teased and draped themselves around him. But women like Natalia Vanspronsen made him feel unhappy. He was too old for cutting critiques and smart creative talents. He wanted women around him who would remind him how radiantly his charisma still glowed; women who would caress his vanity, if not his penis.

'My suggestion was simply that the best form of defence is attack,' said Natalia. 'Dean Farber is basically right. You should deny any knowledge of the virus, or the airplane which brought it over. So what if they do find it on your property? Nobody else knows about it, except you, and me, and your immediate political family. And since you've already set up this research laboratory, you can take the whole thing a step further, and develop the scenario that Walt Seabrook and I worked out between us on the way down here. The laboratory could 'discover' that the virus came from the Merrimack River – a freak pollution that affected one boy, just by accident, and then was passed on from person to person, growing more infectious all the time.'

'Just how is the laboratory going to "discover" that?' asked Reynard, coldly.

'Very easy. Walt can take a virus culture from one of the hyper-polio victims and inject it into a sample of Merrimack river-water.'

'Are you really that unscrupulous?' asked Reynard.

'Aren't you?' Natalia reported.

'I'm not sure,' said Reynard.

'You're not *sure*? Listen, senator, two thousand people have already died. You *have* to be sure. Otherwise, we're all going to go to the political abbatoir together.'

Reynard looked at her narrowly. 'I don't believe you're sincere about this,' he said, and his voice was like a paper bag full of crushed glass.

'You don't expect a woman to suggest anything so unsympathetic?'

'I don't believe you're sincere, that's all. I don't trust you. Is that blunt enough, Ms Aries?'

'So what's your alternative? To sit here, and quake like a jelly, and hope that something will turn up?'

'You're fired.'

'Don't be so ridiculous. You can't fire me; not now. I'll be straight out of the door and down to the *Washington Post* before you can cough.'

'Blackmail?'

'Mutuality.'

'Mutuality, my ass,' Reynard growled. He drank some more wine. He wasn't as angry as he appeared to be, but he felt a terrible sense of political bad fortune all around him, like Macbeth, or King Lear. He couldn't shake it off, and Natalia Vanspronsen didn't make him feel any less doomed, in spite of all her bright and crooked suggestions. He had learned long ago that trickery always brought its own hideous revenge, with bells on. Condor had been the supreme example. After forty years, the spectre of his past had risen out of the ground and blighted his future, and it was far too late now to make amends.

Two thousand Americans had already died: thousands more were inevitably going to follow them. And Chiffon, for God's sake. He had ordered Chiffon's death like a man ordering a new barbecue pit. And in the end, that was what had broken him. That was what had brought him to understand what kind of man he actually was.

'You say Walt Seabrook can mock up a sample of polluted river-water?' he asked, in a tone so offhand that he might have been asking if a decorator could wallpaper his landing.

'That's what he says.'

'He wants to be the Assistant Secretary for Health that badly, unh?'

Natalia nodded. 'I believe so.'

'And you want to be there when they elect me President?'

'Mutuality,' she said.

There was a brisk knock at the door, and Dick Elmwood came hurring in. 'Mr Senator,' he said, as a courtesy, but without saying anything else he picked up the remote control next to Reynard's chair and switched on the television again. They heard the voice first – a voice which Natalia recognized at once. Then they saw the face, Edmond Chandler, with Dr Oscar Ford in the background.

' – from a Nazi bomber?'

'That's right. We found it buried in the woods at a place called Conant's Acre, which is in the southern section of Senator Reynard Kelly's estate.'

'You mean to say that this Nazi bomber had crashed on Senator Kelly's property at some time during World War Two?'

'Yes. Exactly that. It isn't very common knowledge, but aircraft can sometimes bury themselves deep into the soil when they crash, especially at high speeds, and disappear almost without trace.'

'And you think the hyper-polio virus was brought over by this bomber in World War Two?'

'I'm sure of it.'

'Well, just a minute now, we've already got our roving camera team out at Conant's Acre, and, just a minute, yes, here's the first report, hello there, Marcus, have you located anything yet? Can you hear me?'

'Hello there, Dave; yes, we've found it, and let me tell you here and now this is the most spectacular find, we've located the front section of a huge buried airliner here, and most gruesomely of all, if you look here you'll see hanging out of the window the skull of the original pilot who must have flown this airplane here in the 1940s, forty years ago, still wearing his flying helmet and black leather flying jacket. There isn't any question at all that this is a genuine find, this whole airliner is absolutely buried here in the woods, tree-roots still clinging around it, and we have our airplane expert here, Kenny Freo, hi Kenny, you work for the Smithsonian, isn't that right, and what do you judge this airplane to be?'

'Well, there's no doubt about it at all, Marcus, this is the nose section of a Focke-Wulf 200, the Condor, which was an airliner built to fly non-stop from Berlin to New York in the late 1930s, but which was later used to attack British convoys across the Atlantic, you know because of its exceptionally long range.'

'And how would you rate the discovery of one of these Condors buried in a wood here in New Hampshire after all these years?'

'Well, momentous, that's the only word for it. A Condor was supposed to have made a bombing run on Nova Scotia during the war, but that was never proved; but here we have an entire airplane which conclusively establishes that the Nazis did try to reach the United States during World War Two and did actually succeed, which just goes to show how close we were to having World War Two fought on our own soil.'

'Now then back to the studio because Dr Edmond Chandler of Concord, New Hampshire, believes that World War Two has actually caught up with us in the form of the hyper-polio epidemic which is sweeping the nation from East to West . . .'

Reynard switched off the television with the remote-control and sat tense and hunched without saying anything.

'That was the doctor who spoke to us in Concord,' said Natalia.

'Him?' asked Dick Elmwood. 'Dr Edward Chandler?'

'Edmond. Edmond Chandler.'

'How did those people get on to my land?' asked Reynard, dully.

'Does it matter?' asked Natalia.

'Obviously it doesn't,' said Reynard. 'That's the whole trouble with this world today. Everybody thinks they have a right to intrude. Everybody thinks they can go wherever they want, regardless of people's property. They found it, God damn it. The damn thing was buried. Buried! How the *hell* did it get buried? How the hell did they find it? Forty years I've looked for that plane!'

'Senator,' said Dick Elmwood, soothingly. 'There isn't any future in getting upset.'

'There isn't any future at all,' said Reynard. 'They've found the damned airplane. Use your brains, Dick. Don't you think there were maps on the plane, showing where it was supposed to land? A navigator's log?

351

Maybe even instructions, from the German Supreme Command.'

'You *deny* it,' Dick insisted. 'You deny all knowledge. You never saw or heard of that airplane before in your life.'

'But for God's sake, Dick. They found the plane on my land. Two thousand people have died because of that plane. Do you think I can live with that? Do you think I want to?'

'Senator,' warned Dick Elmwood, 'you've got to ride this thing out, one way or another. I mean, think about the alternatives. You were involved with the Nazis during the war? What do you think that's going to do to you? You took money from the Hitler regime? And then Greta's going to say that you rented her services as First Lady-designate, even after you'd separated, and she was living with another man? We're talking about the finish here, senator. We're probably talking about a jail sentence. Watergate isn't going to be anything on this. And what else do you think is going to come out, when some of your trusty aides start plea-bargaining? Chiffon Trent? Ted Peale? Senator, you've got to keep on going, because if you don't, you're sunk.'

Reynard smothered his face with his hands, and sat silent for whole minutes on end.

Then he looked up, and said, 'What can I do? Go on, tell me. What can I do?'

'You have to be cool, first of all,' said Dick. 'You have to stop feeling guilty. You have to tell yourself, this epidemic was all an unfortunate accident because it was, wasn't it? You didn't *want* it to happen. That's the first point. Then you have to say to yourself, this Dr Edmond Chandler is probably being vindictive, right at the start of my election campaign. He happens to have stumbled across an old German airplane buried in my woods, which I knew nothing about; and in some ridiculous way he's trying to connect it with the epidemic. How *could* it be connected? It's all nonsense. There were several attempted Nazi flights to America, and one of them happened to go astray and crash on my property. That's not my fault. Besides, I've already spent thousands of dollars of my own money setting up a research clinic to find out how this epidemic can be beaten. So what do you say to that?'

Reynard said, 'It's no good, you know, Dick.'

'It's no good because you're feeling depressed and guilty. For God's sake have some confidence! All you have to do is *deny* everything, rock solid, over and over again. In the end, they'll believe you; and if your clinic can actually come up with some kind of antidote, you'll be right on top.'

Just then, Walt Seabrook came in. 'Hope I'm not interrupting,' he said. 'But I've just been talking on the phone to some of the medical people in Concord. They're furious, of course, because Dr Chandler has gone right over their heads, straight to the media. And the guy who's most furious of all is Harold Bunyan, he's on the health committee.'

'Well?' Reynard demanded.

'Well, it seems like the redoubtable Dr Chandler doesn't have such a good reputation. He moved to Concord from Manhattan because he killed his girlfriend by attempting a tracheotomy with a restaurant carving-knife. The Medical Association were going to bounce him, apparently, but he called in a few markers, especially with Harold Bunyan, and in the end they allowed him to set up in practice near Concord, attached to the Merrimack Clinic.'

Reynard sat up straighter. 'What are you saying, Dr Seabrook? He's a *killer*?'

'He cut his girlfriend's throat.'

'Would you say as much, on television?'

'It's true, why shouldn't I say it?'

Reynard clapped his hands. 'We've got him, then! If

he's a killer, we've got him! Who's going to believe the word of a killer? A doctor who slits people's throats? We've got him!'

Natalia said, 'You'll ruin him, you know that?'

'My dear, that's the whole idea. What do you think he's trying to do to me?'

'I don't know. Nothing. It seems to me like he's trying to put a stop to this epidemic.'

'Well, first things first. And the first thing to do is to get Dr Seabrook here on network television, denouncing Dr Chandler as a killer and a phoney.'

'Do you know something?' said Natalia. 'I came here today prepared to help you get out of a difficult and dangerous situation. I knew you'd done wrong; but I thought it was one of those long-forgotten things that didn't mean too much. But I think I made a mistake. You supported the Nazis during the war and you haven't really changed, have you, for all of your talk about Medicare and sharing wealth and helping the poor. Deep down, Senator Kelly, my love, you have nothing in your heart but utter contempt for everybody around you. No wonder you supported Hitler. You're an empty, arrogant, careless, and brutal man. And worst of all, you have the gall to sit there and denounce a man who *does* care.'

Dick Elmwood looked across at Reynard with an expression that obviously meant, what are we going to do with *her*?

But Reynard seemed scarcely to have heard what Natalia was saying. He had lost interest in her as soon as she had made it plain to him that she didn't fuck. Well, not him, anyway, and that was all that mattered. He said to Dick Elmwood, 'Make the media arrangements, will you? Get Dr Seabrook here on the first prime-time news this evening. Let's show these people what we're made of.'

'Slugs and snails and puppy-dogs' tails,' said Natalia, and collected her purse and her notes and stalked out.

'You're going to let her go?' said Dick Elmwood. 'She knows all about Condor. She could ruin everything.'

Reynard's left eye twitched involuntarily. 'Yes, well, you're right. Make sure you . . . well, just don't tell me. But make sure. I don't want any repercussions. Not with all this business to take care of. Now then listen, Dr Seabrook, what were you saying about this doctor? What did he do? Cut somebody's throat?'

Walt Seabrook looked anxious. 'You're not going to do anything to Natalia, are you? I mean, I get the feeling that you're thinking of – '

'What?' asked Reynard. He focused on Walt Seabrook as if he were drunk, one eye at a time. 'You got the feeling that we were thinking of *what*?'

'I don't know,' said Walt Seabrook, uneasily. And it was then that he understood for the first time just how far out of his own league he had strayed; and that he was now amongst players who were prepared to give up everything rather than lose; and who would kill to win.

'I don't know,' he repeated. 'I must have – misheard.'

EIGHTEEN

Natalia survived by acting swiftly. Instead of going back to her room to collect her travelling-case, she walked straight out of the front door, across the cobbled court-yard; then climbed into her rented Zephyr and drove out through the gates of Reynard's house with a quick squitter of tyres. One of Reynard's men was on the gate, but Dick Elmwood hadn't yet had time to warn him, and he smiled and saluted as Natalia sped past.

She drove out through English Village and headed north-east for Wisconsin Boulevard, turning south-east through Chevy Chase and into the outskirts of Washington itself. She felt utter fright as she drove, and kept checking her rear-view mirror to see if any of the cars from Reynard Kelly's house were following her.

It was an unnaturally dark afternoon. A heavy bank of cloud had moved in from the west, and even though the sky over the city itself was still bright, and the Capitol shone like some mystical oriental palace, most of the traffic around her was driving on sidelights. She joined the anonymous river of cars that was flowing along Massachusetts Avenue towards the centre.

Natalia was not intellectually sure why she had felt the need to escape from Reynard's house so urgently. But all her life she had been extra-sensitive to atmospheres, to undercurrents of fear, and even when she and Walt Seabrook had first arrived there, she had sensed almost at once that something was wrong. She had remarked to Walt that the house had the same dreadful electricity as Hitler's Bunker, or the White House during the last days of Watergate. There was a closeted, hysterical feeling, with staff rushing around in ever more hopeless circles, while at the epicentre of the tragedy, the once-grand leader sat inert, unwilling and unable to carry on.

They had come down to Washington to present Reynard with their plan to blame the epidemic of hyperpolio on faked-up pollution of the Merrimack River, but even before they had begun to discuss it she had realized that it was all too late. The epidemic had spread much more quickly than Walt Seabrook had expected, and the irreversible fact was that Reynard had given up. There was murder in the air, actual fresh-blooded murder, and Natalia wanted out, and fast.

She checked her rear-view mirror again. Off to the left, a dark-blue Thunderbird with a tan roof was keeping pace with her, although it was impossible to tell in the late-afternoon gloom whether it was the same Thunderbird that had been parked outside Reynard's house. She changed lanes, and the Thunderbird changed lanes behind her. Maybe the driver was just taking advantage of the gap she had left in the flow of traffic. Maybe he was following her.

When she had first arrived at Reynard's house, she had looked around at Reynard's senior staff – Dick Elmwood, Dean Farber, and all of the others – and she had seen for herself why Greta had once called them the Snake Pit. Wherever she had gone, one of them had always seemed to be there, watching coldly, giving her one of their reptilian smiles which were more unsettling than no smile at all.

Greta herself had spent most of the day shut up in her bedroom, talking on the telephone to her lawyers, her real-estate managers, and as many of her friends in New England as she could reach. When Natalia had seen her at lunch she had seemed distracted, almost haunted; although her mood had improved later, after she had spent some time with Walt Seabrook. Natalia suspected that they had either been snorting, or making love, or both.

All the same, it was extraordinary and disturbing how many of the people around Reynard Kelly seemed to be winding-down, and malfunctioning, as if they were automata who depended on Reynard for their power. Natalia could understand it, in a way. Reynard *was* power. He had money, and influence, and position. But now this was all threatened by Condor, and the consensus of opinion among the staff seemed to be that there was no way out of it.

Natalia expected Reynard to try every last twist and turn to avoid the blame for what had happened. But the grinding, incontestable truth was that he had done a deal with the Nazis during the war, and accepted a

357

huge payment for his services in gold bullion. He had also, and more seriously, brought over to the United States a lethal virus which was threatening to destroy the American way of life for ever, and to change the face of the Western world. The damning evidence of his treason had been dug up intact on his own land.

It no longer made any difference if Reynard managed to escape the blame for what he had done – the burden of responsibility which he now had to bear, even for a man as unscrupulous as he was, had become too crushing for him to function as a decision-making politician, or even as a bearable human being.

Natalia's own hopes of fame and glory had died the moment she had seen Reynard's face today. Shifty-eyed, grey, and somehow bloated, as if all the lies he had ever told had decomposed inside of his head.

She took a sudden right off Massachusetts Avenue, southwards down 23rd Street. Two cars followed her, but the blue Thunderbird carried straight on. She pulled over to the side of the road and waited until at least a dozen cars had overtaken her. Then she drew out into the traffic again and carried on south, crossing the Potomac over the Arlington Memorial Bridge, and making for the airport along the Mt Vernon Memorial Highway. Airplanes rumbled overhead, rising from the airport runway with their lights flashing and their wings catching the very last of the sun.

It would soon be curfew time, and without her identity papers Natalia was going to find it difficult to travel. But at least she had her airline tickets, where she had carelessly left them in the Zephyr's glove-box. She thanked God for her one principal personality flaw, her untidiness.

She parked the car right outside the terminal building and left it there. She didn't think that she would be coming back to Washington for a very long time, if ever. Not as long as Reynard Kelly still lived. She went straight to the shuttle desk and found that there was one last shuttle to Boston, leaving in ten minutes. The girl behind the desk didn't even ask to see her ID.

She went to the telephone, and put through a collect call to Dr Edmond Chandler, in Concord. While she waited to be connected, she kept her eye on the terminal entrance, in case she saw anybody she recognized from the Reynard entourage. The last thing she wanted to do was end her life in an airport phone-booth.

'Edmond Chandler,' said his voice, at last; when she was almost about to give up and make a run for her plane.

'Dr Chandler, it's Natalia Vanspronsen. I don't have long, I'm running for a plane. But I'm flying back up to New Hampshire and I'll see you later tonight. The most important thing I have to say to you is this: Dr Walt Seabrook is probably going to denounce you on television as a fraud. Something about a fatal tracheotomy you once performed. Well never mind now. But be warned that's what they're going to do. And also be careful. Reynard Kelly is very desperate now, and I'm worried he's going to stop at absolutely nothing to keep this business under wraps.'

Edmond said, 'You sound kind of strained. Are you okay?'

'Well, let's just say that I got out from under as quick as I could.'

'Call me as soon as you get into Concord Airport. I'll come by and pick you up.'

'I'll see you later, Dr Chandler.'

'Take care, Ms Vanspronsen.'

Natalia hung up. Her flight was being called. She walked quickly across the concourse and through the gate.

Denzil Forbes switched on the lights in the warehouse one by one. It was a huge, dry, airy place; once used for the storing of grain and sugar. Now, however, it was Denzil's special movie location: the studio where he could film the ultimate in eroticism and the ultimate in human agony. In the centre of the floor a large carpet had been laid out, and heaped with dozens of pillows and cushions, and all around this makeshift set there were clusters of lights, and two movie cameras set up on tripods.

What wasn't yet in view was the large jerry-can of gasoline which Denzil intended to use in the final moments of his movie-making. Nor was the fire-extinguisher with which Denzil could prolong the agony at will; dousing and re-lighting the fire again and again.

The five young men who followed Denzil into the warehouse were bare-footed and dressed in a variety of robes and towels; so that they looked like a sorry collection of bathers from a cheap Eastern-seaboard hotel. Piotr wasn't amongst them: he had made an excuse to an irritated Billy Manzanetti about a bad stomach, and borrowed his fare back to New York. Denzil looked the young men over, tightening his necktie as he did so, and said, 'Not exactly the greatest team of studs I've ever laid eyes on; but I guess you'll have to do.'

'Hey, is there any chance of getting something t'eat?' asked one of the young men. 'I'm starved.'

'We'll send out for some burgers later,' said Denzil.

'Char-broiled, hunh?' giggled one of the young men, nervously.

Denzil gave him a stare that could have frozen Lake Muskego hard enough for skating. He was in a state of high tension himself, but when he was in a state of high tension he preferred to stay tense until everything was over. He didn't appreciate wisecracks.

'I just want to say one thing,' said Denzil. 'You boys know what we're doing here, you've been paid big money to do what you're told and say nothing at all when it's finished. Just remember who you're doing business with here. Not some half-assed Hollywood outfit trying to make a few extra bucks. You're doing business with big people. Big people who can reach out and get you no matter where you go. So do me a first-class job today, then go away and forget about it forever. You understand me? *Comprendo*?'

A door at the far end of the warehouse opened, and Mae-Beth came in, leading Chiffon by the hand.

'Hey, she's *nice*,' said one of the young men.

'Jesus,' said another, thinking with excitement and dread about what they were going to do to her.

Chiffon came obediently over to the heaps of pillows, and there Mae-Beth helped her to take off the loose white kaftan she was wearing. She stood where she was, not moving, staring at nothing at all. This was her seventh movie in three days, and at some stage during those seven movies her mind seemed to have switched itself off, so that she did nothing more than eat and sleep and wake up and do what she was told. If Denzil said go down on this man, she went down on him. If Denzil said put more life in it, for Christ's sake, she put more life in it. She couldn't think of anything at all. He had taken away her will, and replaced it with a set of instructions for survival. At least, he had told her it was a set of instructions for survival, and she had believed him, simply because there was nothing else for her to believe.

Denzil's cameraman came in, wiping his wet hands on the back of his jeans. 'Don't you have towels in your head?' he demanded, of nobody at all; and then finished drying his hands on one of the boy's flannel bathrobe. 'Is she ready?' he asked.

Chiffon was standing in front of the cameras meek and nude, her nipples stiffened in the draft which blew softly across the warehouse, her eyes fixed on a point somewhere between infinity and utter forgetfulness. She looked startlingly beautiful this morning, regardless of what had been happening to her, and regardless of her unseeing stare. She could have been a bruised Ophelia, or some minor neglected madonna.

'Let's do it, shall we?' suggested the cameraman, unconsciously repeating the death-house words of Gary Gilmore. He switched on the movie-lights, and the heaps of pillows were transformed into a brightly-illuminated arena.

'Off with the robes, *muchachos*,' said Denzil. He was deliberately needling the one Hispanic among them, a sallow boy with an incipient black moustache. The young men stripped off their robes and shuffled around, uneasy and skinny and naked. One of them, who had shot a whole slew of skin films before, started to masturbate himself enthusiastically into an early erection. 'I didn't ask you to come here to beat your meat,' said Denzil sharply. The young man stopped, and the erection died away. One of the other boys laughed.

They filmed for an hour. The young men were awkward and bashful at first, but as the heat from the lights grew more intense, as Chiffon responded to them with all the sighs and moans and writhings that Denzil required of her, they began to grow more lustful, and thrusting, and to thrill to the total sexual licence which Denzil had given them to ravish this pretty girl in any way they felt like. Two of them crammed themselves into her mouth at once, while two more penetrated her, and the third massaged himself between her breasts. Chiffon twisted and turned amongst the pillows, no longer feeling pain, no longer feeling ecstasy. She was somebody else, playing Chiffon.

As the hour came to a close, Denzil laid his hand on the cameraman's back, which was a signal for him to cut, while they prepared for the climax. The final torture, the final conflagration.

'Take a break now,' said Denzil. 'Let's get ourselves into shape for the big exit, unh?'

The boys climbed up sweaty and panting from the pillows, all except for one of them, who was still waiting red-faced for Chiffon to fellate him to his second ejaculation.

Denzil walked over the pillows and gave the boy a hard kick in the backside with his sharp-toed suede shoe.

'What's the matter with you?' Denzil demanded. 'When I say stop, I mean stop.'

'I didn't finish.'

'Are you arguing with me? Do you want to go the way she's going? They'd like a twosome. Burning and fucking at the same time.'

The boy scrambled to his feet and backed off. 'I'm sorry, okay? I got carried away.'

Denzil turned away; but, as he did so, a door opened somewhere on the opposite side of the warehouse, and he began to turn back again. There was a shuffling, scuffling sound, like soft-soled feet dashing quickly across the concrete floor. Then a sharp snap.

To everybody's amazement, Denzil's head blew apart. A huge chunk of bloody bone and quiffed hair flew right up into the air, and then there was a wholesale splattering of blood and yellowy mush, which was Denzil's brains. The shoulders of his smart grey suit were dark with sudden gore, and he dropped to the pillows as abruptly as if he had been a large marionette all his life, and somebody had suddenly decided to snip his last supporting string.

The five young men turned this way and that in bewilderment. But it was only when there was a rattling burst of sub machine-gun fire that they understood they were being shot at.

'Oh God!' one of them cried out, but those were the only words that were spoken. Mae-Beth dropped to the floor, patterned with red; and then there was a long spasm of fire which brought down three of the five young men.

The Hispanic boy almost made it to the door, but then he was hit in the back again and again and again, and his flesh was torn up as if he were being devoured alive by some terrible invisible creature, muscles and vertebrae and chewed-up ribs.

Denzil's cameraman, more experienced in making quick getaways, dodged and ducked and rolled himself across to the opposite side of the warehouse. A burst of six or seven bullets hammered on the partition wall beside him, and a fragment hit him in the muscle of his upper arm, but he managed to tuck himself down beside a tea-chest full of rubbish and sawdust, and the next hail of bullets that came after him failed to penetrate.

He cautiously raised his head, just in time to see a man in a grey-green combat suit and a grey ski mask run quickly across the warehouse floor.

'Listen!' he called out. 'I give up, okay? I surrender. But this was nothing to do with me, any of this. I was just hired to take pictures. I didn't even know what they had in mind.'

There were more softly-running feet. The cameraman guessed that they were trying to surround him.

'I'll surrender, okay?' he called out again.

'*Idyiti syuda*,' a voice nearby instructed; although the cameraman wasn't at all sure that they were talking to him.

He glanced to his left. There was a door there which led out to the parking-lot. If he could only manage to get it open, and roll out of it, he would have a chance. The problem was that between him and the door there were four or five feet of open, exposed space. They would shoot him down as soon as he appeared.

Then he turned around to his right, and saw the gasoline can which Denzil had brought along for the movie's blazing denouement. That was metal, right? Probably thick enough to deflect a couple of bullets. If he could hold the can up in front of him, he might be able to get out of the door before he was hit. At least it was better than lying here, all crouched up, waiting for them to move in and execute him.

He shuffled backwards until he could feel the large cold can of gasoline against his back. Then he reached behind him and grasped the handle and shifted it slowly forward until it was next to him. Now all he had to do was hold the can in his arms as if it were an oversized, overweight baby, keep his head well down behind it, and make a dive for the door.

A voice, even nearer, said, '*Stoy*.'

But the cameraman lifted himself up on to one knee, embraced the gasoline can, hefted it up a little higher so that his head was protected, and lunged towards the door.

There was a crackle of firing. A shower of bullets boomed and pipped against the side of the jerry-can, and a ricochet shattered the small window in the middle of the door. The cameraman lost his balance, and lurched against the wall, but he managed to reach out and seize the door-handle, and wrench it open.

As he tried to duck into the doorway, however, there was a heavier, louder shot. A .303 round from an AK47, muzzle velocity 2,350 feet per second. It burst into the gasoline can, and the can exploded with a breathy and fearsome *foommff!* The can fell. The cameraman shrieked. And for one moment he was framed in the doorway, his head and shoulders a mass of flames, his hair sizzling, his hands raised like two torches. Then he dropped sideways out of sight.

One of the men in combat suits walked cautiously forward, his Czechoslovakian Skorpion machine-pistol raised in his left hand. He looked down at the burning cameraman for a while, then turned back towards his three colleagues and said, 'Prinyistyi mnyeh devushka.'

Chiffon, shivering, shocked, was brought across the warehouse, one of the towelling bathrobes wrapped around her to hide her nakedness. She stared at the man with blotched eyes.

He said, carefully, 'You have been saved. Do you understand me? We have rescued you from these people.'

Chiffon stared at his faceless ski-mask, and then behind him to the doorway, where the cameraman's body was still burning and guttering like a fatty candle. One of the cameraman's feet was still in sight, and every now and then it twitched as the nerves and the sinews were burned.

'You will come with us and we will give you clothes and medication,' said the man.

'You sound like Piotr,' said Chiffon, in an off-balance voice.

The man nodded. 'We sound like Piotr because we are Russian. Do you understand me? You are safe now.'

Chiffon nodded, her head going up and down mechanically.

'Yes,' she repeated. 'Yes, I understand. I'm safe.'

The clock in the embassy hallway struck three as Humphrey opened the door and cautiously looked around. The hallway was deserted; its polished black-and-white tiles reflected the cold Swedish daylight. His heart pumped and pumped and his hands were sweating, but he had made up his mind to do what he believed to be right. 'This way,' he said to Klaus Hermann, who was standing close behind him, his face as grey as the *Svenska Dagbladet*.

They tiptoed across the hallway, two old men with creaking shoes and creaking joints. Humphrey opened the door which led through to the kitchens, listened for a moment, and then whispered, 'Come on.'

They went through, and Humphrey closed the door behind them. 'Now, follow me,' said Humphrey. 'And for goodness' sake, if we're challenged, just say that you felt unwell, and that I was going to get you a glass of water.'

Klaus Hermann said, 'All right. I understand.'

They crossed the large old-fashioned kitchen with its blue and white painted furniture and its rows of gleaming white tiles. A row of large shining carving-knives hung on hooks along the wall, and there were fish-kettles and saucepans and asparagus-steamers shining in every glass fronted cupboard.

Humphrey unlocked the back door, and the two of them stepped out into the sharp fresh air of the embassy garden.

'If only I could have brought my coat,' said Hermann, with a wry smile. 'It's cold.'

They walked around the side of the building, keeping themselves close to the wall when they passed the windows of the duty officer's room; and then they went through the black-painted gate that led to the embassy courtyard.

Humphrey said quickly, 'That white Skoda across the road. All you have to do is walk across, tap on the window, and the driver will let you in.'

Hermann took hold of Humphrey's hand. 'It is difficult for me to express how I feel for what you have done,' he said. 'I know it was not an easy decision for you to have made. But during the war I always thought that the British were, what did they call it, pukka.'

'Well, yes, pukka,' said Humphrey, anxiously.

'And now I fulfil my part of the bargain,' Klaus Hermann told him. Out of his cuff, he produced a ruled sheet of paper which he had torn from an embassy notebook. It was filled with neat, tiny writing, all in

German, and three bio-chemical formulae. He handed it to Humphrey and his hand was trembling.

'I want your promise that this is genuine,' said Humphrey.

Hermann nodded. 'I think to have been at mortal risk for the first time in my life has led me to understand that life is a precious thing,' he said. 'I have killed too many people in my career; let this be an end to it.'

He held Humphrey close, and squeezed him, and said, '*Auf wiedersehen*, Mr Browne. In other circumstances, you and I perhaps could have been the very best of friends.'

Humphrey watched Hermann limp steadfastly towards the embassy gate. The uniformed guard looked around at him incuriously, and then went back to staring out at Strandvägen. This was just the reaction that Hermann had told Humphrey that he was counting on. The guard was conditioned to prevent unwanted visitors from coming in, not to prevent people leaving. By the time he realised that it was Klaus Hermann who had walked past him, it would be too late. Beyond the embassy gate lay diplomatic safety.

Hermann reached the gate. He walked right through it. Now he was out on the sidewalk of Strandvägen, looking left and right to cross the road; and the white Skoda started up its engine. Humphrey watched Hermann reach the crown of the road, and his fists were clenched with tension. He was almost there. The Skoda driver had reached behind him, and unlatched the rear offside door.

It was at that moment that Bill Bennett stepped out from where he must have been waiting behind a tree in the Nobelpark on the other side of Strandvägen. Klaus Hermann didn't even notice him, he was too intent on reaching the Skoda; but Humphrey did. He watched in hypnotized fascination as Bill Bennett raised both hands, and fired three silenced shots at Hermann, one of which hit him in the face, the next in the chest, and the third in the hip, as he fell.

The Skoda driver revved up his engine, and the car began to pull away. But Bill Bennett simply swung his upraised arms around, and fired one more shot which shattered the car's back window, and hit the driver in the back of the neck. The car swerved, bounced against the kerb, and died.

Humphrey walked slowly out into the road.

'You've got the formula?' asked Bill. He pushed the .38 revolver back into his putty-coloured anorak.

'Yes,' said Humphrey thickly, then cleared his throat and repeated, 'Yes.'

Bill looked down at Klaus Hermann, mouth open against the red tarmac of the road.

'You know he was going to be executed, one way or another?'

'I suppose so.'

'You did the right thing. Saved him some agony.'

There was the braying sound of Swedish police sirens. Hermann's blood began to creep across the road, following the depressions in the road-surfacing with the inevitability of lava. Humphrey couldn't take his eyes off him. To think that only a few seconds ago he had been embracing this man, holding him close.

He looked away; through the trees of the Nobelpark to the dull grey water of Djürgardsbrunnsviken. His eyes watered in the wind and he thought that he must be growing old. His sister would probably bake a Madeira cake for him when he got home, by way of a celebration.

Bill said, 'The formula?' and Humphrey handed it over.

'You'll be rewarded for this,' said Bill. 'A whole lot of very important people in the United States are going to be very thankful about what happened here today.'

Humphrey cleared his throat again. 'I don't think I want a reward, thank you.'

Natalia was woken by a hand on her shoulder. She opened her eyes and Edmond was looking down at her, not smiling, but holding in his other hand a cup of black coffee. The room was dim: the drapes were still drawn, but there was a sharp chink of sunlight in the far corner which told Natalia that today was going to be one of those bright New Hampshire days when the sky is as blue as paint and the trees are as vivid as gold.

'What time is it?' Natalia asked him. She was naked underneath the blanket, and she drew it up to her chin.

'Eight o'clock.'

'My God, I wanted to be up at six.'

'It's this couch. It's more comfortable than it looks. Besides, you probably needed it.'

'Have you heard the news yet?' she asked him.

'The epidemic's worse,' he told her. He drew a chair over so that he could balance her coffee on it. 'Well over two hundred dead in Merrimack County alone.'

'And nationwide?'

He went over to the window and drew back the drapes. Natalia shielded her eyes from the brightness with her hand.

'Six, maybe seven thousand. And it seems to be getting faster all the time, just like Dr Corning said it would.'

'Aren't you going in to the clinic?'

He shook his head. 'First thing this morning, your friend Dr Walt Seabrook made an announcement from Washington, as the newly-appointed man in charge of Senator Reynard Kelly's hyper-polio research unit. He told everybody that it was arrant scandal-mongering for me to suggest that the virus had originated from the German airplane on Senator Kelly's land; and that Senator Kelly had been as surprised as anyone else

370

when the plane was dug up. He said it was sheer fluke. The Germans must have made several attempted landings in America during World War Two, and this one must have crashed on his property, and that was all. Can you believe that?'

'Knowing just how much he was implicated, that makes me *retch*.'

'Well,' said Edmond, 'this'll make you feel even sicker. He's already cordoned off his property to keep away sightseers and television reporters; and he's said that he's going to commission a properly supervised archaeological expedition to salvage the plane. This, he says, could take weeks, maybe months. And all the time people are going to be dying of hyper-polio, just to save his neck. Not even that. Just to save his damned *career*.'

Natalia said nothing, but sipped her coffee.

Edmond said, 'One more little stab, of course, was that Dr Seabrook reported that I was a dangerous quack, and produced medical records to prove that I performed an unsuccessful tracheotomy in a New York restaurant. He produced medical examiner's photographs, too, showing the girl's neck wounds, just in case people didn't get the point. About an hour ago, I had a call from Mr Eldridge, of the New Hampshire Health and Welfare Department, telling me not to bother to practise medicine in New Hampshire any more, or words to that effect.'

Natalia sat up, wrapping the blanket tightly around her. 'But that's *criminal*.'

'Yes, it's criminal. But not as *criminal* as the fact that Senator Kelly is allowing thousands of innocent people to die, for no other purpose than to save his candidacy for the White House.'

Natalia said, 'I don't think he knows what he's doing any more. Every meeting they had down there in Washington, it was all so unreal. Reynard and Dick Elmwood and the rest of them, they kept talking about 'sorting people out', as if they were intent on murdering half of the political population of the District of Columbia.'

'You really think they would have tried to kill you?'

She put down her coffee cup. 'I wasn't going to stick around to find out, thanks very much. This is good coffee.'

'Blue Mountain.'

Natalia ran her hand through her hair. 'I guess I'm going to have to stand up and be counted. Go to the media and tell them everything I know.'

'Kelly will deny it all, of course,' said Edmond. 'And if you've got any skeletons in any closets whatsoever, he'll dig them out and try to ruin you. But – if you can stand that . . .'

'I can stand anything to stop all those people from dying. I had an abortion once. I think that's about the worst thing I was ever guilty of.'

'You didn't have to tell me that. I wasn't prying.'

'I'm not ashamed of it.'

Edmond came and sat down beside her. 'I hope we survive this,' he said. 'Both of us. I think I'd like to get to know you better.'

'I'm not sure you're the right kind of man to get to know, Dr Chandler. One lady dead from a throat operation, the next dead of disease.'

If she had said it in anything other than a sharp and teasing tone of voice, it was the kind of comment that could have been tasteless and crass. But the way she looked at him, and the way she put her head a little to one side, provocative and questioning, and the smallest smile which touched the side of her mouth, all these things redeemed it, and gave it a different and intimate meaning. She liked men who were prepared to stand up for what they believed in, more than she liked winners. Maybe that was why she and Reynard Kelly, even if Condor hadn't come to light, would never have worked smoothly together. Reynard was a winner, but he didn't believe in anything.

Edmond said, 'Everybody's entitled to one or two mistakes.'

Natalia touched his wrist with the tip of one finger, a gentle touch that asked for forgiveness. 'You're hurting, aren't you?'

'I don't have anybody else to blame but myself. But when you love people so much that they mean everything to you; and you hurt them and hurt them and can't seem to stop hurting them, no matter how hard you try . . . well, that's when you begin to wonder whether you're any good at love at all.'

Natalia couldn't help smiling. 'Don't you know that it happens to everybody? You're a doctor, you should know that.'

'I'm not qualified in the repair of broken hearts.'

'Don't ask too much of yourself,' said Natalia. You can't be perfect, you can't accept all of the blame for everything.'

The telephone rang. Edmond reached across the back of the couch and picked it up. 'Dr Chandler,' he said, tucking the receiver under his chin.

It was Oscar. He sounded very tired and his voice was rough as glasspaper. 'E.C.? Sorry, but I've got some bad personal news for you.'

'Not Malcolm,' said Edmond.

'I'm sorry,' Oscar told him.

Natalia laid her hand on Edmond's shoulder. 'What's happened?' she asked.

Oscar said, 'He went off the bridge, about an hour ago. Right off Manchester Street into the river. The police say he was probably doing seventy-five, maybe eighty.'

Edmond took the phone out from under his chin and held it in his hand. 'Was it instant?'

'Must have been. Broke his neck as soon as he hit the water.'

'Oh, Christ,' said Edmond.

'Don't blame yourself,' Oscar put in. 'I ran a test and he definitely showed signs of hyper-polio. He would have died anyway.'

'You're not just saying that to make me feel a little less guilty?'

'Come and look at the autopsy report yourself. You think I'd do anything to make a quack like you feel less guilty?'

'Okay, Oscar. Thanks.'

'I'll drop by when I can,' Oscar told him. 'Meanwhile, you know, fight the good fight.'

Edmond put down the phone.

'You want to talk about it?' Natalia asked him.

'I don't know,' he replied. 'In a while. I think I need a drink first.'

The call came for Reynard Kelly at six that evening. By then, hyper-polio had spread so far across the United States, and so many people had died, that the President was considering putting the entire continent into quarantine. The government's special bio-chemical task forces had failed again and again to make any impression on the hyper-polio virus, despite having tried a whole variety of lipid solvents, from ether to termazine and having bombarded it with X-rays and ultra-violet.

Reynard Kelly had been listening to news of the epidemic hourly, sitting in front of the television in his drawing-room with the drapes drawn and lights dimmed. He was seeing no visitors, apart from Dick Elmwood and his immediate staff, and only taking the most critical of phone calls. He refused to talk to Greta, but he also refused to let her out of the house; so she and Walt Seabrook spent the evening together in the morning-room, tense and wound-up and clean out of cocaine.

Dick Elmwood came into the room on silent feet and leaned close to Reynard as if he were imparting a forbidden secret. 'There's a call for you, senator.'

'I'm not taking any more calls today, Dick. I think I've taken enough calls for one day, don't you? Done enough.'

'This call, sir, I think you ought to take.'

Reynard looked up. One eye reflected the flickering light from the television. 'Well?' he said.

'It's from somebody who says that he has proof that what Dr Chandler was saying on television was true.'

'Somebody's been talking to that Natalia woman, that's it, isn't it? You let her go, for Christ's sake, and now she's been opening her mouth to anybody she can get to listen.'

'We know where she is, sir. She's with Chandler, in Concord. But we don't think she's been talking to anybody, at least not yet. There haven't been any more reports on television about Condor; and nothing in the newspapers, either.'

Reynard nodded towards the telephone. 'Then – who's this on the line?'

'I don't know, sir. But it sounds genuine.'

'Pick up the extension, listen in,' Reynard told him. Then he lifted up the receiver, and said impatiently, 'Yes, this is Senator Kelly speaking. Who is this?'

There was a crackling pause, and then an accented voice said, 'Good evening, senator. I have some good news for you. Tremendous news!'

'What tremendous news? Who are you?'

'My name is Cerenkov, I'm calling you from New York. I'm happy to be the first to tell you that your friend is still alive. Not very well, admittedly, but still alive.'

'What the hell are you talking about?' Reynard demanded. 'Is this some kind of a joke?'

'Not at all, sir. You remember Ms Chiffon Trent, surely?'

'Chiffon Trent? Don't be so damned disrespectful! Ms Trent was a dear and close friend of mine and now she's dead.'

'Oh, no, senator! Chiffon Trent isn't dead. Chiffon Trent is here with me now, 555 Madison Avenue. Whoever died in that car wreck, it wasn't her. We found her in Milwaukee, Wisconsin, where she was being forced to star in what I believe you Americans call a "snuff movie." Fortunately, we arrived in time to save her from the "snuff." '

Dick Elmwood glanced across at Reynard uneasily. Reynard was white, and his knuckles showed white spots of bloodlessness on them because he was clenching the phone so tightly.

'What do you want?' Reynard demanded.

'*Want*? My dear senator, we don't *want* anything. Except, perhaps, to inform you that Ms Trent will always be prepared to testify to what you told her about co-operating with the Nazis during the war; and that if you are fortunate enough to survive the present scandal, which it seems as if you remotely might, then we will always be here, ready with our testimony, in case you should turn out to be as aggressive and as uncooperative towards the Soviet Union as some of your predecessors. Of course I'm not personally in a position of sufficient influence to be able to say what we might ask from you at a later date; but it could well be something like the withdrawal from Europe of cruise missiles, or perhaps less interference in Central America.'

Reynard, without warning, banged down the phone. Then he picked it up again, receiver and cradle and all, and tore it out of the wall, and threw it on to the carpet, and stamped on it, so that it smashed.

Dick said, 'Senator Kelly, I have to tell you that I had no idea that Ms Trent was still alive . . . I commissioned people in whom I had every reason to be confident . . . I mean, this comes as just as big a shock to me as it does to you . . .'

Reynard stared at him, his face shuddering, spit flying from his lips 'It's Condor,' he raged. 'The whole thing started with that damned airplane. Well, that's the only solid evidence they've got. If we get rid of the solid evidence, if we get rid of that evidence once and for all, then by Jiminy they won't have any way of proving what happened, and that means no way at all. So I'm going to tell you what we're going to do. We're going to fly back to Concord tonight, Dick, that's what we're going to do, and we're going to blow the whole damn airplane right out of the ground, and then we're going to blow it into miniature pieces, and then we're going to blow the miniature pieces into miniature pieces.'

'Senator, listen – '

'Don't tell me to listen!' Reynard screamed. 'I've listened long enough! None of this would have happened if it hadn't have been for you, and the rest of the morons who spend all of their time spending my money and sucking my brains and treating this whole damned campaign like a carnival! I want explosives, that's what I want! Where can we get explosives?'

'Senator, please – '

'Where can we get explosives?' Reynard shrieked at him. 'Where? Where? I want explosives!'

'Well, sir, there's a demolition contractor in Washington who might be persuaded to help. He was a friend of someone I knew in Seattle; and –'

'I don't want your goddamned life history,' Reynard shouted at him. 'I want explosives. Do you understand me? And I want a man who knows how to use them. Got that? Got that, Dick? And I want them now. And we're going to fly them up to Concord, and we're going to – '

'Senator, we're going to have to charter a jet. We won't be able to take explosives on board a commercial airliner.'

'I've got my own jet, damn it.'

'Sir, that's in Concord, undergoing – '

'Then just get one, for Christ's sake. Do I have to think of every damned stupid little pusillanimous detail around here?'

'No, sir.'

'And I want to leave tonight. You with me? Tonight.'

'There is a curfew, sir.'

'Damn it, Dick, I'm Reynard Kelly. I'm the man who started the damned disease! It's because of me that they've got themselves a curfew in the first place!'

'Yes, sir.'

'Yes, sir,' Reynard mimicked.

Dick Elmwood left the room. He didn't close the door behind him, and when he looked across at it in annoyance, Reynard suddenly saw why. It was Greta, in an emerald-green cocktail dress, standing watching him, silhouetted by the light from the hallway. Her hair shone, she wore diamonds. He could smell her perfume even from the other side of the room. Eau de Joy. Some joy, he thought.

'What do you want?' he demanded, with undisguised impatience.

'I just wanted to see you.' Greta's voice was very soft.

'I'm busy. I don't have any time for talking now.'

'Oh, I didn't want to *talk* to you. I just wanted to *see* you. I just wanted to see how a great man can bring himself down to absolute ruin; just by failing to recognize the needs and hopes of the people around him. Nobody can be great on their own, Reynard. You could have been great, if you had looked at other people a little more closely, and a little less selfishly. But you didn't have it in you, did you? Personality problem. In some people, you know, being selfish is an affliction. You make it a way of life.'

Reynard turned his back on her, and examined the draped window as if it were an exhibit at the J. Paul Getty Museum. 'Have you finished gloating?' he asked her.

'I don't think I ever will; not quite,' she told him. He hated the sound of amused malice in her voice.

'I'm flying back to Concord,' he told her. 'I'm going back to do something I should have done sooner. I'm going to destroy that airplane, blow it up.'

'Are you mad? That won't solve anything. What do you think the media are going to say if you start blowing it up?'

'I don't care what they say. It's their only piece of solid evidence.'

'But Reynard – '

He swivelled around fiercely and glared at her as if he could happily hit her with anything to hand. 'You're all the same, all of you. All full of rotten, weak-kneed, clumsy advice. And for all these years, I've been stupid enough to listen to it, and act on it, and look where the hell it's got me.'

'You betrayed your country long before you ever met me.'

Reynard shouted, *'Agh!'* in a speechless fury. He seized the bodice of her cocktail dress and tore it away from her, leaving her with one breast bare and deep scratches across her chest.

'You bastard!' she screamed at him. 'You ineffectual bastard!'

Reynard grunted, and seized her again, pulling off her bra. Then he slapped her open-handed across the side of the face, and then back again, with the back of his hand, across the other side. Her pearls broke and poured on to the carpet. Reynard's heavy rings cut and bruised her face and her right eye swelled up almost at once.

Screaming and screaming, Greta tore at Reynard with her fingernails. He slapped her again, then again, and she fell back against the couch. She tried to get up, but he had the upper hand now, and every time she raised herself he slapped her again, once across the bare breasts.

His temper died down, and he turned his back on her. He was breathing heavily, his nostrils flared.

'After all these years,' he said, inexplicably.

Greta could do nothing but weep. She tried to stand up, but she couldn't, and so she knelt on the floor and wept and wept.

'After all these goddamned *years*,' Reynard repeated.

Edmond was almost asleep when the telephone warbled. He groped around in the dark, and at last he found it, and picked it up.

'Dr Chandler.'

'Dr Edmond Chandler?'

'That's right. Who's speaking?'

'This is Greta Kelly, Reynard Kelly's wife.'

Edmond sat up in bed, and fumbled for the light. 'How did you get my number?' he asked.

'It's in the Concord telephone directory, Dr Chandler, it isn't difficult.'

'Well, what can I do? Are you all right? You sound – well, I don't mean to be personal – '

'My husband just beat me, Dr Chandler. He beat me, and then he left Washington to fly back to Concord.'

'I see. Well, as a matter of fact, I *don't* see. What has that got to do with me?'

'Dr Chandler, he's crazy. He's gone hysterically crazy. He's rented a jet, and he's flying up to Concord with a whole cargo-hold full of high explosives. He says he's going to blow up that Nazi plane and destroy the evidence against him.'

Edmond rubbed his eyes. 'Then what I guessed about the plane was true?'

'Fundamentally, yes. But you've got to stop him, Dr Chandler. He's going to end up killing somebody unless you stop him.'

'Mrs Kelly, I don't really see what I can possibly – '

'Please, Dr Chandler, do something. He'll be arriving at The Colonnades in less than a half-hour.'

Natalia came to the bedroom door. The sound of Edmond's voice had woken her up. 'Is something wrong?' she asked him.

Edmond put down the phone. 'The world has just happened to lose its last remaining marble,' he said. 'That was Mrs Greta Kelly, and she tells me that your erstwhile employer is flying up Concord with the intention of blowing that Nazi plane to bits.'

'Is he mad, or what?'

Edmond tugged on a pair of slacks, and took a shirt down from his wardrobe. 'Let's put it this way. I think the strain of hiding this secret for forty years or more has finally proved too much.'

'What are you going to do?'

'I don't really know what the hell I *can* do. The first thing I'm going to do is call Oscar. After that, who knows?'

It took Oscar almost five minutes to answer the phone. When at last he did, he sounded as if he were still dreaming. Edmond told him about the call he had received from Greta Kelly.

Oscar said, 'The answer's easy.'

'What do you mean, the answer's easy?'

'The answer is, we prevent him from landing on his own property so that he has to divert to Concord Airport, or someplace else. At the same time we alert the cops so that they can pick him up wherever he lands.'

'Why not just call the cops straight away and tell them what he's up to?'

'Because Senator Kelly is Senator Kelly, my dear friend; and because the Commissioner is not going to risk sending a dozen of Concord's finest beating their way across Senator Kelly's private land without a warrant and without reasonable grounds.'

Edmond said, in exasperation, 'How the hell do we prevent him from landing?'

The LearJet whistled low over the Merrimack River and began its turn towards East Concord. It was three o'clock in the morning now, and the sky was clear and cold. Reynard peered out of the window watching the familiar landmarks pass underneath him, the Soucook River, Horse Corner, the Loudon Road; and off to their left the winking lights of Concord Airport.

Dick Elmwood sat next to Reynard chewing nervously at his lip. He had taken almost everything into account in his career with Reynard, except the possibility that Reynard might one day break down, and act the way that he was acting tonight. The fact that they were carrying nearly 1,500 lbs of high explosives in the back of the airplane didn't do much to relax him, either.

The pilot said, 'Fasten seatbelts, please, senator.'

Reynard looked up, frowned, and said, 'What?'

'Your seatbelt,' Dick repeated.

'Ah,' said Reynard.

In the seat behind them, a crop-haired man in a chequered shirt sat glumly looking down at Concord through circular spectacles. This was the explosives expert whom Dick had managed to persuade to fly north with them to deal with the Condor. He had only agreed to lose a night's sleep on the promise of $10,000 cash on the barrelhead.

The LearJet lowered its undercarriage, and sank below the treeline. The tarmac runway at The Colonnades was on the north-east side of the house. When he had bought his first jet, nine years ago, Reynard had arranged for the land to be drained specially, and a full-length tarmac runway constructed. The grassy surface of Conant's Acre had been too rough for jets, and in any case it was more profitable under the plough.

Reynard could see the house now, symmetrical and white. 'Home,' he said to Dick, and Dick nodded and gave an unintelligible hmph of acknowledgement.

They waited until the last moment, their cars hidden side by side in the long grass of the orchard. Edmond and Natalia sat in one of them; Oscar was in the other. They kept radio silence between them, in case their short-wave frequency was picked up by anybody in the house, and instead they signalled to each other with pre-arranged waves of their hands. One wave meant, I see the jet; two waves meant go like hell; three meant let's get out of here.

About ten minutes ago, the bright parallel lines of lights along the runway had been switched on, and through the lines of pear trees they had seen lights go on inside the house. Natalia had said, 'It must be any moment. The servants getting ready to welcome their homecoming lord.'

Edmond had said nothing. He wasn't at all convinced that obstructing Reynard's landing was a good idea. He wasn't even sure it was necessary to stop him blowing up the Condor. They hadn't finished examining the airplane yet, and there could well be vital evidence left inside it; but there wasn't any doubt in Edmond's mind that if Reynard blew the airplane to pieces, he would be doing nothing more than confirming his own guilt.

And what was he going to do with all of the pieces? Bury them again? Grind them up and scatter them over the sea?

But he remembered what Greta had said. *'He's hysterically crazy,'* and if that was true, then Reynard was probably capable of doing anything to anybody, including blowing himself up along with the plane. In the dreariest sense of the word, Edmond felt that he had a duty towards Reynard and to the city of Concord itself to try to prevent him. He was still a doctor, after all.

They heard the LearJet before they saw it. A low whistling, coming from the south-east. Then suddenly, much lower and from a different direction than Edmond had expected, the blinking lights of the plane itself. Oscar's hand waved; both of them switched on their headlights, and with a slithering of tyres on wet grass, they roared and bounced out of the orchard towards the runway. Natalia said, 'Oh God, I hope the plane can pull up now. It seems incredibly close.'

Suspension jolting, Edmond's car reached the tarmac itself. He spun the wheel, and punched the gas pedal, and drove head-on down the runway towards the descending jet, Oscar's car was only a few feet behind him, off to his left.

'It can't pull up!' screamed Natalia. *'Edmond, for God's sake!'*

Edmond saw the Learjet's lights, the silhouette of its wings. It seemed to fill up the entire windshield, and he had no doubt in his mind at all that they were going to collide head on. Natalia covered her face with her hands and bent herself double, too terrified now even to scream. And the whole world was drowned out with the thunder of jet engines, and a slamming noise like a hundred airtight doors being closed at once.

Then, through the deafening noise, Edmond realized that the plane had climbed over them, and was still

384

climbing, at full throttle, and that now they had reached the end of the tarmac, and the LearJet was climbing, climbing, trying to clear the tall trees at the far end of the meadowland, turning off to starboard.

People were running out of the house towards them, but they stopped their cars, both of them, and climbed out, and stood in the breezy morning air watching the Learjet climbing and turning against the pale eastern sky, listening to the aching thunder of its engines as it struggled to gain height.

'It's okay,' said Oscar hoarsely. 'It's okay, he's going to make it.'

But almost as soon as he had said that, there was a dying note in the engines that affected Edmond right in the bottom of his stomach, and the jet seemed to drop sideways. They saw its wingtip catch a tree; and then it suddenly spun and fell to the ground.

There was a dull thumping sound, oddly subdued. Some of the staff began to run towards the plane, not shouting, not calling out, quite silent. But then there was a massive and overwhelming explosion, one-and-a-half thousand pounds of high explosive detonating at once; a roar that blotted out all conscious thought and made Edmond's ears sing with deafness. A lurid orange fireball rolled swiftly up into the sky, and then vanished, a sudden genie. Then, one by one, like a flock of birds that had died in the sky, the pieces of airplane began to fall all around them, rustling through the orchard, clattering on to the tarmac. Among those pieces was Senator Reynard Kelly.

Oscar said, 'God.' He turned away at once, and began to walk back to his car.

Edmond and Natalia stayed where they were. Edmond couldn't take his eyes off the blazing wreckage. Natalia held him close, and tugged the lapel of his jacket across his chest to keep him warm. She had begun to understand that he needed it.

The following morning, a few minutes after eight o'clock, Piotr was eating a breakfast of Bran Buds and black tea when there was a buzz at his doorbell. Wiping his mouth with the back of his hand, he went to the front door of his apartment and called, 'Who is it?'

'It's Chiffon.'

He unlocked the door and opened it. Chiffon was standing in the gloomy hallway in a red belted coat, with a scarf tied around her head. Both her eyes were bruised, and there were crimson marks around her mouth, and on her neck. She wore impenetrable dark glasses.

'Chiffon,' he said, so quietly that she could hardly hear him.

'I only came by to say thank-you,' she said. 'They told me that it was you who called them. The Russians, I mean. Mr Cerenkov.'

'They didn't hurt you?'

She shook her head. 'They took good care of me. I was a valuable asset, after all. You know, considering what I knew about Reynard.'

'But they let you go?'

'Haven't you heard the news this morning?'

'Not yet. My television's in for repair.'

'Well, Reynard's dead. He was flying back to New Hampshire and his plane crashed. Reynard, and that other creep Dick Elmwood, both of them killed.'

'You'd better come inside,' Piotr suggested.

'No, I won't stay.'

'At least have a cup of tea.'

'Well . . . for a moment.'

She stepped into his tiny sparse apartment, with its severe black-and-white photographs of Russia and its framed sketches of theatrical costumes. The morning sun shone on the bare polished floorboards. He guided her through to the kitchen by her elbow. Scarcely touching her at all.

She said, 'You saved my life, you know. They almost killed me.'

'You know what I was doing there? In Milwaukee?'

'Cerenkov told me that, too. It doesn't matter. I'm a little too far gone to worry about things like that. I'm a little too far gone to worry about any kind of relationship with anybody.'

'Are you . . . ?' he began to ask her, but he knew that the question was more than either of them could take. Are you hurt, was what he meant. Are you damaged, traumatized, shocked? She wouldn't sit down. Instead she stood beside the table in that ill-fitting red coat, twisting the belt around and around in her bruised and swollen fingers.

'I called Dr Emery first thing,' she said. 'He couldn't believe it was me, not at first. Well, of course, he thought I was dead. But when I told him about the last examination he did on me, he believed me then. He said maybe I needed hospital. You know, just for a while.'

'Yes,' said Piotr. He looked down at his half-eaten breakfast. 'I only hope you understand how sorry I am.'

'It wasn't your fault. I got caught up in something that was bigger than I was, that's all. Just like you. When the elephants do battle, the mice get squashed, isn't that right? Didn't somebody once say that? Shakespeare?'

'I don't know. It doesn't sound like Shakespeare.'

'Well, whoever,' said Chiffon.

Piotr said, after a while, 'I find it hard to believe that Reynard's actually dead. A plane crash? I suppose it was quick.'

'Quick, slow, who cares?'

They stood side by side in silence for almost a minute. Then Chiffon said, 'I won't have any tea, if it's all the same to you.'

387

Piotr frowned at her as if he had never mentioned tea. But then he nodded, and said, 'Ah, well.'

'You look terrible,' Chiffon told him. 'You haven't been sick, have you?'

'Well,' he said, 'I had some delayed bad news.'

'You didn't get the Olsen part?'

'No, no. From Russia.' He held up an aerogramme letter, and then dropped it back on the table again. 'They censor it, you know, and so it always takes such a long time to get here. This letter was mailed in Moscow on May 5 – almost six months ago.'

Chiffon stared at him, without speaking. He tried to smile at her, but in the end he couldn't manage anything except a shrug of emotional acceptance. 'My mother died in April. In April! She had pleurisy. They cremated her two days later, and that was it. No word, no ashes. All I had was this.'

He gently shook the envelope, and out came a small lock of fair hair, bound with faded blue ribbon.

'That was mine,' he said, with tears in his eyes. 'I remember the day my mother cut it. She was baking that day, *Pozharsky*-style patties, and bread, I remember the smell. And when she cut my hair, somebody in the yard outside started to slaughter a piglet. The squeals! You wouldn't believe them.'

Chiffon raised a hand towards him, and touched his sleeve. Then she withdrew it.

'I'm sorry,' she said, 'I have to go now. I have a friend waiting for me downstairs. I only came to say thank-you.'

'You have nothing to thank me for. Our fates were all twisted up together.'

She left the apartment and he stood by the door as she walked quickly down the stairs to the street. He heard the street door bang, and then there was silence.

'*Da svedahniya*,' he told her softly.

The Press were already waiting for Greta as she was hurried out of the house and across to the long white limousine, which seemed incongruously festive for carrying a woman who was only a few hours widowed. There was a sustained flicker of electronic flash, like autumn lightning; and the *meep-meep-meep* of self-winding cameras. Four Secret Servicemen kept the reporters and the jostlers away from her; all shoulders and tight expressions and bulging jackets; but before she was able to climb into the car one of the *New York Times* reporters managed to struggle forward and shout out at her, 'How do you feel, Mrs Kelly? Upset?'

Greta's eyes glittered through the black lace of her veil, and she gave him a look which would appear time and time again as the face of the year, the grieving politician's widow. 'I'm devastated,' she said, 'Reynard Kelly was America's last hero.'

Almost immediately afterwards, Walt Seabrook came hurrying out of the house, his face half hidden by his upraised raincoat. He climbed into the Cadillac next to Greta, and one of the Secret Service officers slammed the door. 'Jesus Christ,' he blasphemed. 'I didn't think I was able to make it. You see those *crowds*?'

Greta laid a black-gloved hand on his wrist. 'It's over now. One way or another.'

'Hm,' said Walt. 'Until somebody's behind with their rent, and decides to sell the whole story to the *Washington Post*.'

'Oh, we can take care of that. Reynard always did. Did you ever read a bad word about Reynard in the papers?'

'Did you ever read a *good* word about Reynard in the papers?'

'They can't do anything to harm us now,' said Greta, taking hold of Walt Seabrook's arm. 'Every grieving widow is entitled to seek some conciliatory company.'

Walt sat back in his seat as the limousine bounced

out of the driveway, crept slowly through the crowds, and then abruptly squealed away towards the airport. Its tyres sounded like Piotr's childhood pig.

'I've learned one thing,' Walt remarked, as they sped along Bradley Boulevard, through Bethesda.

'What was that?'

'Play in your own league, that's what I learned. Reynard was too heavyweight for me. My league is the State legislature; department of health and welfare. No higher. I don't have the head for it.'

'You'll make it one day,' Greta told him. 'You just wait and see.'

'Unh-hunh. Not me. I'll just stick with what I know.'

'You've lost your ambition, just because of what happened to Reynard?

Walt shook his head, wryly. 'Let's just say that I've seen myself for what I really am; and for what I'm really not.'

'Coward,' she teased.

'No,' he said. 'Realist.'

'Well,' said Greta, after a while 'maybe Reynard should have learned that lesson, too. He certainly wasn't in Herr Hitler's league, was he? After all these years, Hitler finally caught up with him.'

'Maybe,' Walt replied. 'Maybe Reynard finally caught up with himself.'

They watched the suburbs of Washington unravel past them, a flat and dusty diorama. Then Greta said, with self-betraying sharpness, 'You'll stay with me, won't you?'

'You think I wouldn't?'

'I don't know. Tell me. Go on, reassure me.'

'All right, I'll stay with you.'

She clasped his hand, so tightly that her diamond rings cut into his skin.

'Well,' said Walt, 'maybe we both turned out to be

390

weaker than we'd imagined ourselves to be. It doesn't do anybody any harm to recognize their limitations.'

Greta said, 'It's the foolishness of it that embarrasses me so much.'

'Foolish? You shouldn't think that you were foolish. You called Dr Chandler, didn't you, and that wasn't foolish.'

'It wasn't heroic, either.'

'Standing up for what you believe in is always heroic, no matter how late in the day you do it.'

Greta said nothing for a long time, but at last she leaned her head against Walt Seabrook's shoulder and said, 'I feel like a child, Walt. Either a child or a very old woman. Help me, Walt: just through this part of it.

Walt Seabrook nodded, and kissed her hair, and that was all that Greta needed.

Humphrey awkwardly manoeuvred his new green vinyl suitcase out of the doors of the bus, and set it down on the wet sidewalk while he made a performance of turning up the collar of his coat and unfurling his umbrella and tugging on his string-and-vinyl gloves. Beside him, the bus clashed its gears, closed its doors, and bellowed off on the Bakewell road, giving one last pneumatic sneeze before it disappeared behind the higgledy-piggledy stone houses and the overhanging oaks.

The rain came down in that soft, persistent curtain that characterizes the Derbyshire Dales in autumn. Low grey clouds moved silently eastwards over the glistening rooftops, a procession of depressing and indeterminate dreams; and the puddles in the roadway were circled and circled by raindrops.

Across the triangular green, beyond the stone war memorial, was the terrace of houses where Humphrey and his sister lived. He stood under his umbrella staring at it; and he was surprised how it seemed to have

391

shrunk, in only a few weeks, and how dingy it was. The guttering at the front was still broken, and he thought of the old house on Pilogatan where Klaus Hermann had first led him. The front garden gate was still hanging off its hinges, and the grass was bright and overgrown. His sister hadn't got out the Flymo, then. Maybe in her heart of hearts she had always suspected that he would come back.

He was about to pick up the suitcase when he saw the front door of his house open, and his sister emerge; wearing a transparent plastic rainhood and a maroon raincoat. She put up her umbrella, walked out of the front gate, and made her way towards the Corner Shop & Post Office, carrying her bright yellow polythene shopping-bag.

Humphrey watched her in unhappy fascination. He saw her reach the shop, and even heard the tinkle of the bell as she opened the shop door. He stayed where he was, with the rain pattering on his umbrella, unable to move; paralysed by what he had seen and lived through, unable to take the first step which would enable him to rejoin his everyday life.

How could he tell his sister what had happened to him in Sweden? How could he explain what he had felt when Bill Bennett had shot Birgitta? Or when Angelika Rangström had cut her wrists with his fishing-blade? What would his sister possibly understand about pain, and blood, and the terrible embrace which he had been given by a man who had killed three thousand people?

He waited and waited in the rain. In the west, towards Longstone Moor the sky began to lighten a little, a yellowish smear of autumnal sunshine.

And just then, its roof reflecting that sunshine as if it were a sign from the angels, the Chesterfield bus appeared over the brow of the hill, heading back the way in which Humphrey had come. Without thinking of anything at all, his heart tight, Humphrey picked up his suitcase and walked across the road to the bus-shelter, standing in line behind two old men in wet tweed caps and a ruddy-faced young woman with a squalling child, enormous breasts, and a folding buggy.

Humphrey mounted the wet brown steps of the bus, and fumbled around in his coat pocket for his fare. He wrestled his suitcase on to the rack. Then he sat down beside a fat woman who smelled of saddle-soap and onions; but he didn't look back.

The bus was pulling away from the kerb when he saw his sister come out of the corner shop. He thought to himself: goodbye, my dear. You will have to believe that your brother Humphrey is dead, and perhaps that will be all for the best. Live out your small, diminished life, my dear, with your church bazaars and your craft sales and your mint imperials at Holy Communion. A new life is waiting for me, somewhere in the rain, out beyond Chesterfield's twisted spire; out there in the wide and vicious world.

The next stop was Nether End. The bus drew into the side of the road, and the driver waited patiently while a very old lady was helped up the steps. The doors were open and Humphrey could smell the rain, and the dales.

He looked at the fat woman sitting next to him. She stared back at him, unsmiling, very Derbyshire. He got up out of his seat, struggled towards the front of the bus, and retrieved his suitcase.

'Getting off, chum?' the bus driver asked him. 'Tha's paid as far as Chesterfield bus station.'

'I – ahem,' replied Humphrey, indistinctly. He manhandled his suitcase off the bus, and stood back, turning up his coat collar again. All the passengers stared at him out of the rain-beaded windows as the bus drove off. In a minute it was gone, leaving no trace behind it of Humphrey's imaginary future but tyre tracks on the muddy verge, and the smell of diesel.

Humphrey suddenly realized he had left his umbrella on the bus.

He changed his suitcase from his right hand to his left, and began the long walk back home. The rain was lighter now, but still steady enough to soak his shoulders, and cling to his eyelashes.

He remembered as he walked the line in *Lolita* which described why twelve-year-old Dolores Haze had crept back into the arms of her middle-aged lover (yes, covertly, Humphrey had read *Lolita*).

The line was, 'You see, she had absolutely nowhere else to go.'

And as he walked, and as he remembered that line, Humphrey had to lift his suitcase so that he could wipe his eyes with the back of his hand, in case anybody realized that his cheeks were not wet with rain, but with tears.

Bill Bennett was sitting at the bar of the Sheraton drinking dry martinis and nibbling peanuts when the small narrow-chested man in a grey suit came across and sat down next to him; no hesitation, no apology, despite the fact that there were plenty of other empty barstools.

'Well, well,' said Bill, taking another small handful of peanuts. 'I was wondering when somebody was going to get in touch.'

The man took off his horn-rimmed spectacles and wiped them clean with one of the paper coasters. He stared at Bill with bulgy, unfocused eyes, and then pushed his spectacles back on again. 'We didn't meet in Haiti?' he asked. 'In 1971, when Baby Doc took over? At the Toussaint Hotel?'

'Not me, pal,' said Bill. 'Are you going to buy me a drink?'

'Sure. My name's Welby. As in Marcus, M.D.'

'Nice to know you.'

Welby reached inside his coat pocket and produced

a long white envelope, which he passed over as if it were a gift.

'Your cheque,' he said. 'Also, your assignment papers.'

Bill tucked the envelope into his windbreaker.

'Aren't you going to open it?' asked Welby.

'And let you see how much I make?'

'I know how much you make.'

'Well, then, I still don't need to open it, do I?'

Welby beckoned the bar-tender over, and said, 'My friend here will have another martini, please. I'll have a beer. Lätl.'

'You drink that piss?' Bill asked him.

Welby ignored the question, and said, 'Don't you want to know where you've been posted?'

'Why should I? They promised me a Stateside posting; and if it isn't a Stateside posting, then I'm going to quit.'

'I don't think they'd like it very much if you quit.'

'They promised me a Stateside posting, that's all; and if they're not going to keep their promises, then I'm not interested.'

Welby coughed. Then he said, 'You know how things are. Times change, policies differ.'

'What does that mean?' Bill demanded.

'It means that we have to be circumspect, that's all.'

'And circumspect means that I don't get the job they promised me? Is that it?'

'Well . . . there are problems. The Swedish security people complained to the State Department. And – well, you know. The can has to be carried back by someone.'

Bill said sharply, 'I did what I was told. I did what I was instructed to do, and I did it within the parameters of my authority.'

'I know, yes,' said Welby, soothingly. 'But all the same, there was kind of a mess. You know? We're not blaming you personally, but someone has to carry the can back; and be seen doing it.'

'Meaning me.'

'Well, you were the agent in the field, after all. And the last thing we want to do is upset the Swedes.'

The bartender brought their drinks. Bill prodded at his olive, then fished it out and ate it.

'Where are they sending me?' he asked, at last.

'You have a choice.'

'What kind of a choice?'

'Costa Rica.'

'That's the choice? Costa Rica?'

'Do you want it or don't you? We think Gulderhof could be there.'

Bill said, 'The choice is, either I go to Costa Rica or I don't go to Costa Rica?'

'Well, yes.'

He sipped his drink. Then he turned to Welby, and said, 'Gulderhof?'

'We've had a tip-off.'

Bill shook his head. 'I don't think I want to go to Costa Rica, okay?'

'That's your privilege.'

'And that's all?'

'What else do you want?'

'Well, I don't know – maybe some other kind of assignment?'

Welby said, 'I'm sorry. Costa Rica is all we have.'

'Can I change my mind?' Bill asked him.

'You mean, can you change your mind and accept?'

'Yes.'

'If you want to.'

Bill hesitated; and then he said, 'No. I don't think I want to go to Costa Rica.'

'That's your privilege.'

'That's all, then?' Bill asked.

'That's all.'

They drank their drinks in silence. Then Bill excused himself and went back up to his room. He stood with his back to the door and tore open the long white envelope. It contained a certified cheque for $62,500 and a letter on plain paper saying simply, DEP ARLANDA 11.00 HRS: ARR SAN JOSE COSTA RICA 15.45 LOCAL.

He crumpled the paper up in his hand and tossed it across the room. Then he went into the bathroom and stared at himself. Was this it? The end of his whole career? Squeezed out of the service like a teardrop squeezed out of an unfriendly eye? No fuss, no argument. Just occluded from the world of secrets and sudden death as if you had never existed. Or as if that world had never existed.

He suddenly felt very ordinary. He felt as if, somehow, Humphrey's mundaneness had affected him, tarnished his personal glamour, scuffed his ego. He had a strong urge to call up Humphrey and speak to him – either to shout angrily at him or to tell him that all the time, *he*, Humphrey, had been right about everything, and particularly about betrayal.

He drew back his jacket and looked at the butt of his holstered .38. He thought to himself: this is it. This is the instrument of betrayal. And if killing is a way of life, maybe it's a way of relief, too.

Quick, black, silent. What more could anybody wish for? Killing was almost better than love.

Except that he was too much of a soldier; too much of an egotist; and, in the final analysis, too much of a coward.

That was the worst thing that Humphrey had done to him. Humphrey had shown him that he wasn't brave.

There was a knock at the door. It was the chambermaid, asking him if she could make up his room.

'I'm leaving,' he told her; and of course he was.

The following day, under a warrant issued by the Supreme Court of New Hampshire, police and pathologists and forensic examiners came with shovels and picks and lifting gear and began to excavate the carcass of the Condor. It rained all day, a fine drizzle which silvered the grass, and clung in drips on to the brims of the policemen's caps.

One of the first important finds was within the rear part of the Condor's fuselage. Neither Edmond nor Oscar were there to see it, because they were still undergoing questioning at police headquarters; but Greta had flown up to Concord early that morning, and they sent an officer to the house to ask her if she wanted to see it.

Young Bernie was there, too, with his bicycle, chewing gum; unnoticed by the sodden crowd of diggers and scientists and policemen.

They kept the discovery under a plastic awning, so that its peculiar fragility wouldn't be damaged by the rain. Greta came forward and stood and stared at it for a very long time.

It was the mummified body of a young woman, in a coat that must once have been maroon. She wore black fur-lined boots, presumably to keep the cold out during her long flight; and a black feathered hat. In her arms she still clutched a wizened little creature in a faded and tattered blue suit. It was the mummy of a boy, perhaps four or five years old, although he had shrunk so much that it was difficult to tell.

In the woman's luggage they discovered a letter from Reynard Kelly, telling her how much he loved her, and that he hoped one day to see her again. Ilse, my dearest.

Greta said to the police officer next to her, 'That was my husband's first mistress.'

The police officer looked embarrassed, and glanced back towards his sergeant for reassurance. The sergeant shrugged. Who cared, let her ramble.

'And that child,' added Greta, 'if this airplane had landed safely, and if its mission had been successfully accomplished – that child might very well have grown up to be the first Führer of the United States.'

HYPER-POLIO Ko'd by K-SOLVENT

Hyper-polio can now be brought under swift and effective control, thanks to the discovery of a 'K-Solvent' which wipes out the virus with 100% effectiveness.

Assistant Secretary of Health David R. Snoman said in Washington today that the Federal government were financing urgent and widespread treatment of hyper-volio victims, and the immunization of everybody in affected areas with dead viral material.

The miracle breakthrough was effected by the government's special bio-chemical research team with the assistance of information on viral research sent from Germany.

Mr Snoman said, 'We are confident that this terrible epidemic will soon be nothing more than a nightmare memory.'

STAR BOOKS BESTSELLERS

THRILLERS

RETURN OF MORIARTY	*John Gardner*	£2.50
A KILLER FOR A SONG	*John Gardner*	£1.25
THE BACK OF THE TIGER	*Jack Gerson*	£1.95
THE INFILTRATOR	*Michael Hughes*	£2.25
SPECTRE OF MARALINGA	*Michael Hughes*	£1.95
BILLIONAIRE	*Peter James*	£2.25
CONDOR	*Thomas Luke*	£2.25*
AIRSHIP	*Peter Macalan*	£2.50
IKON	*Graham Masterton*	£2.50*
DOCTOR JEKYLL AND MISS HYDE	*Jeremy Scott*	£1.95
DOG SOLDIERS	*Robert Stone*	£1.95*

WAR

BLAZE OF GLORY	*Michael Carreck*	£1.80
MEN OF BLOOD	*Wolf Kruger*	£1.80
SLAUGHTERHOUSE	*Wolf Kruger*	£1.95
TASK FORCE BATTALION	*Tom Lambert*	£1.60
PANZER GRENADIERS	*Heinrich Conrad Muller*	£1.95*
THE RAID	*Julian Romanes*	£1.80
GUNSHIPS: THE KILLING ZONE	*Jack Hamilton Teed*	£1.25*

STAR Books are obtainable from many booksellers and newsagents. If you have any difficulty tick the titles you want and fill in the form below.

Name _____

Address _____

_____

Send to: Star Books Cash Sales, P.O. Box 11, Falmouth, Cornwall, TR10 9EN.

Please send a cheque or postal order to the value of the cover price plus:
UK: 55p for the first book, 22p for the second book and 14p for each additional book ordered to the maximum charge of £1.75.

BFPO and EIRE: 55p for the first book, 22p for the second book, 14p per copy for the next 7 books, thereafter 8p per book.

OVERSEAS: £1.00 for the first book and 25p per copy for each additional book.

While every effort is made to keep prices low, it is sometimes necessary to increase prices at short notice. Star Books reserve the right to show new retail prices on covers which may differ from those advertised in the text or elsewhere.

*NOT FOR SALE IN CANADA